THE UNNATURAL

Books by Alan Nayes

Gargoyles

The Unnatural

Return to Underland
(children's book)

THE UNNATURAL

A L A N   N A Y E S

A TOM DOHERTY ASSOCIATES BOOK
NEW YORK

This is a work of fiction. All the characters and events portrayed in this novel are either fictitious or are used fictitiously.

THE UNNATURAL

This book is printed on acid-free paper.

Book design by Michael Collica

A Forge Book
Published by Tom Doherty Associates, LLC
175 Fifth Avenue
New York, NY 10010

www.tor.com

Forge® is a registered trademark of Tom Doherty Associates, LLC.

Library of Congress Cataloging-in-Publication Data

Nayes, Alan.
The unnatural / Alan Nayes.—1st ed.
p. cm.
"A Forge book"—T.p. verso.
ISBN: 0-765-30613-1
1. Women psychiatrists—Fiction. 2. Human experimentation in medicine—Fiction. 3. Young women—Crimes against—Fiction. 4. Immortalism—Fiction. 5. Cryonics—Fiction. I. Title

PS3614.A94U56 2003
813'.6—dc21

2003049149

First Edition: October 2003

Printed in the United States of America

0 9 8 7 6 5 4 3 2 1

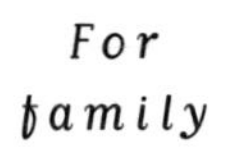

For
family

Acknowledgments

I wish to thank the following persons, who generously lent their time and/or expertise to this book:

Michael Hamilburg
Joanie Kern
Brian Callaghan
Alfa Creative Service and Staff
Linda Mackey
Isabel Salam
Blaine L. Smith, M.D.
Michelle Renee Harrison
Ava Solis Altina
John M. Dunkin
Adel H. Hagekhalil
C. Scott Carrier
Ed Stackler

All factual errors are mine.

PREFACE

THE UNNATURAL

Science, Fiction, Progress, or Perdition?

Science can be a double-edged scalpel. The biotechnological advancements in the fields of medicine, pharmaceuticals, and bioengineering have been staggering—far surpassing what Jules Verne or H. G. Wells might have envisioned. Over the last millennium, Homo *sapiens*, arguably the most intelligent species on the planet, has witnessed a race for knowledge whose pace has steadily accelerated at an indefatigably exponential rate—the Renaissance, the machine age, circumnavigation of the globe, space exploration, quantum physics, and molecular biology. We've watched ourselves reach into the deepest, darkest trenches of the five oceans as well as walk on the moon. Diseases, once the bane of mankind, have been conquered, even extirpated completely, increasing longevity. Reaching the century mark is approaching the commonplace. In another hundred years, who knows what might be attainable under the right conditions.

Scientific discovery is wonderfully awesome. Yet, just as a diamond-sharp scalpel can slice away a malignant tumor, this same blade can also sever a life-sustaining artery. How we use these discoveries is every bit as important as the actual discovery (if not more so). In the H. G. Wells classic, *The Island of Dr. Moreau,* a mad scientist transforms animals into the pitiful Beast People. Eight decades earlier, Mary Shelley described how Victor Frankenstein created a horrific creature from body parts surreptitiously obtained from graveyards and charnel houses. Of course, both treatises are fiction, yet each illustrates the ramifications—some unforeseen—of the unquenchable thirst for scientific knowledge. This same thirst continues today, only on a scale unmatched in recent history.

On one level, *The Unnatural* is a story of just such a thirst—a craving to learn and discover so strong, all other desires become obsolete. Here, on the eve of the fiftieth anniversary of the most significant biomolecular discovery of the twentieth century—James Watkins and Francis Crick's deciphering of the structure of DNA—body parts are being cryopreserved. Human beings are being frozen—not just heads and brains, but entire corpses. Is cryogenics an exact science? Far from it. What is the effect of long-term cryopreservation on Watson and Crick's DNA molecule? No one knows with any certainty. Yet there is no disputing the fact that the logistics of cryonic suspension have advanced far enough to convince some individuals—even a major league baseball Hall of Famer—that the time will come when bodies can be thawed and rejuvenated. If and when this time arrives, what will these bodies be like? Will they be the same . . . or different in some totally unpredictable way? Better, or worse? More intelligent, or less? Stronger, or weaker?

Mary Shelley's Victor Frankenstein created a monster. Are we on the verge of creating our own monsters? Dr. Moreau's island might be nearer than we anticipate. With the recent completion of the Human Genome Project, speculation on future genetic research has run rampant. We produce genetically identical sheep and monkeys from single cells, we splice virus genes into bacterial chromosomes, bacterial genes into yeast chromosomes, yeast genes into mammalian chromosomes. Stem cell research has renewed hopes of eradicating such infirmities as diabetes mellitus, heart disease, cancer, Parkinson's disease, even Alzheimer's. Manipulation of the genetic code might one day allow us to reach that double-century mark. Or longer!

Is there a dark side to these discoveries? Can there be a darker side to such scientific achievements? *Booklist* compared my first novel, *Gargoyles,* to a modern-day *Rosemary's Baby*. As our knowledge to control and modify genes expands, the ramifications, both known and unknown, will also multiply. Yes, one day we might possess the ability to create perfect babies. But what happens when the human race has the ability to create perfectly imperfect babies? Rosemary's dilemma might one day become reality.

In only half a century, the biotechnology revolution has advanced at warp speed. And this race has only barely begun. How and in what directions this race is run remains up to us.

Late Spring

. . . The dream reveals the reality which conception lags behind. That is the horror of life—the terror of art . . .

—Franz Kafka
1883–1924

One

Ignacio stood in the shadows in his faded, baggy chinos and tennis shoes, doing his best to keep dry in the May rain. He'd pledged an oath to Roberto that he'd take care of her. And like most homeboys in the barrios of East Los Angeles, he meant to keep his oath. Roberto was gone, at least the Roberto he'd grown up with, but Ignacio waited, sheltered under the eaves of a building he didn't know the name of, in a city he'd come to despise, performing the job he'd promised.

A police car approached, rain angling across its twin beams like tiny silvery darts. Ignacio pushed against the brick. The black-and-white passed and pulled into a Circle K convenience mart a half-block down. Ignacio waited for the uniform to enter the store, then turned back to resume his vigil.

Although the nursing school stood just around the corner and across the street from where Ignacio waited, he had a clear view of its front steps. One of his hands rested on the handlebars of the stolen bicycle at his side; the other caressed the small-caliber pistol in his windbreaker pocket. He usually preferred something heavier like a 9mm or a .38, but a .22 packing long-rifle hollow points could be just as effective. Especially at close range.

Ignacio stood perfectly still, waiting for her to show. She was late. He ignored the raindrops creeping down his hair and neck, moistening the T-shirt that now clung to his back. A crack of thunder startled him. Behind him, a car revved. Ignacio swung around.

Good, the uniform was leaving.

When the woman stepped out of El Centro Medical College, she realized it'd been a mistake to leave her umbrella at home.

She worked for Tempstar Personnel Services during the day, cleaning soiled sheets, greasy kitchens, floors, and toilets. At night, she attended school, studying to be a licensed vocational nurse.

One month shy of twenty-six, she had a honey brown complexion, full lips, and dark eyes that made her a much sought-after commodity by the local barrio pimps. Of course she'd have none of it, even if it meant extra money for Roberto's care and Carlito. She considered herself religious and had a steady boyfriend.

The rain was cascading down in sheets and it was now late, past ten-thirty. She weighed the decision to make a dash for her car. Her class in intravenous techniques should have ended at ten but she had stayed an extra thirty minutes to practice drawing blood on Nancy. She had already missed the mannequin's large plastic vein twice this week. To make matters worse, she'd blown the same vein again tonight with a twenty-gauge angiocath. The teacher had called her effort "suboptimal."

Three months ago the teacher's critical use of the word "suboptimal" would have had little effect on her. But now it seemed synonymous with her younger brother, who could neither speak nor feed himself. Roberto had been reduced to a shell, ignored by an uncaring, unmerciful God. It wasn't fair, but *la vida no siempre es justa*. Life isn't always fair.

As if a higher power had been listening, the force of the rain suddenly eased. It was time.

Switching two of her five textbooks to her right hand and

with her purse hanging from her right shoulder, the woman hurried down the twenty steps to the sidewalk. Once on the wet pavement, she picked up her pace as the downpour resumed.

A streetlight flickered some fifty yards ahead at the corner of Sheridan and Louis. She had parked midway down Louis.

As she took a right onto Louis, a white Chevy four-by-four honked and went by. She didn't recognize the truck. Probably the school's security guard. He was always the last to leave.

A half-block away, she could see the silhouette of her old Honda Civic next to the curb. She'd purposely parked under a street lamp, but as luck would have it, the one she'd picked had burned out, leaving her car in the dark.

"Mierda," she cursed.

She always spoke her birth language when she became upset. If the evening didn't change for the better, she'd never speak English again.

Overhead, another crackle of thunder followed a short lightning burst. As the flash illuminated her car's interior, she stopped midstride. For a split second, she thought someone was sitting in her front seat. Reflexively, she put all her books under her left arm and reached into her purse for her .38 Smith and Wesson. She'd purchased it at a local gun shop, filing the proper papers one day after her brother's accident. Fifteen days later, she had become a gun owner. Could she actually shoot someone? Standing on the sidewalk drenched to the bone and on her own, she suddenly knew without a doubt she could pull the trigger if things became nasty.

She stepped into the street, ignoring the rush of water that filled her nursing shoes as her feet fell into a torrent running along the curb and into the sewer. She crouched for a better view, blinking the water from her eyes. As another flash of lightning froze the car's back window in a silvery veil, she felt foolish.

"Get some sleep, *señorita*."

What she had thought was someone's head was nothing more than her headrest. She released the pistol and searched her purse. Finding the key chain with the whistle, she approached her car.

At the other end of Louis Street, another vehicle turned the corner. Its headlights illumined her as it crawled her way. She'd just unlocked the door when the car stopped. A spotlight bathed her in a white light.

"Need any help, miss?" The voice sounded friendly.

She turned and squinted.

The vehicle was a police car. The officer moved the light out of her eyes.

"No, thanks, officer. I was studying late. I'm leaving now."

The policeman studied her lab coat briefly. He was young, perhaps late twenties. "Sure thing, ma'am. Drive carefully. It's wet out here."

The officer rolled up his window, turned left, and was gone.

The woman wasted little time in climbing in out of the rain. She tossed her books and purse to the passenger side and slammed the door shut, locking it.

"Finalmente." She leaned her head on the steering wheel and inhaled deeply.

Suddenly, she jerked her head up at a loud grating noise. It sounded like metal on concrete. She could see nothing but the rain sluicing down her windshield. Then she heard—even felt—it again. She looked to the left. The side window was fogged. Quickly, she turned the key in the ignition and the Civic's little engine fired.

Almost simultaneously, a third metallic clang resounded from the center of the street.

She turned on her headlights and wipers, illuminating nothing except wet pavement. Only when the car shook did she realize she was no longer alone. She attempted to shift into gear.

Two powerful blows shattered her driver's-side window. She

screamed as she felt her head violently yanked through the shards of glass. Her scalp burned where the long black hair was torn out by its roots.

"No, por favor, no!" she cried. *"Ayudame, por favor, ayudame!"*

With brutal force, her body left the seat and she was pulled halfway from her car.

"No, ayudame!"

A thick arm encircled her neck, choking off her air.

She tried to turn her head but saw nothing except rain and broken glass. As she struggled in vain against her abductor, her nostrils filled with a horrifying stench. It smelled worse than a dying animal.

With one final, hyperadrenalized effort, she managed to reach into her purse. She clawed for her pistol. A single earsplitting explosion blasted into the night. Then the pistol left her hand. The woman cried out in dismay.

She'd missed.

La vida no siempre es justa. Life wasn't fair.

Two

*Medic 13 backed up the emer*gency ramp at California University Medical Center with its siren still wailing. Their pickup, a young Hispanic woman, had been reported by two cops who had found the patient screaming some sort of gibberish. She had since lapsed into unconsciousness.

ER Nurse Gwen Ferris and Dr. Purvis Skinner, a third-year resident, opened the rear doors. IV bag in hand, EMT Jack Cole squatted at the head of the stretcher and wheeled the patient out. The woman's face exhibited prominent bruising. One eye had completely swollen shut and mud and grime caked her forehead, matting her long black hair and clothing. The scene reeked of raw sewage.

"Last BP 110/60, pulse 120, respirations 24," Cole reported. "Fails to follow any commands, though her pupils do respond to light."

Dr. Skinner reached for the woman's wrist, and grimaced at the stench emanating from under the ambulance blanket. "God, where'd you find this one, the sewer?" He found her pulse. "Tachycardic."

Cole nodded. "Been that way since we picked her up."

"Let's get her inside," Skinner said.

With Cole in the lead, they wheeled the woman up the ramp and toward the sliding hydraulic ER doors. With a *swoosh,* they entered the raucous cacophony of voices and noises of a busy emergency ward in full swing.

CUMC emergency room had treated over three hundred thousand patients the previous year and at the rate the homeless and illegals were flooding in, a new record would be set in '03. There were fourteen curtained exam rooms, four trauma rooms, a radiology suite, two minor surgery suites, and three cardiac rooms. At twelve-thirty at night on this particular Wednesday, half the exam rooms and two cardiac rooms were occupied.

Periodically a voice would boom over the overhead paging system for some doctor to report to surgical ICU or a lab tech to report to one of the hospital's wards.

Cole slowed near the central nursing station. "Which room, Doc?"

Nurse Ferris checked the triage board where all new admits were noted in red, black, or blue marker. She motioned toward the nearest trauma room.

Skinner nodded. "Trauma A." He ordered the necessary lab work including blood and toxicology screens. "We know who she is?"

"No ID." The paramedic pointed at her ripped and bloody clothing. "She was found alone about a mile from the hospital, near the intersection of Brooklyn and Soto. There was no car and from what I've heard, no witnesses either."

As Cole swung the stretcher around and Dr. Skinner made a quick detour into a cardiac room, a dirty, grimy hand shot from under the ambulance blanket and gripped Cole's wrist.

"What the—"

The Latina patient let out a bloodcurdling scream.

Nurse Ferris dropped an IV bottle in shock. The glass shattered on the tile floor and the patient shrieked again. Before Cole could restrain her, she sat up, flinging the blanket away.

She gripped Cole's arm with her other hand. *"Por favor, no!"*

"Hold her. She's crawling all over me," Cole yelled to his partner.

The other EMT had the patient by the shoulders, but she writhed out of his grip.

She twisted and turned, causing the stretcher to bounce. *"No, por favor, no! Ayudame!"*

"What's she saying?" Cole asked the nurse.

" 'Please, no, help me,' " Nurse Ferris translated. She reached for the patient's back but the woman's shredded blouse ripped, revealing more bruises and cuts.

Two muscular orderlies entered the fray.

"Where's the doctor? Dr. Skinner! Dr. Skinner!" Nurse Ferris yelled.

An elbow slipped past an orderly and caught Cole just above the left eye, opening a one-inch gash.

Cole winced. "Get her arm, someone get her arm!" He felt something warm trickling down his face.

"Dr. Skinner!" Nurse Ferris yelled again.

Dr. Skinner came through the curtained partition and, for a second or two, just stood there with an electrocardiogram dangling from his fingers.

"Do something, Doc," Cole yelled. "Before she whips all of us."

The two orderlies had the patient by each shoulder, trying their best to force her to lie down. Cole snaked one arm around her neck, while the blood from above his eye dribbled down the patient's chest.

Fumbling with the restraints, Nurse Ferris couldn't get a clean grip on the patient's wrists because of the mud and grime.

"Jesus frickin' Christ," Dr. Skinner muttered.

Dr. Todd, assistant chief of the CUMC emergency department, burst from one of the surgical suites at a full run. He entered Trauma A just as the overhead page blared. "Security Code One, ER. Security Code One, ER."

The woman screamed again. *"Por favor, no!"*

"Dr. Skinner!" Cole and Nurse Ferris yelled almost simultaneously.

Dr. Skinner tried to hold one of the patient's kicking legs.

Dr. Todd assisted with the other leg. "I see you got a live one here."

Dr. Skinner started to warn him to hang on tight, but before he could, the patient's leg slipped from his grasp. With a cry, she kicked with all the strength her hip, thigh, and calf muscles could muster. Her foot caught Dr. Todd flush on the nose with a sickening thud. Blood spurted from both nostrils as he fell.

Nurse Ferris knelt at the injured physician's side.

Outside Trauma A, where a horde of clerks, receptionists, and other hospital personnel watched, a male nurse in a white lab coat shoved through.

With Cole controlling her head, the orderlies on each arm, and Cole's partner restraining the midsection, Dr. Skinner threw himself across both legs.

"Ten of diazepam," he grunted. "Stat!"

The patient's wheezing and gasping noises sounded only half human.

"Ten milligrams of diazepam!" Nurse Ferris called from next to the injured Dr. Todd.

The male nurse made for the medicine cart as the patient struggled more fiercely.

"Hurry!" Dr. Skinner yelled. "Shit!"

Cole looked down at the back of the woman's head. "Jesus." He hadn't seen it earlier. A large chunk of hair was missing. The patch of denuded scalp looked like a pint of swollen, overripe strawberries.

The patient cried out again, spittle flying from her mouth.

"Dammit, where's that diazepam?" Dr. Skinner was tiring.

The nurse passed the syringe to Nurse Ferris. While the orderlies helped ease the patient over, Nurse Ferris stuck the needle in the struggling woman's fleshy left buttock. She pushed the plunger down.

The woman's eyes widened. *"No, no . . . por favor . . . no."*

Her voice weakened quickly as her eyelids fluttered and struggles ceased.

"It's working." Dr. Skinner relaxed his grip.

"Thank God." Cole wiped blood, grime, and perspiration from his face.

While the orderlies finished applying the restraints, Nurse Ferris capped the syringe and deposited it in a red plastic needle dispenser. "I've never seen anything like it. It was like she suddenly went crazy."

"Or strung out on phencyclidine," Cole said, studying the strained lines of the girl's face.

Nurse Ferris turned to Dr. Todd, who remained on the floor. She and another nurse helped him to his feet. He could only groan.

"Let's get him to X-ray," Nurse Ferris said, leading him out.

Dr. Skinner followed them. "Get Dr. Charmaine on the line," he ordered the nearest ER clerk.

"I'm not sure she's on call," the clerk said.

"Just get her."

The patient lay perfectly still. Her breathing was regular. The diazepam was doing its job. Next, she'd be cleaned up, examined, and the appropriate laboratory tests completed.

As the paramedics returned to their vehicle, an elderly custodian wheeled his housekeeping cart into Trauma A. He'd observed the entire fiasco from the registration clerk's desk. It reminded him of the young gangbangers and addicts who would come in strung out on PCP. But this girl wasn't on PCP. He could tell. Call it a gut feeling. Gut feelings weren't mentioned in any medical texts, but the custodian had mopped and cleaned the urine, vomit, and excrement off CUMC floors for over forty years. No, they wouldn't find PCP, LSD, crack, methamphetamines, or any other generic street drugs in her blood.

He bent down to pick up some of the larger pieces of the shattered IV bottle. No, this girl had been scared. Terrified really. Scared to almighty death. He'd swear to it. Something or someone had frightened the poor woman out of her fucking mind.

Three

The worms crawl in,
The worms crawl out,
Worm Man plays pinochle on your snout.
It's getting dark, no time for fun,
Worm Man is coming,
Everybody run!

The nightmarish riff bounced inside her skull like an errant pinball. Twisting deeper into her sheets, she couldn't escape its childish melodic pull any more than she could will herself awake. She tossed and turned on a cold sea of floating dollhouses and papier-mâché figurines reaching, reaching . . .

Julie was fast, Janine was faster.
Julie was last, Janine was first.
But in Worm Man, first was dead.
Janine, Janine!

At 12:55 A.M., her phone rang.

Dr. Julie Charmaine's eyes snapped open. There was no abandoned toolshed, odors of wet earth and insecticides, or bloodied finger pulps to greet her. Asleep less than an hour, the dream hadn't been given the chance to take root and germinate. It had only progressed to the laughter stage. She'd wait another night to relive the anguish. But not tonight.

"Go to hell, Worm Man," Julie muttered. Fully alert, she reached for the phone before the end of the second ring.

As a staff neuropsychiatrist and supervising physician of CUMC's prestigious Sleep Diagnostics Laboratory, she'd grown accustomed to calls in the middle of the night, as much as she'd grown accustomed to her older sister's nocturnal visits each spring.

She could live with the dreams. After all, she treated patients with emotional scars far worse than hers, especially since agreeing to serve as director of the medical center's Battered Women's Unit.

"Hello," Julie answered, wondering briefly what Sigmund Freud would say to a physician ranked near the top of her field who sometimes heard nursery rhymes while she slept.

"What time?" she asked, deciding just as quickly she could do without the deceased psychotherapist's opinion. "How bad is she? . . . Is she stable? . . . I'm on my way."

Julie hung up the phone, her mind instantly focused. A young woman brought into the emergency room by paramedics had been viciously beaten. The good news was she'd been found alive.

As a list of admit orders formed in her head, the fatigue rapidly dissipated from Julie's limbs. Yawning, she pushed aside a handful of dark hair from her forehead and stretched.

Had it only been three hours since she'd left the Amphisphere? The quasi-elite discotheque catered to aficionados of the L.A. rock scene—not one of the first places Julie would choose to spend a Tuesday evening. She had gone to the club to conduct interviews, of all things—part of her ongoing research into the esoteric world of the subconscious and dreaming.

Since early childhood, dreams had captivated her. Once scary and frightening, certain visions had terrorized her as a young girl.

Later, education and learning had provided the cushion for a soft, wakeful landing. Her dreams never frightened her anymore. Irritated, yes. Disturbed, only on the darkest and rainiest of nights.

Julie had chosen the Amphisphere and its clientele because of the bartender's description of his friends as creative individuals with an uncanny ability to recall their dreams in vivid detail. It took only two interviews for Julie to realize her mistake. Hallucinations from drugs and alcohol don't count as dreams. The evening wasn't a total loss, though. Four of the interviews had yielded intriguing material for her research.

Lifting the sheets aside, Julie swung her legs over the side of the bed. In the dark, she heard the muffled padding of four paws on the bedroom carpet. Jake, her pet golden retriever/shepherd mix, rested his heavy head across her thigh.

Julie gently cupped his ears with both hands.

"Don't wait up for me."

The steady drizzle ran off the roof of the abandoned Honda Civic. Shards of glass sprinkled the street on its driver's side. Some were stained with blood and wisps of hair, although the rain had washed most clean. What little blood remained would soon find its way into the gutter. From there, it would flow into the city's wastewater disposal system, a complex and intricate system of sewers and underground conduits, some twelve feet or more in diameter. These man-made caverns were not only home to the foul wastes of humanity, but also to myriad living organisms, including viruses, bacteria, rats, snakes, and other creatures that chose to shun the light.

Officer Jeff Beamis wasn't interested in the inhabitants of L.A.'s sewers that stormy night, but he *did* intend to check out the blocks around El Centro Medical College. When he had heard over the radio that a woman had been found assaulted five blocks from the nursing school, he played a hunch and decided to check out the little Honda he'd seen some hours earlier. He specifically recalled its attractive driver and her late-night departure.

He switched off the windshield wipers. The rain had slowed considerably. From Sheridan he took a right onto Louis and played his spotlight's beam off the shattered fragments of glass on the wet concrete. He unsnapped his revolver in its holster.

Stopping twenty feet behind the Civic, Beamis reached for his radio.

Julie silently observed the unconscious woman in Trauma Room A of CUMC's emergency ward. If it weren't for the wrist restraints and her bruised and swollen face, Julie would have thought her asleep. Assuming no other more serious injuries took precedence, this patient would be admitted under Julie's care after the appropriate medical specialties were consulted, if indicated.

In addition to supervising the Sleep Diagnostics Laboratory, Julie's position as interim head of the Battered Women's Unit dictated she oversee the evaluation and treatment of all CUMC female victims of violence. The former chairman had just retired and Julie, in light of her largely female clientele, had assumed those responsibilities. She didn't mind; in fact she enjoyed it, in spite of the wee-hours emergency calls. Victims of assault and battery required specialized care and counseling and Julie was more than willing to put in the necessary time.

Julie stepped back out of Trauma Room A, pulled the curtain, and looked for the patient's medical chart. She'd had a few words with the ER clerk about the case but she wanted to see the history and EMT report herself.

She walked past two empty exam rooms and made for the nurses' triage station, searching for Dr. Todd. He would be the staff ER doc on duty, but so far she hadn't seen his energetic body bouncing in and out of exam rooms, barking orders like, "More lidocaine here," "Start an aminophylline drip here," or "Catheterize the man in room twelve." She didn't see him in the central triage area either.

"Dr. Charmaine," Nurse Ferris called from the otolaryngology room. Only patients with ear, nose, or throat injuries entered this room.

"Morning, Gwen. You guys look busy." She noticed the earliest signs of a bruise forming under the nurse's right eye. "What happened to you? A patient not like your advice?"

Nurse Ferris touched her cheek. "We got a crazy one for you tonight. You think this is bad, you should see Dr. Todd."

"Dr. Todd?"

Ferris motioned to the closed otolaryngology room. "A comminuted fracture of his nasal bridge. The ENT doc's ordering a CT scan now to rule out a blowout fracture of his left orbit."

"That doesn't sound encouraging." Julie pushed the exam room door partway open and glanced in. A man—she guessed it to be Finny Todd, although a large supportive dressing virtually covered his face—lay on an exam table. His eyes were closed and there was an IV in one arm. He looked sedated.

Julie stepped back out.

"Finny looks bad," she said.

Ferris took Julie's arm. "Could be out for six weeks if the CT is positive, two if negative. Bad news. Dr. Todd's a good physician."

The nurse handed Julie the medical chart she was looking for.

Julie began to study the ER admit notes. She checked the medical history. "So she's still a Jane Doe."

"That's gonna change."

"How'd it happen?" Julie asked, referring back to Dr. Todd's injuries.

Nurse Ferris led toward the triage station. "It was incredible. Like the woman had the strength of five men. We were trying to restrain her when Dr. Todd caught her foot flush in the face."

"Ouch."

Ferris nodded. "You be careful. I've never seen a patient more frightened. She was terrified out of her mind."

Julie had seen frightened. She patted Ferris's shoulder. "Don't worry, I like my nose the way it is." She motioned once again to her shiner. "You really should get some ice on that, you know."

"Thanks. I will."

Giving Nurse Ferris one last reassuring look, Julie started back across the triage arena toward Trauma A with chart in hand. Just as she was about to pull the curtain to Trauma A aside, she heard her name.

"Dr. Charmaine. Julie." It was Dr. Purvis Skinner.

"Hear it's been an interesting night. Or should I say morning?" Julie reached out and shook his hand. She'd worked with Purvis Skinner several times during his residency and considered him bright and professional.

Skinner feigned a grin. "Been like this since midnight. Hey, thanks for coming in. Guess Ferris filled you in."

"Some."

"Well, we got a real intriguing case here. I'll let you decide," Skinner said.

Translated this meant he was glad as hell he could dump this one in Julie's lap. Most ER docs hated "interesting cases." They wanted simple and boring. People didn't die when cases were simple and boring. Not usually, anyway.

"We had to sedate her with ten of diazepam," he said, almost apologizing.

Julie suppressed a groan. She disliked having her patients heavily sedated. It made her work of reaching them that much more difficult. But then if Dr. Todd's nose was any indication,

Skinner in all likelihood made the right call with the intramuscular diazepam.

"Let's see what you have for me," Julie said, reaching for the curtain, and immediately decided it would be less offensive on her olfactory nerves if she breathed through her mouth. The faint but unmistakable stench of sewage hovered above the hospital bed like an invisible cloud.

Skinner noticed Julie's expression. "That's nothing. You should've been here when they brought her in."

Julie simply nodded. Her eyes remained fixed on the young woman on the white sheets, who stared impassively at the ceiling. Both her hands and wrists were secured to the guardrails with leather restraints. Each ankle was tied to the foot of the bed. Julie stepped up to the side bars.

Behind her, the ER resident kept his distance. "She was found screaming incoherently in an alley by two cops. They summoned an ambulance and Medic Thirteen transferred her here. Tentatively, we have her registered as a Jane Doe."

"Tentative?" Julie asked, gazing down at the woman's face. One eye was completely swollen shut, resembling more an overripe plum than flesh and blood. Flakes of coagulated blood were caked to her right nostril and lower lip, also swollen.

"Yeah, tentative was how Ferris just put it. It seems a patrolman found a Honda Civic behind El Centro Medical College. It'd been broken into. The car is registered to a Ms. Irene Inez, a twenty-five-year-old Hispanic female. Her age and description are similar to this patient. The police are awaiting a copy of her DMV photo."

Julie studied the woman's beaten face. "I'm not sure it's going to help."

Skinner shrugged. "She looks bad, but none of her physical injuries are serious, at least not life-threatening anyway. She's sustained multiple bruises and abrasions. Also two punctures to her right thigh. But there's no evidence she was raped."

"Thank goodness for small miracles."

"Her most serious injury is a nasty scalp avulsion involving about twenty-five percent of her posterior parietal and occipital area."

Julie bent closer to the large gauze dressing wrapped around Irene's head, if in fact this woman was Irene Inez. "Was she trying to run?"

"Maybe. If she was, she didn't run fast enough. Whoever did this pulled out a good chunk of her scalp along with her hair."

Julie studied the woman's one remaining open eye. It seemed to be fixed at some invisible point on the ceiling. "Drug screen?"

Skinner pulled several lab slips from his coat pocket. "All negative. Everything. I would've given ten to one odds she'd been positive for coke, PCP, or at least marijuana. But no. There was no evidence of alcohol, ice, ecstasy, other designer street drugs, or even any prescription meds. Nada."

"Other lab work?"

Skinner watched as Julie aimed a small penlight into first one eye of the patient, then the other, checking for consensual and direct pupillary light responses.

"X-rays of her skull, c-spine, chest, and ribs were also normal. CBC, SMAC, urinalysis, lytes, all within normal limits."

"CAT scan?"

"Been ordered. Both the 9800 and the GE Signa are tied up now. Neurosurgery's got a guy who lost control of his Harley. He and his girlfriend came in unconscious and on spine boards. As soon as the next scanner opens up, your patient's next."

Julie continued her preliminary neurological exam. Everything seemed to be in working order. The woman's lab tests were all normal and her vital signs were stable. Even her cranial nerve exam fell within normal limits. At least cranial nerves two through twelve. The patient's sense of smell would have to wait till she regained consciousness.

Julie stepped to the head of the bed and placed both hands over each ear of the patient. Gently, she rocked the woman's head, first to one side then the other. She was testing the woman's doll's-eyes maneuvers, another bedside neurologic exam.

Skinner yawned. "Ever since she KO'ed Todd, she's just stared at the ceiling. Think she's catatonic."

"It's too early to tell."

Julie knew what Skinner meant, but going into an extensive explanation of catatonia would've taken too long. The actual dictionary definition of catatonic referred to a form of schizophrenia marked by excessive and sometimes violent behavior and excitement, or as in this case, excessive inhibition. However, a diagnosis of catatonic schizophrenia was impossible to make without knowing something about a patient's history and especially impossible to determine in five minutes. Besides, there was something else different about this case.

"Watch her eyes," Julie said, motioning Skinner closer. "Her extraocular movements are all intact." She swung the woman's head back and forth so Skinner could see. "However, if you hold her head still, you'll notice some very fine rapid horizontal eye twitches. There, see?"

Skinner bent closer. "It almost looks like nystagmus."

Julie removed her hands. The woman's eye continued to exhibit a fine vibration. "It's similar, but too fine. It's closer to what you see in REM sleep."

"What, you saying this woman's asleep?"

"Of course not. But it is odd. It's almost as if she's dreaming."

"If she is, it's a helluva nightmare."

"Has she responded to any verbal stimuli?"

"Nothing."

Julie moved around so she faced the woman. "You said her tentative ID is Irene Inez."

"So far."

Julie placed a hand on one of the patient's restrained wrists. "Irene, Irene can you hear me? I'm Dr. Julie Charmaine. And this is Dr. Skinner. We're here to help you."

The woman continued to stare blankly at the ceiling. There was no visible response. Except for the rapid eye movements.

Julie placed two of her fingers in the woman's hand. "Irene, squeeze my hand. Squeeze my hand, Irene. *Aprieta mi mano. Aprieta mi mano.*"

Still no response.

A look of concern crossed Julie's face. Irene's injuries, although significant, did not appear to be severe enough to warrant this type of nonresponsiveness. Unless of course, the CT scan revealed a subdural or epidural hematoma or some other anatomic defect that the physical exam had missed. Julie doubted it would, as the patient's neuro exam had been essentially normal. Her reflexes were intact, and all anyone had to do was ask Dr. Finny Todd about her muscle tone.

"How long ago did she get the diazepam?"

"Over an hour. Just prior to your page."

Julie took out her stethoscope and listened to the patient's heart and lungs. The woman's chest was clear and her heart was beating regularly. While Julie finished her exam, an older nurse pulled the curtain aside and brought in another bottle of D5W. The five percent dextrose in water was a common IV solution used in the emergency department.

As the nurse stepped by Julie, she removed a small alcohol packet from one pocket. This would be used to clean the connector before it was inserted into the new IV solution bottle. The original bottle hung by the Medic 13 crew was almost empty.

As the nurse ripped open the alcohol packet, the patient suddenly began to shake her head.

Skinner immediately stepped forward. "Watch it Julie, something just woke her up."

"She's restrained," Julie reminded him, but moving back a step anyway. She motioned for the nurse to stop what she was doing.

"Irene," Julie said, "Can you hear me? *Me holles?*"

The patient flung her head more vigorously. *"El se . . . el se murio. No . . . no chango."* She began to fight the restraints.

Julie quickly glanced at Skinner. "Has she said anything else since being brought in?"

"Only *por favor.*" Skinner was getting a little nervous. The image of Todd's misshapen nose was still vivid in his mind. "You want more diazepam?"

"No," Julie shook her head. "Irene, it's okay. You're in the hospital. *Me oyes?* Can you hear me?"

The patient's struggles intensified. She didn't appear to hear anything Julie said.

"Irene," Julie tried again. "Irene, we're here to help you. *Esta bien. Esta bien.*" Julie placed a hand on the woman's forehead. This only made her struggle more.

"No . . . chango. No. No!" The woman's voice sounded terrified. There was a pleading shrillness to it. *"No, por favor."* It sent a single shiver up Julie's spine.

"Irene. *Escucheme por favor.* It's okay. We're here to help," Julie said. She nodded for the nurse to continue.

Using the alcohol, the nurse quickly cleansed the intravenous connector, completed exchanging the new for the empty IV bottle, and left without a word.

Ten seconds later, the Hispanic woman lay in her trance-like state again, totally oblivious to her surroundings.

Skinner shook his head. "What was that all about?"

"I don't know, but something sure set her off. I'm going to

begin my admit orders. As soon as the CT's done, I want her transferred up to the sixth floor."

The faxed DMV photo did not help a great deal. Though grainy and dark, it described a woman with brown hair, brown eyes, five foot six, and weighing one hundred ten pounds.

Julie had to agree with the two officers who'd been at the scene. Her patient, in spite of the temporary facial deformities resulting from her injuries, was indeed Irene Inez.

The officers could provide no additional useful information other than the woman had initially appeared intensely terrified before lapsing into her current semicomatose state. They'd collected samples from under her nails and the patient's clothing had been dispatched to the forensic crime lab. An investigator would be by in the morning to attempt further questioning, provided Irene's status changed.

Nurse Ferris tapped Julie on the shoulder. "Dr. Charmaine, radiology's ready."

"Great, let's do it."

Nurse Ferris nodded. "There's also a woman in reception requesting to see you."

"A woman?"

"She says she knows this patient."

The woman was Soccoro Chavez, Irene Inez's aunt. Julie introduced herself and led the woman, who looked to be in her early fifties, to one of the four physician offices in the emergency department. Each was modestly furnished with a desk, two chairs, a phone, and some generic medical-reference texts including Harrison's *Principles of Internal Medicine* and a *Physician's Desk Reference.*

It became immediately apparent to Julie that she needed an interpreter, as Soccoro Chavez spoke little English and Julie was not confident enough in her medical Spanish to carry on without one, especially when the subject was an ill relative.

As the woman spoke to the translator, Julie watched her, noting her nondescript blouse and plaid skirt, worn rain gear, her lack of makeup, not even lipstick, and graying hair pulled back in a bun. Her features looked plain, though not unattractive. It was obvious her fifty-odd years had not been easy ones. She worked as a cleaning woman for some janitorial service. And she was understandably upset.

Señora Chavez had become concerned when Irene was late in returning home from El Centro Medical College where she attended night classes. Señora Chavez watched Irene's son, Carlito, and Irene was always anxious to pick him up. The aunt had contacted the local police but was informed a person had to be missing for twenty-four hours before anything official could be done. No sooner had she hung up than she'd received a call from her son, who lived with her. It was just after midnight and the young man was frantic, saying that Irene was in desperate trouble and needed his help. He told her to call the local hospitals to see if Irene had been brought in. By the time she found Irene at CUMC, it was almost two in the morning. She'd taken a taxi—she didn't have a driver's license—and had come straight to the emergency department where Nurse Ferris found her.

Julie empathized with the woman. She could see the worry and tension in the lines of her face, which made it even more difficult to have to inform her that she could not see her only niece at precisely this time, but reassured her that Irene was stable and everything possible was being done to make her comfortable.

Julie didn't want the older Chavez to see Irene for two reasons. First and foremost, a visit would only delay the CT scan and Julie's number one priority was getting Irene Inez's medical workup completed as efficiently as possible. Secondly, this poor woman was already on the brink of a nervous breakdown and seeing her niece in her present condition would only make the situation worse. Julie embraced her, as did the interpreter. She even offered to pay for her taxi home, but the older Chavez refused. Politely. She was a proud woman and Julie admired her for that.

Julie suggested that the aunt have her son talk to the police about what he'd heard and seen. Señora Chavez said she'd try and promised to return in the morning. Before leaving, she gave Julie her phone number.

By three-thirty, the CAT scan was completed and found to be within normal limits by the staff radiologist on call. With nothing more physically serious than an acute scalp avulsion, the patient was admitted to the sixth floor, a general surgical ward. Irene Inez's admitting diagnoses were large scalp avulsion, acute post-traumatic stress disorder, and multiple minor abrasions and contusions.

After ensuring Ms. Inez was stable and would be closely monitored throughout the night, Julie left University Hospital. The rain had lessened considerably. She arrived home and was promptly in bed by four-thirty Wednesday morning. The week was barely into its third day.

Four

*The Shilden Hotel stood for*lornly against the cloud-studded sky, its broken façade a stark reminder of nature's capricious moods. The Northridge earthquake had destroyed what little customer base had remained on that early January morning, sending the building's owners into bankruptcy court and unleashing a string of lawsuits and countersuits that years later still prevented the demolition crews from attacking the cracked brick and mortar seams.

A half block down from the three-story edifice, Vicki Zampisi yielded to a postal delivery truck, before pulling her van next to the curb. A span of nearly twenty years had passed since she'd last set sight upon the stone-arched entryway that once led to the hotel's lobby. With one hand, she shielded her eyes from the few rays of sunlight that had managed to find kinks in the early morning sky's overcast. The immediate neighborhood looked much the way she'd remembered it, a cluttered assortment of residential bungalows, convenience marts, and liquor stores. Though the few trees lining the street offered more shade and many of the structures appeared newer, the entire scene still spoke of economic depression and lost dreams, containing a sense of futility only the homeless could exude. The few passersby looked elderly or unemployed. On the opposite curb a man sat at a bus stop, his expression listless as he rested his chin on the handle of his grocery cart.

Vicki opened her purse and pulled out an opened pack of Montclairs. Finding her lighter, she lit up her third cigarette of the morning and stepped out onto the concrete. The air felt heavy with humidity and smelled of smog and exhaust, a total antithesis to the pine-scented freshness of Washington state, where she'd spent the last five years, living with her mom and working as an assistant to an insurance adjuster for a large Seattle insurance company. Until recently, the job had provided decent security. The sudden budget cutbacks had taken everybody by surprise, although the loss of income was not the reason Vicki had arrived in Los Angeles a week ago.

She strolled up the sidewalk. In her sunglasses, blue skirt, sleeveless pullover, and shoulder-hung purse, she could've been just another tourist. Except the Shilden Hotel area had never exactly been a hotbed for tourists. She passed a beverage mart, was tempted, but continued to where the chain-linked fence began.

The hotel grounds occupied an entire street-corner lot, lying between a laundromat on one side and the liquor mart on the other. The six foot fence, sagging in places, extended around the entire structure.

Water from the previous night's storm puddled on the entrance walk and lawn, more weeds now than grass, and Vicki noted with a vague sense of sadness the hotel's landmark wooden gazebo was missing. Many of the twenty units' windows were broken or missing completely and the heavy padlock and chains festooned across the French-door entrance told her she'd have to find another way inside.

She walked three-quarters of the length of the fence, letting the tips of her fingers fall across the metal links. She passed five or six NO TRESPASSING signs. Out of the corner of one eye, she saw a police car stop at the corner, then proceed. Initially, Vicki thought she might spy a security guard, but there was none, unless inside, and from the state of disrepair of the structure, she doubted that.

The only violation of the fence's perimeter lay at the rear of the lot, in an alley where the asphalt appeared to have been dug up. Orange warning cones marked the area and the faint stench of raw sewage wafted from the alley along with men's voices. She spied a city sanitation truck and the bright orange traffic vests worn by city employees.

Her eyes moved from the construction work, through the fence, and across the weeds, dirt, and trash, to a first-floor unit. It wouldn't take much effort to scale the low balcony and break in. Once inside, she'd have no difficulty locating room five.

The very thought of stepping across the same floor where she and Ben had spent so much time together gave her a rush. She no longer felt sinful or vile. Years of therapy allowed one to rationalize anything. Feeling her skin blush, Vicki allowed herself a shameful smile.

One of the men spotted her and whistled. Two of his companions cheered lewdly.

Vicki pretended not to hear and returned to her van. She'd come back when it was dark. It wouldn't take long. If not tonight, then tomorrow night or the next. Two or three days wouldn't make any difference. And if it wasn't there, well, she'd tried.

The drive back to her apartment took her past CUMC. The sight of the sprawling complex shocked her. When she'd worked for the foundation, there'd been maybe four buildings in addition to the main hospital. Today, she stopped counting at twenty. It was almost as if a city within a city had been born. The western-most boundary now extended to within three blocks of the Shilden Hotel where she and Ben had consummated their relationship.

Vicki parked on the street next to her apartment building. The complex didn't provide a carport. She climbed the stairs to her upper-level unit just as the locksmith was completing work on the front door.

The man looked young, and he eyed her in an obvious attempt not to stare. "You the renter who requested the dead bolt?"

Vicki removed her sunglasses. "Yes, I'm Vicki Zampisi."

The man checked a requisition slip. "That be the name." He flipped the lock several times before depositing a key in Vicki's hand. "Want to give her a try?"

Vicki slipped the key into the slot. The metal bolt slid smoothly. "Seems to work fine, thanks."

"Here's an extra key and my card if there's any problem. Kwikset is a trustworthy brand. Most outlive the owners," he said.

"That's reassuring."

He grinned. "Well you know what I mean."

Once inside, she slid the dead bolt back into place. It wasn't that she was being paranoid. Nobody even knew she was back in Los Angeles yet, except her mother. But today that would change.

She opened the blinds, allowing some light into the small living room. The unit also included a single bedroom and adjoining bathroom and kitchen. All furnished. She considered herself fortunate to have found the place so easily. Though blue-collar, the neighborhood appeared well kept and the landlord, an elderly widow, had agreed to forego any lease commitments if Vicki paid three month's rent in advance. The amount was not excessive and Vicki had agreed. The location was convenient and she doubted she'd be staying for any length of time. Much would depend on her next phone call.

Vicki went to the kitchen and dropped her purse on the counter. On the round Formica kitchen table, a saucer served as an ashtray. Beside it lay a book of matches. She noted the slight trembling of her fingers as she retrieved a half-smoked Montclair and struck a match. She wasn't too concerned about her shaking hands. She had a cure for that.

Inhaling the tobacco taste, Vicki blew a puff of gray smoke and reached for the fifth of Ezra Brooks Kentucky Whiskey on top of the refrigerator. She poured herself a good antitremor shot-and-a-half and sipped it slowly. Vicki relished the warm feeling the ninety-proof whiskey gave her throat. Soon that same warm feeling would spread throughout her entire body, even to the tips of her fingers. It wouldn't be long before the shaking would cease.

Vicki rose and walked down the short hall to her bedroom. She purposely avoided her reflection that flashed in the dresser mirror. Her cranial-facial surgeon had said he could make her look normal. He'd been only partly correct. After multiple surgeries, she did look *more* normal, though her skin hadn't aged quite as well as she would've preferred. But then tobacco and booze had never been christened the fountain of youth. Her bleached-blond hair only accentuated her forty-two years.

Her mind drifted to a photograph surreptitiously taken twenty years earlier and discarded in a hotel room in a fit of anguish no human should be forced to bear. It had been a foolish wish to think she could ever forget. Every day and night since her tumultuous departure she'd thought of that picture, the only tangible evidence that she and Ben *had been*. Yet it was the photo's absence that had prevented her from forgetting. Ben had been nineteen when the picture was taken. And Vicki, barely twenty-two, still a virgin.

What had later happened between them could never be explained or justified in a court of ethics and morality. She could accept that. When you're born with eyes too far apart and a skull more appropriately designed for a cartoon character than a living person, you tended to observe your own existence from a warped plane. Being physically touched in a world that had always turned away in disgust blinded one's desires. Kovacs had seen it coming and she'd let it happen. The training had gone too far.

"Damn you, Kovacs," Vicki cursed, taking one last puff and crushing out the cigarette.

In her closet, she retrieved a secondhand briefcase. The vendor had promised the combination lock worked and it did. She worked the code and opened it, exposing a thin folder of Xeroxed papers. The originals she'd kept back in Washington. Her fingers avoided the papers as if they carried an electric charge and unsnapped a small side pocket. She removed a worn business card. The professionally printed letters were old and faded. At one time they'd read PHOENIX LIFE EXTENSION FOUNDATION. She knew the address was the same. The phone number wasn't. The 411 operator had provided the updated version.

Shutting the briefcase, Vicki went to the nightstand and sat on the bed. She pulled the phone closer. She hesitated. After all these years, why had she suddenly returned to the scene in her life that had started her long downhill slide? The answer was simple. The foundation was moving. At least that's what she'd read in a tiny Associated Press article from the *Seattle Sentinel*. And a foundation move was a scenario she'd never envisioned. She could live with the nightmares, but not without making one last attempt at closure. And destroying the man who'd almost destroyed her.

Vicki picked up the handset. Dr. Wesley Kovacs would not be expecting her call. She dialed.

A male voice answered on the fifth ring. "Hello."

The fact there was no secretary unnerved Vicki some. Maybe it was still too early. "Is this Dr. Wesley Kovacs?" She knew it was.

"Who is this?" The voice was rough, but wide awake.

"Dr. Kovacs."

"Who . . ." There was a pause. "Vicki, is that you?"

She closed her eyes. Of course it's me you bastard, she wanted to say. Instead, "Yes, it's me, Vicki Zampisi. I'm back in Los Angeles."

A longer pause followed. She could well imagine what he was thinking.

"It's been quite some time. How have you been?" he asked.

"I'm still having the nightmares, if that's why you're inquiring."

"I'm sorry to hear that." There was a silence and for a moment, Vicki thought he'd disconnected.

"Is it true you're moving the foundation?" she asked.

He didn't answer.

"We need to talk." Vicki could hear him breathing.

"The foundation's concerns are no longer yours." An impersonal hardness had entered his voice.

"I think they are."

"Do I detect a threat?"

"Listen to me," she hissed. "I played your game. Now it's my turn."

"I realize—"

"You don't realize shit. Nothing," Vicki shot back. She tried to slow her breathing, not wanting to lose control when she dropped the bombshell. "Listen carefully," she said. "I want to see Ben."

"My God," Kovacs said. "You're insane. You know that's impossible."

"No more bullshit. When do I see him?"

"Don't push it," he said, the menace in his tone obvious.

"When do I see him?" Vicki persisted.

"I must warn you. The foundation suffered a minor problem, a setback—"

"When?"

"Reconsider, Vicki."

"And if I don't?"

More silence ensued before Kovacs spoke. "The past is best left undisturbed. Stay away from the foundation, Ms. Zampisi. Good-bye."

Vicki hung up the phone with both hands. Her tremor had returned.

Five

The alarm woke Jake first. It took a full ten seconds of the golden retriever's coaxing before Julie finally crawled out of Stage III sleep into Wednesday morning's semiconscious state. She'd barely slept two hours, fitful sleep at best. Though she couldn't recall any images, she knew the dream had returned by the disarray of her bedsheets.

Science called it psychomotor stimulation. The dream triggers the release of neurotransmitters in the cerebral cortex which in turn stimulates the release of acetylcholine at the motor neuron endplates, resulting in muscle contractions. Sometimes these contractions could be quite intense. In severe cases, Julie had actually witnessed dreaming patients injure themselves, though Julie had never sustained any physical injuries herself during one of her sleeping episodes. Occasionally, she'd been embarrassed, like the time at an all-night sorority party when she awoke screaming, "Worm Man, let go of my sister!" Luckily she was able to blame the outburst on the forty-proof fruit punch.

Rearranging the bedspread, Julie stopped long enough to observe Jake watching her with his all-too-knowing dog stare.

"Okay, let's have it, I talked in my sleep last night, right?" she said.

The dog turned on all fours and sat on his haunches.

Julie scratched his neck. "They'll be over soon, Jake," she said, mentally calculating what day the anniversary would fall on this year.

She walked toward the stairs. "I promise."

After a fast shower, some toast without butter, and coffee, Julie set the house alarm and let Jake out. She lived in a neat two-story stucco home in an upscale neighborhood of Monterey Park. Her large backyard was perfect for a dog with its lush vegetation and eucalyptus trees.

Once she'd ensured Jake had plenty of water and food, Julie fired up her blue Ford Thunderbird and took the Santa Monica Freeway west to work, and the CUMC complex.

The main hospital, University Hospital, was a sixteen-story building that from the outside resembled a huge hotel more than an acute care hospital. It was a thick L-shaped structure with the shorter leg of the L housing the emergency room, radiology suites, extensive laboratory facilities, and several outpatient surgery wards.

Over the years, a score of other modern buildings had been added to meet the ever-demanding community's health-care needs. One of these buildings, Psychiatric Hospital, was conceived in the early fifties at the end of a large tuberculosis epidemic. Originally a separate sanitarium called Old Red because of its red brick, the hospital later expanded to include the seven-story building serving as a treatment facility for psychiatric problems. Old Red now served as a document storage center only and no longer saw patients.

Adjacent to Psychiatric Hospital stood the medical center's distinguished sleep laboratory. Building Two East, as it was called, connected to the east side of Psychiatric Hospital at the second floor with a concrete crossover.

Only three other facilities rivaled the CUMC sleep lab in sophistication, innovation, and technology. These were the University of Chicago Sleep Disorders Clinic, the Bethesda Hospital

Sleep Center at the U.S. Army Medical Center in Bethesda, Maryland, and the Sleep Disorders Clinic in Oxford, England. The California University Sleep Laboratory, however, was the only one that owned the highly specialized computer hardware and software needed to visually interpret dreams.

Julie stepped off the elevators on the third floor, where most of the other staff psychiatrists also had their offices. The psychiatric clinics didn't open till 9 A.M., so hers were the only footsteps that echoed down the halls as she proceeded past a small waiting area and a conference room. The lights were on so the isolation didn't bother her.

Setting her briefcase down, Julie found a key in her purse and unlocked the two oak-paneled doors.

She stepped inside the outer administrative office and shut the doors behind her. Off this main suite stood six small faculty offices. Julie unlocked the door marked with her name and hung her lab coat on the brass hook behind the door. She opened her briefcase and removed her dream notes from the Amphisphere, which she placed in a file labeled MISCELLANEOUS DREAM SEQUENCES.

Her first call was to the eighth floor in the main hospital, the otolaryngology ward. After a brief conversation with the head nurse, she learned that Dr. Finny Todd had undergone a two-hour operation to repair the comminuted fracture of his nasal bridge as well as the medial wall of his left maxillary sinus. She was pleased to hear he'd tolerated the procedure well and was expected back to work in the emergency room in two to three weeks.

A few calls later, Julie returned to the first floor and the short concourse that connected the Psychiatric Hospital to University Hospital. By this time the halls of the main hospital were bustling with the activities of nursing students, medical students, interns, residents, CUMC staff physicians, respiratory therapists, and a diverse crew of other hospital employees.

Julie stopped at the nurses' station on the sixth floor of the general surgical ward. Irene Inez was in room 618.

The ward clerk looked up. "Morning, Dr. Charmaine."

"Hi." Julie stepped behind the counter toward the chart rack. "How's the new patient in room six-eighteen?"

"Quiet." The clerk swiveled around to face Julie. "I read your ER admit note. They have any idea who did it?"

Julie shook her head as she checked the nurse's notes from the previous night's shift. "No, not yet. If you need me later, I'll be in the sleep lab."

Julie tucked the chart under one arm and stepped the short distance down the hall to room 618.

Irene lay in the far bed in the semiprivate room. The near bed, separated by a partition, was empty.

Julie set the chart on a hospital tray beside a bottle of peroxide, some gauze four-by-fours, and tape. Inside a pink biohazard plastic bag, she saw Irene's old scalp dressing. The surgical intern had already been by to cleanse and evaluate the head wound.

Julie paused by the IV stand. Irene's dextrose drip had been slowed to a maintenance rate of 125 cc per hour. Moving closer to the head of the bed, she studied the calm lines of Irene's face. Nothing seemed to have changed since Julie's first visit, except for some minimal decrease in the swelling of her right eye. The female patient continued to stare blankly at the ceiling. Julie took out her penlight and shined it in each of Irene's eyes. The pupils reacted properly although she saw no visible evidence that Irene had consciously seen the light. After the brief neuro exam, Julie returned to the nurses' station. Irene would not be answering any questions today.

Julie sat at an open cubicle near the rotating chart rack and opened Irene's chart to the last progress note. It was written by the surgery resident. Irene's scalp avulsion was granulating nicely and there was no evidence of infection.

Julie glanced back at the open door of room 618. Something was not right about the woman she'd just examined. Irene Inez was not going to be just another routine post-traumatic stress syndrome patient. By this time, she should've been, at the least, responding to simple verbal commands.

Julie had barely started her note when her beeper sounded. She recognized the number of the sleep lab.

The two interns and three medical students looked down through the four-by-eight glass window in one of the six viewing bays in the CUMC Sleep Diagnostics Laboratory. Each bay held a ten-by-ten-foot sleep room similar to those found in the main hospital, except these used soundproof walls. A single hospital bed abutted one wall, with the foot of the bed facing the window. This ensured that the face of the subject would always be visible.

In this particular bay, a pretty girl of approximately sixteen years lay asleep. Multiple electrodes were attached to her head, chest, and extremities. An array of instruments, including an EEG and electrocardiogram, several oscilloscopes for monitoring brain waves as well as heart rhythms, an electrooculographic scope, an electromyogram, and two computer terminals compiled computer data. A video camera mounted on the inside wall could be remotely directed to cover every inch of the sleep room.

Behind the glass, viewers watched from an observation deck.

The console below the window held a computer terminal linked to the central station's supercomputer. It was an augmented version of the Cray J916 system, one of the most advanced and fastest computer systems in the world. It took every bit of the Cray's power to run the sophisticated VEROC software program that was the heart of the lab's dream studies.

Above the window hung a seventeen-inch SVGA monitor. A

speaker system allowed audio communication between the outside observers and the interior of the sleep room.

Jim Nelson, the technologist, sat at the console. He was a slight man with thinning hair, and at least fifteen years older than Julie. He was busy punching some keys on a computer keyboard. Behind him, the medical interns and students watched in silence and scribbled notes. No one turned when Julie entered Bay #3 and picked up Melanie Balsam's thick medical chart.

She slipped up to Jim's left shoulder. "Our patient's ready?" she asked.

Jim never took his eyes from the computer screen. "She'll be taking another run at REM shortly. No visualization yet."

Julie nodded as she studied the six irregular, sharply wavy lines that coursed continuously across one of the oscilloscopes. Each wave corresponded to one of the six electrodes taped to the girl's head—two on her forehead, one over each temple, and two barely visible on either side of her occiput near the base of her skull.

Julie's eyes left the oscilloscope for a moment and settled on the pretty face of the teenager sleeping on the other side of the glass partition. Melanie appeared relaxed and comfortable. Her long brunette hair lay loosely on the pillow, partially concealing the wires and leads coursing away from her scalp.

Julie motioned the interns and medical students away from the window a moment. They were here to observe and learn and Julie enjoyed teaching. Prior to this meeting, Julie had obtained Melanie's permission for her session to be witnessed.

"Any questions so far?" she asked the four observers.

One of the students raised her hand. "What's this patient being treated for?"

Julie spoke softly but clearly. "Melanie Balsam is a sixteen-year-old asthmatic who suffers from major depression with melancholic features. She was admitted three weeks ago after an attempted suicide. She's been my patient for over two years and until only recently, say the last one or two months, her mood features have been characterized by a loss of interest or pleasure in virtually all of her activities." Julie motioned toward the sleep room. "By utilizing the recent advances in sleep technology, we hope to better understand not only Melanie's condition but various other mental dysfunctions as well."

The same woman raised her hand again. "By analyzing dreams?"

The interns and other students also looked doubtful.

Julie wasn't bothered by the beginning doctors' skepticism. In fact, early on Julie had been skeptical as well, but with the development of VideoTech's software, she'd since become more convinced than ever of the validity of her research. There was no doubt that the advanced software program and new computer system stood on the brink of the breakthroughs she'd been hoping for. She might even have considered submitting herself to a dream study. If she thought it could change the past.

"Dream analysis has come a long way since the days and nights of Sigmund Freud and Carl Jung. In fact, it was Freud who said," Julie smiled, "and don't quote me, 'Dreams are the royal road to the subconscious mind.' Of course, we know now that dreams are much more. The process of sleep visualization, or dreaming, is actually a blueprint of all our subconscious thoughts, desires, and even fears. And there is increasing evidence that dream interpretation, if properly understood, can be utilized to treat certain forms of mental illness."

"Dr. Charmaine." It was Jim. He motioned at the oscilloscope where Melanie's six wave patterns, which previously had been the characteristic slow *delta* and *theta* waves of non-REM sleep, were now gradually transforming into the low-voltage sawtooth-like desynchronized waves indicative of the onset of rapid-eye-movement sleep.

Julie explained as the medical students and interns stepped closer for a better view. "Normal sleep patterns can be divided into five distinct stages. These include rapid-eye-movement sleep or REM sleep and the four stages of non-rapid-eye-movement sleep, stages one, two, three, and four." Julie pointed to the oscilloscope screen as Jim continued to monitor the wave forms. "In the past, the process of monitoring sleep was called polysomnography and consisted of measuring three specific electrophysiologic parameters. One of which was, and still is, the electroencephalogram or EEG brain waves which you see here. If you look closely, you'll see that Melanie's brain waves have taken on a roughened appearance indicating she has just now entered a period of REM or rapid-eye-movement sleep. In a typical subject, REM sleep occurs cyclically, alternating with NREM or non-rapid-eye-movement sleep about every eighty to a hundred minutes, and it is during these REM periods that the majority of our dreams take place."

Julie next motioned to another screen. This one was smaller and was located just to the right of the larger oscilloscope. "We also measure electrooculographic activity which you see here. These leads indicate any electrical activity in the six extraocular eye muscles." Julie stepped around one of the interns and pointed to an instrument with four needles that extended out over a roll of graph paper. "This instrument monitors any electromyographic activity of the patient's limbs and trunk muscles. When she moves, it keys a corresponding movement of the needle, which then contacts the graph paper. When the instrument is turned on," Julie paused to turn a dial. The graph paper began to roll causing one of the needles to make a low amplitude deflection on the paper. "Any activity can be recorded. Here you can see the chest lead, indicating Melanie's respiratory pattern. Presently her breathing is perfectly normal."

"Dr. Charmaine, look," one of the interns said, pointing.

They could all see the irregular nervous jumping of Melanie's eyelids.

"That twitching is characteristic of REM sleep," Julie quickly explained. "It corresponds to the underlying activity of the muscles that control a person's eye movements."

The electrooculographic waves on the smaller oscilloscope were bouncing off their baselines.

As Jim began to punch in some numbers on the console keyboard, the same intern commented, "I was under the impression most sleep studies were done at night."

Julie nodded. "They are. In general. However this case in particular is not so much a sleep study as it is a dream analysis."

"There's a difference?" one of the medical students asked.

Julie nodded again. "Sleep studies are used to evaluate primary sleep disorders such as insomnia, hypersomnia, and narcolepsy. In dream analysis, we are more interested in evaluating a patient's dream content. And since the majority of REM sleep falls during the morning hours, early morning studies are not uncommon since it is during these hours that the majority of the subject's dreams occur."

The woman who asked the first question pointed down into the sleep bay. "What's that black box for?" She was referring to a six-inch-square box on a small shelf with numerous fine wires running from it to the two electrodes attached to the back of Melanie's scalp. A larger-diameter cable exited the top of the box and entered the wall just behind Melanie's bed.

"That," Julie answered, "is called a transducer. Its job is to convert every single EEG wave into a series of zeroes and ones. These digitized brain waves, so to speak, are then fed into our computer network where they can be analyzed."

Julie left the explanation at that, though she was thoroughly familiar with the history behind the new VEROC software, a computer program developed by VideoTech Corporation and designed to assist in dream analysis. Based upon hundreds of patients and thousands of hours of interviews, researchers discovered certain relationships existed between various patterns of brain-wave activity and the subject's dream images. Using advanced computer graphics, VideoTech then created scenes as close as possible to the visions recounted in the dreams and recorded them. It wasn't long before VideoTech had collected an entire film library of sample dream images—people, animals, landscapes. They dubbed it the generic Dream Bank.

Next, each specific image was assigned a nine-digit code so that it could be digitized, stored, and retrieved by a computer.

This same nine-digit combination was also assigned to the specific brain-wave pattern that initially triggered the image. When the electrodes were attached and the computer recognized a portion of the dreaming subject's EEG pattern, the image would be instantaneously retrieved from the generic Dream Bank and projected onto a video screen where it could be seen and recorded. It was like watching TV. Almost. And since the EEG electrodes over the occipital region of the skull yielded the most accurate data, the program was christened VEROC, an acronym for Visually Evoked Responses of the Occipital Cortex.

Julie moved behind Jim. She watched as his fingers moved across the keyboard, punching in the various combinations of letters and numbers necessary to run the computer program. She motioned to the seventeen-inch television screen mounted above the observation window.

"If all of you will observe the display overhead, we'll see if we can't peek into Melanie's dream state and actually see what she's dreaming," Julie said.

As all eyes left Melanie and targeted the monitor, the screen's static faded to a kaleidoscope of blacks, grays, and whites.

Julie explained as the students and interns watched in silence. "VEROC is a first-generation dream-imager. I know this sounds like it's right out of an Orson Welles movie, but with the VEROC software, we are capable of crudely imaging dreams."

A burst of red color formed in one corner of the screen. It quickly broke apart like oil droplets in water.

"How does it work?" A student asked.

"VEROC records electrical impulses from the visual cortex," Julie answered. "In this case, these impulses are represented by Melanie's brain waves. Our database has over three thousand images and each image is assigned a code. When the computer isolates a match between a brain-wave pattern and an image in our database, this image is then projected on the screen."

Jim punched a key. A burst of *ah's* erupted from the students and interns.

A blend of deeper reds now filled the monitor, giving way to a generic image of a man and woman undulating briefly in the red sea of color before fading out.

Julie put a hand on Jim's shoulder. "Melanie's angry."

"Red is anger?" the intern asked.

Julie nodded as she quickly scanned the monitors recording Melanie's vital signs. Her blood pressure, pulse, and respirations, though increased, were well within normal limits. Routine.

Julie looked back at the monitor. "It used to be said that people only dream in black and white. We now know this to be incorrect." Though Julie could have embellished her point from personal experience, she didn't. She continued, "Humans display the same wide variation of feelings in their subconscious lives as they do in their conscious lives. These four basic emotions, love, hate, fear, and anger, have all been consistently correlated with various shades of three primary colors. Blues are associated with feelings of comfort, harmony, love, or well-being. Yellows indicate fear or terror. And red symbolizes hatred or anger. Also, reds have been associated with feelings of deceit." Julie glanced back at her patient. "When we wake Melanie later, we'll show her the video and attempt to get her interpretation of what we've just witnessed. I'll then be able to use this information to assist in her therapy."

"Who were the man and woman?" the tall intern asked.

"Good question," Julie said. "At this point all we can accurately say, at least according to Melanie's electrical activity, is that some male and female, represented by a generic image encoded on the VEROC software for man and woman, appeared in Melanie's dream and this specific image elicited anger or hatred in her subconscious mind."

The phone on the console lit up.

Jim picked it up. "Sleep lab," he answered. "Sure, she's right here." He handed the phone to Julie. "Surgery ward, University Hospital."

Julie took the receiver. "This is Dr. Charmaine." A look of concern crossed her face as she listened. "Yes, I'll be right there." She hung up the phone.

"What's up?" Jim asked.

Julie swallowed. Her mind was racing. "The patient I admitted last night just suffered a massive cardiac arrest."

Six

Julie barely remembered racing to the elevators and rising to the sixth floor. She saw the Code Blue team standing outside room 618. Julie recognized Dr. Kurtzer. He was the anesthesiologist on call responsible for IV access and intubation. Seeing him standing idly in the hall was not a good sign.

Terry Kalone, the ward nurse on for the day shift, intercepted Julie, Irene's chart in one hand. "Dr. Charmaine." Terry appeared shaken up. "She became hysterical. It was so sudden. I was only changing her dressing. Suddenly Ms. Inez began to cry and struggle."

"It's okay, Terry." Of course it wasn't okay and it sure as hell wasn't routine. But what else could Julie say?

She reached for the chart while Terry continued to elaborate. "She was quiet the entire morning, vital signs all normal, then it was like she just went crazy. She started to seize. A minute later, everything just . . . stopped."

"These things happen." *Very rarely.*

The internist on Code Blue team duty approached them.

"I'm sorry, Julie," he said, visibly perspiring. "We never got her out of ventricular fibrillation."

"Irene had no history of cardiac disease, at least according to her aunt. What happened?" Julie asked.

He shrugged awkwardly. "A Code Blue was called around

eight-fifty. I was in the middle of a teaching conference. When the team arrived, she'd completely stopped breathing and was in asytole." The internist shrugged again. "After some adrenaline, a lidocaine push, and calcium, we were able to generate a fine v. fib. But that's as far as she went. We worked on her at least an hour."

"It doesn't make any sense." Julie shook her head.

Inside the room, she stopped. If she hadn't seen the numbers on the door, she'd have thought she was in the wrong room. Room 618 was a disaster. The vacant bed near the door was thrust up against one wall. The curtained partition was pulled back. And Irene's bed was angled out toward the center of the room allowing plenty of room on four sides for easy access to the patient. Spent syringes and ampules of epinephrine and sodium bicarbonate cluttered the floor. A central-line kit was open on a hospital tray. Irene's sheets were tossed in the bathroom.

Julie stepped over a small spot of blood to Irene's bed. Julie's patient was no longer restrained. An endotracheal tube protruded grotesquely from her mouth. Several IV angiocaths remained taped in place on each arm.

Julie examined Irene's head. Terry hadn't even had time to apply the new dressing before Irene seized. The scalp avulsion was open but it appeared clean with no evidence of infection or sepsis. Julie lifted a bottle from near Irene's head and sniffed it. It smelled like alcohol. Terry must've been using it when the seizures began.

"Dr. Charmaine."

Julie turned.

It was Terry. "They're ready to take her," the nurse said.

Behind her two men in white waited.

Julie motioned the orderlies in. Irene Inez would make one last trip down the hallowed halls of University Hospital. But the autopsy wouldn't be performed in the medical center's morgue. That was because Irene had expired within twenty-four hours of being admitted, thus classifying hers as a coroner's case. From the hospital she'd be taken to the L.A. County morgue, one block away.

As the orderlies pulled the sheet over Irene's head, Julie found the conference room on the east wing of the general surgical ward where she could spend a moment alone. The next of kin—Soccoro Chavez—would need to be notified, never a pleasant task. After that, Julie planned on reviewing the chart in meticulous detail. Healthy people just don't die of cardiac arrest.

Julie leaned back, staring at the ceiling. *Dammit, Irene, why today? You were so young.* She shut her eyes.

Only in such situations did she find herself reflecting on her career choice. Not that she would ever change. She loved what she did.

Even as a shy, introverted five-year-old, growing up in a Dallas suburb, Julie had dreamed of becoming a physician. Janine would be the actress and Julie the actress's shrink. That's how their mother used to joke. Though Julie was younger by two years, she was always looking out for her older sister. Occasionally, especially this time of year, Julie found herself wondering if Janine would have been as successful in achieving her career aspirations as Julie had been at hers.

Like her dad and grandfather, both of whom earned accolades for their respective research and technical skills in surgery, Julie exhibited the superb physical talents required to excel as a surgeon. Instead, she chose psychiatry. Partly because of Janine, but even more so she relished the challenge of delving into a patient's mind, probing for those inscrutable secrets that contribute to an individual's mental blueprint, more than exploring a distended abdominal cavity searching for an inflamed appendix or ruptured gallbladder.

A tormented mind could never be healed with simple excision. Irene Inez was an extreme case in point. Such a waste.

Julie suddenly felt older than her thirty-four years. Life was too damned short. Just ask Janine.

There was a light knock at the door. Terry stepped in. "Dr. Charmaine."

Julie attempted a weak smile.

"You okay?" Terry asked.

"I'm fine. It's just not a real pleasant way to start a day."

"I hear you." Terry paused briefly. "This may not be the right time, but did you know you have a visitor?"

Julie stood up. "Relative?"

"Don't think so. Say's he's a detective."

Julie glanced at her watch. It was 10:15. "Tell him I'll be right there."

"Sure." Terry closed the door behind her.

Julie took two deep breaths. She wanted to make the meeting quick. She still had Melanie's sleep session to evaluate and a clinic full of patients this afternoon. Plus her research. And Irene's next of kin and chart review. It never ended.

Outside, she found a man politely examining one of those inexpensive reproduction hospital pictures that adorned the walls of University Hospital. When he turned, she saw he was unshaven and wore wrinkled clothes, yet he possessed a certain ruggedness that touched her. Her eyes settled momentarily on an inch-long scar above his right brow.

"Hi, I'm Dr. Julie Charmaine. I presume you're here to discuss Irene Inez."

"Matt Guardian." He held out a large hand that had smooth mounds of scar tissue over the fourth and fifth knuckles. "Robbery and Homicide, LAPD."

Julie shook his hand. The grip was firm but not too firm. "Detective Guardian, if you're here to question Ms. Inez, I'm afraid you're too late."

"How so?"

"She . . . we're not really sure what happened. But this morning at approximately nine-fifty, Ms. Irene Inez was pronounced dead."

"I guess her injuries were more serious than you thought."

Julie didn't take offense, though his demeanor exhibited a certain aloofness. She assumed he was a very busy man. "No, that's what's so puzzling. The CT scan last night was normal and all her other lab work's been within normal limits. Besides that, Irene was so young, and at least according to her aunt, she had no history of any medical problems. It just doesn't make any sense."

"Any guesses as to a preliminary cause of death?"

"Cardiorespiratory arrest." Julie returned Matt's steady stare. "As to what caused her heart to stop beating, we'll have to wait for the autopsy report. I can tell you Irene was suffering from some type of post-traumatic hysteria."

"Something like shock."

Julie nodded. "That's correct. Irene experienced something that she was unable to emotionally accept."

"Was she raped?"

Julie shook her head. "There was no evidence of that. However, that doesn't mean she wasn't sexually abused."

"The police report mentioned Ms. Inez talking some sort of gibberish. Do you recall her saying anything?"

"Nothing that made any sense. She said, *'el se murio,'* something related to death or dying. Oh, and she said *'chango'*."

"That's it?"

"Other than *por favor* and *no.* It almost sounded like she was pleading."

After a few uncomfortable minutes of silence, Matt's attention returned to the picture. Julie would've thought he was daydreaming except for the intensity in his green eyes.

"You know my ex-wife used to paint," he said. "She'd spend hours on the beach just painting waves. Can you believe that crap? Hours."

The abrupt change in subject matter momentarily caught Julie off guard. "Painting can be relaxing," she said. "We even use it for therapy at times."

"Do you paint?"

"No." Julie watched Detective Guardian continue to stare at the picture. She could tell his mind wasn't on his ex-wife's waves. Neither was hers. "Well, detective, I have to get back to work." She turned back for the nurses' station.

Matt took a step after her. *"Chango,"* he said.

Julie stopped and faced him. "It's a Spanish slang word for monkey. What Irene meant by that, your guess is as good as mine."

"Monkey," Matt repeated. His tone reflected an attempt to decipher some hidden meaning from the simple phrase.

"Irene's aunt's name is Soccoro Chavez," Julie said. "I suggested she call your department. Now I have to call her to say her niece died."

"Those calls aren't easy."

"No."

"We'll be contacting her." Matt started for the elevators.

Julie called after him. "Detective Guardian."

He stopped.

"Let me know if I can be of any further assistance."

Matt smiled thinly. "Sure, Dr. Charmaine. And I am sorry about your patient."

Julie watched as the elevator doors closed behind him, then returned to room 618. In the stillness, she tried to visualize the scenario leading up to Irene's cardiac arrest. Terry had reported Irene's condition stable until she'd attempted to clean her scalp wound. Julie looked around and found the disinfectant bottle Terry had used just prior to the Code Blue call. She read the label.

The bottle contained seventy percent isopropyl alcohol.

Seven

Matt found Sokol Ramani, his partner of three years, at his desk on the third floor of Parker Center, home of the Robbery and Homicide Division of the LAPD. Ramani was the total antithesis of Matt's rugged good looks and rock-hard 195 pounds on a six-foot-one-inch frame.

At barely five foot six, Ramani's one redeeming physical attribute was his jet black hair. When most men were complaining of hair loss, his scalp at forty-three was thicker now than when he was twenty. It matched his waistline, which almost matched his age. And with shoulders that dropped from his ears, Ramani still failed to see what Isabelle, his third wife, saw in him.

The nascent file lay open before Ramani. Irene Inez was officially theirs.

"So Blocker found the lady hysterical in some alley off Cincinnati," the shorter detective said. "That's at least five blocks from where her Honda Civic was parked. Blocker and Officer Joyce Pearce were probably bouncing old Car Fifty-four pretty good when they got the disturbing-the-peace call."

"So Blocker's still banging Pearce."

Ramani ignored Matt and studied Blocker's notes. "The victim looked like she'd been worked over pretty good. Odds on a jealous husband or angry boyfriend. Or maybe both. But what's this Blocker says about her being covered with some sort of crap when they brought her in?"

"Like she'd been in a sewer," said Matt, who was intimately familiar with the file.

"I thought Blocker found her in an alley."

"He did, but ten feet away, a manhole cover sat half open. And if you'd smelled her when the medics brought her in, you'd figure she'd been in the sewer too. At least according to Pearce. They bagged some samples for forensics."

"How thoughtful."

"It's a start." Matt returned to his desk, checked for incoming messages, and heard one from Blocker—the Inez girl had expired. What's new? Matt made a quick call to the coroner's letting them know he was on his way and left the office.

With no witnesses thus far, the case's resolution would greatly depend on information gleaned from the victim. The fact she was dead was not encouraging. However, there were indications she'd put up quite a struggle during her ordeal. The coroner's evaluation of swabbed material taken from under Ms. Inez's nails might provide additional leads. Matt hoped so.

The energy required to solve a homicide in the City of Angels increased exponentially each day that passed without a suspect.

And though Matt, an ex-boxer, figured he had adeptly transferred his pugilistic energy to a different kind of ring, he also realized he was fighting in a ring without ropes or Queensbury rules. In this ring, encompassing more than four-hundred square miles and 3.5 million people, a loss didn't mean a number in a right-hand column, but a fast trip to the county coroner.

The world was getting to be a tougher place to live and even tougher to control. Every hour of every day, a man, woman, or child was either beaten, burned, stabbed, shot, raped, abused, tortured, mutilated, or murdered in L.A. And not one, but many. Crime was a vicious animal that was impossible to cage, much less destroy.

Matt was an ex-fighter, ex-husband, and one day he'd be an

ex-homicide detective. That thought seemed all the more enticing on days such as today.

The Los Angeles County coroner was located in a three-story brick building on North Mission Road. Matt parked his Monte Carlo and walked up the short steps to the large glass doors, humming "I Love L.A." as he passed the sign that read:

DEPARTMENT OF THE CORONER
–MEDICAL EXAMINER
–FORENSIC LABORATORY
–PUBLIC SERVICES

Matt flashed his badge at the receptionist and found the stairs to the second floor and the deputy medical examiners' offices. He was looking for one in particular, Dr. Dan Dorfman's.

Three offices down he walked through an open door with Dorfman's name on it and into an office, more of a cubicle really, cluttered with charts and folders.

Matt knocked on the desktop. "Anybody home? Dorfman?" Matt had worked on and off with Dorfman for over five years. He wouldn't exactly call the deputy coroner his best drinking buddy but he did not hesitate to call Dorfman "thorough."

A half-filled coffee mug showed a fat bear dressed in a Rams NFL jersey drinking a beer and watching TV. The Rams insignia was passé. The team sold out to St. Louis in 1995. Matt stuck one finger in the coffee and found it cold.

"That's a good way to get burned."

Matt licked his finger and turned. "I've been burned before."

A large, middle-aged, balding man in a white lab coat filled the doorway. The extra-large coat barely covered his gut. Up close the skin on Dorfman's puffy face looked crisscrossed with red and blue veins. When the pathologist became excited or exerted himself too much, these vessels would fill and swell. Ramani and some of the other detectives sometimes joked about what these same veins did when Dorfman moved his bowels.

Dorfman moved by Matt and around his desk. "So who you poking these days, Guardian?"

"No one you know."

"I hope she's female." Dorfman took a sip of the cold coffee and spit it in the trash. He offered the rest to Matt. Matt declined. Dorfman turned and opened the window behind his desk and tossed the remaining coffee outside.

"Doesn't that stain the wall?" Matt asked.

"Building's due for an overhaul." Dorfman placed the mug on a shelf of books next to one wall. "Kind of like the coroner's department."

"How old's Contrera?" asked Matt, referring to the chief examiner.

"Sixty-one."

"You next in line?"

Dorfman exhaled through thick lips. "Depends on the Board of Supervisors. You know I helped crack the Death Angel case."

Matt nodded. Dorfman had been instrumental in nailing Johnny "the Angel" Bogata. It was Dorfman's piecemeal forensic work that linked the four murders by potassium cyanide ingestion from San Francisco to similar homicides committed in L.A. And Dorfman was quick to tell anyone who'd listen, including Johnny "the Angel" himself, if he'd been given the chance.

Dorfman reached under a stack of office memos and pulled out a thin manila folder. "How's that shit-dump partner of yours?"

"Ramani?"

"You know any other shit-dumps?"

"Not really." A lie, Matt knew plenty. "He and Isabelle are still fighting."

Dorfman shrugged. "Those Latina bitches can be hot, real hot."

Matt tried not to imagine how Dorfman acquired this pearl of

Latino culture. "You get a chance to look at that stuff Blocker sent in from last night?" the detective asked.

"Follow me."

Dorfman led Matt down a short corridor to another hall where they took a right toward the forensic lab. Partway down the hall Dorfman slowed. He ducked into a break room. Matt heard the jingle of change as Dorfman slid some coins into two of the vending machines.

The deputy coroner returned with a Snickers bar and a cup of coffee and led Matt past the drug laboratory and through two swinging double metal doors that read FORENSIC PATHOLOGY.

Dorfman stopped at a long counter mounted with several microscopes. Here, gross tissue specimens were prepared for microscopic examination by the deputy medical examiners.

"So what's the latest odds?"

"Twelve to one," Dorfman said as he grabbed a glass slide from a box marked simply with a number, 807B. "You interested?"

"Maybe."

Prior to his career in law enforcement, Matt had dropped out of community college to pursue a career as a professional fighter. He fought six years as a light heavy, winning twenty against two losses. The second loss, a decision to a man who eventually climbed to the number-two contender, resulted in a detached retina and ended his ring days on the professional circuit. Now at thirty-eight, Matt still followed the local fight game and he and Dorfman occasionally made small bets on fights at the Olympic Auditorium.

Dorfman focused the microscope. "Take it or leave it."

The fight pitted a welterweight rising star from the streets of L.A., Harvey Gipson, against an older journeyman from Detroit, a guy named Ranier. Gipson was black. Ranier was white and a twelve-to-one underdog. Supposedly, though, Gipson had a glass jaw.

Matt figured the bet was safe. "Take it," he finally said, meaning he'd go for Ranier with twelve-to-one odds. Make the fight interesting.

Though Dorfman remained quiet as he studied the slide, Matt knew he'd taken his bet. Dorf liked betting almost as much as Matt used to like to fight.

The pathologist pushed back from the scope. "Hell, you and Ramani have really outdone yourselves this time. Here, take a seat and look."

Matt sat down and attempted to focus.

"This is from the samples sent over by Blocker and Pearce," Dorfman said. "This particular slide was made from stains from the girl's clothing. I believe the note said she might have been in a sewer."

Matt said nothing as he stared at the dark amorphous shapes intertwined with some fine white filaments. "What's the white?"

"Cloth threads. Appears to be cotton. Definitely not nylon or other synthetic fibers."

"And the black shit?"

"Wait." Dorfman removed the slide and put in another. "This slide was made from the bag marked NAILS. Since there was no keratin or cuticle present, I assume Blocker meant from under the nails. That would make more sense."

Matt looked back into the scope as Dorfman talked between bites from his Snickers bar. "Now here it starts to get a bit more interesting. This sample was prepared in paraffin and sliced down to one one-thousandth of an inch thickness. As you can tell, most of the specimen resembles what you called it earlier, black shit. However if you focus down close, you begin to see vague shadows and outlines. But if you switch to high power," Dorfman turned the lens for Matt, "you begin to appreciate various structures."

"What the hell am I looking at?" Matt saw some cylindrical forms and several flat structures with irregular outlines.

"That's just it, I'm not sure. I did a quick review of one of my histopath texts and I'd swear some of these slides look very close to skin cells and striated muscle fibers." Dorfman paused to finish off the Snickers.

Matt exhaled as he pushed away. "It still looks like shit to me."

"Well, most of it is. Actually sewer sludge, what you'd find running under most L.A. streets at this very moment. And even that slide you're looking at, which by the way is the most revealing, is nothing more than necrotic tissue, if that."

"I thought you said you could make out skin and muscle."

"Maybe. But even if it is, it's all decaying. Never hold up under intense scrutiny from an opposing expert witness."

"Prints?"

Dorfman chuckled. "Get real, chief."

Matt stared back at the scope. "So you're telling me Inez scratched a corpse, not some jealous boyfriend."

"Nah." Dorfman licked a pudgy finger. "Not unless he's a rotting sonuvabitch. I'm having a few slides prepared for SEM analysis."

"SEM?"

"Scanning electron microscopy. Might give us a few more clues." The coroner shifted his bulk down one stool. "Before you rush out, take a gander at this. Took me over an hour to find it."

He moved aside so Matt could position himself before the stereoscopic binocular microscope.

Dorfman assisted with the focus. "That's magnified one hundred times."

Matt recognized the miniature overlapping scales resembling the wood shingles on a roof. "A hair," he said.

"A hair fragment," Dorfman corrected him. "A very tiny hair fragment."

"It looks orange."

"More red actually. The magnification does that."

"Human?"

"Possibly, though the sample's really too small to determine source purely on scale count. The medulla, the central core of the shaft, might even be considered large enough to classify as animal in origin. I'll defer final analysis to the trace evidence lab."

Matt took one last glance at the slide and shot from the hip, recalling his earlier conversation with Julie. "What about a monkey?" he asked.

"You think a monkey attacked the girl?" Dorfman asked incredulously.

"Just asking."

The coroner leaned forward for a second look. "Can't give you an opinion. I'm not a forensic primatologist. I can inform you, the laboratory gurus will require a hell of a lot more hair than this to determine what type of animal it came from, if in fact it's eventually determined to be an animal hair. And even if it is animal in origin, considering the sewer source, it probably won't contribute much. Might not even be related to the case."

"I appreciate your optimism." Matt started for the door, pausing momentarily. "Those other slides. You mentioned striated muscle."

"I wouldn't wager my medical license, but yes. Remember the state of the tissue was far from optimal."

"That'd make the scratches deep."

Dorfman appeared to suppress a belch. "Let me illustrate it this way. If this girl had gotten hold of your face, you'd no longer be a candidate for LAPD poster boy."

"Scarring?"

"Quite possibly."

Matt briefly touched the scar above his right eye before heading back for the exit.

The pathologist called after him. "Hey, chief, what was your girl doing crawling through a sewer?"

Without turning Matt said, "Don't know, but you'll get a chance to ask her."

"Yeah?"

"Yup." Matt stopped at the door. "Coroner's case." Then he disappeared down the hall.

Eight

In the dark, the infrastructure appeared more imposing than during the daylight hours, the deep edges of night effectively concealing the earthquake-damaged brick and mortar walls. If it weren't for the fence with its NO TRESPASSING warnings, Vicki might have thought only the lack of electricity prevented the Shilden Hotel from conducting its usual business.

She turned right at the corner and parked in front of the all-night laundromat. She kept the engine idling and opened the window. The rap music from someone's boom box blared from the laundromat's entrance where several men jostled and talked. Next door, on the steps of a closed consignment shop, she saw a glowing ember shift back and forth in front of a couple sprawled on the shop's steps. The softly pungent scent of marijuana drifted her way.

Vicki debated pulling closer to the alley behind the hotel. She and Ben had always used the more familiar rear entrance, never the front. Kovacs would drop them off in the clinic van, and the odd couple, as the old nightman used to jokingly refer to them with just enough fear in his eyes to keep a healthy distance, would sneak inside under the blanket of darkness. Once safe in their room, which Kovacs had leased for research purposes, Vicki would instruct Ben on the chores of daily living. Kovacs usually picked them up after only a few hours, but later, he'd allowed them the entire night together, sometimes not returning until early the next morning. The hours from 2 A.M. till dawn had been the best. She had never felt as secure as when wrapped tightly in Ben's arms, savoring the strength in his fingers as they pressed against her rib cage just under her breasts.

Years later, she still wondered if she'd ever rest as soundly again.

Vicki decided she preferred the laundromat's better-illuminated spot—the neighborhood wasn't exactly Mayberry RFD—and shut off the ignition.

An older man and woman walking a small dog passed on the opposite curb. They didn't look her way. In the distance, Vicki heard a siren and another dog begin to bark. She waited for the wailing to stop, using the time to secure the band around her head. She'd tied her blond hair back in a ponytail, exposing her ears. The surgery had corrected their lopsided appearance, but deep scars remained. It was night so Vicki didn't care.

Momentarily she sensed a weakening of her resolve. Was the photo worth risking an arrest? Only she and one other individual even knew of its existence. And more than likely, after all the intervening years, the picture had already been discovered by some housekeeper, and discarded as a joke, or perhaps destroyed in the earthquake. But without the photograph, who would believe her?

Watching a girl enter the laundromat gave Vicki a start. The woman wore a white nurse's uniform. She carried a bag of clothing.

The image jarred Vicki in a way that was both uncomfortable and disturbing. She'd almost been a nurse, too. *Before.*

The siren's wail had ceased but Vicki didn't move. She mouthed the word, *before.*

It was strange how her life could be so sharply partitioned. Before it happened. After it happened. A single sharp incision in the fabric of her existence separating the before from the after.

The before. She'd been Ben's teacher and later his intimate companion. And the after. Her blood turned cold.

Yes, she wanted that damned picture.

Vicki entered the alley from the sidewalk, walking with a sense of purpose. If she were being watched she didn't want to appear sneaky or hesitant. Dressed in dark pants, shirt, and black waist-pack, her attire blended well with shadows. She stepped around a puddle of water and approached the gap in the fence. Though the city truck was gone, the construction cones remained. A barricade was set up, enclosing the black pit. A ladder led underground. She could hear seeping water and the air smelled faintly of rotten eggs.

Wood planks had been laid around the construction zone and Vicki used one to slide between the barricade and the fence, allowing her to enter the back lot of the hotel. She relied solely on the half moon's glow as the building's silhouette blocked all illumination from the streetlights. Fortunately, there were few clouds and with her eyes properly adjusted to the dark, she sidestepped the stacks of plywood, bricks, and other debris that littered the lot. She moved cautiously, careful not to step on a nail or twist an ankle.

Vicki found the rear entrance nailed shut under a sheet of plywood so she approached the nearest first-floor unit, the one she'd seen that morning, and climbed up on the balcony. The railing was loose and creaked when she swung her legs over. When she placed her feet on the floor, pieces of plaster cracked under her weight. The noise made her stop. She listened but heard only the evening street traffic, shielded some by the building. She waited a full half-minute before unzipping her waist-pack and removing a small flashlight. Another thirty seconds of relative silence strengthened her belief she was alone and she turned it on, partially blocking the beam with her free hand.

Sizeable chunks of ceiling plaster from the second-floor unit and broken pottery covered the balcony floor. The skeletal remains of a potted tree shadowed one corner. In separate piles, beer and soft-drink cans reflected back at her, as if someone at one time had attempted to collect them but never returned.

For no apparent reason, Vicki shivered. Wiping a few strands of hair from her forehead, she felt her skin crawl with perspiration. She took a deliberate step forward.

More sheets of plywood replaced the sliding glass door. Several hung loosely, their warped edges holding the rusted nails that had once secured the wood in place. They'd been ripped free, exposing an entrance.

Aiming the beam, Vicki checked the metal door frame for any glass edges, and finding none, she stepped across the threshold, careful to avoid the nails.

Inside, the air smelled wet and dank. Again, she stood quietly and listened. Excluding the few chirruping crickets, she heard nothing else living. Every so often an inanimate creak or groan betrayed the building's fragility, but she figured since the hotel had stood this long since the quake, it wasn't going to pick tonight to implode.

With purposeful swings of her light, Vicki made a brief survey. Even though this unit wasn't *the room,* the familiarities of the layout gave her an odd sense of security. She'd been here before. A bed abutted the wall to her right, a dresser to her immediate left. Cracks spiderwebbed across the mirror's surface. Opposite her, she saw the closet, bathroom, and door leading into the hall. Other than the color of the carpet, green now versus brown, and the pattern of the bedspread, it was all the same. Even the same monotonous faded yellow wallpaper plastered the walls.

As opposed to the building's exterior, the interior demonstrated little obvious structural damage. Vicki detected no large cracks or pieces of plaster lying about. More debris littered the carpet—cans, liquor bottles, cigarette cartons, and Styrofoam fast-food containers. It was obvious the trespassing warnings had done little to keep out the homeless and loiterers.

Only when she started across the carpet did Vicki note the floor was canted from horizontal. The foundation sloped away from her and her beam reflected off a shallow puddle of water pooling in one corner. She stepped around the foot of the bed and reached for the doorknob. Mud caked its brass surface and Vicki used an old rag from the dresser to wipe the grime away. The door swung open easily to the halfway point then stopped, its hinges wedged in position.

She slid sideways into the hall and again marveled at how the passage of time seemed to have skipped the first floor of the Shilden Hotel. Though rain-stained, the carpet appeared in decent shape and pictures still adorned the walls. Using the light, she could read the numbers on the doors to the three nearest units—one to her left and three and four to her right.

Vicki propped a cardboard carton against the door to the second unit to prevent the door from swinging shut behind her and started down the hall. In spots, water squished under her shoes and she noted black smudges staining the carpet fibers at regular intervals. She would have guessed footsteps except for their oddly amorphous shapes. Walking the corridor, she found more evidence of damage—cracks in the walls, fallen Sheetrock, and above the door frame to the third unit, she had to step around a splintered wood beam that had crashed through the ceiling. Water dripped from exposed wiring and when she pointed her flashlight up, she glimpsed two furry shapes dart from view.

Vicki picked up her pace. With each step her mind traveled back through the years. She heard her own laughter and turned suddenly, only to realize the gaiety originated in her imagination.

Vicki found the door to room five lying in the hall, its wood panel splintered down the center. Standing in the doorway, she let the beam be an extension of her fingers, playing it across the dresser, the mirror, the nightstand, and finally the bed. *This had been our room.*

Vicki moistened her lips with her tongue. In distinct waves, the images played out in her mind.

She saw Ben watching her in the mirror. His odd expression was one of intense curiosity. She had no idea he was sexually aroused until she heard him make that strange noise way down in his throat. She'd never heard it before, a deep guttural sound that initially frightened her.

Of course she had no idea Kovacs was observing them as she slipped her sweater up over her head. Ben just sat on the bed, never taking his eyes from her. His keen attention to her every movement made her feel beautiful. She'd never had a male stare at her with such rabid fascination. There was no doubt he wanted her that night and for the first time in her life, she saw herself as a desirable woman, not a freak in a carnival sideshow. Ben didn't care that she had a misshapen skull or eyes separated by too much bone.

And she loved him for it. She turned and faced his hunger, unclipping her bra and letting it dangle from her fingers before dropping to the carpet. She stepped closer, allowing Ben's fingertips to explore her. He nuzzled her nipples, which by then were as hard as pebbles, sending titillating shocks of electricity into her groin. That first time she recalled she'd been menstruating and this only seemed to fuel Ben's passion, like pouring gasoline on a fire.

He reminded her of a diffident child, timorous at first, then curious, and finally growing in confidence each night together, until near the end, he was hunching her from behind with the heated urgency of a prisoner on death row, so desperate was his desire to please her. Multiple times she thought she would explode into a thousand tiny fragments and even now, twenty years later, she wondered if this unnatural act would have been consummated, if not for the heavy doses of antipsychotics Kovacs had administered to her.

Maybe, probably, no, who the hell cared. It happened, and it continued to happen, with Kovacs, the opportunistic voyeur, videotaping each session from the peephole above the bed. For research. The perverted bastard.

Vicki tried to swallow but the lump remained in her throat. She moved to the headboard and saw that the wood was still firmly anchored to the wall. A strip of duct tape had been placed over the peephole. She tossed a beer can aside and placed one knee on the mattress. The worn springs creaked under her weight. Using the light, she searched for the one spot where she could leave a picture and be confident no tenants would discover it. It had been raining heavily that night and she and Ben had been forced to leave in a hurry. Someone had complained to the night manager about the noise.

Positioning the flashlight against the wall, she aimed the beam down. She knew where to look and quickly found the place where the wood did not firmly contact the wall, a narrow seam separating the Sheetrock from the headboard. Brushing away a cobweb, she leaned closer, cocked her head to the side, and looked into the slivered space.

It was there, just as she'd left it, wedged upright and resting on two wood pins anchoring the bed frame to the wall. Hurriedly, she tried to force her fingertips into the seam but lacked a good three inches. She flashed the light around the room, searching for something she could use to grasp the photograph. Bottles, more cans, and cartons, yet she saw nothing useful. She kicked a box out of her way and checked the bathroom. The cabinets were missing as was the sink. Mildew stained the bathtub which held an inch of rainwater. She returned to the room.

More plywood barricaded the sliding glass doors, obstructing any way to the balcony. Vicki cursed, scanning the carpet. Her light reflected off a six-inch-long narrow shard of glass.

Careful not to cut a finger, she retrieved the fragment and turned, only to freeze in her tracks. She stared at the bed. Someone had gathered up pieces of debris, wood, and Sheetrock and piled them on the mattress, creating a circular barrier. It reminded her of a huge bird's nest. The center of the exposed mattress was imprinted with a large black stain. She moved the light. More stains darkened the wallpaper above the seam, creating an image of dirty fingers clawing after the photo.

Vicki felt her skin prickle with goose bumps. The aura of the past suddenly evaporated and she wanted to leave. But not without the picture.

Using the glass, she forced a jagged edge against the photo's edge, wedging it next to the wall. Slowly and carefully she pulled upward. The glass rose along with the photograph.

Vicki was concentrating so hard she barely noticed the fleeting astringent odor. After two attempts, she held the prize in her hands.

"Thank you, God," she murmured, examining the photograph in the light's beam.

Sobs swelled inside her chest but these were quickly extinguished by the onset of a horrendous stench.

Stifling a gag, Vicki tucked the picture in her pants and rose, making a retreat for the door. In her haste, the flashlight bumped against her thigh, disrupting her grip. It fell on the floor. She reached down to pick it up.

Even before she heard the heavy steps in the hall, she realized she was no longer alone. Grabbing the light, she lunged for the open doorway and nearly collided with the intruder.

A tight grip closed around her free wrist and Vicki screamed. In the beam, she glimpsed a shiny surface partially covering a thick arm and with all her strength, she swung the flashlight up and around like a club, connecting with something solid. The flashlight flew from her hand, landing several feet down the hall.

With the same hand, she seized her attacker's forearm. She felt a thin rubbery material under her fingers, as if the arm was wrapped in a skin-tight raincoat.

The grip loosened and Vicki wrenched free. Stumbling against the doorjamb, she recovered her balance and ran. Though she couldn't see him, she heard her attacker shuffling after her. As she passed over the flashlight, its beam illuminated her from behind, casting her shadow in front of her.

In her mad dash, Vicki misjudged the fallen beam midway down the corridor. Her leg struck the splintered wood, ripping her pants. A stabbing pain momentarily paralyzed her left knee. She groaned and fell face-first onto the wet carpet.

Instantly, she leapt to her feet, just ahead of the heavy steps.

"Stay away from me!" Vicki cried out, her heart pounding.

She dodged into room two and slammed the door behind her, locking it. In the dark, she groped her way around the edge of the bed and snaked through the plywood exit onto the balcony.

Behind her, Vicki heard the explosion of splintering wood as the door ripped from its hinges. Ignoring the throb in her knee, she clambered over the railing and limped for the alley. Her breaths now came in shallow gasps.

She fell again, this time on the wood plank, but maintained her balance well enough to avoid a serious slip into the construction pit.

Once on solid asphalt, she stopped to glance back at the abandoned hotel, but detected no movement. The balcony appeared deserted and the horrible smell had vanished.

When she turned for the street, a blinding light hit Vicki flush in the face.

A man's voice called out. "Hold it right there, miss."

• •

"How do you feel?" Julie asked.

"Fine. A little tired, I guess." Melanie Balsam's voice sounded subdued.

Julie nodded. It usually took Melanie all day to recover after a sleep study, though this session was running much later than usual. She ran the video forward several frames.

Undulating waves of red filled the monitor, different shades flowing into one another. Then without foreshadowing, the vague images of a man and woman appeared, moving as if beneath many feet of sanguinary water. The images on the screen froze.

"Do they mean anything to you?" Julie asked.

The pretty sixteen-year-old wrinkled her forehead in concentration.

"Try to remember," Julie coaxed.

"I am. I really am."

Julie felt sure the images were significant, possibly related to the teenager's past history of child abuse. This had been the third instance in which Melanie's brain waves had matched with VEROC's man and woman images.

She waited. "Anything?"

Melanie finally shook her head no. It was plainly evident she'd tried.

Julie pulled her chair closer. "Okay, let's call it an evening. We'll try again in several days."

"Sorry, Dr. Charmaine."

Julie clasped one of Melanie's hands, just below a fresh scar on the teenager's wrist. "Listen to me," she said. "We're making progress. And we're going to continue to make progress. But it takes time. Hang in there."

After dropping Melanie off at her room in the in-patient ward at Psychiatric Hospital, Julie returned to her office. She'd just filed Melanie's chart and dream video when the phone rang. She answered, recognizing the ER triage nurse's voice.

Gwen Ferris said, "Now why am I not surprised at finding you still here? Don't you ever sleep, Dr. Charmaine?"

"Sure, one or two days a week," Julie said jocosely. She glanced at the wall clock. Almost 9 P.M. It *was* late. "What's up, Gwen?"

"This isn't an official hit," the nurse explained, referring to an admission, "but Dr. Skinner asked me to ring your office concerning a patient he's seeing."

Julie guessed the call regarded her position as supervisor of the Battered Women's Unit. "I was just leaving," she said. "I'll stop by on my way out."

Julie waited at the triage desk while Nurse Ferris and another nurse completed an IV setup for a patient. She glimpsed Dr. Skinner in one of the minor surgery suites. All she could make out of the patient was an exposed knee and lower leg. She had to force an image of a deceased Irene Inez from her mind.

Next to the coffee dispenser, a uniformed officer scribbled on a clipboard.

Julie played a hunch and walked over and introduced herself. "Evening, officer. I'm Dr. Julie Charmaine."

The officer stopped writing. "Ron Kincaid."

"You wouldn't happen to be here with the patient Dr. Skinner's seeing?"

The policeman cast Julie a quizzical glance, then nodded. "Yes, and you must be the dream doctor."

"What?"

"No offense intended. I heard the ER doc discussing something along those lines with the woman before asking the nurse to call you."

"Is that why the patient's here?"

The officer shook his head no. "In violation of Civil Code

Six-oh-two. Trespassing. Ms. Zampisi was picked up at the Shilden Hotel."

"Is that the old hotel near El Centro Medical College?"

He affirmed with a cynical nod. "The vacation spot of the drugged and homeless. Claims she heard someone call for help, went inside, and that's when the alleged assault took place."

Julie looked back at the surgery suite. Skinner appeared to be finishing up. "Are her injuries serious?"

"Not that I'm aware of. In fact, my partner and I were unable to corroborate her story of any attempted attack or struggle, and we certainly found no one in need of assistance. Other than cracked beams and a couple of possums, we came up empty. Except for a flashlight that Ms. Zampisi identified as hers." Officer Kincaid rested a palm on the butt of his revolver. "I suspect she went inside for some unknown reason, maybe a place to sleep, I don't know. Anyway, she became frightened, ran and fell, and that's when she cut her knee. We had the Medic unit transport her here because she seemed too upset to drive. Her van's parked just down the street from the hotel."

"How will she get back?"

"The hospital has a crisis intervention service. They'll give her a ride once she's ready for discharge."

"And the trespassing charge?"

"In all likelihood, it'll be dropped. The owners and city have bigger legal troubles with that building."

Julie nodded. "Thanks for the report, officer," adding, "I won't keep Ms. Zampisi long."

Prior to the introductions, Julie reviewed Skinner's notes while the emergency physician updated Ms. Zampisi's status. The initial diagnosis had been laceration/contusion—right knee. Prior to suturing the wound, though, Skinner had removed a two-inch wood splinter from just above the kneecap, thus amending the original diagnosis to laceration/contusion/status post foreign body—right knee. Ms. Zampisi had been given oral pain meds, antibiotics, a medicated dressing, and ice pack. She'd declined the use of crutches or a cane, instead requesting a pill to help her sleep. Skinner had warned Julie he may be overreading this patient, but he was glad Julie was willing to take a look. The woman's bruised wrist and the Shilden's seedy history had made him concerned that she'd been beaten, though she wasn't talking much about it.

"That looks sore," Julie said, now alone with her patient.

The woman sat up gingerly on the stretcher. With a friendly smile, Julie noted her odd appearance. Though the woman's blond hair hung loosely over her ears, Julie recognized the characteristic facial asymmetry of craniosynostosis. Her plastic surgeon had done an extraordinary job. Ms. Zampisi could be considered seductive in an unnaturally provocative way.

With a grimace, Vicki straightened her injured leg. "He said the splinter just missed entering the joint."

"You were fortunate."

Vicki gave Julie an approving gaze. "You seem young to be a doctor."

"I appreciate your candor." Julie was used to statements like this. "I completed my residency at UCLA in 1996 and from there went on to a fellowship in sleep disorders. I've been at CUMC since 1998." When Vicki didn't comment, she asked, "Do you feel comfortable talking about tonight?"

"You mean about the Shilden?"

"What happened?"

With a wince, Vicki adjusted the position of her knee. "Thank God for pain medicines." She exhaled thorough pursed lips.

"You okay?"

"I will be when I get home." She met Julie's attentive gaze and forced a smile. "I guess I just fell wrong."

"Dr. Skinner was also concerned about your bruised wrist."

Vicki's eyes shifted to the policeman waiting in the triage area. "He didn't believe me, did he?"

"Just because his investigation failed to turn up anything substantive doesn't mean an assault didn't occur."

Vicki nodded, fidgeting with the ice pack.

Julie sensed she wanted to speak but was holding back. She stepped closer. "Vicki, I treat innocent victims of violence every day. And each case is unique, requiring its own set of guidelines. But no matter what circumstances are involved, there's always help out there. All you have to do is ask."

Vicki smoothed the tape over the dressing. "Someone else was in that building, Dr. Charmaine, I'm not making this up."

"I believe you," Julie said, studying the taut lines of the woman's face. She placed a card in Vicki's hand. "Here's my clinic number. The hospital can reach me twenty-four hours a day. Call if you ever need to talk."

"I appreciate your offer. Right now, I'm just not up to discussing it."

"I can accept that. Anything else I can help you with tonight?"

Vicki stared at the card's tiny lettering. Her tense expression had softened. "Dr. Skinner said you're a dream researcher."

"Neuropsychiatrist. My research interests lie in the study and interpretation of dreams."

Vicki smiled wanly. "When that cop brought me in, I was pretty upset. My knee hurt like hell and I was scared and I guess I was running off some at the mouth. My mother tells me nightmares are indicative of an active imagination. It's amazing what a shot of alcohol and a little imagination can do to a night's sleep."

"Do you have these dreams often?"

"Some. I can live with them."

Julie knew the feeling. She watched Vicki's expression turn pensive.

"Dr. Charmaine, do you believe nightmares can predict the future?"

Julie chose her words carefully. "I feel the manner in which an individual perceives her nightmares can affect a person's future. But," she added, "in my experience, I've seen no consistent relationship between what a person dreams and what actually happens."

"How about inconsistent relationships?" Vicki asked, attempting a grin.

"Dream research is only in its infancy."

Vicki brushed back some loose bangs. "That's an honest answer." She promised to consider setting up an appointment later.

Though the informal interview had ended on an up tick, Julie departed, unable to shake the vague impression that there was far more to this woman's pain than just the knee.

Nine

Ten miles west of CUMC by way of the Santa Monica Freeway, Detective Matthew Guardian sat with his feet on his desk and an open folder containing Dorfman's preliminary findings from Irene Inez's autopsy.

According to the coroner's report, Irene Inez had been in excellent physical shape. Her coronary arteries were clean, kidney and lungs working well, reproductive organs functioning normally, evinced by her incipient pregnancy, and there'd been no liver or other organic disease. Other than the scalp avulsion and some scratches and bruises, nothing seemed out of the ordinary. Except she was dead.

Dorfman had told Matt over the phone earlier that he was going to list the cause of death as cardiac arrest, at least until the microscopic and toxicology portions of the post-mortem were complete. Presently the line for cause of death was left blank.

Matt shut the folder. The autopsy had also confirmed Dr. Charmaine's and the ER doc's findings that she wasn't raped.

Across from Matt's desk and nearest the coffeemaker lay Sokol Ramani's three-by-eight-foot home away from home. Pretending to read, Matt couldn't help but overhear the onslaught his partner exposed himself to every evening he worked late.

"Isabelle, Isabelle, would you hold on a minute? Jesus, give me a . . ." Ramani stared at the receiver. "She disconnected me."

Matt dropped his feet to the floor and tossed the autopsy folder toward Ramani's desk. "Maybe she's not getting what she wants."

"I do her twice a month," Ramani said, finally hanging up.

"Well stud, she's your wife. Try substituting a little passion for sense of duty." Matt said this with a straight face, though they both knew Matt was the last one qualified to be giving matrimonial advice.

"Dorf says you took Ranier by the sixth." Ramani knew nothing about boxing but from his tone it was obvious he thought Matt had made a sorry bet.

"Sixth or seventh, makes no difference. Gipson's black, mean, hungry. But he also has a chin of glass."

"Kinda like you, champ." Ramani removed one of the forensic photos. "She's not a bad-looking lady." He'd been working the case from his end while Matt had been at the coroner's.

"Wasn't," Matt said. He opened the bottom drawer of his desk and pulled out a small Nike gym bag containing his shorts, jock, socks, sweats, and a pair of speed-bag gloves.

Ramani checked another photo. "The story made the evening *Times.*"

Matt had seen it too. The reporter had already coined a phrase, the sewer murder. Matt could easily visualize where this would lead. If there were a second.

"You know," Ramani started, but belched. "This Inez girl wasn't your typical low-rent slouch. She was studying nursing at El Centro. Planned on starting a clinical rotation at the medical center this fall. Her teacher claims she was better than average. Even described her as motivated. She wasn't close to any of the other students in her class and none of them, at least those contacted so far, knew much about her. Most weren't even aware she had a son." He checked some notes. "A security guard at the school recalled seeing a girl walking down Louis just prior to ten-thirty. Can't describe her in detail, but he did mention she had long dark hair and was slender. Nice figure."

"Think it was her?"

"Probably. Jibes with the police report filed by Beamis. He actually spoke with the victim. Waited till she'd unlocked her car before driving away."

"Too bad he didn't stick around."

"Yeah." Ramani shuffled through the remaining photographs. "Ms. Inez had been dating some guy about six months, but not seriously. A Guillermo Onteveras. He's clean. Was working till two A.M. at some local club spinning vinyl. Says he wants to be a morning deejay."

Matt zipped the workout bag shut. "How'd he take the news?"

"Her death upset him . . . seemed sincere."

"Any word from the aunt's son?"

"Nothing. But this might be interesting. According to the aunt, the son kept a pet python. A big one."

"So?"

"So every couple of weeks he'd feed it a rabbit."

"Rabbits don't tear out half a girl's scalp and leave her for dead." Matt couldn't say the same for big pythons.

Ramani picked a food particle from his front tooth. "No, but last week, the aunt said her son tried to feed *El Jefe*, that's the snake, a dead skunk. Supposedly the skunk had died from noxious inhalations. Some asshole had spray-painted the varmint's head with orange acrylic. What do you think?"

"I feel bad for the skunk."

Ramani leaned sideways and spit into a trash can. "I agree it's probably nothing, but I'll have Dorfy check that hair fragment from the Inez case for any foreign substances."

Matt reached for the bag, then paused. "Did *El Jefe* eat the skunk?"

Ramani grunted. "Would you eat something spray-painted with orange acrylic?"

"I guess not." He started for the door. "Come on down and hit the big bag."

"No thanks, champ. I'll work it out with a cheap bottle of wine, a bag of egg rolls, and a hot Latina who's yearning for some passion."

Old City Gymnasium was one of those workout arenas straight out of *The Prizefighter,* that cable classic starring Anthony Quinn about a washed-up fighter on his way down. It was six blocks from Parker Center in the heart of downtown L.A. Its sole proprietor, Pepe Rodriguez, had been a welterweight contender decades ago.

Matt liked it because parking was accessible, it had a fighter's atmosphere, and it wasn't usually crowded unlike the spandex and chrome, flex-and-strut Family Fitness and Golds workout centers.

Old City Gym had a weight room, free bar and pulley systems, locker and shower stations, and three canvas rings for sparring. Along one wall hung six heavy bags ranging from sixty to two hundred pounds, and at least ten speed bags. The interior air smelled of heat balm, sweat, leather, and moldy towels.

Many of the fighters who worked out here and paid their hundred dollars a month fee dreamed of fighting Oscar De La Hoya or Lennox Lewis in Olympic Auditorium. Most were in their teens or early twenties, some had fought in the Golden Gloves, and a few, if very lucky, might one day see the lights of a professional ring.

Pepe had a score of trainers and, although always on the lookout for the next De La Hoya, he mostly kept busy just keeping kids off the streets and drugs.

Soaked with sweat in the first two minutes, Matt pounded

the hundred-and-fifty-pound bag. He'd do this for ten minutes, jump rope for ten, then finish up with speed-bag drills. Three times a week, he'd also throw in some bench presses and arm work.

Tonight's workout wasn't going well, though. Matt found it difficult to concentrate as he squared off before a speed bag.

For some indefinable reason, he felt drawn to the Inez case. He couldn't explain why. Irene Inez was statistically no different than a hundred other homicide cases he'd handled in the past—single female, brutally assaulted, just another victim of a random act of violence. Then why?

His thoughts drifted to Ms. Inez's treating physician. He could still see Dr. Julie Charmaine in her black slacks and silk blouse, her lab coat barely concealing her feminine figure. Was she the difference? Did he want to solve this homicide for the wrong reasons? To score points with the victim's attractive female doctor?

His shoulder muscles burning, Matt paused to catch his breath. No, he decided. The Inez case would be solved, not because of any misguided chemistry, but because he'd taken an oath to uphold the law. Plain and simple. Justice would prevail for Ms. Irene Inez because that's what his professional duty demanded.

His unease only slightly mollified, Matt attempted to reset his stance and resume his workout.

So far inquiries around the local emergency rooms had failed to turn up any admissions for treatment of deep scratches. And the coroner's finding of dead flesh under the girl's nails defied routine explanation, though other possibilities surely existed. All bad. L.A. didn't need another sicko setting up shop.

The sharp rhythmic popping of leather did little to resolve Matt's disquiet.

He still had a bad feeling about this case. He didn't like bad feelings.

Ten

Jezebel Humphries had been, without a doubt, the prettiest girl at Compton High. She was voted Most Beautiful her senior year, which is why it was such a disappointment to her divorced mother when Jezebel, her only daughter, dropped out of a local community college after only three semesters. Instead of continuing her studies in broadcast journalism, Jezebel had begun work as a cocktail waitress at Scene I, a semi-trendy night spot several rungs below the Amphisphere.

Jezebel waited for the light to turn at the corner of First and Myers Streets. From where she stood she could see several cars crossing the Fourth Street river bridge. She was late—her shift started at 9 P.M. and it was rapidly approaching midnight. Still, her spirits soared. She was scheduled to meet with a movie producer, a cousin of Scene I's owner, who always kept his eyes open for an exotic face. And Jezebel was exotic. Half-black, half-Mexican, with jet black hair and a light complexion, she possessed a model's face on a foldout's figure. In her red satin heels, a black miniskirt, purple fishnet stockings, and blue iridescent bodysuit, *exotic* would be the first word to come to the producer's mind.

She hit the button on the light pole impatiently. As if responding to her, the light turned green. Despite her heels, Jezebel broke into a semi-jog across Myers. Three blocks up was Fourth Street. She could cut ten minutes off her walk by taking an alley that snaked behind two rows of retail outlets and pawn shops. She'd taken the shortcut before because she was frequently late.

Halfway down the alley, she noticed a bum sleeping between two cardboard boxes. She quietly stepped by him.

As she reached the middle of the alley, Jezebel cringed at the stench. It'd never been this bad before. Must've been the rain. Or the street people were using the alley as a huge outdoor toilet.

She stopped short. Five feet in front of her, a gaping, black hole yawned skyward. The manhole cover lay to one side.

"That ain't cool," she mumbled as she started to take a wide berth around the sewer entrance.

The smell was stronger and obviously coming from the sewer's dark maw.

Detecting an odd noise, she paused.

The drunken bum fifty yards away never heard a thing because Jezebel never screamed. She left only a single red satin pump lying on the asphalt.

It would be some time before her name was officially removed from the missing person's list at Parker Center. And when her body was finally discovered, no one would ever have believed Jezebel Humphries's mother's claim that her daughter was once the most beautiful girl at Compton High.

Using her little finger, Vicki transferred a few drops of whiskey from the glass to the surface of her lower lip. Her tongue moved the liquid the rest of the way into her mouth.

Before her, the photo sat on the kitchen table, propped up by the bottle of Ezra Brooks, the same bottle she'd popped the cork on a week ago, her first night in L.A. Now it was almost empty. A fifth a week wasn't that bad. She'd done worse.

Vicki felt no regret about lying to the cop. Far more damaging would have been the truth. No one would ever believe she'd entered a condemned building for a twenty-year-old photograph.

Vicki reached to clean a smudge from the picture's edge and experienced a sharp pain in her leg. Since arriving back at her apartment, the throbbing in her knee had intensified, more so over the last several hours. The doctor had warned her this might occur once the local anesthesia wore off. Vicki unscrewed the cap off the prescription bottle, then chased the Darvocet down with a swig of amber liquid. She promised herself there'd be no dreams tonight.

In the beginning, shortly after moving to Oregon, the nightmares had awakened her at regular intervals, leaving her skin crawling under a layer of cold sweat but her mind incapable of recalling specific images or content. Then for years they vanished, allowing Vicki to fractionally forget the past. Fractionally because only a state of being as final as death could ever grant her the ultimate escape. Only recently, in Seattle, the nightmares had resurfaced, elevated to the edges of Vicki's consciousness as if buoyed by a vengeance of their own.

Precipitated by the recent knowledge of the foundation's impending move, the nightmare's recurrence forced Vicki to accept she could no longer run from what had long lain dormant under the guilt and denial. No one other than Kovacs knew of the depth of her relationship with Ben. Perhaps the old night watchman had suspected, but by now he'd be long past talking to anyone. If word ever got out, she'd be branded insane for sure.

Vicki took another long drink. Well, fuck it. She'd taken the first step toward recovery tonight. She'd retrieved the photo.

Confronting Kovacs and the foundation would carry considerably more risk. But she wanted that signature. She thought of that cruel evening years ago and how she'd carelessly ripped the medical consent form in half when she'd yanked it from Ben's chart. Silently, she berated herself for not being more careful. Her only consolation now was knowing Kovacs had far more to lose today than when the foundation was in its early existence. What means he'd justify to stop her, Vicki could only guess, but regardless, she would confront her former employer on any playing field he proposed. Ben deserved that at the minimum.

Earlier, in the emergency room, when the doctor had examined her for swelling in her right wrist where she'd been grabbed, Vicki had contemplated the notion that Kovacs had orchestrated the entire assault himself. Her biggest mistake would be to underestimate Dr. Wesley Kovacs.

Vicki downed the shot, set the photo facedown, and went to her bedroom. She checked the window, ensuring the latch was secure, before going to her nightstand and opening the top drawer.

The .380 Back Up fit nicely in the palm of one hand. Deftly, she checked the safety and the clip, made sure a round was in the chamber, and a second clip was loaded and ready. Next time she was confronted she'd be packing more than pepper spray.

Returning to the kitchen, Vicki laid the pistol beside the photo. She poured herself another shot, no ice this time. She was down to her last Montclair.

The despair began soon after the whiskey warmed her throat. Having the photograph in hand did nothing to block the rising tide of panic spreading before her face, as untouchable and ubiquitous as the cigarette's acrid haze.

Vicki pressed the heel of one hand to her eye, wishing with all her soul she could float back in time and undo the past. Her sense of futility coated her insides like a toxic film. The snowball had begun its tumultuous roll downhill and when it finally crashed later tonight, Vicki would awaken drenched in cold sweat, wishing she were dead.

Eleven

Julie's thoughts returned to Vicki Zampisi when she read the case summons for "Grand Rounds," the weekly teaching conferences that began at 7:30 A.M. every Thursday. Today's case concerned a woman who'd sustained a minor wound to her leg that had become infected. Two weeks later, the patient, a diabetic, succumbed to overwhelming septic shock. Perhaps it was the fatal outcome of that conference's particular subject matter that put Ms. Zampisi in Julie's unsettled mind. She hoped Vicki's knee healed well.

Back at her office, Julie found Irene Inez's preliminary autopsy findings in her in-box. On any terminal case Julie handled, she requested the postmortem report. But to get one without requesting it seemed odd. Especially since it was a coroner's case.

Momentarily, she experienced a stab of guilt, reading her patient's name on the cover sheet. She wondered if the coroner had found anything in his exam that she'd missed. If she'd handled the case any differently would the outcome have changed? Though she realized in medicine, even hindsight was never always twenty-twenty, this did little to lessen her sense of loss.

Julie also had two phone messages, one from Detective Matthew Guardian, the other from a man who wouldn't leave a name or number with the hospital operator.

Julie had barely sat down at her desk when the phone rang.

"Dr. Charmaine?" It was the operator.

"Yes."

"You have an outside call. He won't give a name."

Occasionally Julie received calls from present or past patients who, for whatever reason, refused to give their names.

"Okay, I'll take it."

Julie waited as the operator put the caller through. The last time she'd received a call like this, it'd been a suicide attempt. Julie had spent two hours successfully convincing the teenager otherwise. She hoped this call wasn't similar.

"Hello." The voice belonged to a man, a young man. He sounded tense.

"Hello, this is Dr. Charmaine."

"Is this the doctor who took care of Irene Inez?" His pronunciation of Irene's surname sounded Hispanic.

"Yes. Ms. Inez was my patient."

"How she is?"

The man had obviously missed Julie's use of "was." Julie hesitated too long.

"I asked how she is?" the man asked again, urgency in his tone.

"May I ask who's calling?" Julie asked.

"You talk to the *policia*?"

"Yes, I've spoken to the police." She then repeated the sentence in Spanish.

"I speak English." Then silence.

For a moment, Julie thought the caller was going to hang up. This lasted two or three seconds.

"Irene hurt bad, yes?" he finally said. It was a statement. "I talk with Mother. She told me Irene bad."

"Soccoro Chavez is your mother?"

"*Sí*. I call her Tuesday night."

"Have you talked to her yesterday or today?"

"No."

That explained the caller's lack of knowledge concerning Irene's current expired status.

"You are Irene's cousin then," Julie said.

"*Sí.* I try to help."

Julie suddenly sat up straight. "Help? You saw her attacked?"

"I was there." More silence.

"Have you spoken to the police?" Julie asked quickly. She couldn't lose him.

"Don't trust police. *Mi madre* says to trust you."

"Can you tell me your name?" There was a long pause. "If I'm to help, I must know your name," Julie repeated.

"We meet," he said.

"Where? *Donde?*"

"Chicago and Marengo. *Poquito* cafe."

"Alberto's. Good taquitos." Julie knew the place.

"Nine-thirty, *Doctor,*" the young man said.

"Wait—"

"Nine-thirty." He sounded final.

"Yes, *sí,*" Julie confirmed. But he'd already hung up.

Julie sat at her desk in a mild daze. She checked her watch. It was 8:45. Alberto's wasn't even open at this hour. And for all she knew, this guy was the same maniac who'd beaten the hell out of Irene Inez.

Julie dug into her purse for the scribbled phone number Irene's aunt had given her the night she'd been admitted.

She dialed it. *"Bueno."*

"Señora Chavez?"

"Sí."

The ensuing conversation with Irene's aunt lasted barely a minute and confirmed that Señora Chavez did indeed have a son. His name was Ignacio and he was twenty-two. Julie told Mrs. Chavez about the call she'd just received. The older lady sounded very tired and she had simply asked Julie to please have her son call her when she met with him. Julie assured her she would.

Julie's next call was not so successful.

"Central Division, Robbery-Homicide. Detective Bergin."

"Yes, I'd like to speak with Detective Matt Guardian."

"He's not available, ma'am. May I take a message?"

"Yes, this is Dr. Julie Charmaine. I'm a physician at CUMC and I'd spoken with Detective Guardian regarding a patient of mine. Irene Inez. She was assaulted two nights ago. I believe Detective Guardian is handling her case." Julie added, "Also if this will help, he attempted to contact me at my office earlier this morning."

"I can have him paged for you."

"Please do, it's important."

"Yes, ma'am."

"Thank you, detective."

In a vain attempt to calm her nerves, Julie scanned Irene's autopsy report. But before Matt returned her call, she had to leave.

Julie waited by the pay phone outside the convenience store on Marengo. Her surveillance position provided a clear view of Alberto's on the corner just across the street. It was little more than a hot-dog stand serving authentic Mexican food at economical prices. Julie ate lunch there at least twice a month and she liked the food. Today the gnawing in her stomach came purely from nerves.

Ignacio was five minutes past the agreed-upon time when Julie saw two young men at the intersection. Both were riding bicycles, nothing fancy, the kind with no gears and fat tires. One, the smaller of the pair, wore a long-sleeved beige shirt rolled to his elbows and unbuttoned, a plain black T-shirt underneath. He looked younger than twenty-two. The other man appeared several years older because of his shaved head, and held Julie's attention even longer. He was so large, his body dwarfed the bicycle mounted between his thick thighs. A well-worn Los Angeles Raider's sweatshirt with the sleeves cut off was stretched tautly across his wide torso, leaving naked and visible a forbidding pair of arms and forearms that bulged with muscle and sinewy veins. She guessed his motley collection of tattoos had taken years to accumulate. He fixed Julie with a baleful glare.

The smaller man pedaled his bike through the red light on Chicago, jumped the curb, and stopped in the parking lot of Alberto's. He set the bike down on its side and sat at the table nearest the order window. The other man remained rooted across the street, straddling his bike.

Julie went into the convenience store, bought two iced teas, and walked out to the traffic signal. The man seated at the table was watching her. She waved, assuming this was Ignacio. He simply nodded.

Attempting to appear casual, Julie crossed the street and took a seat at the table. As she set down the drinks she could see a vague resemblance to Soccoro Chavez, especially in his eyes. When Ignacio reached for a tea, she could see he sported a tattoo of a woman with flowing hair and large breasts on his neck.

"Hola," Julie said, casting a furtive glance across the street.

"We talk *inglés.*" He didn't smile, but he wasn't unfriendly. Detecting her concern, he made a sharp motion with his chin in the direction of his companion. "Arbol not bother us."

Julie forced a smile, instantly recognizing the appropriateness of the name. *Arbol* was the Spanish word for tree. Hell, Ignacio's friend was as big as a tree.

"I treated your cousin," she said, keeping the conversation on track. "You are Ignacio?"

He nodded.

"What kind of *doctor* are you, Julie?"

"I'm a neuropsychiatrist by training."

Ignacio smiled briefly. "You fix that head shit, right?"

"In a way, yes."

"What kill my cousin?"

So Ignacio did know Irene was dead. Why didn't he reveal this over the phone? Julie's pulse increased just a little as words like revenge and vindication crept into her mind. She didn't relish the thought of being around when either Ignacio or his brutish friend became angry.

"I'm truly sorry we couldn't do more for Irene," she said. "Frankly, we aren't sure what killed her. Her injuries were not that serious. Yet . . ." Julie paused. She felt as if she were suddenly making excuses for something that was not her fault. "Sometimes in medicine, things happen that we can't explain."

"Sorta like the street. *Mierda siempre pasa.* Shit happens."

"Yes, it does." Julie nodded and took a sip, thankful she had something in her hands.

"Did you tell police about me?"

The question caught Julie off guard. She hesitated, but it would do no good to lie. Someone as streetwise as Ignacio would detect any untruths.

"I called the detective investigating Irene's case," she answered candidly. "He wasn't in."

Ignacio drank until he was almost finished. Julie wondered if this impromptu meeting was too.

Ignacio finished the tea. *"Gracias,"* he said. "You know about East L.A. gangs?"

Julie wasn't sure whether he was trying to be polite or a smart-ass. She simply shook her head.

"Me and Arbol been homeboys eleven years. Arrested ten times. Five times to jail. I don't talk to no *policia.* Simple."

"Do you know who did this to Irene?"

The gangbanger shook his head. "If I did, he be dead."

Ignacio leaned closer as if what he was about to say he wanted only Julie to hear, although there was no one else in earshot. "Almost one year ago, I eat lunch with Roberto. Six blocks from here. McDonald's. Roberto, he Irene's brother. My best friend. I remember what he ordered. Fries and Coke. No burger, nothing. Just fries and Coke. Then, bang," Ignacio made a sudden rough gesture to his neck, "bullet hit him here. Blood everywhere, all over fries, Coke, me." Ignacio looked at his hands.

Julie waited for him to go on.

"Roberto, he wasn't no homeboy. That bullet, that was for me."

While Ignacio fiddled with the empty tea bottle, somewhere a car honked, but neither looked.

"Roberto fell on the floor. Everyone was running, screaming. Roberto told me to protect Irene. Make sure she okay. So I watch her back."

Ignacio took the bottle and whipped it into an empty litter barrel a few feet away. "Roberto, he never the same after that. His *madre* take him home to Mexico. He can't eat, talk, think. Can't shit by himself. Bad, real bad. Someday I go to see him." He stared into Julie's eyes. "Irene was gonna be a nurse, help Roberto."

"I'm sorry, Ignacio."

He accepted Julie's apology with a shrug. "Sometimes I followed Irene. She didn't know, but I do it for Roberto. Irene, she pretty, like you. Not always careful. Tuesday night, Irene left school late."

"You saw her Tuesday night?"

Ignacio held up one hand to let him finish. "After ten o'clock, she still didn't leave school. I waited in the rain. I seen a cop car so I go into a Circle K down the block. When I gone back to school, all the lights were off. I called Irene, but she didn't answer. I figured she was already gone. Then I hear a scream. And another scream. With thunder and rain I didn't know where it come from. I call, 'Irene, Irene. It's Ignacio.' But she didn't answer. So I go around the block."

Ignacio slowed to catch his breath. Julie could see him getting more anxious the more he talked. She already knew he'd have to repeat his story to the police.

"I find her car," Ignacio started slowly. "The door open, motor running, window broke. But no Irene. I call her name again. But she wasn't nowhere. I shut the car off. I was careful, didn't leave no prints."

"And you didn't see who did this?"

"No. I just waited in the rain and lightning and I cry, man. I cry for Roberto, I cry for Irene."

"Can you think of anything else? What else did you see or hear?"

Ignacio started to shake his head, but abruptly stopped. He made a face. "Bad smell. All over street there was *olor a muerte.* Dead smell, shit. I get out of there."

"When did you decide to call me?" she asked.

"I been looking in the paper. I saw Irene was dead. *Mi madre* say you good, you trusted."

"Your mother would like for you to call her." Julie reached for Ignacio's hand. He didn't pull it away. "You realize you must tell this to the police."

"*You* tell to police. That why I told you. You tell police."

"What will you do?"

For the second time Ignacio smiled. But this grin was cold, calculating, and cruel. Very much like the streets he was raised on. "I look for him and I kill him."

"No, Ignacio, let me help. I'll go with you to the police."

He stood up suddenly, so fast that Julie jumped. One hand went into one of the deep pockets in his baggy pants. "I give you this, case it helps."

Julie swallowed, watching his hand.

Ignacio withdrew a white cloth. Wrapped around a hand-sized object. He set it on the table.

"This was Irene's," Ignacio said, anger in his voice. "You give it to the cops."

Ignacio checked that they weren't being watched, then he unwrapped the cloth which turned out to be a pillowcase. Inside lay a .38 caliber revolver similar to the one Julie kept in her nightstand. Only this one was dirty. A black coat of grime covered the cylinder and barrel.

Ignacio pointed to the gun. "I found it in the street, by the sewer. She shot it one time. Cops'll know what to do."

Julie looked from the gun to Ignacio. "I can't take this."

"You take, Señorita Julie."

Julie started to protest but it was too late. Ignacio was already picking up his bike.

"Ignacio," she called after him.

He hopped on his bike, waved, and disappeared into the traffic with Arbol.

Twelve

Julie waited for Matt Guardian in the lobby of Psychiatric Hospital.

"This way, detective," Julie said, using her most professional tone to disguise her nerves. She had no idea how the homicide detective was going to react to what she had to tell and show him.

Matt followed Julie's lead to her office.

"I appreciate you rushing right over," Julie said.

"You said it was important."

"Believe me, it is."

"I believe you."

Julie shut her office door behind them. Matt hung his gray sports coat on the back of a chair.

Behind her desk, Julie took a deep breath, suddenly feeling a sense of relief at the sight of Matt sitting in front of her. He appeared patient, just waiting.

"You okay?" he asked. "You look like you've just seen my ex–mother-in-law."

She took another deep breath. "I'm fine."

As Julie carefully removed the pillowcase holding the pistol from her desk, Matt pointed at the folder containing Irene's preliminary autopsy report.

"You get a chance to see the coroner's report?" he asked.

Julie cleared the center of her desk. "No, I glanced at it briefly, but frankly I was surprised to receive it so early."

"I had Dorfman—he's the deputy medical examiner handling the case—send one over. Thought you might be interested."

"Thanks, I am." Julie started to unwrap the cloth, relieved her hands weren't trembling.

"You know your patient was pregnant."

Julie stopped. "No."

"Three to five weeks. The boyfriend took it pretty hard."

"Is it pertinent, I mean, of course it's pertinent, but—"

Matt held up both hands. "Forget the autopsy. Why don't you—" he paused, "—do you mind if I call you Julie?"

Julie shook her head.

"Great, call me Matt. Now Julie, what do you have to show me?"

Julie unwrapped the pillowcase, exposing the dirty .38 revolver.

Matt stood. "I take it that's not yours."

"No. It was given to me less than an hour ago by Irene Inez's cousin. His name is Ignacio Chavez. He claims he found it on the street where Irene was assaulted."

Matt leaned over the desk for a better look at the barrel which was crusted with some sort of dark material. "Have you touched it?" he asked.

Julie shook her head a second time. "It came to me just as you see it."

"And you called me immediately?"

"Of course. The last thing I need is a concealed-weapons charge."

"It's a misdemeanor. Five hundred dollars. I'd get you off." Matt produced a pen, inserted it into the barrel, and lifted the gun for a better look. "Did you know it's loaded?"

Julie nodded, pointing to the visible brass cartridges. "I own a similar gun. My dad gave it to me."

"Not a bad choice. Light, easy to handle. Packs a wallop."

Matt removed a pair of latex gloves from a pocket of his sports jacket. With gloved hands, he flipped the cylinder open. Four cartridges fell onto the desk. He checked the barrel for any residue or odor before setting the unloaded revolver down.

"Thirty-eight Special. Smith and Wesson," Matt said. He picked up one of the cartridges. "One-hundred-fifty-eight grain hollow points." He looked at Julie. "One's missing, shot, or whoever last loaded it only put in four." He rolled one bullet across his palm. "The owner meant business. This little baby will expand an inch. The entry wound may not look like much but lord help the exit wound."

From another pocket, Matt removed a small glassine bag and dropped the four bullets in. He then rewrapped the gun and pulled it to his side of the desk. "Feel better?"

"Much."

"So you met this character, some guy who refuses to socialize with cops and wouldn't ID himself, in front of Alberto's. Alone."

"I was alone. He came with a friend, a big man, heavily tattooed. Ignacio called him Arbol. Matt, I didn't know what else to do. I couldn't reach you—"

"Great."

"Look, Matt, thinking back I realize it was crazy, but I . . . I had a gut feeling he was telling the truth. You're trained to deal with criminals, I'm trained to deal with stressed-out, mentally dysfunctional patients. He didn't sound off-balance. I didn't want to lose this chance."

Matt watched Julie's eyes drift to the gun and then the autopsy report.

"And maybe you were feeling a little bit guilty too?"

Julie barely nodded. She moved closer. "Listen detective, Irene was my patient. Sure she was attacked but she wasn't critical. There's no reason for her to be dead. I missed something. Something she didn't say, something she tried to tell me but couldn't. Maybe if I'd sedated her more, or—"

Matt dropped his hand on the coroner's folder. "And now she's my case. Julie, quit second-guessing yourself, you have nothing to feel guilty about. You did your best, now Irene's in my hands. Now tell me about the meeting."

"He told me he's a member of some East L.A. street gang—has been for eleven years, since he was *eleven*. He couldn't go to the police." Julie paused briefly as Matt made a note. "It seems Ignacio was the intended victim in Irene's brother's shooting. The brother is paralyzed, mentally diminished. Ignacio felt he owed it to Irene, or rather her brother, to watch her back. So the night Irene was attacked, he was waiting for her outside the nursing school. He was going to make sure she made it home okay. But it was raining that night so Ignacio waited down the block at a Circle K. He heard her scream."

"Did he mention a gunshot?"

"No, just screams. When he got to her car, Irene was gone. He found the gun near the curb. Oh, and he described an extremely offensive odor."

Matt paused. "Odor?"

"His words were *olor a muerte*. Smell of death."

"A veritable poet." Matt looked up from his notes. "And that was all he told you? He rode off?"

"Yes."

"And Ignacio's tattooed goon?"

"We never spoke. The last I saw, they were both on bicycles heading north on Chicago. I lost them in the traffic."

Matt must have read the hesitation in Julie's expression. "There's something else, isn't there?"

"Ignacio said he was going to kill whoever did this to his cousin."

Matt shrugged and closed his notepad. "Understandable. I'd probably feel the same way. Ignacio Chavez, assuming this was in fact Ignacio, is a gangbanger and gangbangers wear revenge like a medal. You shoot my brother, I shoot yours, you rape my sister, I rape yours, you steal my car, I blow up yours."

"You think Irene's assault was gang related?"

"Maybe. It's possible. This," motioning to the gun, "raises more questions than it answers. But then raising questions is what solves cases."

"Where do you go from here?"

"We'll run a trace on the gun, check for prints, and send it to ballistics. I want to know if there ever was a fifth bullet and if so, was the gun discharged as recently as May fifteenth. Also we'll have to round up Ms. Chavez's son and and this Arbol character and have a cordial chitchat man to man."

"Surely you don't think Ignacio could have done this to his own cousin."

Matt shrugged. "In this do-unto-others-as-others-would-*undo*-you city, anything's possible. When Ignacio turned that gun over, he put himself at the top of our suspect list. He and his shy *compañero.*"

Matt placed the wrapped gun in an outside pocket of his sports coat.

Julie accompanied him to the door. "I appreciate your time, detective." She still found it awkward calling him by his first name. "Hopefully all this helps."

Just before leaving, Matt pulled a card out of his pocket. Before handing it to her he scribbled a number on the back. "Three numbers. Department, my pager, and home. You hear anything else, call me."

"I certainly will." She took the card. "There is one other thing. Before leaving the hospital last night, I saw a patient in the emergency room. She was being treated for a lacerated knee, but claims to have been assaulted not far from where Irene Inez was attending school."

"The Shilden Hotel lady?"

"I believe so."

"I read Kincaid's report. He didn't seem too impressed. All the same, we checked out the place this morning. It's a real rats' nest," Matt said. "We found nothing to confirm the woman's story, though. She probably just panicked. She tell you why she was there?"

"We didn't get into it. But I thought it was worth bringing to your attention."

"Any time."

After escorting Matt out of her office, Julie returned to her desk. The receptionist was waiting with a message.

Julie pressed the intercom button. "Yes."

"Dr. Charmaine, you had a call. A Ms. Vicki Zampisi."

Thirteen

Julie blocked out an hour of her afternoon in anticipation of meeting with Vicki Zampisi. The appointment had been scheduled for 2 P.M. At 2:20 Julie began to think her new patient might be a no-show.

Over the phone, Ms. Zampisi had sounded calm, but her insistence on a same-day appointment made Julie wonder.

When the receptionist finally buzzed to signal Vicki's arrival, Julie asked her to send her in.

As the secretary/receptionist showed the patient in, Julie stood and straightened her lab coat.

"Hello," Julie said, motioning to a chair. "Please make yourself comfortable."

"Thank you." Walking with a noticeable limp, Vicki came in. She wore a loose cotton shirt, sleeveless vest, and white slacks with flat heels.

"How's the knee?"

"Throbbing's less. I think the antibiotics are helping." Vicki smoothed a wrinkle on her slacks. "I appreciate your taking the time to see me on such short notice."

"It was no problem."

Vicki looked about the office, stopping momentarily at the wall of diplomas. "I used to work in the medical field."

"What did you do?"

"A medical assistant. Not anymore though," Vicki answered.

She pretended to adjust her vest. "It's been years since I've actually taken care of anybody. If you don't include my mom." Vicki tried to smile. "I moved away from L.A. in 1985. Spent some time in Oregon and Washington. Been living in Seattle for the last five years with my mother." She paused. "You know, I worked at this hospital for a brief time. It was in an old red building not far from here."

"Really?"

"For a doctor, Wes Kovacs. You ever hear of him?"

Julie shook her head, taking notes. "No. Did he work for the medical center?"

"Sort of, for a while. Dr. Kovacs was a psychiatrist."

Julie stopped writing. "That hits close to home."

Vicki smiled uneasily. "I suppose it does." She hesitated, fiddling with her clothing again. "Dr. Charmaine, I wasn't completely honest with you in the emergency room when I casually said I could live with my nightmares. I guess I was trying to give you the impression I was fine. But," she paused, biting at her lower lip. "I'm not okay. Last night they came again."

"Do your dreams always occur at night?" Julie never used the word nightmare with her patients. The word somehow made her feel less a doctor, as if suffering from chronic nightmares could make a person less than whole.

From Vicki's expression it was obvious she thought all dreams occurred at night.

"People can dream at any time," Julie explained, "although the majority of dreaming does happen at night or very early morning. Only because most people sleep during these periods. But some individuals describe flashbacks. These are images that can occur at any time, night or day. Even while watching TV or a movie."

Vicki seemed to understand. "Yes, they . . . my dreams always happen at night."

Julie made a note. "When did they start?"

Vicki reached down and touched her purse which was on her lap. After a second's hesitation, she opened it and partially removed what looked like some sort of notebook or journal. Instead of removing it all the way, Vicki simply stroked it once and then slid it back inside. It reminded Julie of the way a child feels the wall before venturing into a dark room, needing to touch something tangible before entering the unknown.

Vicki inhaled slowly. Her eyes were still on her purse. "I guess you could say they really started after the accident. I hadn't had one in a long time."

"The accident?"

Vicki glanced at the clock. A visible tremor began in her hands.

Julie leaned closer. "Don't worry about the time. I'm here to help you and you can take as much time as you need."

Vicki swallowed. "Dr. Charmaine." She spoke slowly. "What I'm about to tell you, I've never talked about with anybody before. Not even Mom. I'm not even sure where to start because I was having nightmares before I moved away from Los Angeles, but after several months, they finally stopped. For years. Then one night, it was this last March, I believe it was a Sunday, I'd taken Mom out to eat, and we argued about my drinking and smoking and everything else a mother can find wrong with her daughter. Mom and I are pretty close. I guess raising a child with problems, especially a girl, was very difficult for her. Anyway, I was buzzed and when I went to sleep that night, around eleven, I felt this strange premonition that something dreadful was about to happen. And the next morning I woke with this terrible headache. Like a hangover." She smiled weakly. "Then two days later, I read an article in the paper concerning a company I used to work for. The company was moving. I guess the news upset me and that night I had the first one. And God, this one was so different from the ones I'd had in the past."

"How was it different?"

Vicki wet her lips. "I'm getting ahead of myself. Is it all right if I start at the beginning?"

"Of course."

Vicki closed her eyes, briefly.

"Twenty years ago, I was twenty-two. I was a young, naive woman working for who I thought at the time was the most intelligent, compassionate doctor in the entire world. His name was Dr. Wes Kovacs. He was a psychiatrist. I believe he was even on-staff at the medical center here for several years, though I'm not sure. As his assistant I became . . ." Vicki stopped and stared into space.

For a moment, Julie thought she'd lost her breath. "Are you all right?" she asked.

Vicki appeared not to hear. "I'm fine," she finally said. "I'm sorry, where was I?"

"As his assistant."

"Yes. While working as Kovacs's assistant I became particularly close to one of his research patients. His name was Ben. Ben Simmons." Vicki took a deep breath. "Dr. Kovacs had been using Ben in his studies."

Julie wrote inconspicuously.

"Anyway, when Dr. Kovacs sold his clinic to the medical center, he left the psychiatric center and took his research with him. Ben was a large part of that research. Of course, I followed Dr. Kovacs too."

Julie studied her patient's expression. For a moment, Vicki was twenty-two again. Julie saw a self-contained excitement, yet underneath the passion, Julie detected a frailty. And fear.

Vicki turned her purse over in her lap. "For several months, Dr. Kovacs had been expressing concern about Ben's wild mood swings. To me, Ben was doing well, he learned quickly, I even taught him to dial the phone, but for some reason Dr. Kovacs thought otherwise and scheduled him for a session of shock treatment."

"Electroconvulsive therapy."

"Yes," Vicki folded her hands together. They were trembling again. "Dr. Charmaine, this sounds so bad." She wet her mouth again. "During the procedure, which was carried out at Kovacs's private clinic, Ben suffered a grand mal seizure. The doctor tried everything but couldn't control it." Vicki wiped at one moist eye. "Ben died choking on his own vomit."

"I'm sorry, Vicki."

Vicki swallowed back a sob. "It was terrible. I kept suctioning his mouth, but the vomit kept coming. Ben wasn't supposed to have eaten, but the food kept filling his throat. I couldn't keep up. It was a living nightmare." Vicki was crying now.

Julie listened in silence.

"Until that moment, when I saw the panic in Ben's face, I'd never realized I'd developed such strong feelings for him." Vicki found a Kleenex in her purse. She caught the tears and mascara halfway down her cheeks.

Julie waited for her patient to collect herself.

Vicki sniffled and looked up. "Sorry."

Julie nodded reassuringly. "That's what I'm here for, Vicki. And you think this accident is the cause of these dreams?"

"Initially, yes, I do." Vicki paused to gaze out the window. "I used to laugh so hard. Ben would make these weird faces and funny noises when I was sad or feeling down. I'd laugh and laugh. Sometimes I think Ben thought I was the crazy one."

Julie stood and walked around her desk. "It sounds like you and Ben were very close."

Vicki nodded weakly.

"You should know," Julie said, "that certain types of dreams can be expected after severe psychological trauma. It's not abnormal and your case is definitely not unusual. Sometimes these subconscious images can even recur. But eventually they fade away." Julie knew there were exceptions to the norm but to state this aloud would provide no benefit for her patients.

"Six months ago," Vicki said, "I would've believed you. This may sound crazy and you'll probably think I'm a total lunatic, but . . ." She looked into Julie's eyes and smiled, almost sheepishly. "I don't know how to explain it, but my dreams, my nightmares, they're so real." Her voice was soft. "I'm trapped in a dark room, no light anywhere. The air is heavy and stifling and when I breathe it's like sucking syrup through a straw, I feel like I'm drowning. And the most terrifying part is I know I'm not alone. There is someone else in the room, very near, who wants to hurt me."

"Is the dream always the same?" Julie asked, keenly aware of her own breathing.

"Yes, pretty much so. And I always wake up with this tremendous sensation of guilt. Sometimes I want to die."

"What about last night?"

"That nightmare was the worst. Even after waking up, I couldn't get rid of this sensation that I'd smelled something terrible and frightening." Vicki smiled wanly. "I even looked under my bed."

Julie stopped writing a moment. "Was this sensation new?"

"Yes. I thought it was because of the assault."

"The episode at the Shilden Hotel."

"Yes."

"Do you feel like talking about it?"

Vicki touched her knee. "I wasn't totally truthful with the cop when I said I'd heard someone calling for help. I didn't hear anything. I thought I was alone in that building."

"What did you think you'd find?"

Vicki took a moment to answer. "Ben and I used to go there. We'd always stay in the same room." She shrugged. "I guess I was searching for a piece of my past."

"Did you find what you were looking for?"

"Sometimes what you're looking for isn't the answer you're seeking." Vicki's stare returned to her lap. "It happened when I was leaving the room. Just like my dreams, everything was dark, except for my flashlight. When he grabbed my wrist I swung at him and hit him with the light. I was able to break free and run down the hall. That's when I hurt my knee."

"Did he say anything?"

"No, nothing. But I'll never forget that horrible smell. And the bed. Something had been on the mattress. It was stained and it had that same rotten odor. It was disgusting."

"Similar to the odor in your dream."

Vicki nodded. "Two smells, actually. I remember just before I knew I was no longer alone, there was this strange, almost aseptic smell. Then came the bad smell. It was so strong it made me gag."

"Did you tell this to the police?"

Vicki shook her head.

Julie studied her notes. Something was missing, an important piece of the puzzle. She turned to the past about Dr. Kovacs. "Why did you return to Los Angeles?"

At first Julie thought her patient hadn't heard the question. Vicki sat perfectly still with both eyes shut, massaging her wrist before speaking.

"I'm not really sure, maybe the guilt. I don't know. Sometimes I think it should have been me who died, not Ben."

"Vicki, no. It wasn't your fault. The accident was an accident. It was a long time ago. It—"

"You don't understand, Dr. Charmaine." Vicki's tone turned unnaturally calm. "I was all Ben had."

Long after her patient had departed, Julie remained alone in her office. Though she'd evaluated and treated hundreds of cases of sleep disorders, today's interview had hit uncannily close to home. An accident, a death, perceived guilt, nightmares.

If I'd just opened the damn door, Janine would be thirty-six.

Though the sudden temptation to call her mom was strong, Julie resisted the urge to pick up the phone. It would be close to 8 P.M. in Dallas. Her mother would be ensconced in the family-room chair reading the latest John Grisham legal thriller and her dad, now a semi-retired surgeon, would be studying his latest medical journal or swimming laps in the backyard pool.

She didn't talk to her parents enough. Next week she'd make the time.

Julie finished her notes. Vicki Zampisi had touched her on a deeper level, a personal plane she didn't entirely feel comfortable with. She worried whether this was in her patient's best interest.

She closed the file, still debating how to proceed.

In the end, she had simply prescribed Vicki a mild sedative-hypnotic to help her sleep. She usually didn't do this, but had made an exception in this case. When she spoke with Vicki again, she'd ask her permission to enroll her in a dream study. She'd also thought it'd be prudent to have Vicki discuss her assault with the authorities again. Maybe Matt's investigation at the Shilden Hotel had missed something. At the least, Vicki's coincidental description of the offending odor and the near proximity of the Shilden and El Centro Medical College made it worth looking into. Julie hadn't forgotten Irene Inez's state when she'd been brought in, nor Ignacio Chavez's *olor a muerte* "dead smell" comment.

Julie needed one other piece of information in order to reach a more complete understanding of Vicki's condition, especially if she chose to continue treating her.

She reached for the phone and dialed a four-digit number.

After two rings, a receptionist answered. "Medical records."

"This is Dr. Charmaine. How would I go about finding a chart on a patient that might have been treated here a long time ago?"

"How old?"

"Say twenty years."

"That's not old. That's ancient."

"Can it be done?"

"Patient files are generally maintained for thirty years. But anything over ten years old is on microfilm. You don't need this information now, do you?"

"No, no, but I would like it as soon as it's convenient."

"Name?"

"Ben Simmons. His treating doctor was . . ." Julie checked her notes. "A Dr. Wes Kovacs."

Fourteen

Vicki nearly missed it, the ivy had grown so tall. Bundled clumps of vines obstructed the five and much of the two.

She slowed near the corner of Pacific and Forty-sixth, studying the Huntington Park address. Even after eighteen years, she'd had no trouble recalling the route from downtown Los Angeles, south through Vernon, into this mostly industrialized suburb between Maywood and Southgate.

The light turned red and Vicki stopped. On her right was a manufacturing plant and a business complex. These structures hadn't been there in the mid-eighties when she'd last frequented 225 Pacific.

The light switched to green but Vicki didn't move. She feared how she might react. Would she cry? Would she get sick? At least the interview with Julie Charmaine had boosted her resolve, even if she hadn't been entirely truthful. But what the hell, she felt better. And she wasn't crazy. Nightmares were normal after severe psychological trauma. Her new doctor had said as much. Vicki found herself wondering how normal it could be, though, to dream of being trapped in the dark, in constant terror of meeting someone so frightening she'd awake, drenched in cold, salty, sticky sweat.

The long rectangular warehouse on her left and across the intersection of Forty-sixth looked similar to how she remembered it. For the longest time, she'd dreaded this moment, her first sight of where it all happened.

And yet, now perspiring in her van, staring at the gray, one-story building, Vicki really felt no reaction at all. There it was. The Phoenix Life Extension Foundation. The place where Vicki Zampisi last saw Ben alive.

Of course alive and living were relative terms. A cucumber could easily be classified as alive and living. So it was with Ben, on December 10, 1985, when Vicki said good-bye.

A tow truck honked behind her, but Vicki waved it by. The light turned yellow, then red again.

How did you say good-bye to someone you once loved? How did you say good-bye to someone hanging upside down in a nine-and-a-half-foot cylindrical aluminum canister, bathed in liquid nitrogen like an oversized obscene popsicle?

The light turned green again. Vicki took her foot off the brake and the van inched forward. She stayed in the right lane and when she was opposite the entrance to 225 Pacific, she turned right into the parking lot of the business complex.

She parked between a white Cadillac Seville and some small foreign sports car. Across Pacific Avenue, the parking lot of the warehouse was virtually empty. One car, a white Lexus, was parked out front and in the back near a delivery entrance, she saw a mid-sized U-Haul and a pickup.

Vicki lit a Montclair and studied the length of the building. She had no idea what Kovacs would be driving now, but it could very well be the white Lexus. Luxury cars and large homes appealed to his ego.

Vicki had argued against the clinic's original move out of the shadows of the main medical center. Though not privy to all the underlying politics, Vicki had seen Kovacs's emphasis shifting from the treatment of mental illness to the bizarre field of cryonics and its effects on living tissue. She even complained to Ben about the move but Ben had seemed indifferent. He didn't understand.

A thin man wearing glasses exited the foundation's warehouse. He sported a lab coat over a shirt, tie, and casual dress pants. In an instant, Vicki knew he wasn't Kovacs. He carried a briefcase and a separate small stack of files under one arm. He appeared to be in a hurry as he unlocked the Lexus and climbed in.

Vicki guessed Kovacs was still inside. It was at precisely this point, though, that her plan began to change.

It wasn't that she feared Kovacs, although she knew the man could be cold-heartedly brutal if it served his best interests. If anything, Kovacs should fear her. After all, she *knew.* Everything.

No, it was because of the man in the Lexus. That and all the empty parking slots and the U-Haul. Kovacs had been evasive about his plans for moving the foundation again during their brief phone conversation. Vicki wondered why. Was it because *there was a slight problem,* as he'd intimated? What kind of problem?

She finished the cigarette and dropped it outside. She watched as the man backed out and took a right onto Pacific. Then without even being aware she was doing it, suddenly Vicki found herself on Pacific three cars behind the white Lexus. It proceeded north to where Pacific curved west and crossed Alameda and Long Beach Avenue. When he took another right on Central, so did Vicki.

She nearly lost him when he sped across the Amtrak tracks just before the crossing guards dropped. Fortunately, the train was only five cars long and Vicki was able to quickly catch up again when the Lexus was stopped at a red light.

At this point, just past the Interstate 10 overpass, something odd happened. The Lexus turned into a Denny's lot, but instead of parking out front where there were plenty of spaces, the driver pulled around back. Not wanting to be conspicuous, Vicki found a self-serve service station next door and drove to the farthest pump, where she could see the back lot of the Denny's.

The Lexus was parked and Vicki saw the driver tearing some papers and tossing the scraps into a Dumpster. The entire incident lasted less than fifteen seconds. The driver promptly returned to his vehicle and drove back onto Central.

Vicki waited for two cars to pass and then followed. Seven blocks up at the corner of Sixth and Central, the Lexus pulled into a liquor store, a place called Happy's Discount Mart, and again disappeared around the back. With no other easily accessible parking alternative, Vicki turned left into Happy's and stopped out front.

She waited until the Lexus reappeared, looking closely at the driver. He wore sunglasses and appeared nervous. She saw his head jerk oddly. Their eyes met and for a moment neither looked away. At the first opening, he darted into the northbound lane of Central.

Vicki jumped out of her car and ran to the curb. She glimpsed only a portion of the license plate before he was lost. GE64 and two other numbers. She thought they were a 2 and a 5 or maybe another 6.

She turned and walked around the side of the liquor mart. Empty cases and cardboard boxes cluttered the back. She stepped around the wheel of a bicycle. The Dumpster was situated in a corner, butting up against a graffiti-decorated cinder-block wall.

Vicki approached the bin. One half of the top was swung open at a hinge, forcing her to stand on her tiptoes to look inside. It was only one-third full and much of the paper and trash was soaked with moisture. She saw a pile of torn white office paper but couldn't read the print.

Vicki stepped away, looking for something of use. Lying behind the grocery cart, she saw a cracked broom handle. It was close to four feet long. She retrieved it and tried to lift several of the papers out of the Dumpster, missing on several attempts.

"Damn it," Vicki cursed.

A door opened behind her.

She turned.

A black man with a shaved head stood at the rear exit of the liquor store. Torn jeans and an open sleeveless flannel shirt hung on his skinny but hard body.

Vicki lowered the broom handle. "I lost a receipt," she said.

"No receipts in there, lady." The man studied her face with a curious grin.

Vicki backed away, the broom handle tightly gripped at her side. She'd only stepped four paces, though, when she saw the wrinkled sheet of paper lying on the asphalt. Its white appearance looked starkly out of place in the dirty squalor of the back lot.

Dropping the broom handle, she picked it up. Much of the paper was blank although Vicki could see it was some type of requisition form or invoice. The letterhead indicated EVERGREEN MANOR MORTUARY. OVER THIRTY YEARS OF THOUGHTFUL, CARING SERVICE. It was from a Pasadena address.

Vicki folded the paper and returned to her van. She was tempted to check out the Denny's, but wanted to make it back to the foundation before dusk.

The white Lexus was parked out front in the same space when Vicki slowed at the intersection of Forty-sixth and Pacific. Instead of turning into the business complex, though, she took a left into the foundation's parking lot. Since no other cars were parked near the entrance, she guessed Kovacs wasn't there. Vicki drove to the back and parked next to the U-Haul. Her pulse quickened.

A ramp serving a shallow loading dock led up to a metal door. Before climbing the three steps to the dock's surface, she grabbed her purse and limped over to the pickup. The truck's bed was almost filled with five-gallon plastic jugs. She didn't recognize the chemical names on the labels. Propped diagonally and wedged between the bed's side panel and two jugs lay two blue pressurized gas canisters. A large N was stamped on each. The metal cylinders felt cold to the touch.

Checking first to see she was not being watched, Vicki mounted the steps and was surprised to find the rear entrance unlocked.

It opened into a narrow storage room. An overhead light was on. Though most of the shelves were empty, she saw no evidence of dust collecting on their surfaces. Ignoring the dull throb in her knee, Vicki followed a central aisle to a second door. Before opening it, she first listened, but heard no noise on the other side. The door swung open freely and Vicki stepped into the foundation's laboratory.

Immediately, she was struck by the immensity of Kovacs's private pantheon of research. Running away from her, two long counters lined each wall and the center section consisted of an elongated island. She counted several microscopes and ventilation hoods strategically placed near sinks and various other instruments with multiple dials and gauges. Crisscrossing over her head, numerous pipes of varied diameter created a latticework of complexity that converged into a single pair of larger conduits that disappeared above the ceiling near the front of the lab.

Much of the expansive counter space held boxes and small crates in various stages of packing. The facility's layout was new to Vicki, but Kovacs had obviously spent hundreds of thousands of dollars to advance his research. She realized the file she wanted wouldn't be here. But something else was.

The only sound she heard was the soft murmur of the building's ventilation system. Vicki noted a peculiar *clean odor* to the air that was remotely familiar, though she couldn't place it.

Directly across the laboratory, Vicki saw a double door with windows. Through these windows she made out another corridor and what appeared to be the foundation's administration suites. No doubt Kovacs owned one of these offices.

Her breath caught in her throat when one of the office doors opened. Stepping behind a counter, Vicki recognized the thin man from the Lexus. He carried a briefcase and moved away from the lab and disappeared around a corner.

Vicki wet her lips. The storage facility had to be nearby, most likely directly connected to the laboratory in some way. Creeping up an aisle farther from the windowed doors, she noted much of the equipment appeared to be boxed and crated in preparation for moving. Except for one corner area, where she detected an open box of microscope slides and test tubes—some filled with a red substance she presumed was blood and others containing a translucent milky liquid. She saw two centrifuges and a stereoscopic microscope. Again she detected the faint yet familiar odor.

Beneath a ventilation hood and adjacent to a double sink she saw an aquarium, holding just an inch or two of water.

Past the counter, Vicki ran into a second perpendicular corridor leading to her right. This hadn't been visible from the rear of the lab. The faint odor had grown notably stronger.

Muffled voices erupted from her left and Vicki spun, grimacing at a sharp pain in her knee. She quickly found a large wooden packing crate to slip behind. She kept her eyes on the front and rear entrances. Neither door opened and the voices faded. They sounded like they'd come from the administration suites.

Vicki debated going further. Pulling her purse closer—and the pistol it contained—did little to slow her racing heart. She had no idea what Kovacs would do to her if he caught her. She didn't need another trespassing charge, yet she suspected contacting the police would be the furthest from Kovacs's mind.

Vicki followed the corridor to where it opened into a wide enclave. Across the enclave, she saw what she'd been searching for.

Her pace quickened. As she approached the heavy six-foot-wide, double-walled door, the aseptic smell grew stronger. She froze, suddenly recalling where she'd smelled it before. The Shilden Hotel, just before her assault. Could Kovacs really have had her followed?

Vicki continued, passing a three-foot-tall aluminum canister. She glanced inside but it was empty, swabbed clean.

She walked past what she recognized to be a heart-lung machine, an oxygen canister, a resuscitator, and a computer workstation with two large-screen oscilloscopes. In the vault-like door, Vicki saw a tiny viewing window at eye level. It emitted a low-intensity blue light.

She saw no visible door handle and the heavy insulation lining its edges told her the door was hermetically sealed.

Momentarily, she felt her nerve slipping away. So close. Vicki inhaled deeply and stepped up to the window. Her breath fogged the wire-reinforced glass. When she wiped it clean, she jumped at its frigid touch.

Everything inside reflected blue through the thin veil of mist that filled the massive vault from floor to ceiling. Vicki counted at least ten adult-sized canisters or storage dewars and several more half the size of an adult. Tiny feathers of frost clung to their aluminum surfaces and the tangle of tubes and pipes that surrounded each. Each individual dewar had separate electronic displays. Their red digits shone through the blue mist with surprising clarity. The entire scene appeared frozen in time and Vicki wondered if the subzero interior of an Arctic weather station could look as frigid and inhospitable as this vault.

A series of shelves held more dewars, some no taller than a foot. At the top of each sat additional gauges and turn valves.

One dewar in particular held her attention. It stood at the rear of the vault and was taller than the rest, reaching almost to the pipes crossing the storage facility's ten-foot ceiling.

She felt a sudden chill that bore no relation to the cold. The large dewar was frost-free and leaned against the wall, instead of standing perfectly upright like the others. Vicki thought she saw patches of rust on its outer coat. On the floor beneath it she saw what appeared to be a large rectangular piece of thick cellophane, glossy blue under the fluorescent lighting and torn and tattered at its edges.

Vicki swallowed, trying to remember. She knew the material wasn't cellophane.

"Damn it," she said. What had Kovacs called it?

"What the hell you doing?" The voice came from directly behind her.

Vicki spun and opened her purse in one jerky motion.

A short, thick man in jeans, boots, and flannel jacket walked her way. His shoulders looked as broad as a piano.

Vicki shifted her weight to her good leg. She didn't speak.

"Lady, I asked you a question." The man stopped at the enclave's entrance. His face bore more irritation than animosity.

"Who are you?" Vicki asked.

"You're asking me?" He took a step closer.

Vicki pulled the .380 from her purse, releasing the safety. "No closer."

"You crazy or something?" He took another step.

"You deaf?" Vicki raised the gun, aiming at the man's thick chest. "I said don't fucking move."

"Yes, ma'am." The man's hands dropped to his side.

Vicki motioned him into the enclave, clearing the doorway out. She backed into the hall, keeping the gun on him with one hand.

The man followed her, holding his distance. "Ma'am, if you need some kind of help—"

"I don't need your help."

"You want me to call the police?"

"Call 'em."

He gave an awkward shrug, his eyes dull.

Once in the laboratory, Vicki turned and rushed for the rear exit.

"Hey, Doc," the man called out behind her.

Vicki stumbled down the loading-dock stairs, but maintained her balance. She didn't look back until safely locked in her van, the engine idling.

On the loading dock, she saw the man and the driver of the Lexus. Neither moved to intercept her.

Vicki shifted out of reverse and raced out of the foundation lot without looking back.

The thick man scratched at a dry scab on his forearm. "You want me to follow her?"

The Lexus owner watched the van disappear down Pacific. He'd seen the same van in the parking lot of Happy's Discount Mart.

"No," he said. He turned and went back inside.

Fifteen

*The two-story Tudor-style man*sion at 357 Roseview Place, its Bermuda lawn, gardens full of Josephine coat and Olympiad roses, and guest house sat on an acre of high-priced Southern California real estate in the area known as Elysian Heights. The lot's perimeter lay in the shelter of towering eucalyptus trees in the front and thick, vibrant sago palms in back. The entire estate was surrounded by a ten-foot-high wrought-iron fence with an electric sliding gate at the entrance.

A black Mercedes backed out of the four-car garage onto the concrete circular drive. The man behind the wheel sipped coffee and savored the smooth rumble of the finely tuned engine. Dr. Wesley Kovacs was a big man at six foot four and although his cholesterol topped 260, as did his weight, he drank at least eight cups of caffeine a day. His sixty-three-year-old frame was literally addicted to the drug's energizing ability.

To hell with heart disease, arteriosclerosis, cerebiovascular accidents, even diabetes and cancer. In another hundred-and-fifty years the medical community would have developed cures for many of mankind's afflictions and if Kovacs's plans played true to his scientific theories, he would be around to see it.

Kovacs set the coffee cup in a plastic holder on the dash and shifted the car into reverse. As he backed out and swung around a small fountain in the center of the drive, he took a few moments to admire the morning sunshine falling on the lush landscaping and neatly manicured yard. It seemed as if his two-month sabbatical to Arizona had never taken place. But it had. And with a modicum of success. He and a small group of investors had purchased a fifty-thousand-square-foot facility that would work out just fine for the foundation. In another month, the transfer of all equipment, records, and clients would be complete. And the seemingly endless string of clashes with city, county, and state agencies would lie in the past.

Kovacs slowed as he approached the heavy gates. He looked to his left at the large eucalyptus tree. Two nights ago, during a rainstorm, he was positive he'd seen a raccoon or some other large rodent shielding itself in a hollow at the tree's base. It held his interest not because he claimed to be an animal lover, but because Kovacs would gladly submit any such creature to one of his scientific experiments. Just ask Tom and Jerry, a pair of twenty-plus-year-old rats. The hollow, or perhaps the ravine behind the guest house, would be as good a place as any to set a trap.

Kovacs waited impatiently as the gate slid open on its metal runners. He'd planned on working in his lab all day, but after being informed of Vicki Zampisi's unexpected visit, Kovacs realized his once-trusted assistant had become more than just another nuisance.

Melting into the morning rush-hour commute, Kovacs cradled his cellular phone in one palm and dialed a number.

A woman answered. "Evergreen Manor."

"Johnny Devlin, please."

"He's not available yet. May I leave a message?"

"Yes. Have Mr. Devlin call the foundation as soon as he's available. He has the number."

Kovacs disconnected and dialed a second number. He waited for the pager to activate, keyed in his car phone number, and hung up.

Sixty seconds passed, giving Kovacs a minute to dwell on the bizarre pieces of data he was receiving back on the Tom and Jerry rat experiments. Of course, the entire picture was not yet complete, so forming any type of conclusion at this early stage would be premature. Regardless, his concern for possible severe adverse effects during the preservation process had increased substantially since reviewing the initial results.

His cellular phone rang.

"Case, I've made a decision," Kovacs said.

"And?" A male voice waited.

"Ms. Zampisi must be convinced it's in her best interests to return to Seattle."

"And if she's not so easily convinced?"

Kovacs delivered his prepared line. "Under no circumstances will the foundation abide interference from anyone."

The caller took only a moment to absorb the inference. "Understood."

Kovacs locked his car and entered the one-story rectangular structure. The front third of the warehouse consisted of the administrative section, which was vacant with the exception of several pictures and four pieces of out-of-fashion furniture. Kovacs crossed the small reception and paused at another door. This one was locked. He hurriedly opened it. It led down a hall with two offices on either side, and an additional room which held a copy and fax machine. Kovacs found his office, the first one on the right, the large one, and shut the door behind him.

At the end of this hall, a double door led to the large laboratory area and its spacious workstations. A constant low-pitched drone echoed monotonously from the intricate network of aluminum and PVC piping that crisscrossed the ceiling. These pipes were not for the air-conditioning system, but they *were* used for cooling nonetheless.

The nondescript warehouse was, until only recently, wholly owned and operated by the Phoenix Life Extension Foundation. However, the real story had begun more than a quarter of a century earlier.

In 1975, Dr. Wesley Kovacs was a thirty-six-year-old clinical psychiatrist who'd just completed two years of post-graduate study in low-temperature molecular biology. But it was actually two years earlier, in the fall of 1973, when Americans were still burning their draft cards and the nation was locked in the midst of the Watergate scandal, that the Phoenix Life Extension Foundation was actually conceived.

Two scientific articles were published that year, one in the *Journal of Nature* and the other in the *British Journal of Medicine.* The *Nature* article described how rats were conditioned to fear the sound of a bell when the bell was consistently accompanied with an electric shock; subsequently, they learned to leap off the shock pad when only the bell rang, even though no electricity was involved. This was called an operant conditioned fear reflex and this fear reflex usually lasted ten to twenty trials without the shock before it would wear off or, in the parlance of the study, become extinct.

However, if the rats were subjected to an abrupt and prolonged decrease in body temperature for a finite period of time (one hour in this particular trial), this extinction process occurred much more rapidly with fewer "false" bells. In fact, after being brought to near-freezing, it only took exposure to a single bell minus the electric shock to completely abolish their fear reflex. It was suggested the cold played some role in the abolition of the neural reflex arc transmitting the reflex. The article ended by indicating that further studies would have to be conducted to further clarify their results.

The second research paper, published in the *British Journal of Medicine* in their 1973 October issue, described how an English terrier named Pesky was nearly frozen alive for almost an hour—fifty-eight minutes to be exact—in a liquid nitrogen chamber, then subsequently thawed successfully.

Over a very short period, Pesky's core temperature had been lowered to thirty-eight degrees Fahrenheit and sustained at that temperature for fifty-eight minutes. Then, using warmed intravenous saline lavages and warming blankets, she was brought back from the brink of death to a normal core temperature of one hundred degrees Fahrenheit.

This feat, lowering a subject's core temperature, was nothing new. It was used, to a degree, in cardiothoracic surgical procedures. What made the trial so special was the length of time and degree of low-temperature exposure undertaken.

Although both these published reports seemed related only in their experimental lowering of a subject's core body temperature, the young practicing neuropsychiatrist and part-time staff physician at California University Medical Center immediately began to envision the potential uses of low-temperature therapeutics in medicine, especially in the treatment of mental illness.

If the rats' brain circuitry involving the processing and perceiving of an emotion as primitive as fear could be manipulated and eventually abolished with low temperature, why couldn't the same results be achieved in humans?

Dr. Wesley Kovacs believed they could. In fact, he believed so strongly in the potential therapeutic effects of low temperature on psychiatric dysfunctions such as depression, mania, and schizophrenia that he took two years off from clinical medicine in order to complete an intensive research fellowship in low-temperature biology called cryogenics. He studied under the well-known cryobiologist of the time, B. J. Luyet, at the prestigious cryolab on the University of California at Berkeley campus.

It was during these two years that his fascination with cryonics, the science of freezing and reviving animals, became almost an obsession. He always kept a copy of the *British Journal*'s Pesky paper within easy reach. If a dog could be nearly frozen for fifty-eight minutes, why not two hours, or a day? Or a month? Or even years?

In June of 1975, Dr. Wesley Reginald Kovacs earned a PhD in cryobiology. For his doctoral dissertation, he anesthetized a rhesus monkey that answered to the name of Cheetah and replaced Cheetah's blood with a 1.4 molar saline-buffered alcohol:glycerol solution. The primate's body temperature was lowered to zero degrees Fahrenheit, some thirty-two degrees below freezing. The cryoprotectant solution flowing through Cheetah's veins acted as a sort of antifreeze, thus preventing the formation of lethal ice crystals in the monkey's cells. Exactly twelve hours later, the process was reversed and Cheetah was revived with no adverse side affects. Five years later, Cheetah was alive and well, the official mascot of the cryolab at Berkeley.

With a PhD postscripting his medical doctorate and an ambition bordering on the fanatical, Dr. Kovacs returned to CUMC, rented space in the basement of Old Red, and unofficially founded the Phoenix Life Extension Foundation. Officially he called it Community Psychiatric Center, specializing in the treatment of mental disorders. The year was 1975.

Ahead of his time in a psychiatric profession that still clung to the beliefs of Carl Jung and Sigmund Freud, Wesley Kovacs was convinced that every mental illness could be explained by minute deviations in the brain's neurotransmitters. These large and small molecular-chain proteins with names like serotonin and norepinephrine were responsible for the psychic makeup of individual personalities.

His hypothesis, which stemmed from the cold rat experiments and ran against the scientific grain of every mental-health organization in the field, theorized that cold could be used to induce changes in the brain's neurotransmitter levels and these changes could be used to therapeutic advantage in treating mental illness.

Two problems. First, the research technology of the late sixties and early seventies could not measure neurotransmitter levels in individual brain neurons unless the subjects were sacrificed first—an impossibility, even for the driven Kovacs.

Second, the biotechnological ability to freeze animals was not yet at a stage conducive to long-term survival.

Kovacs tackled the second problem first. If he were to be successful in proving his hypothesis, he first had to perfect a method of freezing whole-bodied animals in a way from which they could be successfully resuscitated. And he tackled this problem with all the fervor of a Dr. Jekyll or a Dr. Frankenstein. After a full schedule of seeing manic-depressives, insomniacs, and schizophrenics during the day, at night he'd close the doors to his Community Psychiatric Center and sequester himself in the basement amongst the Erlenmeyer flasks, insulated canisters, liquid nitrogen vats, and various derivatives of alcohol/glycerol solutions.

He started with tadpoles and amphibians, usually toads, of which there was always a plentiful supply behind his small house in Vernon, and soon progressed to small rodents, rats, and mice, eventually succeeding in freezing cats and dogs. All this required time and money. Fortunately, Kovacs's clinical practice grew at such a rate that he could hire three full-time psychiatrists and a battery of clinical psychologists and social workers to see the patients, thus freeing him to devote all his time to his "mission."

By 1977, Kovacs owned five clinics under the Community Psychiatric Centers' name and employed more than a hundred people, including thirty full-time and per diem psychiatrists and twenty psychiatric nurses. Each mental-health clinic functioned as a gold mine, generating millions of dollars in revenues and accumulating more resources to support Kovacs's cryonics research.

Over time, the administrative hassles, family leave, sick leave, malpractice insurance, employee health coverage, and retirement plans also took their toll, so in 1978, Dr. Kovacs sold a seventy-five percent interest in his medical enterprise to California University Medical Center for twenty-five million dollars. The match was perfect for both parties. CUMC maintained use of the Community Psychiatric Centers' goodwill, gaining easy access to a high-volume patient referral source for its new, state-of-the-art Psychiatric Hospital. Kovacs became a multimillionaire.

One clause of the clinic's sales contract, though, stipulated that Kovacs relocate his research laboratory. The regents of the California University system had not been eager to maintain an affiliation with the doctor whom certain esoteric, quasi-science magazines described as the man who could wake Rip Van Winkle from cold storage.

Relishing the freedom from prying bureaucrats, Kovacs promptly plunked down three hundred and fifty grand for a forty-thousand-square-foot warehouse at 225 Pacific Boulevard. He spent another hundred-thousand dollars converting the one-time food-storage facility into the most advanced cryolab on the West Coast. It surpassed even the research laboratory at Berkeley, had those at Berkeley known, but initially Kovacs remained secretive about his work. From humble roots in treating mental illness, the psychiatrist quickly realized his research could one day touch every field in science and medicine, from organ transplants to space travel. The race was on. The sky was the limit and Kovacs had the greatest head start. Once he successfully cryofroze a human, he'd be awarded the Nobel Prize for science.

He didn't even put the name of his investment on the door, although Kovacs did file a D.B.A. license with the city of Huntington Park as Phoenix Life Extension Foundation. The clerk filing the name figured it was some sort of religious organization and no further investigation into the workings behind the walls of the nondescript warehouse would take place for more than two decades.

Kovacs thumped the thick briefcase down on top of the mahogany desk and rested his heavy frame in his cushioned executive chair. Even though the inside temperature was maintained at a cool sixty-eight degrees Farenheit, he was perspiring. Wiping his forehead with a handkerchief with one hand, he began to sort through some journal articles. It wasn't long before he heard the reception door close in front. As no one else possessed a key, he presumed his associate had returned.

Kovacs waited for the knock. The office door opened.

"Wes," Dr. Christian Eisler greeted his superior. Thin and scholarly, always clean shaven, he wore his wrinkled white lab coat and carried his clipboard as usual.

"Take a seat." Kovacs opened his briefcase and took out yesterday's *L.A. Times.* He tossed it to Eisler. It landed on the clipboard.

"You read yesterday's latest?" Kovacs asked.

Eisler shook his head. Kovacs knew he never read the paper. Eisler didn't care about the outside world. He didn't care who the president was, he didn't vote, could care less what the Big Seven's latest monetary policy was, or who led the NFL in rushing. None of it mattered, as long as he could conduct his research. But with a master's in biothermal engineering and a doctorate in cryophysics, Dr. Eisler was well qualified for his position as associate director at the Phoenix Life Extension Foundation.

Kovacs pointed. "Turn to page twenty."

Eisler did, and found the headline: PHOENIX FOUNDATION THINKS DEAD HAVE FUTURE.

Eisler briefly scanned the article, a rehash of an investigative report written seven months ago after a Phoenix Foundation delivery driver suffered an accident on the 405 Freeway, spilling an ice chest–sized vat of liquid nitrogen and closing off the carpool lane. By the time the authorities arrived, the liquid nitrogen had all but evaporated, and a woman's pet ferret, Binky, which the foundation had been contracted to freeze, had begun to thaw.

Panicked, the driver quickly departed and it was left up to Eisler to transport the woman's ferret, in a chest of ice from a local 7-Eleven, back to headquarters. Meanwhile, Kovacs himself drove to the woman's estate in Beverly Hills and assured her that Binky's present condition was still perfectly suitable for cryonic preservation and that her twenty-five-thousand-dollar fee was well spent. In the next millennium when Binky was finally thawed and revived, kidney failure in ferrets would indeed be curable.

Though the woman had been satisfied, a flood of questions and investigations had ensued. The final straw came when a copy of a cryonics contract between the Phoenix Foundation and a rich Newport Beach octagenarian suffering from severe Alzheimer's leaked to the press. Just prior to his official death, the man's power of attorney granted the foundation the right to freeze him upside-down inside an eight-foot thermos until a cure for Alzheimer's was finally discovered, when the contractee would be thawed and healed.

The furor had led to Kovacs's trip to Tucson two months ago. He had always enjoyed Arizona's low humidity and clean air and he was convinced the foundation needed a fresh start. It took only a week to finalize the purchase of a forty-acre rundown winery with its expansive warehouse and in-house laboratory. He also promptly filed all the necessary business papers and applied for the required licenses that would begin the Phoenix Foundation's move east.

The latest article concluded with a quote from Tucson's mayor. "We welcome any and all business as long as they maintain a certain touch with reality!"

Eisler returned the paper to Kovacs's desk. "The journalist's a cretin," he said with a shrug.

Kovacs had to suppress a grin. A cretin. Not an asshole, not a shithead. But a cretin. Vintage Eisler.

Eisler turned a page on his clipboard. It was back to business. "The electricity has been paid till the end of the month. Next week, all vats and dewars will have their liquid nitrogen replenished so that any heat contamination during the eight-hour transport will not adversely affect the subjects. Assuming an ambient air temperature range of sixty-five to eighty degrees and transfer under optimum insulating conditions, that will eliminate any convective and conductive heat gains. The vessels' internal core should not rise more than two degrees Centigrade."

"Minus one-hundred-ninety-four degrees Centigrade." Kovacs stated the obvious.

Temperatures of minus 196°C were required to halt all metabolic and biochemical activity. At least that's the number they'd initially determined. But recent data Kovacs had not yet shared with Eisler were a new source of worry.

Eisler misread Kovacs's concern. "Statistically speaking from a biothermal perspective, the two-degree rise over eight hours will have virtually no negative consequences. It's insignificant."

Two weeks ago Kovacs would've agreed. But Tom and Jerry changed all that. Killing a subject's metabolism without killing the subject was proving more difficult than initially anticipated.

With his associate's help Kovacs had no doubt the cryoproblem would be solved. He was a genius, but Christian Eisler was a genius's genius. For that very reason he'd delegated the responsibility of transporting all fifty-three of the foundation's current clients, including former pets like Binky the ferret, seven *Homo sapiens* brains, thirteen adult human subjects, and the thirty-plus whole-animal body suspensions, to Eisler. Meanwhile Kovacs had overseen the more practical matters such as construction of the specially fabricated reinforced-steel vaults that would later house the subjects in their new home, meeting with Tucson officials, hiring ancillary staff, and transferring all scientific records.

Kovacs pulled his briefcase closed. He popped open the latches and pretended to fumble with some papers. Since his return three nights ago, there was one subject they'd both carefully avoided. Unfortunately, though, with the unexpected entrance of Vicki Zampisi, the subject could no longer remain unspoken.

"And case two-twenty-five," he said without looking up. It was actually a question.

"Taken care of."

Kovacs nodded. "I have a call in to Devlin. He's to notify either you or me of any unauthorized requests for information regarding the subject's disposition. I don't mind paying this prima-donna grave digger good money, but I want results."

"You think she'd actually go to the mortuary?"

"She came here didn't she, damn it," Kovacs exploded.

Eisler flinched. "I didn't know I was being followed."

Kovacs forced himself to maintain control, pinching the bridge of his nose. "The mortuary invoices were all fabricated, the name's been altered, hell, the foundation wasn't even listed as the primary purchaser. No irreparable harm done, I suppose. The only link Vicki Zampisi has between us and the hill is seeing you. And if she didn't discover the Evergreen Manor name in the trash heap, that link becomes nonexistent.

"Oh, there is one other minor detail," he added.

Eisler continued to stare at a table of biothermal-tissue gradients on his clipboard.

Kovacs resisted the urge to smack his associate's balding pate. "I delegated Ms. Zampisi to Case. You're positive he got a good look at her?"

This brought Eisler's head up. "You don't easily forget a face like hers. Besides, she had a gun for god's sake."

"Yes, that does tend to sharpen one's focus." Kovacs would have smiled if so much wasn't at stake.

Eisler cleared his throat. "Wes, just how dangerous is this woman?"

"Physically, not at all. She's a depressed drunk who never got married, who I suspect has manufactured an ax to grind. But," Kovacs leaned his heavy bulk closer to his desk. "She does know just enough to seriously compromise the foundation's near-term agenda."

"Simmons?"

"She's aware of the subject's existence."

"Damn, Wes, she was standing right outside the unit."

Kovacs's voice softened. "Case assured me she had no time to see anything. And by this hour tomorrow she'll be nothing but a minor memory in the foundation's glorious history."

Eisler's squint narrowed. "What do you mean?"

"Relax. I'm referring to her return trip to Seattle. The foundation's emphasis leans toward preserving life, not extinguishing it."

Eisler exhaled deeply. "For a moment—"

"Christian." Kovacs stepped around his desk. "I've arranged a meeting with the University of Tucson Medical Center board as soon as the foundation's move is complete, probably sometime next month. Our goal will be to get you on staff. Maybe teaching a basic science elective in thermal biology or something related. The options are varied."

"Thank you. That would be much appreciated."

Kovacs rested a big hand on Eisler's shoulder. "It will also increase the foundation's chances of receiving additional grants for cryo research. We'll get it done, Christian. All in good time."

Though Julie had driven by its cracked façade a hundred times on her commutes to work, she'd never paid much attention to the structure on the corner of Faraday and Lemon. Until today.

With no premeditated desire to stop, she nevertheless found herself slowing and pulling next to the curb.

The Shilden Hotel sign still hung across its arched entrance, precariously canted off-center. Studying the boarded-up windows and weed- and trash-strewn lot, Julie couldn't imagine herself invading the condemned building's dark halls at any time, much less after sundown.

The last time she'd allowed herself inside an abandoned structure had been when Janine was found. Or rather when she found Janine. Even today, any odor of insecticides uncovered long-dormant images and sensations she'd prefer remain buried. She would just as soon let a spider spin its web than reach for a can of Raid. Yet Vicki had done what she could never do, challenging the hotel's NO TRESPASSING warnings in daunting fashion and suffering a nasty knee laceration in the endeavor.

Julie respected her patient's intrepidness, though she questioned Vicki's motives. What could have prompted Vicki to risk arrest and personal injury by entering the Shilden's premises? Had she been searching for something tangible or was her quest more a fishing expedition for answers? Perhaps regarding her nightmares.

Julie suddenly felt compelled to take a closer look at this broken, vacated building that had lured one of her patients into its damaged cavity, then spit her out in one terror-stricken breath. What had Vicki witnessed inside? Simply a transient looking for a place to sleep or was it like the cops had said, the woman just panicked?

Julie waited for a city truck carrying a load of asphalt to pass before stepping out onto the street. She walked along the sidewalk until she came to an alley.

She gazed over the top of the chain-linked fence at the Shilden's upper floors. Sheets of plywood sealed many of the windows and several of the balconies slanted at unnatural angles. Though the sun had set, leaving the sky a deep purple, there was still enough light to make out the ugly cracks snaking down the exterior brick and mortar walls.

Janine! Janine!

Julie, run, it's Worm Man!

From behind her, Julie heard a shrick followed by laughter. Without warning, two kids on rollerblades sped by dangerously close, forcing her against the perimeter fence.

"Hey lady," one yelled. "Kurt Cobain's ghost sleeps on the second floor."

Julie watched the speedsters vanish around the corner. She doubted it'd been the dead singer's spirit that had caused her patient's injuries. Or her dead sister's voice.

She moved further down the alley until the faintly pungent scent of raw sewage made her stop. Abutting the hotel's back lot, she saw an abandoned construction zone. A line of orange cones extended into the alleyway and barricaded a large pit. Chunks of asphalt lay piled next to a John Deere backhoe.

Across the fence, pools of stagnant water puddled the ground's uneven terrain and the entire lot was littered with refuse, Sheetrock, and piles of wood. Some of the weeds reached heights of several feet.

Scanning the boarded-up first-floor units, Julie wondered which one had been Vicki's access of entry. In the waning light, all appeared impenetrable. A car horn shattered the relative solitude of the hotel lot, followed by the squeal of tires, and for an instant she expected the crunching sound of metal and glass to fill the alley. There was none, just a pickup zipping by on the street.

An odd sensation crept over Julie as her attention returned to the defective three-story structure before her. She almost felt that if she stood in its shadows long enough, intimate details of the Shilden's history would be revealed that would assist her in understanding Vicki's problems. And her own past. She stood motionless, only her eyes picking out the black holes that once were windows. Along the second-floor balconies, she could almost imagine hearing the mellifluous keening of an ailing Kurt Cobain.

Julie sensed the man's presence even before he spoke. When she turned, he was standing no more than six feet away. Stooped at the shoulders, he was short and emaciated, and dressed in layered pieces of dark fabric and cloth that at one time might have been shirts and trousers. Deep lines wrinkled his face which was covered in coarse gray whiskers. Stale remnants of his last meal still clung to the hairs around his lips. Tucked tightly under an arm, he held a paper sack.

"I seen it." He spoke with vocal cords rife with phlegm.

Reflexively, Julie stepped back. She saw fear mirrored in the derelict's irises as they darted toward the hotel.

"I seen it," he repeated. With a noticeable limp, he shuffled around her in the direction of the backhoe.

"What?" Julie called after him.

The man's incoherent babble was lost amid the muted sounds of city traffic. He hobbled between the construction cones, teetering for an instant on the brink of the pit, then disappeared behind the John Deere where the alleyway once again intersected the sidewalk. He leaned right and vanished into the shadows.

Turning, Julie walked briskly back to her car. Vicki Zampisi would remain her patient.

Sixteen

"Case" Mitchell Beeden pulled the collar of his flight jacket up around his ears and stepped from behind the wheel of the stolen Jeep Wrangler. The former owner, a businessman in pinstripes and Rockports, was probably still nursing a nasty headache from the clip he'd taken on the back of his skull two hours earlier. Since this particular operation had precluded Case from driving his own car, he'd chosen the Jeep because all the other vehicles in the Boyle Heights parking garage had names like Toyota, Nissan, and Mercedes. Case preferred never to patronize foreign manufacturers, even if it meant not stealing their products.

Once his employer had provided the name, it'd been relatively simple for Case to obtain the target's Los Angeles address through the phone company. He'd simply waited until the woman exited her apartment, then followed her van to this Lucky's grocery store a few blocks away. She'd been inside now for two minutes.

Case, a sobriquet from the time he'd won a redneck strongman event by holding a case of bottled Budweiser at arm's length for six minutes, shoved both hands into his jeans' front pockets and angled toward the deserted van. He moved fluidly and quietly in the dark, a rhino in satin slippers. A panhandler who shuffled a few steps his way experienced a change of heart and backed away.

The van sat next to a cement island under a parking-lot light. Case found an abandoned shopping cart and casually approached the passenger-side door. He waited while another vehicle drove away, then popped the van's lock and climbed in. The fact that the woman had neglected to activate any type of car alarm told him he probably wouldn't be sitting alone long.

Case squeezed over into the backseat and forced his squat body as low as possible below the headrests. The floorboard carpet was worn and gave off a musty odor. With only his forehead and eyes visible, he watched the store's entrance.

The woman appeared, carrying a small grocery sack. He recognized her face from the foundation headquarters, the wide-set eyes, the flattened forehead. Her nose was nice, though, and he'd always had a preference for blondes. In jeans and a tight pullover, her silhouette cast a seductive figure. Case felt the blood pulse in his veins and he began to relish his executioner's role. There were no rules that stated it had to be fast. Just permanent.

She waited for a car to pass, then proceeded toward the van.

Case ducked lower, folding an arm across the lump in his chest. The Colt 357 Magnum would remain in its shoulder holster for the time being. As he listened for her footsteps, he slid a Swiss-army knife from a sheath strapped to his belt. He unfolded the four-inch blade. A sharp point of metal, however small, always did wonders for a woman's cooperation.

She stopped outside the driver's-side door. Case heard the jingle of keys and he sucked in his breath.

Vicki tossed her purse to the passenger seat and slid in behind the wheel. Before closing the door, she examined the sack's contents. It was hell to drive all the way home and find out she'd forgotten something. However, tonight all the essentials were accounted for—a carton of Montclairs, a bottle of Tawny Porto wine, a half-dozen eggs, and some Aquafresh hair spray and shampoo. Tomorrow she'd get whatever else she needed. Shopping in the evening depressed her. Late at night the grocery aisles seemed to attract only the lonely and socially maladjusted.

Vicki pulled the door shut and backed out. Because she was already somewhat buzzed, courtesy of a light dinner consisting largely of easily prepared Ezra Brooks, she experienced more of a subdued shock than true fear when the cold metal pressed into the right side of her neck.

She braked and reached up with her left hand. She touched the blade, which rested between her internal jugular and trachea.

"Lock your door, release the brake, and drive. Real slow." The man's voice had the flat affect of someone medicated on psychoactive drugs, perhaps a barbiturate or lithium.

Vicki's eyes moved to the rearview mirror.

The blade dug deeper. "No, not yet. Now drive."

"Where?" Vicki asked. She drove toward the exit, her eyes frantically darting across the nearly vacated lot. She saw a homeless man pushing a grocery cart. He was headed away from her.

A heavy hand gripped her left trapezius. "Don't signal. You're in the medical field. You should know how rapidly, or slowly, depending on your point of view, your carotid artery bleeds."

Vicki slowed at the streetlight.

"Nothing funny now, Vicki. I'm very good at what I do," the man warned. "Do exactly as your pretty ass is told or I'll fill up this fucking van with your blood. Do you believe I can kill you?"

"Yes."

"Do you believe I *will* kill you?"

"What do you want?"

"I want you to turn left on Clarence. Blinkers, no speeding, no horns, nothing to draw attention. Are you hearing me?"

"Yes." Vicki waited for two cars to pass—neither of them cops, she lamented—before pulling into the right-hand lane.

The man's grip loosened, though the pressure from the knife blade remained the same. Vicki felt sure the steel had cut her skin.

She glanced in the rearview mirror but could see nothing of her abductor.

"Where are we going?" she asked.

"Find Fourth, take a right, and drive toward the river."

Vicki kept well under the speed limit of forty. Unfamiliar with its darkened silhouette, she passed El Centro Medical College. One intersection later she turned left on Louis. Approaching Fourth Street, she slowed even more, hoping to catch a red light. But the signal remained green.

"Signal," he said.

Vicki flipped the right-turn flasher. "Sorry, I forgot."

"Don't."

She turned right onto Fourth. To her dismay, the traffic was even lighter. Lining either side of the street, industrial warehouses and small businesses stood cramped together in concrete rows. The street lighting was dim and the only real illumination she saw was that provided by the local buildings' security lights. Every structure looked shut down and locked for the night. She prayed for a security guard or other passerby but saw no one.

The man spoke as if reading her thoughts, "What'd you think, I'd escort you to the Coliseum on Dodger night?"

Vicki didn't answer. There was something oddly familiar about the man's voice. She didn't know whether to be relieved or more frightened. "You work for Kovacs," she said.

The knifepoint didn't flinch. "Score one for the bimbo."

It *was* relief Vicki felt. She could deal with Kovacs, even secondhand. A would-be rapist, a random kidnapping, scared her far more.

"Are you a patient?" she asked, slowing at the next intersection. She could count one more before the bridge.

"That's two for the bimbo. I guess all blondes aren't cracked from the same mold," the man said, chuckling. "That's a joke. You do have my permission to laugh."

Vicki feigned a smile. "I guess I should be asking what Kovacs wants."

"Right now, lady, it's what I want that's important." For the first time, he sat upright, resting a square chin beside Vicki's handrest. "And what I want is to sit in the front seat where I can see your pretty face. I bet that's a first, being called pretty."

Vicki disregarded the insult.

Case laughed. "Well, makes no difference. I'm going to climb over now. If you try anything, I'll cut off your nose. Do you believe I'll cut off your nose?"

"Yes."

"Then we have an understanding. Stop the van."

"The light's green," Vicki said, entering the intersection.

"I said stop the fuckin' van."

Vicki braked to a halt. She saw no vehicle in either direction.

"Don't make a noise, lady."

Suddenly, his left hand grasped a handful of hair and jerked Vicki's head back, extending her neck. The knife blade pressed against her trachea. Stifling a scream, she stared straight out the windshield.

"Don't kill me," she said.

"The bimbo would like her nose in her palm, maybe?"

Vicki shook her head as best she could, but didn't speak.

"That's better. We're back to our understanding."

Maintaining his locked position on Vicki's head and neck, he squeezed a thick thigh and then his wide chest and torso over. His left leg followed last.

Vicki could smell his breath, a nauseating mixture of onions, beer, and marijuana, as he twisted into the front seat. He pressed close as he released his grip on her head.

Vicki inhaled several times to clear the fog.

"Drive," he said.

She pulled forward, aware of every sensation in her body. Her right ankle hurt from pressing so hard on the brake. The throbbing in her knee had returned, full-blown. Her nose itched but she dared not touch it.

"See the bridge?" he asked.

Vicki nodded.

"You can talk now?"

"Yes."

"On the right, just before the bridge, there'll be a service road and a place to stop. Pull off and park next to that clump of oaks."

Vicki nodded.

"Did you hear me?"

"Yes," Vicki said, feeling his hard stare.

"Then say it, bimbo."

"I'll park next to the clump of oaks," Vicki said, searching for the trees. Her earlier relief had begun to abate. She swallowed and felt the sharp edge of the knife blade.

"My name is Case," he said, shifting the point back to the jugular area. "And you . . ." He pressed.

"Vicki Zampisi."

"I know that," Case said. "I know all about you. Kovacs told me how you want to fuck up his prize project. Did you really know this Simmons character?"

"Yes."

"And did you fuck him?"

Vicki clenched her jaws. Case obviously wasn't entirely informed about the experiment. She felt a hand grope her breast.

"I asked you, bimbo, did you fuck Mr. Simmons?"

"Yes."

The hand remained on her breast. She felt the fingers crudely searching out her nipple. An index finger and thumb squeezed.

Vicki grimaced, jerking the wheel.

"Careful, lady. I can just as easily chop off a nipple as a nose," Case said. He released his grip and pointed. "There."

Vicki saw the rise of the bridge and the ramp leading down to the service road, vanishing behind a growth of vegetation. She pulled off, slowing next to a stand of trees.

"Stop," Case said.

Vicki braked and shifted into park.

"The engine too, bimbo."

She switched off the ignition and lights. The only sounds were the traffic on the nearby Santa Ana Freeway overpass and the swirl of water in the river below. She could make out the L.A. skyline and the concrete embankments of the river basin ahead of her.

"Crack the window," Case ordered.

Vicki turned the handle one quarter and instantly felt a dank breeze cross her cheek. The air smelled of raw sewage and stagnation.

"Look at me," he said, grabbing her wrist.

Vicki turned with the knife and stared into a flat oblong faceful of whiskers and menace. His eyes looked like black divots torn from his head and his neck sloped out from the ears in thick cords of muscle.

"Now we talk," he said. "You know, you're really not too bad looking. How much of the scalpel did it take?"

"More than you could afford," Vicki said icily. She broke from his gaze and glanced at her purse lying on the passenger floorboard.

In an instant, Case released her wrist and grabbed the purse, tossing it to the rear of the van. "No pistols tonight, hotshot," he said, slapping Vicki sharply across her cheek before finding the opening under her pullover top.

"No," Vicki said.

"Shut up." Case's hand dug under the underwire of her bra. He twisted.

A weak shriek escaped Vicki's lips. "Please let me go," she pleaded.

His grip loosened. "Dr. Kovacs requests that you return to Seattle immediately. Are you hearing me? A nod will suffice."

Vicki nodded.

"He also requests you forget you ever heard the name Ben Simmons. There was never any such patient, never any experiment, and you never worked for the foundation. Do we still have an understanding?" He squeezed.

"Yes," Vicki said through pursed lips.

"I don't believe you, Ms. Zampisi." He twisted again, sending a searing pain into Vicki's armpit.

"Don't, please."

"I don't believe you, lady," Case said louder, lunging against her. He pinned her body against the door.

Vicki felt the knife drop away, only to be replaced by the same hand on her neck. Her airway pinched off.

She choked, gargling a scream as his other hand dug into her flesh.

Case's breath smothered her face. She began to grow faint.

"You want me to fuck you, don't you?" he said. His grip loosened. "Don't you? I want to hear you!"

Vicki's breathing came in heavy gasps.

"Answer me, bitch!"

Coughing, she sputtered. "Fuck me, Case. Fuck me hard."

He followed with his head and tongue, licking her neck and chin in wet vulgar slurps.

Vicki pressed her head against the glass, waiting for her chance. It came when he found her mouth.

She bit down hard, sending both front incisors through his lower lip. She could taste his warm blood and she spit a mouthful into his face.

Case pulled back instinctively, holding his loose piece of lip in place.

Vicki twisted and released the door lock. He lunged just as she pulled the door handle and both of them tumbled to the asphalt.

Screaming and kicking, Vicki somehow slid away from his grasp and turned and ran. She sprinted down the service road leading to the bridge.

She could hear his heavy footfalls close behind.

"You fuckin' bimbo!" Case screamed.

Vicki followed the asphalt under the bridge, dashed between two cement columns, down the embankment, and past a large concrete culvert where shallow patches of algae and moss forced her to slow. Her knee could betray her at any moment. If she slipped and fell, he'd catch her. If he caught her, she was dead.

A sharp quick movement over her left shoulder took her completely off guard. Terror gripped her. How had Case closed the distance so fast? She veered away from the flowing water and ran back up the embankment on the other side of the bridge. For just an instant, a wave of raw offensive stench rolled by her and then it was gone.

Vicki glanced back and saw Case angling diagonally across the cement slope after her. His thundering steps sounded like racing hoofbeats. He reached the culvert with one hand still clutched to his mouth and his face contorted by pure rage. Momentarily, he vanished in the dark shadows of the overpass. Vicki thought she heard him stumble.

She continued her climb at breakneck speed, reaching the service road again but not before hearing a muffled curse behind her. An abbreviated scuffling noise ensued and then there was only the sound of flowing water.

Vicki didn't slow until she was back on Fourth Street. There were no passing cars to signal so she jogged fifty yards to an illuminated spot under a street lamp. She turned and faced the bridge, expecting to see Case appear at any moment. She felt confident, even with her injured knee, she could outrun the far heavier man on flat ground.

Vicki waited ten minutes. When Case failed to show, she slipped cautiously back to her van. If the bastard fell, she hoped he broke his goddamn neck.

Twenty-five feet underground, a scheduled maintenance cleaning of the East L.A. Interceptor sewer entered its second day. The Department of Public Works construction crew thought little of the spiked red pump and woman's gold bracelet they found intermingled with the sludge and debris. But in accordance with city policy regarding anything of potential value found in the sewer, the shoe and jewelry were passed up to the supervisor in charge.

Seventeen

*The only major new piece of evi-*dence in the Inez case came in the form of the .38 revolver given to Matt by Julie. As Matt had suspected, it had been fired once. Fingerprints on the gun matched those of the victim. Police technicians also lifted two smudges that could have been prints but remained unreadable. A warrant for Ignacio Chavez went out to all eighteen precincts of the LAPD, but the guy had simply vanished.

A Dorfman call had created another piece to the puzzle. Further trace-evidence examination had turned up tiny fragments of an unknown polyurethane substance in several samples taken from under Ms. Inez's nails. Continued evaluation to determine type and possible sources was ongoing. The bad news was the hair fragment had been a dead end. No foreign substances had been detected, acrylic paint or otherwise, and because of its severely altered state, identification as either human or animal was impossible.

And a recent development threatened to complicate the crime picture even more.

The shift commander was a guy named Bert Signelli. Lieutenant Bert Signelli had devoted thirty years of his life to law enforcement, twenty-three with the LAPD. Nicknamed Wopman for his penchant for pasta and Arturo Fuente cigars, he was tame as a pussycat when cases were closing but could be a royal pain in the ass when suspects still walked the street.

Signelli approached Matt with a folder in one hand. He barely glanced at Ramani's empty desk.

"Where's the guru?" Signelli asked, referring to Ramani's Indian heritage, as in India, not Native American.

"Isabelle had chest pains."

"So?"

"So he took her to the doctor."

"Sunday evening?" Signelli sounded perturbed.

"No law says a person can't have chest pains Sunday evening." Matt still hadn't looked up.

"Look at me, Guardian. I'm fifty-two, three months from fifty-three, forty pounds too thick, enough cholesterol to butter a loaf of bread, and I don't get chest pains."

Matt looked up slowly, pausing at Signelli's trademark belly. "Keep telling you to come to the gym. Before you strain your back kissing Osshoff's ass."

"Fuck you."

Matt shrugged. Osshoff was the captain and Signelli would be the last to kiss his ass.

The lieutenant shoved some of the clutter on Ramani's desk aside and sat down. "No, seriously, Isabelle is really sick?"

"Had chest pains."

"She's too young for chest pains."

"She lives with Ramani."

Signelli pondered Matt's words a moment. "You got a point."

Lieutenant Signelli sat with the folder across one thigh. He was using one corner to scratch his opposite leg.

"What's that?" Matt asked, suddenly suspicious.

Signelli stopped scratching. "I'm about to give you and Ramani more chest pains."

He dropped the file on top of the one Matt was already looking at.

Matt saw the blue stripe taped across one edge. He shoved it away. "No way. I'm up to my puke-green eyeballs in sewer shit, and unless we track down this kid from the barrio, this hospital homicide is gonna be open six months from now. And now you're gonna dump a fuckin' blueball on my ass. What about Heraldson or Lee? Or hell," Matt thumbed at a gangly detective henpecking on a typewriter. "What about Rosen? He and Jensen land all the easy shit."

"Fuck you, Guardian," Rosen said.

"Shut up, Rosen, you skinny prick," Signelli half-joked. He shoved the file back at Matt. "It wasn't my idea. It comes down from above."

"A blueball. Great, just fucking great." Matt leaned back in his chair. It creaked as he stretched his tight neck and back, which were destined to get tighter.

In its most primitive sense, a blueball case meant the investigator pursued relentlessly any and all leads until his balls turned a deep shade of blue or the case was closed. So far Matt hadn't actually experienced any blueballs, including his own, but there'd been some close calls. Blueball cases were reserved for special situations, such as when an officer is shot or a high-ranking official is the victim of some violent crime. The assault and stabbing of an L.A. city councilwoman several years back was a prime example of a blueball. The tag usually carried with it a string of twenty-hour days and constant reports to superiors.

Matt reached for the file. "Why do I get the feeling I'm getting fucked?"

"Cause you are. But look at it this way. The captain fucks me, I fuck you, and you get to fuck Ramani. Hell, I've never even fucked a real guru."

"A regular circle fuck." Matt opened the file. A model-quality black-and-white glossy of a beautiful, light-skinned black woman made him suck in a breath. "Whoa babe . . ."

"You like her?" Signelli read his expression. "Then find her."

Matt lifted the picture. Underneath he found a Missing Person's Report form. "Hold it, Lieu, this is missing persons. In case that cigar smoke has disoriented that pre-senile mind of yours, this floor is homicide."

"Says so right on the door. Homicide," Ramani said shuffling in, wearing a coffee-stained shirt, no tie, and wrinkled pants. He passed Rosen and indiscriminately punched a key on Rosen's Selectra.

Rosen shoved his arm away. "Fuck you, shithead."

Ramani paused only long enough at the coffee machine for a half cup and pulled his chair back.

Signelli shifted around. "How's Isabelle?"

"She had chest pains."

"So how is she?"

Ramani sat down. He looked tired. "She'll live to love another day."

Matt held up the eight by ten glossy.

"Who's that?" Ramani asked, leaning forward.

Matt indicated the blue-edged file.

Ramani pushed back. "Ah, goddamn fuck, no way Signelli. If I get another blueball, Isabelle will divorce me for sure."

Matt fingered the Missing Person Report form. "She's missing."

Ramani shook his head, more out of incredulity than exasperation. "Come on, Lieu, what gives? A missing person. Hell, find a body, then toss it to us."

"All right, shut up, both of you," Signelli said. He moved to an unoccupied desk where he could face both detectives. "This is what went down. Either of you familiar with the name Clotilda Paris?"

Matt shrugged. Stewing, Ramani just swallowed his coffee.

Signelli took these as signals to continue. "Clotilda Paris is a legal secretary over in the D.A.'s office. She works with Assistant District Attorney Rothchild. Prior to that, Assistant D.A. Barnes, and prior to that, the list goes on and on. She's been employed in some capacity or another by the City of Los Angeles for over twenty-five years."

"Sounds like you," Ramani interrupted.

The lieutenant ignored him. "Clotilda Paris has a sister. Her name is Clovis Humphries. And Clovis has, or rather had, a very pretty daughter, named Jezebel."

Matt tapped the eight by ten glossy.

Signelli nodded. "Last Wednesday evening, Jezebel Humphries was late for an interview at Scene I, some trendy yo-yo nightclub off Fourth Street. She never showed. That night, her mother called missing persons who gave her the usual spiel, your daughter's not missing until it's been twenty-four hours. Thursday she was officially declared missing and hide nor hair of her pretty head has been seen since. Supposedly Jezebel and her mother had an argument Wednesday just prior to the daughter's departure to work."

"So why us?" Ramani asked.

"Clotilda says the girl is temperamental and has run away before, but Clovis, her mom, is convinced Jezebel's been kidnapped by guys or drug lords or monsters from space, hell, I don't know. Anyway, Clovis is pressuring Clotilda who's pressuring Rothchild in the D.A.'s office who called the chief who kicked it down to Osshoff who then dropped it on me."

Matt tossed the file to his partner. "I already got open files on my desk. Am I safe to assume you feel this added burden is in some way related?"

Signelli shifted his weight. "You always were a regular Sherlock Holmes. And yeah, you and Ramani will be pleased there is a method to the department's madness. Friday morning, one of the girl's pumps—"

"Pumps?" Ramani asked, not looking up.

"Yeah, Ramani, pumps. They're shoes, ask Isabelle, she'll tell you."

"We ain't talking."

"One of the girl's red pumps," Signelli continued, "her left, was found in an alley off the corner of Myers and First. It was only a few feet from the entrance to a sewer vault that parallels Myers."

It was barely perceptible but Signelli saw both detectives come to attention.

"And number two, and this is where it really gets sticky, a girl's gold bracelet and shoe, an identical right red pump, were found in some debris during a routine maintenance check of the East L.A. sewer. The kicker is these last two items were discovered over a mile away underground. Anyway, an astute supervisor familiar with the bulletin on Jezebel Humphries notified department dispatch yesterday. The bracelet and shoe were sent over to missing persons and lo and behold . . ."

"They're hers," Matt finished.

"Yep, they're hers. Positively I.D.'ed by Clovis."

"Her aunt," Ramani said.

"No, Clotilda's the aunt, Clovis is the mom."

"Right." Ramani stood corrected.

Matt shut the Inez file. He didn't much believe in coincidences. This girl's shoe was found near a manhole cover in some alley and her bracelet and other shoe located over a mile away stashed in some sewer. Irene Inez was dragged through a sewer. Coincidence? No fucking way.

"You're awful quiet, Guardian."

"He's thinking, Lieu," said Ramani, who shut the Humphries file and tossed it on Matt's desk. "He's thinking 'bout how he's got less than six hours till the end of shift and how he wished bunko Rosen would learn to half-assed type. He's also thinking 'bout life's little inequities, how in the last twelve hours Jensen and Rosen have already closed two cases any schoolyard detective could solve and the next call that comes in is a drive-by dunker with a victim, a weapon, enough evidence to fill a courtroom, and a confession, and how this drive-by slapshot lands smack in Rosen's desk. That makes three murders, three down, and it's not even the end of the shift for Rosen. On the other hand, we got some Latina literally scared to death, and now a blueball with all the brass tailings of a political dump. No witnesses, one weapon, a victim's shoe, a bracelet, some psycho, one body, and another missing."

Rosen stopped his henpecking long enough to mutter, "Ramani, you sure bitch a lot for a little guy."

"Try bitching on this," Ramani said, grabbing his crotch.

Matt ignored the banter, putting the Humphries folder on top of the Inez file. Two files, two open cases. In time, with some hard work and plenty of luck, each would be closed. He just hoped it didn't get worse before it got better.

Eighteen

"Stop!" Vicki screams.

He dissolves out of the darkness before her, a putrid wreck, desecrated by underworld events known only by the nonliving.

"Please, what do you want?" Vicki pleads.

He floats just above the floor and she realizes the deepness of the gloom is no longer her impenetrable wall of protection. He sees her and moves in with the methodical gait of a wrecking ball.

SLSHSH. SLSHSH.

"Oh God," Vicki cries. "What are you—?"

The smell and stench are physical and the putridity of the air squeeze her entrails to the breaking point. She vomits and pushes away, bare hands and feet raw and bleeding from the wet and slippery stone under her.

He stops and looks down, whispering something unintelligible. The switchblade hovers at his swollen fingertips.

Vicki focuses only on the mouth, a lower lip ripped away and teeth resting in sockets with no visible support.

"No, stop!" she screams again. "Stop!"

She lies frozen in fear until he begins to pull. Her head feels on fire and he yanks and she begins to move.

The pain physically contorts her. This time she cannot escape.

"It hurts! It hurts!" Her cries echo from walls she cannot see.

SLSHSH. SLSHSH.

Deeper into the cavern of blackness they descend. Furry crea-

tures scurry across her legs. She struggles and is restrained. Her shirt and pants are tugged. Vicki fights back, screaming. "No! No!"

She lies exposed. Her body is roughly groped.

Then she feels him!

"No!"

She writhes in vain.

"I'm sorry. I'm sorry!" she wails.

But he doesn't stop. Her flesh rips.

She fights and recognizes the face.

"No! No! No! No! No!"

Vicki Zampisi jerked awake, struggling to catch her breath and feeling as if she were inhaling from an icy vacuum. Drenched in cold perspiration, she felt her eyes sting from the sweat.

The glowing digits on her clock read 4:30. By the window, the drapes moved with the first early morning air currents. Drizzle pattered the alley outside. The light rain had begun soon after she'd departed the Fourth Street bridge and continued her entire drive back to her apartment. There was no thunder or lightning, nothing remotely violent or tumultuous in the skies to suggest what Vicki had recently experienced. She thought again of calling the police and again shelved the idea. The incident was hours' old, her assailant far from the scene by now, and rousing any type of investigation would only further cripple her goals.

Vicki pulled the clammy sheets aside and sat up, looking to the pistol on her nightstand. If Case followed her here, she'd kill him.

For minutes, the intense images of the nightmare replayed themselves in gory detail. Vicki was helpless to tune them out. Pulling her knees to her chest, she watched in the dark, mesmerized by the vivid brutality and vehemence. She heard her own cries of agony and felt the searing pain of ripping flesh.

The final conclusion neared and Vicki looked into the mirror, waiting for the face to appear, a face she would recognize despite its lacking human form or emotion.

At the last moment, though, she became frightened and shut her eyes, to no avail. The apparition burned right through her eyelids.

Cringing, Vicki cried out.

The image was not of Case.

He slogs along in the black sludge and goo, the dank humidity coating his skin and hair like a rime of soggy cellophane. Like a piece of weathered luggage he can't discard, he carries with him blurred fragments of his past, indistinct slices of his prior self. He pauses to sniff the moisture-laden air, as motionless as a layer of mist hovering over a windless sea, and detects nothing but the raw putrescence of things no longer living. Rotting and bloated corpses of dogs, cats, rats, and other vermin.

He presses on, his pilgrimage taking him along dark corridors that have come to symbolize his own cold twisted mental perambulations. Cement walls, cinder blocks, and vitrified clay coated with decades of fungal growth and layers of mold mark his pathway. With mounting distraction, he discovers his mind is a Byzantine maze of the past and present, leaving the timeline of separation nothing but a vague squiggly stinking smudge, not unlike the stench enveloping his feet and ankles.

Still, stored images in his brain, stored scents, stored memories drive him toward his ultimate destination. He moves on atavistic instinct alone, an innate drive that will only be satisfied by visual, taste, and tactile sensations of familiar things and places he once held. He screams out for his teacher. He must find his teacher.

He's not lost, just confused.

Not bitter, just afraid.

Not out for indiscriminate revenge, just an insatiable desire to set things right.

He slogs forward, every step driving him nearer. And nearer. And nearer.

Nineteen

Four black-and-white patrol cars parked in the patient unloading area told Julie this day would be anything but routine as she arrived at work. She'd slept soundly the night before and had awakened feeling more relaxed than she had in the past several weeks. She knew her nights would get worse though, at least until the first of June, and was prepared, looking upon the relative equanimity as the calm before the approaching storm.

What she hadn't been prepared for that morning was the hubbub of activity near the hospital's main entrance. A fire engine and ambulance waited along one curb. Julie recognized a Channel 4 News van, where a reporter was speaking into a minicam.

Several uniformed policemen were standing by the open door of one squad car. They appeared to be having some sort of conference.

At the entrance, a tall policeman stopped her. A badge revealed him to be Officer Blocker.

"I'm Julie Charmaine," she said. "I'm one of the physicians at CUMC. What happened?"

"You're Dr. Charmaine?" The officer's eyes narrowed just a little.

"That's correct."

Blocker nodded. "You're the doctor who treated the girl we found last week. Detective Guardian filled me in. I'm sorry."

"What's happened here?" she asked, indicating the crowd of law-enforcement and media personnel.

"A serious, well, incident, for lack of a better word, occurred early this morning on the medical center grounds. I would tell you more, but we're under strict orders to say as little as possible. I believe the hospital's administration department is preparing a statement."

"Whose orders?"

"The detective in charge of the case."

Julie's eyes met Blocker's. "And who might that be, if I may ask?"

"Detective Guardian."

"Is Detective Guardian here?"

"Yes ma'am. He's in the basement."

"The Tunnel. So that's where this incident happened?"

"I can't say. Sorry."

"I understand."

Behind her, Julie could hear the network news reporter getting the same script from another officer. She went inside.

On the second floor, Julie met Dr. Skinner coming down the hall from the recovery room. He looked tired, but less tense than when she'd seen him in the emergency room the previous week.

"Morning, Purvis. How's ER treating you these days?"

"I'm on nights. And not too bad. Had a gunshot come in about three A.M. Stabilized him and rocketed him to the cutters on the second floor. Just checked. O'Brien says he'll walk out of here minus two feet of colon, but otherwise salvageable."

"Could be worse."

"Hey, you hear?"

"You mean the cops?"

Skinner nodded. "About five A.M. it seemed all hell broke loose. Bunch of cops came busting into the ER like it was a drug bust or something with all the sirens. I thought a goddamn plane had crashed."

"Everyone seems hushed about what happened."

"No one's saying much. I haven't a clue what's going down."

Julie could see Skinner was a little wired from being up all night. "Go home, get some rest."

"Righto. Hey, Finny Todd came by yesterday. Wanted to make sure the ER was still running okay without him. He's got this big white cast on his nose. Looks like a goalie."

Julie smiled and continued to the Department of Psychiatry, which she found already open when she tried the double doors. Inside, the office to the chairman was also open. As Julie shut the door behind her, Dr. Oswald Schwartz materialized in his doorway. A short, rotund individual with a heavy gray beard and compassionate eyes, she always thought he would have made a great holiday Saint Nicholas.

"Julie, I was hoping to catch you here early," he said.

"Morning, Dr. Schwartz." Julie always referred to the department chairman by his professional name. Harvard educated and seventy-one, he was actually a better administrator than clinician.

"I'd like to have a word with you." Dr. Schwartz waved her into his office.

Julie took a seat, surrounded by walls adorned with an array of diplomas, certificates, and civic mementos commensurate with the chairman's title.

"That's quite some excitement we've had this morning," Dr. Schwartz said.

"Yes, it is."

Dr. Schwartz's voice took on a more somber tone. "Julie, according to what I've ascertained so far, one of our hospital's employees was abducted while on duty early this morning. There's going to be an intensive investigation. They, being the investigators involved, feel there might be some correlation to one of your patients, Irene Inez. I just wanted to inform you as you will, in all likelihood, be fielding some questions."

Julie nodded. "I'm up to it."

"I know you are."

The phone rang on the chairman's desk. Dr. Schwartz picked it up and listened for several seconds, then waved good-bye to Julie.

Outside, the department secretary had just arrived and was making some fresh coffee.

"Morning, Connie."

"Dr. Charmaine, did you hear the news?"

Julie wasn't sure how much to say. "I saw the police outside."

The secretary appeared genuinely shaken. "One of our nurses was just found beaten to death near Hollenbech Park."

"Who?"

"A Brenda something, I'm not sure."

Julie tried not to look too shocked—no use upsetting Connie further. She went into her own office and shut the door. Her thoughts returned to Irene against her will. Now a woman bludgeoned to death. Inside, she felt a cold spot form just below her heart. May was not going to be a good month.

The corpse emerged bruised, battered, and lifeless inside a rain sewer at the north edge of the small Hollenbech Park. A county gardener found the partially clad female body at 6 A.M. It happened one hour after Al Loren, the chief of security at CUMC, received a call at home from a night-shift security guard concerning a mess found in the Tunnel under University Hospital.

By seven, the dead woman had been ID'ed and Al Loren had told his wife. Soon after hanging up, his wife had promptly called her neighbor who happened to be the mother of Connie Rivas, the secretary in the psychiatry department. Once Connie told a friend, the rumor mill shifted into high gear.

To the chagrin of the homicide investigators and the hospital's PR department, the name and occupation of the dead woman spread through the medical center population like a flu epidemic. By 9 A.M., a brief hour and forty-five minutes after Julie's meeting with Dr. Schwartz, Brenda Nixon was already being eulogized as one of the finest nurses to ever grace the hospital's surgical suites.

Matt stepped by two T.V. news reporters, ignoring their pepper spray of questions. The press were calling Brenda Nixon the second known victim of the Sewer Stalker. The carnival atmosphere of the media only added another layer of tarnish to an already sordid situation.

He signaled to Blocker with a curt nod and entered the hospital. The basement elevators opened into a boiling cauldron of field-evidence technicians, criminalists, investigators, coroner's people, photographers, and uniformed police.

Matt stepped from the elevator into the Tunnel and met Ramani halfway.

Security Chief Al Loren made a half-assed attempt to intervene. "Any idea what happened down here?"

"The girl had worked here in nursing for four years," Ramani told Matt, "the last one in surgery. She was last seen alive at just past three this morning."

"Here in the basement?"

"She'd been called to the operating room for a gunshot case and was getting an extra set of surgical scrubs. Supposedly they're kept down here in the Tunnel."

"Who saw her?"

"Two people."

Matt stopped. "Two. We got this whole goddamn hospital and only two people were in the basement at that time."

Loren saw his chance and took it. "The medical center runs a skeleton crew from eleven to seven," he said. "That includes housekeeping and custodial services, both of which are headquartered in the Tunnel. Been that way even since the budget was slashed. Add to the fact that at three in the morning most of the personnel will be upstairs, your lack of witnesses is readily explainable, unfortunate as that may be."

Ramani continued as if Loren weren't there. "An older custodian passed two girls on his way back to the elevators. He'd come down for supplies. He said they looked like nurses. One of the girls, a nurse named Charlotte Guyan, recalled seeing the custodian, Gus Cochrin, but denied seeing anyone else down here during that time. And she was the last one to see the victim alive."

Matt put both hands in his pockets. His major problem now was tying this grisly hospital scene to the scene he'd just examined, not a hundred yards from a little-league diamond four miles away in Hollenbech Park.

"How'd she look?" Ramani asked, referring to the deceased.

"Like she got the holy fuck beat out of her," Matt said, taking in the entire basement scene. "She's getting a free ride to Mission Street now."

"Must've been one helluva fight," Loren said to no one in particular.

Two housekeepers, both Hispanic women, began to mop some of the dark stains from the cement floor.

Matt pointed at the housekeepers. "What are they doing?"

Loren shrugged. "Doing what they get paid to do. Clean up this sludge. We got quite a mess down here."

Matt eyed the security chief. "Mr. Loren, we, and that includes you, have a girl, one of your employees I might add, dragged almost twenty city blocks from your hospital through the dark to a quaint city park where the biggest hit is usually from a marijuana cigarette. And amazing as this may sound, no one saw a thing. We have no witnesses, *nada,* once the victim left the medical center." Matt pointed to a black smear on the floor. "And now you have your crew destroying what may be the only evidence we have."

"It was an unfortunate accident," Loren said.

"Accident, my ass. Ramani might've been an accident. I probably was an accident." Matt waved a hand. "But this was no fucking accident. This is a homicide. And I own this scene. Just like I own the scene at Hollenbech Park. They're mine. And no one touches or disturbs so much as a tiny piece of loose crap till I give the say-so. Capeesch?"

"Capeesch." The security chief, humbled a notch or two, guided the housekeepers away from the splatters of sludge and debris.

Ramani showed Matt his pocket notepad, which contained three diagrams. One sketch showed the relationship between the elevators, the housekeeping corridor, and the Tunnel, as the hospital personnel called the mile-long concrete artery under University Hospital.

Matt looked up and down the housekeeping corridor. "What are the closest exits?"

Loren stepped over a pile of scrubs from the nearby uniform rack. "One exit in housekeeping. Stairs and an elevator." He then turned in the direction of the Tunnel. "Or you can return to the Tunnel and take the elevators you came down on or proceed past those elevators back under the main body of the hospital. I believe there're four or five stairwells and elevators servicing the other departments in the basement." He ticked them off on his finger. "Plant Management, Medical Records, Patient Property, and the hospital morgue. There's also the corridor to the Psychiatric Hospital."

Ramani scribbled something. "And if we follow this hall back to the Tunnel and go left—"

"You enter the medical center's physical plant where we were standing earlier," Loren finished. He led the two detectives in that direction. "This area includes the generators for the air-conditioning and heating systems. They're located behind the two heavy metal doors." Loren had to speak over the drone of the turbines.

Ramani added a phone located across from the generator doors to his second sketch, which was a rough diagram of the physical plant layout.

Matt moved by a crime photographer who was finishing up in a room adjacent to the generators. "What's this used for?" he asked, pausing in the doorway of the ten-by-ten-foot room.

Inside, the floor surrounding a large central drain was splotched with mud and other foul-smelling debris. A short stool lay on its side.

Two forensic techs were working over a particularly putrid pile near the thirty-two inch drain. The drain was covered with a metal grille that appeared not to have been cleaned in more than forty years. The entire room reminded Matt of a gigantic dirty shower stall.

Loren cringed at the odor in the room. "We call this area the generator access room. At one time it was the hospital's sole noninfectious disposal system. See that drain there?" He pointed. "It leads into a large underground vault that transports wastes into one of the city's main sewage lines. About the only thing that goes down that drain now is excess runoff water created by the four hospital generators. And that other door there." Loren motioned to a metal door situated at the right rear corner. "That allows us to access the two generators in the back. It's always locked."

The third sketch in Ramani's notebook was this room. Ramani refined his rendering of the door and the large central drain.

"Any way out of this end of the basement, other than the elevators back by housekeeping?" Ramani asked.

"None. To get out of here, you have to retrace your steps back past the generators."

Matt looked back down the physical plant hall. Even at 3 A.M. it would have been virtually impossible to drag a woman from this point to outside the hospital, without someone seeing or hearing something. There had to be another way out.

He stepped over by the large sewer drain. Its rusted collar appeared to be wedged securely into the concrete. The closer he got to its metal grille, the worse the odor.

"It usually smell this bad down here?" he asked.

"No," Loren answered. "But we usually don't have this type of mess down here either."

Matt and Ramani both examined the metal grille. Most of the quarter-inch latticework was dry, albeit corroded and rusted.

Matt leaned over and spit. A second later the sound of a plop echoed lightly from below. He kicked at the metal but it didn't budge. He motioned for Ramani, and both detectives tried to pry it up.

"The damn thing's not giving," Matt said.

"My back is," Ramani groaned.

Matt counted the housekeeping crew in the immediate area. Six.

"What other departments did you say are in the basement?" he asked.

Loren thought briefly. "The largest is housekeeping. That includes the custodial crew. There's also various plant-management departments, medical records, and probably several others."

"But the largest is housekeeping."

"Yes."

"At three A.M. how many on each crew?" Matt asked.

"Offhand I couldn't say exactly, but ballpark, maybe twenty or so housekeepers and ten custodians."

"I need a list of everyone working last night."

"Everyone?"

"Everyone."

"I'll need to check with Personnel."

Matt reached into his wallet and pulled out a card. "Here's where we can be reached."

Loren pocketed the business card without a glance. "I trust you'll expedite this investigation."

Ramani cleared his throat.

Matt said, "We'll do our best."

"What about the other scene, where the girl was found?" the security chief asked.

Matt shrugged. "All we have is a body."

Ramani caught Matt's eye. There was more, but Matt wasn't saying.

"Yo, Guardian."

Matt turned to Cecil Giamoco, a crime scene investigator with the coroner's department, who was squatting next to the sewer-vault opening.

"What color was the girl's hair?" the investigator asked.

Matt kneeled beside him. "What do you got?"

Using a small forceps, Giamoco lifted a threadlike filament from the basement floor. "We've found three, but this one's the longest."

Matt only had to glance at the foot-long hair strand to know it didn't come from the victim. She'd been dark-haired, while the hair in the forceps looked more reddish blond or rust-colored.

"Not hers," he said.

"It's a keeper then." Giamoco sealed it in a paper envelope and passed it to an assistant. Then, standing, he produced a Zip-locked plastic forensic bag from one pocket.

"Whaddaya make of this?" he asked, handing the bag to Matt.

Matt examined the irregular piece of fleshy tissue inside. "What the hell-shit is that?"

"From the contour of the pinna," the tech said, "I'd guess it's a human ear."

"Shit," Loren said and turned away in disgust.

Sure enough, using a little imagination Matt could almost make it into an ear.

"From the Nixon woman?" Matt didn't remember her missing an ear when they'd rolled her over in the park's bloodstained cement culvert.

"No way," Giamoco said. "Unless she'd already been dead a few days."

"You are kidding."

"He better be kidding," Ramani added. "We don't need any more curve balls, chumpo."

Giamoco retrieved the bag. "All kidding aside, gentlemen, and I use that term very loosely, this ear is in early stages of necrosis. Believe me, I've been in on enough decomp cases to recognize recently living from not-so-recently living tissue. And this baby is dead plus three or four days."

While Ramani drove to the coroner's to observe the Nixon girl's autopsy, Matt returned to the phone across from the generator doors. After dialing the hospital operator, he waited for the connection.

"I'm not interrupting, am I?" he said.

Julie sounded a bit surprised at hearing his voice. "No, Matt. Are you still at the hospital?"

"The basement. Listen, I had a matter I wanted to discuss with you. Mind if I run up?"

"No, but I was on my way to Medical Records. I can meet you down there, if it's more convenient."

"I'll be waiting by the elevators."

Matt passed the hall to housekeeping and arrived at the elevators in time to escort Julie past two techs dusting for prints.

She stepped carefully around their trays and brushes of carbon powder and rolls of transparent acetate tape. When she'd first come on-staff at CUMC, Julie had hated traversing the isolated Tunnel corridors. The air always smelled *unfresh,* there was always faint odors of dirty linen, custodial supplies, and diesel fuel. And another smell she could never pinpoint, like something not quite dead. Huge isolated pockets of mold and mildew came to mind. She could easily visualize a large ceiling fan mounted over a pool of stagnant water yielding a similar olfactory picture.

"How's the investigation?" she asked, masking her disquiet.

"Still in the evidence-collection stage," he said, leading her away from the crowd. He stopped at the corridor to housekeeping, noting Julie's rapt attention as she watched the flow of crime investigators. "You ever seen a real crime scene?" he asked.

"Once," she said. "A long time ago."

"We can talk elsewhere if you'd be more comfortable."

"No, Matt, I'm fine." Julie looked past him to where two men were measuring distances between the generator doors and spots of sludge on the concrete floor. "Is that where it took place?"

"I'll show you."

Matt had to speak louder to be heard above the generators. "Recognize the smell?" he asked, watching Julie's expression change.

"Like raw sewage." It had never smelled this intense before.

"Did Ms. Inez smell this bad when she was brought in?"

"Not this strong. But I wasn't there when she was first admitted." Julie stepped over a small pile of debris. "Is that what you wanted to discuss, Irene Inez?"

"Partly. The lab results returned negative. Dorfman's gonna rule her death a cardiorespiratory arrest. It's gonna be up to the

D.A. as to whether it's prosecuted as a homicide." Matt pointed to the entrance to the access room. He led. "This is where it really gets noticeable."

"That poor woman," Julie said, looking at the sordid filth contaminating the floor. "She was dragged through here?"

"We think." Matt let an investigator slip by before motioning Julie into the room. "My biggest dilemma is figuring out how the hell she left the hospital." He saw Julie gazing at the heavy drain cover.

"Already considered. That top's been corroded in place for years," he said. Matt grabbed a mask from Giamoco's kit. "Wear this."

"Are we going to be down here long?"

"You won't."

"Thanks." Holding the mask over her mouth and nose with one hand, Julie stepped over and studied the necrotic contents of a plastic bag on the forensic investigator's tray. "Is that what I think it is?"

Matt stood beside her. "For what it's worth, it's not from the nurse."

Julie simply shook her head and moved back. This was worse than she'd imagined.

From where he stood, Matt couldn't help but notice the intense blue of Julie's eyes. He looked away. "I wanted to ask you about Vicki Zampisi. She still a patient of yours?"

"Yes, in fact I'm meeting with her again next week."

"Kincaid—he's the officer who responded to the trespassing call, which, by the way, has been dropped. Anyway, in Kincaid's report he made a brief mention of Ms. Zampisi describing a peculiar smell just before her alleged assault. Do you recall her mentioning anything similar?"

Julie took a moment to answer. "Yes, she did. But she initially described smelling a clean smell at first. I believe she used the word 'aseptic.' That was rapidly followed by a horrible odor so strong it made her gag." She looked up at Matt. "You think there's a relationship?"

"It's probably not significant, but I wanted to ask."

Julie touched Matt's arm. "There's something else. Yesterday after work, I dropped by the old Shilden Hotel."

His eyes registered objection.

"I know, you don't have to say it," Julie said, "but I thought I might be able to gain some insight into Vicki's actions."

"Did you?"

Julie shook her head. "But I saw this homeless man. And he said the oddest thing. He told me he'd seen it."

"Seen it? What?"

"I don't know, he didn't say."

"You think this bum's responsible for your patient's assault?"

"No. The man appeared so old and weak, I doubt he'd pose a threat to anyone. I was more concerned with what he was referring to."

"I'll have some men check it out." He added, "And the next time you entertain pulling a crazy stunt like that, I'd appreciate a call first."

"I will. Can we go now?"

Matt led her back to the elevators. "Enjoy the tour?"

Julie's expression turned somber. "What a terrible way to die."

"There's no good way."

Twenty

Vicki wanted answers, and fast.

Not just her well-being but Ben's would depend greatly on her actions today. The .380 was in her purse, a round in the chamber. If she confronted Case again, she'd be ready.

She turned left at 225 Pacific. The white Lexus wasn't there. She parked next to a black Mercedes.

The front entrance was unlocked, which she did not expect. She rang the buzzer at the window. The office now appeared vacant. The file cabinets had disappeared from along the back wall. Vicki thought of the U-Haul and wondered where the records were.

She buzzed again. A door opened somewhere and heavy footsteps approached, deliberate and methodical. Even before she saw him, Vicki knew who they belonged to.

Kovacs stopped in the doorway, both hands in the pockets of a white lab coat. Momentarily, no recognition registered, then an expression of surprise crossed his face. "It's reassuring to see you still know how to use a front door."

"I met your attack dog."

"I suspect you're referring to Case. A patient for over ten years, though occasionally he gets his synapses crossed. I haven't seen him in days."

"That was real stupid. It's not like you to play dumb."

"This isn't an act. I warned you once. I don't want you anywhere near the foundation."

Vicki saw that perspiration had broken out on his forehead. "Or what, you'll call the police? Why not give Mr. Case a second shot?"

Kovacs shifted his weight. "Don't push it, Vicki. Case is not one to be taken lightly, especially when he's not taking his lithium. He'd make Ben seem like one of Santa's helpers."

Vicki smirked. "Ben would've eaten Case's lunch and spit it on him."

"Enough," Kovacs said, closing the door behind him. "Why did you come here?"

Vicki squared her shoulders. "I came to see Ben." She never would've predicted his response.

Kovacs put his head back and laughed. When he finally stopped, she no longer detected blatant hostility. It was as if a switch had been thrown. Kovacs actually smiled at her.

"Your hair," he said, "it's becoming. And your new face."

"The miracles of modern medicine."

"Ben wouldn't recognize you."

"I didn't do it for Ben."

"I suspect that's not entirely true. Come." Kovacs opened the door and led her down a hall.

Vicki saw no sign of the foundation's impending move in Kovacs's office. The showroom-quality desk and furniture were still there along with his elaborate display of wall photos and diplomas. In one, he and several politicians stood before one of his Community Psychiatric Centers. That had been before Kovacs sold his majority interest to CUMC. Other photos depicted the early years of the Phoenix Foundation.

One in particular gave Vicki pause. It showed a young Kovacs decked out in his safari attire. Beside him stood a group of naked children playing on a squalid dirt street. An anemic cluster of decrepit thatched huts stood in the background.

Vicki touched the glass. Dust came off on her finger. "Where was this taken?" she asked.

"Borneo."

"That's where Ben was from."

"Originally, yes. A very poor island. A good psychiatric nurse makes in a day what those kids' parents make in a year."

Kovacs opened a mahogany credenza and poured two glasses of red sherry. One he filled, the other he half-filled. He walked over and handed Vicki the full one. "What's it been, eighteen years?"

"Not long enough."

Kovacs returned to his desk and sat. The chair groaned under his weight.

Vicki settled in the chair farthest from the desk and nearest the exit.

"Tell me about the move," she said.

Kovacs held her with an impassive gaze. "The foundation recently purchased a winery in Tucson. The cost of doing business in Southern California was becoming too prohibitive, both financially and legally. Once the transfer is complete, we'll be in a position to accommodate twice our present census."

Vicki set her glass on the desk without taking a sip. "So you're still growing."

"The demand for our services has never been greater."

"I had another dream last night," Vicki said.

"Another one?"

"Each nightmare gets worse than the one before. *He* was in this one."

Kovacs nodded as if understanding her concern. "Guilt can be a burdensome weight to carry, Vicki. Please don't forget, I feel bad too. Terribly. But dreams are just dreams. Simple mental releases. Nothing more or nothing less. You will get over them."

"Where is he?" she asked.

"I think you know, Vicki."

"He's dead."

Kovacs's moment of hesitation was affirmation enough. "There was nothing I could do. Absolutely nothing."

"I want to see him." She now realized why the nine-foot aluminum canister she'd seen in the cold unit had appeared in a state of disrepair.

"Why did you leave, Vicki? The experiment had just begun. It wasn't like you to run out on me. Or Ben. Especially Ben."

Vicki reached for her wineglass, suddenly thirsty. "I had no choice. If I'd stayed, I would have driven myself insane."

"He trusted you. I was only his guardian so to speak, but you, you were his teacher, his mentor."

"It was wrong what I did."

"You enjoyed it."

"You enjoyed watching," she said and quickly finished her sherry, holding the glass in both hands. As much as she tried, she couldn't control the tremor. "I wanted to forget. I needed to forget everything."

"And clearly you did not forget."

"No." Vicki looked from her own empty glass to Kovacs's cold, opaque stare. "I need to see him. That's why I'm here. I came back to take Ben." *And destroy you.*

"I really believe you are crazy."

"Where is he?"

"There was a malfunction, an accident," Kovacs started slowly. "Two or three months ago, I don't recall the date, my assistant detected a tiny nitrogen leak."

Leak. The word hit Vicki like a freight train.

"By the time it was discovered," Kovacs went on, "the damage was irreparable. There was nothing else I could do. It had to be disposed of."

"It?"

"I'm sorry, Vicki. I'm truly—"

Vicki rose, her face feeling flushed with heat. "Goddamn you. When exactly? I want to know when."

"Does it matter? Does anything that happened almost twenty years ago matter anymore? He's gone, Vicki. Ben is gone. Please, it's finished. Go home, wherever that may be. You're a disgrace. I no longer need you. The foundation no longer needs you. And God knows, Ben no longer needs you."

Stunned, Vicki took a step back. She wasn't going to see him after all. And she'd promised herself. But when it came down to the wire, she couldn't even keep a simple promise.

Kovacs stepped around his desk, his hands held out as if in supplication. "We're making tremendous progress. But accomplishments of this magnitude require sacrifices. Sacrifices the foundation must be willing to accept, even foster, if our goals are to be achieved. There can be no roadblocks. Any strike against us now would be a strike against all humanity."

The gun appeared in Vicki's hand before she realized what she was doing. But once she crossed the threshold, it was easy not to turn back.

"Bastard," she snarled. "Take me to him."

"Do you know what you've just done?" he asked, the color draining from his face.

"Yes. I do." Her fingers hadn't felt this steady in days. With a sharp flip of her gun hand, she motioned Kovacs into the hall. "The storage unit."

"You're more of an animal than Ben."

"Shut up."

Vicki kept two paces behind Kovacs, warily watching for Case or anyone else.

Kovacs opened the door to the laboratory. "I told you there was an accident. Ben is no longer here."

"You're lying. I saw his dewar," she said.

In the narrow corridor to the storage unit, she detected the same aseptic odor she'd smelled when she'd had her first run-in with Kovacs's human security blanket.

"Where's Case?" she asked.

"I wish I knew," Kovacs said. "He's not answering his pages."

"I'm real concerned," she said sarcastically. "Did you know he tried to rape me?"

"I'm sorry."

"I bet you're sorry. Sorry he failed twice, starting at the Shilden Hotel."

"I don't know what you're talking about."

"I think you do. Other than you, I'm the only person who's aware of all the dirty details of the foundation's *grand experiment.* How much money did you make off Ben?"

Kovacs remained silent.

They stopped and over Kovacs's shoulder, Vicki saw the bluish glow through the cold unit's viewing window.

"Does what I know make you uncomfortable?" she asked.

"I'd feel less uncomfortable if you'd put away the gun."

Vicki gestured her pistol at the vault door.

"How do you get inside?" she asked.

Kovacs pointed to a digital keypad. "A code electronically breaks the seal. Two revolutions of the handle will mechanically disengage the lock."

"Do it."

"It's minus-forty degrees in there. You'll freeze in under five minutes dressed like that."

"You mean *we'll* freeze." Vicki pointed the muzzle toward Kovacs's head. "Open the goddamn door."

"I'm not going in there."

Vicki took aim at an oscilloscope. The shot's echo stung their eardrums as the monitor's face shattered, showering Kovacs in tiny shards of glass.

Cowering, the scientist covered his head. "You bitch, that's a twenty-thousand-dollar instrument."

"Was." Vicki aimed at Kovacs again. "How much was Ben's life worth?" She could see him trembling under the lab coat. "Or yours? Now open the goddamn door."

"I told you Ben's not in there." Panic had crept into his booming voice.

"Three, two . . ." she began to count down, lowering the gun to Kovacs's fat thigh. "One." She gritted her teeth.

"Okay!" Kovacs yelled. "Okay." His fingers flew over the pad.

Vicki heard a prolonged sibilant sound. Instantly, the air temperature of the annex began to drop.

Kovacs rushed over to the vault door and twisted the huge rotating handle. It reminded Vicki of a ship's wheel.

The door edged open an inch, sending a blast of frigid air across the room. Vicki began to shiver. A thick mist climbed the viewing window, dimming the blue light.

"Let's go, you first," Vicki ordered.

The scientist's face had turned a deep red. Vicki could see him weighing options.

"Wait," he said. He went to a rack and removed two insulated bodysuits. "The small one's my associate's. It should fit you. At least we won't get frostbite."

Vicki watched how he put his on. Then, backing away and carefully maintaining her aim, she slipped into hers, and zipped the front. The hood fit snugly so that only her eyes were exposed.

Kovacs proffered a pair of goggles.

"Set them on that tray." Vicki took them and slid them on with one hand. "After you," she said. Her own voice echoed in her ears.

The scientist swung the massive vault door open halfway. He started to enter.

"Kovacs," Vicki said. "No tricks. Or I swear I'll kill you."

He simply nodded, looking like a fat blue snowman under the vault's fluorescent glare.

Even through the insulation, Vicki felt the piercing cold which sent tiny jabs of pain into her skin. Her eyes watered and she had to blink to clear her vision. Each breath caused her chest to heave. Somehow the frigidity made the air seem thicker.

"What if we get locked inside?" she heard herself ask.

Kovacs didn't look back. "Impossible, the vault can only be sealed from the annex." He slowed. "Are you entertaining second thoughts?"

"Which one is Ben's dewar?"

Kovacs pointed with a gloved hand. "In the rear. The large one, leaning against the wall. But like I said, Ben's—"

"Shut up and show me."

Vicki felt like she was wading underwater in an antique diving suit. Every shadow was cast in blue and frost sprinkled every surface, making each object appear as if it were covered in a thin layer of finely ground quartz.

Dewars of various sizes lined the aisle, their cylindrical shapes supported by metal racks. The voluminous maze of tubing and pipes made Vicki feel as if she'd invaded a snake's den.

The rough surface of the floor offered good traction, which helped Vicki overcome the clumsiness caused by her increasingly stiff knee. She glanced up to find the source of a constant low-grade humming noise, but saw only more pipes crossing behind the fluorescent lighting.

"Don't touch anything," she heard Kovacs warn. He stood six feet in front of her beside the largest dewar in the vault, the same dewar she'd seen through the viewing window on her prior visit.

"How many people do you have in storage?"

"Our client list is confidential."

Vicki stepped over a piece of gray plastic sheeting and moved to within a yard of the dewar. She felt her pulse quicken, and even in the sub-zero temperature, she could feel the perspiration covering her skin. She was this close.

"Would he have felt any pain?" she asked, mesmerized by the aluminum canister's dull luster and brown rust-colored patches.

"No," Kovacs said. He pointed to a silicone connector between the upper and lower half of the storage dewar. "There's where the nitrogen began to leak."

Vicki wasn't listening. Condensed memories flooded her with a sense of euphoria and well-being she hadn't experienced in years. She no longer felt the frigid cold of the vault, but only the warmth and pleasure of his body next to hers. He'd accepted her unconditionally, like a small child, and now she wanted to touch him, and if that weren't possible, then at least touch the cylindrical tomb that had been his home for the past twenty years. Underneath the insulated hood, Vicki smiled. The most difficult and risky portion of her plan had been accomplished. She'd found Ben.

She watched Kovacs remove a side panel from the dewar's midsection.

"Look," he said.

Vicki stood in a daze.

Kovacs thrust his hand through the opening. "Look," he repeated harshly. "And tell me what you see."

Bending slightly at the waist, Vicki gazed past the gauges and thermostat, into the deep blue depths of the dewar's interior. *Ben, I came back for you.* She felt herself pulled closer and closer until the nauseating stench of necrosis overwhelmed her senses.

She gave an anguished groan. Dewar #225 was empty.

• •

The mud and sludge under his feet oozes between his toes with the viscosity and color of melted tire treads. In places the layers of decades' old waste accumulations reach almost to his knees and he wades forward using his hands much like the prow of a boat to clear a path. Mostly though, the thick goop settles around his ankles, creating little forward resistance.

Once, he was so close he could smell her—her skin, her hair, her hormonal surges—such simple recollections are what drive him to states of vicious and unrelenting frenzy. And any within reach pay dearly. However, he's unable, or unwilling, to recall whether these scents are now or then. Some things he understands. He understands a physical attraction so primitive and pleasurable the drive for consummation transcends time, and he understands his loss of this precious object of his desire.

He also understands, as much as he's capable of understanding, things will never be as they once were—the laughing, the playful cajoling, the learning, the touching, and the trust. His teacher will make everything right, though. He'll make her hold him close, like she used to, her sweet scent enveloping him like his favorite blanket, and he'll do things to her only a beast would do because his teacher was naughty, she hurt him. She hurt him real bad.

Above him, past concrete and rebar, distant sounds of the city filter down through passageways and corridors devoid of light, reminding him of where he's been and how far he has to go. As he climbs streetward, the rusted rungs of the ladder strain at their metal brackets, unaccustomed to such sheer mass and bulk. He pauses, both cuprite eyes penetrating the thick dark air until he detects the fine rays of sunlight squeezing through the vault's overhead seal. Then he backs down.

He'll wait for dark.

Twenty-one

Although a scant few inches of water flowed from the Hollenbech Park culvert that served as Brenda Nixon's last cradle of death, Matt's notes showed that the waterline had been six inches higher when the victim was discovered.

He and Ramani stared down at the runoff as it wound its way around small piles of debris and litter. Across the four-by-five-foot culvert, a six-foot wire fence separated the park from an undeveloped piece of land. The only evidence that this cement creek bed had once been a temporary grave were the brown patches staining the far wall where the victim's head had rested.

Ramani lit up and tossed the match into the sewer ditch.

"That's a two-hundred-dollar fine," Matt said.

Neither detective was in a particularly good mood. Isabelle was threatening to move out if Ramani didn't spend more time with her. The workload was also beginning to get to Matt. Their blue-ball case, the Jezebel Humphries investigation, still hadn't turned up the missing body.

For all Matt knew, the Humphries girl might at this time be lying somewhere under this great city of brotherly love. For three days, the entire route and the area underneath, from her apartment which she shared with her mom to her place of employment had been turned inside out. No one saw or heard anything. The news and television bulletins turned up zilch. Ditto, too, with the questioning of fellow employees, friends, relatives, and past boyfriends. Matt even went so far as to mark on a map beside his desk the sewer entry points near her walking route. All but two were on busy streets. One was on a drive behind a mom-and-pop grocery store, and the other in an alley that intersected Myers.

At least in Brenda Nixon, they had a body to work with.

Matt walked downstream a few paces to where the murky water flowed into an underground channel. "According to Dorfman, the Nixon girl was killed somewhere between one and three hours prior to her being found."

Adding to the macabre puzzle, Brenda Nixon's lungs had been partially filled with water, meaning she was still breathing when her body was tossed into the concrete ditch. She'd been left to die.

The post-mortem also demonstrated a large expanding epidermal hematoma caused by a fractured skull. In all likelihood, complications of this massive blood clot were what killed her. Also, prior to her death she'd been raped and sodomized. Matt had seen for himself the rectal and vaginal tears and massive echymoses and bruising of her abdomen, face, and chest while the victim lay on the cold autopsy table.

Matt watched as Ramani's match lodged against a dog turd near the park's gutter. The yellow tape was gone, the patrols were finished canvassing the residents living nearby, and what little physical evidence had been present was collected, bagged, and labeled. No witnesses claimed to have seen or heard anything suspicious, there were no prints recovered, and, excluding the necrotic tissue found under the girl's nails, the only hair and blood samples collected belonged to the victim. With the exception of the three isolated hairs found in the hospital basement. Thus far the laboratory evaluation on these had not been completed, though early returns indicated at least two of the hairs might not be human in origin. Why the delay? The extremely damaged nature of the samples was confounding their analysis.

This persistent lack of concrete evidence was beginning to feel like an ingrown toenail to Matt. "How the hell do two victims get dead tissue lodged under their nails?"

"The sewer?" Ramani said.

Matt shook his head. "Doesn't jibe. Dorf was real specific on that point. He said necrotic tissue, separate from what you find in sewer sludge. Unless both victims scraped their hands across a corpse—"

"Like some kind of ritual maybe?" Ramani interrupted. "I read about one case where a new member of a devil worshipping cult had to skin a cat and gut it with his hands. Say the inductee himself were also sacrificed . . ." he paused, raising his palms.

"You're inferring some sicko piece of shit is in some depraved way using body parts or corpses on these girls, then assaulting them?"

Ramani shrugged. "Hey, Milwaukee had Dahmer."

Matt saw his partner's point. If there was one city in the entire U.S. that could produce a killer higher up on the sadistic psychopath chart, it would be Los Angeles. And to have that investigation land smack dab in the middle of his caseload . . . wonders never ceased.

Matt returned to surveying the park.

Only two streets were visible from where the detectives stood—Fourth Street to the north and Chicago to the east. A tall grove of oaks blocked the view of the southbound Santa Monica Freeway to the west, but not the traffic noise.

Matt spit into the culvert. His shoulders were sore. Not even twenty minutes on the heavy bag earlier that morning had loosened him up.

"You're right," Matt said as if his partner had just spoken again.

"I am?"

"Even at three or four in the morning, some dick would've

been concerned about carrying a body across the baseball diamonds and being spotted by some other dick driving on Fourth or Chicago."

Matt was assuming everyone out at three or four in the morning was a dick. In that area, it was a fairly safe assumption.

Ramani pointed to the fence. "And there's no way the girl was tossed or carried over six feet of fence without getting a drop of blood anywhere."

Matt squatted down for a better look. He could smell the dog turd now. "It has to be the goddamn sewer."

He could see where the water dropped ten feet or so into a vault. It was dark under the cement overhang. He'd forgotten his flashlight but on his initial visit four days ago, the CSI boys had pried open the iron plate—it took two to lift—and climbed down and looked around. They'd found nothing. The underground vault was serviced by a forty-inch sewage pipe that carried almost a foot of water. They'd stopped their search there. Any evidence would have long since been carried to God knows where by the time the body bag was zipped shut.

Ramani pointed at the turd. "That my match?"

Fatigue was getting the best of them.

Ramani inhaled one last time and tossed the cigarette into the water. It missed the turd and disappeared underground. "I'm going to call Public Works. They must have some sort of blueprint or map that tells where all these pipes go."

Ramani's beeper interrupted any further discussion.

Matt waited while his partner stalked across one corner of a baseball diamond for his car. He returned, looking like he'd been hit with a sucker punch.

"That was Heaton," Ramani said.

"What the fuck does he want?" Matt knew it couldn't be good news. Heaton was a senior investigator with the coroner's office.

"Says he's on a case with Rosen and Jensen."

"So let Rosen and Jensen handle it."

"Says Signelli thought we might be interested."

"What makes Signelli say that?"

Ramani fumbled with his keys. "Heaton says they just pulled two more bodies from the sewer."

"Shit."

Matt parked behind Ramani on Santa Fe Avenue. One half of the block between Fourth and Sixth Streets was cordoned off. Four squad cars were parked there, their lights flashing.

A temporary setup consisting of a tripod with electrical attachments and lights hung over a sewer well. A flexible vacuum snaked out from somewhere below street level. It was attached to a generator.

Rosen and Jim Jensen were talking with two men, one of them Randy Heaton. He'd been a coroner's investigator for fifteen years. Dorfman had never criticized Heaton's work and that was all Matt needed.

The other man was older. He was dressed in the characteristic yellow city-waders' outfits that the sanitation crews wore when they worked underground. The city van was not far away. Another sanitation employee leaned against the van.

The older man in the waders looked upset, waving his arms like he couldn't say enough with his mouth. Heaton put a quieting hand on his shoulder and then made his way toward Matt and Ramani. The forensic investigator's dress pants and shirt were covered with filth.

Heaton shook Matt's hand, nodded to Ramani. "Days like this make me wish I'd been a perfume salesman." He took out a pack of cigarettes.

Matt declined.

Ramani accepted and then motioned at the two other detectives in Signelli's squad. "What's with them, they don't like talking to us?"

"Rosen thinks you guys get all the easy cases," Heaton said.

"Bullshit." Ramani caught Rosen's eye. Rosen waved. "Bullshit," Ramani repeated.

Matt silently acknowledged one of the policemen and walked over toward the stretchers. Even after ignoring the all-pervasive stench that filled the air, he didn't like the smell of the situation.

Each of the two nearby stretchers carried a large black plastic garbage bag, the kind homeowners used to collect residential refuse or grass cuttings. The tops, though closed, were not tied shut.

Matt leaned over and opened one. The stench hit him like a strong right hook. Inside, all he saw were partially clothed, mangled body parts.

The other bag held the same sort of goodies.

Ramani almost gagged. "Shit, a goddamn decomp."

"Two decomps," said Heaton.

Matt shook his head. "What happened down there? Those two look like they went through a meat grinder."

"You'd look that way too, if you were stuffed headfirst into a sixteen-inch pipe," Heaton said.

"How'd you get 'em out?"

"Piece by piece. Logan over there," Heaton pointed to the older city employee talking with the other two detectives, "was in charge of locating a possible sewage obstruction. Took him several days, but it appears he found the source. He was using what's called a grinder. It's basically a giant roto-rooter. Anyway, he felt something dislodge from the connecting sewer pipe he was attempting to clear and when he withdrew it, lo and behold, he had himself a human foot. He didn't hear any screams of protest so he figured the foot's owner was probably in as bad shape as the foot. He called LAPD. And here we be."

Heaton dropped his cigarette and stamped it out. "We got two bodies, one female, the other male. From the looks of things, both were down there at least a week and possibly longer. It's a bloody fuckin' mess."

"Wonderful." Ramani eyed the bags.

"That makes four," Matt said.

"How so?" Heaton said, glancing at only two garbage bags.

"Four bodies." Matt was talking to Ramani. "Irene Inez, Brenda Nixon, and a John and Jane Doe."

Ramani kicked at one of the stretcher's wheels. "Tell me how you jam two adult bodies into a sixteen-inch pipe."

Heaton couldn't answer.

Matt could. "I guess the same way you take 'em out . . . piece by fucking piece."

"How did she react?" Eisler asked.

He and Kovacs stood outside the foundation's entrance, having just locked up the premises. The air was cool and both men glanced at the moon that seemed to float above the skyline like a giant ivory eye.

Kovacs shivered slightly. "Like she'd seen the devil's wrath."

"You actually allowed her to examine the dewar."

Kovacs took offense at his associate's tone. "I did the same thing you would've done if she'd had a gun pointed up your ass." He started for the Mercedes.

"Wes, I didn't mean it that way." Eisler walked faster to keep up. "Think she'll go to the police?"

"No."

"What will she do?"

Kovacs stopped abruptly. "Ms. Zampisi is a drunk and a loser. She's also frightened. So she'll do what all drunk losers do when they become frightened. She'll run. I suspect she'll run back to

Washington to be with her mom." Kovacs resumed a more leisurely pace to his car. "When she walked out of here this morning, Christian, it was like I didn't exist. She looked like a fuckin' zombie who'd lost her last friend in the world. She didn't say a goddamn word, nothing. If she were a patient, I would have seriously considered the woman suicidal."

"Wouldn't that be convenient."

Any grin was lost in Kovacs's furrowed brow.

"What?" Eisler asked.

"Case never came in to pick up his prescription renewal today. You know how he gets when his medicine drops below therapeutic levels. Has he called you?"

Eisler shook his head. "He was just going to scare her, right?"

Kovacs didn't answer. He set his briefcase on the cement and unlocked his car door. "It's not like Case to ignore my pages."

"What should we do?"

"We'll wait." Kovacs set his briefcase inside. "If you hear from him, contact me immediately. Also I'm still expecting Devlin to call."

Eisler tried to sound assertive. "Don't worry about Devlin. Everything's under control at the mortuary."

"There can be no mistakes. A failed research experiment at this juncture would be devastating." Kovacs watched Eisler closely, searching for any clues that his younger colleague suspected anything other than what he'd been informed regarding Ben's interment. He saw none.

"What will we do if . . ." Eisler hesitated.

"If what?" Kovacs's gaze turned intense.

"What if she goes to the mortuary?"

Kovacs placed a hand on Eisler's shoulder. "Then, my friend, we'll let her bury him."

Twenty-two

The game was called Worm Man.
Any number could play but optimally the number of children participating ranged from four to eight. Occasionally, in the Charmaine neighborhood as many as ten would gather under the majestic Dutch elm shading the vacant lot across from the new high school.

The rules were simple. Modeled after the universal Hide-and-Go-Seek, one child, aptly christened the Worm Man, would be blindfolded and count aloud one hundred Worm Mans with his or her forehead pressed firmly against the Dutch elm's gnarled trunk. (This same Dutch elm would succumb to a tiny fungus called *ceratocystis ulmi* four years after Janine's accident.) The other participants would then sprint to a favorite hiding place and try to avoid capture by the child–Worm Man. Any location was fair game except Mr. Ackerby's old place at the end of the block. The first individual found would become Worm Man's first assistant, the next, the second assistant, and so on and so on until only one individual remained in hiding. The searching pack of Worm Men would sprint across neighbors' lawns, crawl under oleander hedges, and even trample over weird Ms. Clayton's tomato patches in their quest for the final fugitive.

To win Worm Man you had to have the best hiding place. Easy-to-find places never created a winner. The game was declared over once everyone was discovered (captured).

Bestowed upon this last lucky individual would be the title Worm Man (which as a child Julie never really understood; who'd want to be called Worm Man? Earthworms were ugly, squirming, wet creatures who shunned the sun, and were almost as bad as grubs and snails).

According to Janine, who held the most titles because she was the fastest, and the speediest runners could always search out the best and furthest hiding places, the Worm Man crown actually represented an individual's ability to elude capture from the *real Worm Man.* And possessing this ability to escape Worm Man meant the difference between life and death, Janine used to claim.

Julie looked away from her notes collected at the Amphisphere. Something had triggered this series of macabre recollections and it hadn't been anything in the research interviews. 'Tis the season, she mused.

Sitting in her study, feeling the heat of the high-intensity desk light on her hands, her thoughts returned to what Vicki Zampisi had said. *I was all Ben had.*

The objectively analytical part of Julie's mind gave in to the sensitively creative side. Her expression grew sullen.

She was all Janine had had on that rainy night twenty-nine years ago. Julie hadn't wanted to play Worm Man, but Janine had convinced her. How would they ever know if they had the ability to escape Worm Man if they didn't play the game in the dark and drizzle, Worm Man's favorite conditions? How did a shy five-year-old oppose an assertive, confident seven-year-old sister? You didn't. She'd played.

Julie shivered slightly. Her chair sat in the path of the air-conditioning vent and with the unseasonably warm spring, she'd been running the air more, even at night. The unit's low-pitched hum woke Jake who'd been curled on his rug in the den. The dog trotted into the study, touched Julie's ankle with his nose, then staked out a fresh area next to her desk.

Janine had invented Worm Man after a second-grade science fair. She and Julie had seen an exhibit illustrating how earthworms burrowed through the dirt, digesting and aerating the soil, in search of food.

That evening when their parents went to bed, Worm Man was born. And Julie had never been so frightened.

Worm Man was as long as a room and thick as a telephone pole. He slithered upright on thick, squat legs when aboveground but under the grass he moved like an earthworm. With his powerful limbs hugged to his sides, he wore a black pullover mask with two slits for eye openings—no one had ever seen his real face—and a black raincoat and black galoshes. His skin was dark brown and always wrinkled, similar to human skin held under the water too long. Worm Man smelled like a pile of rotting vegetation. But the part that had disturbed Julie the most was Janine's assertions that he was always hungry.

When Worm Man tired of eating decomposing earth, he would burst up through the grass and weeds in search of young children because they never put up much of a struggle. He'd drag them, crying and screaming, underground, pack them in a coat of moist dirt, and let them rot, preferably until all the skin fell off.

That wet evening of June first was the last time Julie ever played Worm Man. And until she turned eight, she truly believed Worm Man had killed her sister. In reality, Janine's tragic death had been caused by something far more lethal.

Tiring of the past—it only depressed her—Julie returned to the present and spent another hour reviewing a stack of dream interviews she thought were relevant to her research. After these were logged into her computer, she shut the machine off.

Before going to bed, she drank a small glass of wine and took Jake for a short walk. There was a soft breeze and the temperature had dropped enough for her to consider opening the house up for the night. The fresh air might make sleeping easier. She hoped.

Tomorrow she'd call the Medical Records Department again and issue a second request for Ben Simmons's medical file. Her years of experience had taught her that every patient's recurring nightmares could be crystallized down to one singular *real* event, or *seed*, as she referred to them.

Isolating this seed was the key to controlling the dreams. Julie knew what her seed was, though she'd never told anyone. She wondered what seeds Vicki Zampisi was harboring.

Twenty-three

Saturday morning arrived bright and sunny. And warm. Just the kind of weather that could wreak havoc on a body that had nothing better to do than to lie around exposed to the elements. Even a body twenty-five feet underground. Make that two bodies.

Unlike the forecast, Dr. Dan Dorfman's mood was dark. Last night in the feature bout at the Grand Olympic Auditorium, some no-name white bum calling himself the Ranier Rustler crawled off the canvas at the count of eight and head-butted Harvey Gipson above the right eye. The fight went to the cards and was declared a draw in the sixth round. Not only did the unlikely demise of the gifted black Gipson cause the deputy coroner to lose two hundred bucks to the local bookies, but it left him six-hundred dollars in the debt of one Detective Matt Guardian.

Dorfman would've bitched, but the only ears presently within listening distance lay inside two plastic garbage bags.

While most cognoscenti of forensic science tended to loathe decomp cases, Dorfman simply looked upon them as he would an old puzzle whose pieces were so ragged and tattered that their edges no longer fit. Any recent graduate of pathology could determine the trajectory and path of a .38-caliber slug that entered a body at one point and after traversing bone, arteries, nerves, and muscles, exited the deceased at another point. Simple, basic physics. The same with knife wounds. Was the blade straight or serrated as in the infamous case involving a former NFL football player, or was the weapon curved with no serrations? No challenge.

A completely different picture was painted when the human canvas had been lying dormant underground for a number of days weeks, months, or, God forbid, years. In those cases, one had to be a true scientist of forensic pathology to answer even basic questions such as the time and cause of death and in some cases, gender.

Such was the monumental challenge facing Dr. Dan Dorfman as he stood before the two separate piles of putrefying skin, hair, organs, and appendages that had once been living, breathing, conversing human beings. Like every tried and true forensic expert, Dorfman believed these victims still could and would *talk*.

And Dorfman was a good listener. Though most autopsies could be completed in less than an hour, Dorfman intended to take all morning on these two. He pulled the closest metal gurney from the large walk-in freezer. The one carrying the bag labeled F1096. He promised Detective Guardian he'd tackle the girl first.

Last night Clovis Humphries had tentatively ID'ed her daughter from some forensic photos taken at the scene. According to Heaton, the former beauty queen of Compton High was folded like an accordion when her once-perfect body had been extracted from the sewage pipe.

Dorfman wheeled Jezebel's remains a short distance to an overhead camera. He placed a mask over his face and cut away the plastic. The stench permeated the entire autopsy room in seconds. Even the mask didn't help much. He began to breathe through his mouth as he snapped photos for the autopsy record.

It was 9 A.M. when he transferred Ms. Humphries to the autopsy table. Dorfman positioned the overhead microphone and began the external examination. Every corpse is weighed upon arrival at the morgue but Dorfman always re-weighed his particular cases. The Humphries girl dressed out at 51 kg. or 112.2 pounds. According to the mom, she'd been five foot nine, with a model's figure. Dorfman would take her mother's word for that descriptive gem. There was no way he'd get an accurate length now, not with the shattered long bones of the lower extremities.

Being careful not to dislodge the paper bags tied around the victim's hands, he positioned the corpse as best he could in the normal anatomic position, supine and palms up. The paper bags had been placed by Heaton at the scene to preserve any blood, hair, fibers, or other material beneath the victim's nails. Dorfman removed each bag and collected the dirty black debris fixed under the long red acrylic nails, some of which were broken. It looked similar to the substance collected from the Inez and Nixon girls.

Next, after determining that there were no obvious gunshot or stab wounds, Dorfman removed the victim's clothing. This included purple fishnet stockings, a black miniskirt, and a blue iridescent bodysuit, which was ripped, actually shredded in places, and covered with sewer slime and filth. The victim's gold necklace and ankle bracelet were collected for the family.

By now the stench was no longer bothersome to Dorfman. He was totally involved. As he periodically paused and spoke into the mike, the growing similarities to the prior female victims became unnerving.

The victim was totally nude now and bore little resemblance to the eight-by-ten glossies in the detective's file. Using diagrams and descriptions, Dorfman noted the obvious wounds. Any mark, lesion, or other evidence of trauma, he carefully examined. Each would require an explanation. The difficulty many times in decomp cases was determining what occurred antemortem and what postmortem.

The very act of decomposing involved two processes. Autolysis, or the breakdown of cells and organs from intracellular enzymes. And putrefaction, which is due to bacteria and fermentation. After Ms. Humphries died, the bacterial flora of her gastrointestinal tract spread throughout her body via blood vessels and nerves. And in the warm, moist environment which had been her temporary tomb, this process accelerated. This explained the victim's greenish hue and diffuse swelling of her face, which had to be differentiated from the pre-death injuries—the fractured cheekbone, nose, and multiple lacerations. He noted the missing right external ear or pinna and made a point to reexamine the severed ear found in the medical center basement.

The corpse also demonstrated extensive marbling caused by the hemolysis of blood vessels. Portions of the victim's legs were already turning green-black and in some places her once flawless skin was disrupted with large clusters of vesicles and blisters. In other areas, it'd been actually eaten away, Dorfman guessed by rats.

Each time he moved an appendage, he had to be especially careful not to deglove her. In advanced decomp cases, complete sections of skin and hair could slip from the body, especially at the hands or feet. Not only was it grotesque, but valuable evidence could be lost.

The list of injuries grew. Multiple fractures involving both femurs and her right tibia and fibula and left radius. Fractures of her nose and left zygomatic arch (was the assailant right-handed?), and a hairline fracture of her occiput, the posterior portion of her skull. Dorfman guessed she'd been thrown down on her back or against a wall or some other hard surface. Again determining the time of some of these injuries would be next to impossible. But that was part of the frayed puzzle Dorfman was being paid to reassemble.

The last part of the external exam involved the woman's three orifices. Her vaginal wall exhibited multiple tears but her rectum was intact. Like one of the other female victims, she'd been menstruating. It was usually impossible to isolate any semen once this much time had passed, but the ever-diligent coroner swabbed the victim's throat, rectum, and vagina for any residual foreign material anyway.

The internal exam was initiated with a scalpel and electric saw. Moments later, with the chest plate removed, Dorfman confirmed a collapsed right lung and multiple rib fractures. There was little doubt these were inflicted while the girl thrashed about, trying to escape her assailant. Or hopefully she was already unconscious.

Inspection of the abdominal cavity revealed a severely ruptured spleen. All her internal organs, including the intestines, kidneys, and liver, resembled brownish-black putty, all signs of advanced autolysis and putrefaction. Nothing new was gained from the examination of the heart and internal cranial contents, the brain.

In the end, Dorfman counted two potentially fatal injuries, the collapsed right lung and the ruptured spleen with secondary hemorrhage. But even with these extensive injuries, Jezebel Humphries could still have been alive when she was stuffed into the pipe, which undoubtedly would've killed her. Dorfman hoped for her sake she wasn't.

The victim's clothes were bagged and samples were taken for the trace-evidence lab, including some he planned on sending to the DNA specialty lab in Germantown, Maryland. Finally, the rest of the victim's remains were prepared for the mortuary. It was five past eleven when he wheeled Ms. Humphries back into cold storage.

No matter how Dorfman adjusted the pieces, the puzzle did not come fully together. Something was dreadfully wrong here—not just the fact that three innocent women's lives had been savagely snuffed, but the makeup of the killer himself. The evidence didn't jibe. Necrotic skin under the victims' nails, rotting tissue, the stench. What did it mean?

If a murderer had set out to devise a scheme to muddy the investigation, the perpetrator's goals had at least to this point been achieved. Was there a cryptic message behind the cadaveric clues? He hoped the forensic scientists at the DNA lab in Maryland would meet more success at deciphering the macabre trail of evidence, the critical question being, did all the isolated dead tissue originate from the same body?

Then there were those goddamn hairs from the hospital basement.

Dorfman washed his hands and replaced his mask in preparation for the second metal gurney. If what he was thinking was ever made known to his colleagues, they'd have recommended he return to medical school. When a person dies, he dies, right? That's the way it's supposed to be. What type of killer were they dealing with?

Dorfman shook his head and went back to work.

Julie hoped for a quiet Saturday evening. She felt physically drained. She wasn't on call so she wasn't expecting any emergencies, though she had instructed the hospital operator to page her if Vicki Zampisi called again. Sometime Friday afternoon, Vicki had placed a call to Julie's office, then hung up. Julie had tried twice to reach Vicki at the number given, but both attempts had been unproductive.

Last night while sleeping, Julie had listened to the nursery rhyme again. This time Janine was liltingly trolling the words while skipping rope on the roof of Mr. Ackerby's old toolshed. Julie awoke when she saw her dead sister's hair fly up. Janine was missing an ear. Before falling back to sleep, Julie had whispered a brief prayer for the murdered medical center nurse. She'd also added Irene Inez's name to the list.

Tonight, she added Janine's.

Jake had a clear view of Julie from where he rested on his favorite rug. A small room adjacent to the family room was Julie's home office. It was equipped with a fax, phone, desk, and a pentium PC.

Julie sat before her computer, browsing abstracts condensed from medical journals published on the Internet. She pulled up three on dreams associated with premature death and printed them. She'd study the actual articles in more detail later.

Shutting the machine off, she debated whether to drive over to the records department at the hospital. So far, she'd received no word back on the status of Ben Simmons's medical chart. And that was after two formal requests. Which meant one of several things had happened. The most likely scenario was the medical center had simply lost the file. Unfortunately, this was not an uncommon occurrence when very old records were involved. The second one, which Julie found slightly more appealing, was that Vicki had either given her the incorrect patient name, which seemed unlikely, or that Ben had never been hospitalized at CUMC.

Regardless, she'd just have to go on what her patient had told her during their interview.

Julie moved to the den and turned on the evening news. More gory details of the Sewer Stalker's most recent strikes occupied much of the newscast. One of the two new victims, who were found together, was a missing girl. The other victim was described as a Caucasian male between thirty and forty years old.

Julie wondered if these events had anything to do with Vicki's call Friday afternoon. It was not beyond reason that the Sewer Stalker case had exacerbated Vicki's condition, a concern Julie hoped to address at their next meeting. Lord knows, the violence was enough to trigger sleep disturbances in any sane individual. Janine's missing ear last night proved that.

Though her field of expertise dictated treating the victims of violent crimes, the majority of time Julie couldn't help but wonder what kind of defective mind could wreak such physical and psychological havoc on another human being. The case history of such a miscreant would provide an interesting study in aberrant behavior. But only on a theoretical level. She had no desire to personally sit down face to face with a Hannibal Lecter protégé.

Julie caught herself yawning when the phone rang. For some odd reason she thought it might be Vicki.

"Julie, Matt Guardian."

Her energy level jumped a notch. "Hello. I've been watching the news.

"All in a day's work," he said.

From the tone of his voice, Julie guessed it was going to take much more than a day's work to solve these crimes.

"Say," Matt said. "If you're not busy tonight, there are some things involving the case I'd like to run by you."

His request caught Julie somewhat off guard but she wasn't disappointed. "That's convenient, because there's an item I wanted to run by you, too."

"How's your appetite for Chinese?"

The image of Matt's large hands manipulating a pair of chopsticks amused Julie. "Sounds fine. So what was it you wanted to discuss, detective?" she asked.

"I'll tell you later. How do I get to your place?"

Julie gave him directions and slowly replaced the receiver. Her entire evening had just turned on a single phone call.

Twenty-four

Matt turned his Monte Carlo over to the valet parking attendant and met Julie on the entrance walk. She was wearing a blue lycra top, knee-length navy skirt, and heeled ankle boots. Her leather purse hung over one shoulder.

"Somehow, I'd never guess you were a doctor." Matt had barely taken his eyes off her since he'd picked her up.

"Maybe I should've worn my lab coat." Julie smiled and slipped her hand into Matt's arm. She'd have never guessed Matt was an LAPD homicide detective either. In his sports coat, shirt, no tie, and casual pants, he looked more like a college jock. She was mildly intrigued when he actually triggered memories of a former fiancé.

Matt escorted her inside the Peking Garden, past figurines, tapestries, and banners celebrating the pre-Mao Tse-tung era of Chinese history. Illumination by candles mounted in wall sconces, scents of herbs, gourmet cooking, and traces of exotic incense contributed to the quixotic ambiance that had elevated the Chinese eatery to its four-star status.

The maitre d' seated them on the restaurant's small veranda. Inside, a man played a piano in the main dining room.

Matt waited for the waiter to finish pouring the wine. It was a pink chardonnay from the Vichon Wyland series.

Julie raised the glass to her lips. "Um."

Matt watched the light from the oil lamp flicker off her smooth skin. "I take it you approve."

"What a difference a couple of city blocks and two continents can make," Julie said, savoring the taste.

Matt gave her a quizzical look.

She smiled. "I did some dream research recently at a place called the Amphisphere, one of those quintessential L.A. underground rock nightclubs. It's not far from here, over on Beverly Boulevard."

"How'd it go?"

"Interesting, but I must admit this atmosphere suits my nerves far better."

"So you're not a closet punker."

"The only parts pierced on me are my ears," Julie said, raising her glass for a toast. "To a successful investigation . . ."

"And interesting dreams," Matt finished.

Been there, done that, Julie thought, though in Matt's company she felt perfectly at ease.

Their eyes held each other momentarily but before the silence grew awkward, the waiter returned with their meals.

"You said you had some things to discuss," Julie said, midway through her salt-and-pepper baked crab. "The news is saying the murders are the work of a serial killer. The Sewer Stalker."

"Don't believe everything you read in the paper or see on the tube. The press can never be accused of lack of zealousness when reporting the news. I've seen them jump on dogshit before the flies. On the other hand, all four victims were covered with material consistent with raw sewage. I guess you could classify that as an indirect link. Guilt by association."

"They showed a picture of Jezebel Humphries. She was a beautiful girl."

"Who happened to wander into the wrong place at the wrong time."

"Any identification of the male victim?"

"That's one of the things I wanted to ask you." Matt set his fork aside. "Are you familiar with the drug Haldol?"

"Yes," Julie said. "It's a strong antipsychotic used in the treatment of various forms of psychoses. I've used it occasionally in my practice."

"And what about lithium?"

"Also used extensively in the psychiatric field. Lithium's classified as an antimanic though it's generally prescribed in bipolar disorders such as manic-depression." Julie studied Matt's face. "I think you do have an ID on the fourth victim."

"Mitchell Beeden," Matt said. "We're awaiting notification of next of kin somewhere around Baton Rouge. He carried an old Louisiana driver's license in his wallet."

"Can I assume Mr. Beeden is related to the psychiatric drug questions?"

"An unfilled prescription for Haldol was stuffed in one pocket. The clinic address was torn away. And you know how hard it is to read a doctor's signature? Also two green capsules found on Mr. Beeden were identified as lithium by our toxicology lab. The laboratory results won't be able to confirm the presence of either drug in the victim's system until next week."

"If Mr. Beeden's tests turn out positive, that would mean he was a mental health patient," Julie said.

"Name sound familiar?"

"No, but I can ask my colleagues."

"I'd appreciate that. Ramani's already requested a patient census from the medical center and surrounding clinics for the last year," Matt said, spearing a shrimp with his fork.

Julie started to take another bite but noticed her appetite had waned. "Any relationship between Mr. Beeden and the dead girl?"

Matt reached for his napkin. "None so far. Except they were both extricated from the same pipe."

"A pipe? I didn't hear that on the news."

"Don't mention any of this. We're keeping much of this under wraps pending the investigation," Matt said, washing down his shrimp with his wine. "Beeden was first out, so presumably he was shoved in last. Imagine two adults pressed into a sixteen-inch pipe."

"I'm trying not to." Julie reached for some more wine.

"According to the coroner the time of death for the male victim was anywhere from twelve to thirty-six hours. Ms. Humphries couldn't be narrowed down to less than one to two weeks."

Matt poured her more wine. "I'll spare you the sordid details. Except to say it was Ms. Humphries's ear we found in the basement."

"You've got to be kidding."

"No."

"How bizarre is that?"

"Believe me, it got our attention." Matt's expression remained somber. "Dorfman mentioned some other things that didn't make much sense."

"Like what?"

"I don't even think Dorfman knew for sure. We collected three hair samples that Dorfman swears had to have been pulled from a corpse."

"What?"

"Yeah, a dead body. And two of the hairs appear to be animal in origin."

"Jesus. What about the third?"

"Final results still pending. It's pretty decomposed."

"Decomposed." She didn't know what to make of it.

Matt sensed it was time for a change of subject. "You've been at CUMC how long?"

"Five years."

"During that time, how many patients would you say you've treated?"

"Hundreds. It'd be difficult to guess." Julie was wondering where Matt was going. The next question told her.

"Who was the most violent patient you ever treated?"

"Matt, I can't say. That's confidential information anyway." Julie sat back, piercing the detective with her eyes. "Are you suggesting one of my patients could be responsible?"

"Do any come to mind?"

"No. None at all. Most of my patients are women and sure, any number of the patients I'm treating for psychotic disorders or serious mood disorders, male or female, have the potential to be violent. But . . . this."

"Just asking." He held up his hands in mock surrender. "So far, our current and former employee lists have turned up nothing. There's still a lot to check out, though," he quickly added. "Let me ask you this. Are you familiar with any psychiatric condition in which a person would use a dead body or severed body parts in the performance of a crime?"

Julie's expression turned serious. "That's an odd question." While she gathered her thoughts, Matt replenished her wineglass. She didn't stop him.

"There is a condition called necrophilia," she said, "the morbid attraction to dead bodies. This can range from visiting cemeteries to experiencing sexual fantasies with the deceased. Of course, being a necrophiliac doesn't make you a murderer."

"Are you treating any necrophiliacs?"

"Somehow I knew you were going to ask that," she said, setting her glass down. "The answer is no. In fact, I've only seen one case and that was during my residency. Very sad."

Matt leaned back in his chair. "Let's say you did see a patient, or better yet, let's pretend a patient, not necessarily a necrophiliac, mentioned something incriminating during the time you were treating him." Matt paused a moment.

"Yes . . ."

"Would you tell the police?"

"Depends."

"On what?"

Julie reached for her wine. "A variety of factors. What the patient said, what the crime was, and what—no, who—the investigating detective was."

Matt took the bait. "Say it was me."

"That's somewhat presumptuous, but . . ." Julie emptied her glass. "I am glad you brought up the subject of patients."

"Why's that?"

Her expression grew pensive.

"I think you should consider interviewing Vicki Zampisi."

"The woman of Shilden Hotel fame." Matt's trace of cynicism vanished, though, when he added, "I'm listening."

Julie motioned to her wineglass and waited for Matt to finish pouring. "Thank you." She wet her lips before beginning. "Vicki is deeply troubled about an incident in her past. I believe this is what's triggering her nightmares. However, the woman is adamant about the facts of her assault at the hotel. She swears she was not alone. Remember you asking about how she described that smell?"

Matt nodded. "Kincaid attributed the stench to the city repairing a ruptured sewer line just behind the lot. I saw the construction pit myself."

"You'd be the last to call that a coincidence. Am I right? Look, if Vicki was really assaulted, she might be the only living witness to this Sewer Stalker. I reviewed my notes earlier today. Just before Vicki smelled that offensive stench, she mentioned a clean, almost aseptic smell. At the time I didn't think much of it until I recalled how strongly Irene Inez responded to a nurse's use of alcohol on her IV tubing. I know it's not much but I definitely feel there might be some relationship between Vicki's aseptic smell and Irene Inez's reaction to alcohol."

Matt thumped the tablecloth with his fingers. "Maybe. Why don't I talk to her."

"Would you?"

"If you think it's important. How's she doing?"

"She tried to reach me yesterday, but we haven't spoken since. I suspect these recent killings might be adversely affecting Vicki's condition. She's due to have her sutures removed sometime next week. I'll meet with her then."

"Let me know and I'll arrange an interview," Matt said.

Though the evening ended earlier than she would've liked the drive home was quiet and Julie enjoyed the coruscating lights of the skyline against the dark backdrop of the night sky. The radio was tuned to a classical station and she could feel her skin glow from the wine. She found herself watching the moon, which seemed to follow them, darting in and out of the amorphous silhouettes of skyscrapers, freeway overpasses, and tree limbs.

Matt walked her to the door. Julie could smell his cologne. She thought it was Aramis. In the yellow glow of her entranceway, Matt's face cast a desirable shadow and Julie was surprised at her sudden attraction for this homicide detective who held the small of her back in one hand. And to think only hours ago she was reading medical journal abstracts on the Internet.

Jake barked once from inside.

"Quiet, Jake," Julie whispered.

"He's jealous."

She turned and faced Matt. "Thank you for the evening. I enjoyed it."

The kiss felt too brief yet carried the warm electricity Julie expected. And anticipated.

"Till next time." Matt made a weak attempt of returning to his car, but stopped. For a moment, he stood stock-still, except for his fingers fidgetting with the keys in one hand.

"Yes?" Julie said.

Matt smiled awkwardly. "Nothing." He glanced at the sky. "Actually, I was kind of curious about one thing."

Julie unlocked the door. "Hold it, Jake," she said, blocking his big head with one knee. She gestured to Matt with one hand. "I don't suppose you'd like to come in."

Matt shrugged. "Why not?"

After a formal introduction to her pet, which went smoothly until Matt attempted to pet him, eliciting a deep growl, Julie let Jake out into the backyard.

"I've never seen him act that way around a stranger," Julie called from the kitchen. "I apologize."

"No harm. Just two old men getting to know each other."

"Jake's not old."

"Thanks." Matt heard Julie chuckle.

Above the fireplace hung a haunting seascape of wind-eroded cliffs and frothy seas. Even the gulls in the painting appeared alarmed by the bleak and darkening sky. Matt walked across the rug, noting the familiar artist. Below the painting on the brick hearth sat a collection of intricately carved wood sculptures, mostly of wild animals, bears, otters, and several ducks. The pieces were similar to the types Matt had seen advertised in art collector's catalogues. That was before his divorce.

Oddly out of place, a small papier-mâché ballerina balanced precariously at the hearth's brick edge.

From the kitchen, a cupboard opened, followed by the clink of glasses.

"Can I help?" Matt asked.

"No," Julie called back. "I've got wine, an unopened Tawny Port, or tea, or coffee."

"Coffee's fine." He looked back at the figurine. The face portrayed a young girl, but the body epitomized a mature woman.

Julie returned carrying a small tray with two cups and a plate of cookies and sliced cheeses. She stopped when she saw what held Matt's attention at the fireplace.

"That was my sister's," she said. "Janine collected them, those and dollhouses. She had dozens of them. Our room looked like a miniature city."

"I collected coins when I was a kid," Matt said, returning to his chair. "Until my dad got drunk one night, one of many nights, and lost them all in a Saturday-night poker match. Man, I had over fifty buffalo-head nickels. I could've killed him." He took a sip, followed by a bite of cookie. "Thanks. It's good." He motioned to the figurine. "Your sister a doctor too?"

Julie's expression remained impassive, almost wan. Matt could've easily pictured her at that moment standing at the edge of the cliffs in the painting above the fireplace wearing a flowing windblown white gown. She was that hauntingly beautiful.

"No," she said. "She always wanted to become an actress."

"Did she?"

Julie shook her head. "She died in an accident when she was seven."

"I'm sorry."

"It nearly destroyed my parents." *Not to mention me,* Julie rued silently. She averted Matt's scrutiny by selecting a thin slice of the French Roquefort cheese. She tore it in half and took a small bite. "So what was it you were so curious about?" she asked.

It was obvious Matt had touched on a painful subject and even more evident to Julie that he suddenly didn't appear at ease with himself.

She moved quickly to defuse the situation. "Or was that just a line to get inside my house?" she quipped.

"No, no," he said. "Promise." His spontaneity had returned.

"Then?"

Matt set his cup on the tray and leaned closer, both elbows on his knees. "The other day at the hospital when I asked you if you'd ever seen a crime scene before, this look came over your face that really . . . ah, got to me, I guess. I don't know how else to explain it. Then you said—"

"Yes, a long time ago."

"Yeah, that's what you said. But now after the ballerina, maybe we should talk about something else . . . if there's a connection."

"There is."

"I was afraid of that."

Julie watched him folding and unfolding his napkin. An odd feeling came over her. His unease actually made her feel more comfortable.

"I was the one who found Janine," she said.

"We don't have to go there."

"I'm fine." Julie set her teacup beside Matt's. Since high school, when she'd last discussed her sister's death with her best friend, she'd never retold the story. And she'd never told the *entire* story to anyone. Not her ex-fiancé. Not even her parents.

Tonight that was about to change and she didn't know why.

"Are you familiar with TEPP?" she asked.

Matt shook his head, his eyes locked on hers.

"It's an insecticide. Very potent. The letters stand for tetraethylpyrophosphate. Janine, I, and the other kids in the neighborhood used to play a game called Worm Man, sort of like Hide-and-Go-Seek, but in Worm Man you were fleeing this monster that lived underground and ate kids. Crazy, huh?"

Matt didn't say anything.

Julie nibbled at a cookie. "One night, Janine and I played. I didn't want to but she said, 'What's wrong, Jule, you chicken?' She always called me Jule. She was seven, I was five. I remember it was raining, not hard, just enough so your hair stuck to your neck.

I counted my one-hundred Worm Mans and started the hunt."

Matt watched Julie's eyes drift to the papier-mâché figurine.

"Janine cheated," Julie said, her voice icy. "She hid in an old shed somewhere we weren't allowed to go. There were rumors Mr. Ackerby was a child molester. That was years before Megan's Law. Anyway, I looked and looked and couldn't find her. It started to rain harder and I began calling her name. Nothing. I even walked to the edge of Mr. Ackerby's place. He always had a couple of junk cars parked in his lawn and never mowed his grass. A perfect place for Worm Man to hide. I remember being so scared, but I climbed his fence anyway. I had to find Janine.

"All the lights were out in the house so I figured no one was home. I crept along the side of the house until I could see the toolshed in one corner of his backyard. It was a large yard so I was still thirty yards away. I called her name again. Now I was really frightened. I remember thinking maybe Janine went home and here I was, stupid little sister, still out in the rain. That's when a gust of wind hit my face bringing with it a strange odor. Almost sweet. It was coming from the shed.

"I stood for the longest time staring at that rickety old woodshed. I even walked halfway across the yard for a closer look. The smell was stronger. I wanted to gag. I took one more step toward the door and froze. I swore I saw Worm Man leaning against the fence. I screamed and ran, crying Janine's name all the way home."

Julie threw her head back, closing her eyes. "Damn it, if I'd just opened the goddamn door."

Matt moved beside her. "It's okay."

Julie rested one hand on his thigh. "No, Matt. It's not okay. It was terrible. It was . . . almost a crime. Let me finish. Please."

He nodded. "I'm listening."

Julie composed herself by taking two deep breaths. "Before I ran, I really did go to the door. *All the way.*" There, she'd said it.

Yet she felt no different. "The odor was terrible now because I could smell vomit," she continued. "And I heard this grotesque breathing noise, like a wet gurgle. It was a noise only Worm Man would make. Matt, I didn't open the door because I was afraid Worm Man would leap out and drag me underground. That's when I screamed and ran home." Though she desperately wanted to throw herself into his arms, she settled for her cup of tea. "The police came and I told them about playing Worm Man. Mom and Dad were hysterical. They were sure Janine had been kidnapped. I was positive Worm Man had gotten her.

"Around eight that night, the rain stopped. I took the police down the street to old Ackerby's place. By then, the odor near the shed was almost gone. I called Janine's name. Then Worm Man's. I watched as the police tried the door. Its hinges were rusted so they had to push real hard.

"Janine was curled in one corner. They wouldn't let me go in all the way because of the TEPP vapor, though at the time, I had no idea what the smell was. I did know Janine was dead. I don't know how. The ambulance rushed her to the hospital but all resuscitation efforts failed. Somehow she'd trapped herself inside Ackerby's tool-shed and accidentally knocked over a five-gallon canister of concentrated TEPP. The doctors told my parents she died quickly, painlessly. I didn't believe them, still don't. I remember seeing Janine's bloody fingertips. She'd tried to claw her way out."

Julie turned and faced Matt. "For a week, the investigators had Ackerby's place taped off. I know if I'd opened that door the first time, Janine would still be alive."

"Maybe."

Julie saw none of the toughness in his expression, only a vague unfulfilled longing, almost as if she'd hurt him.

"Are you sorry you asked?" she said.

He tried to grin. His attempt came across clumsy. "You've satisfied my curiosity."

"Thanks for listening."

"You're welcome."

This time the kiss was far more intimate, piquing their emotions on a much deeper level. Julie let him pull her into his arms, accommodating his lips as they pressed against hers. She sensed she was floating as she lifted him with her on a ride neither could have predicted nor would either forget. Closing her eyes she saw a sky around them that was intensely blue, except for one small dark cloud low along the horizon. The flaw wouldn't go away.

Janine had never and would never experience the heated electricity only touching can give. That pained Julie almost as much as the guilt.

Matt drove away long before sunrise.

Twenty-five

Ignacio Chavez crouched low in the dungeon-like blackness of the fifty-four-inch sewer conduit. This was his first—and if things went as planned, his last—foray into the Byzantine Los Angeles underground. He loathed the dank putridity of his surroundings, enveloping him like a rancid abattoir, yet he'd never dishonored an oath before. He wouldn't dishonor Roberto. Even if enacting his revenge required crawling where the sleaze and scum of the City of Angels lived out their daily existence in absolute anonymity.

Ignacio had made the promise. He'd live—or die—by his word.

He paused, allowing Arbol to catch up. His *bato*'s greater dimensions made moving through the sludge more cumbersome. A third figure, the most diminutive of the three, sloshed to a stop behind the bigger gangbanger. Romy, a.k.a. *El Cuchillo*—the knife—barely stood five foot three but when yielding his self-styled six-inch blade, he became a giant. Ignacio had once stood back and watched while Romy sliced off the ear of a rival 'banger during an altercation over an ex-girlfriend. The dude was bad news and even Arbol respected the homeboy's *culinary* prowess.

"Listo?" Ignacio asked.

"I feel like puking," Romy complained in Spanish.

"You wanna go back up?" Ignacio asked, in earnest.

Romy slapped the moist concrete above his head. "I'd slice my nut off first," he hissed.

All three homeboys grinned.

"Then let's finish this," Ignacio whispered.

"We're with you, *buey.*" Arbol nudged him onward.

Ignacio could actually feel their pride and loyalty in the dark and right then he knew he'd never find a better, more efficient pair to watch his backside if he lived five lifetimes. Arbol and Romy were more than friends, much more. They were *hermanos,* brothers.

Ignacio aimed the flashlight's beam along the conduit floor. Unless the man they were following was a ghost, there was little doubt he'd walked this way. And the tracks appeared fresh. Ignacio shut off the light. There was no reason to broadcast their presence.

With one hand in constant contact with the damp clay wall, Ignacio started forward again, maintaining a wide-based stance for balance. He could hear his *batos* behind him. He was surprised at how fast they were able to glide through the darkness. Every so often, he'd turn on the light, more out of a need to placate his nerves than anything else. And each time, other than a few dead rats, he saw only slime and sludge. He wondered if Arbol and Romy were as afraid as he was. He knew they weren't. Neither would back down from anything—unless it was each other.

Three days prior, Ignacio had received the news from a gang-banger friend who'd heard it from a member of a rival Vietnamese gang. Word traveled fast and informally on the streets, especially when it involved manholes in the middle of the Sewer Stalker case.

The rumors were that a strange dude had been seen hanging around the neutral turf of Sixth and Seventh Streets near the Los Angeles River basin. Only two times it had happened, both instances occurring late at night, and on the second occasion the figure, really only a shadow, had been spotted lifting a manhole cover and vanishing below the street. No one had gotten a good look at him.

Though the police were locked out of this tight circle of information, Ignacio had been made privy to the beat. For three nights he'd waited unsuccessfully, but tonight his luck had changed. He'd sat at his position, along with Arbol and Romy, hidden in the shadows of the Seventh Street bridge, for less than twenty minutes when he barely glimpsed the dude, a hulking figure who moved with a swift rambling gait. He'd dropped preternaturally out of the darkness and vanished just as rapidly. Immediately, the sharp twinge in his gut told Ignacio he'd caught up with the one responsible for his *prima*'s death. The hunt had commenced.

With his 9mm tucked in his jeans against his abdomen, Ignacio gripped the stolen flashlight with one hand, crossed himself with the other, and slid further into the darkness. It was well past 2 A.M. Off his shoulder, Arbol's breaths were coming in short gasps.

Ignacio slowed. "Need a break?"

In the flashlight's beam, Arbol's skin glistened with perspiration. "No," he answered roughly.

Ignacio swung the light toward Romy, careful to keep it directly out of the homeboy's eyes. "You?"

Romy's teeth gleamed white. "Not before you, *bato.*"

Ignacio nodded and flicked off the light.

Initially unnerved, he now moved virtually invisible in the sewer passage. He barely felt the prickly sensation on his skin as the cool dark air played with his neck and forearm hairs. Faint echoes of dripping water came from all around him. At least an hour had passed and the urge to gag had diminished. The raw sewage odor did not seem as strong. Or maybe he was just getting used to being underground.

He wasn't sure how far they'd traveled when he heard an unfamiliar noise. Ignacio stopped and cocked his head toward this new disturbance. *Sloshing footsteps.*

Someone was ahead of him. He felt Arbol's soft tap on his back. They'd heard the *presence,* too. Ignacio's free hand left the wall and touched the Beretta in his pants. He turned on the flashlight, shining it at the sewer floor.

The same uneven footprints tracked out of the light's illumination. Momentarily, he stared at the oddly shaped print. The dude was barefoot. There was also something else about the tracks that didn't quite jibe, yet there was no time to dwell on it. He shut the light off and moved on. He hadn't gone more than fifty yards when the unseen walking abruptly stopped, replaced by a new noise. It sounded like the wind blowing through a tunnel. He inched himself forward as the noise increased. Unable to restrain his hand, he flicked on the flashlight.

Just ahead, he could see where the sewer entered a tunnel with a much larger diameter. It was huge. And black as a cavern.

"Shit," Romy whispered.

Arbol stopped. "Fuck."

Ignacio told himself it was only his own fear he was hearing in their tones. Yet for the first time since dropping below the street's surface, he knew this wasn't entirely true.

As Ignacio approached this underground intersection, he pulled the Beretta. It took all his willpower not to call out, "Hey, fuck, why you kill *mi prima*?" Instead he remained silent. Only the three men's breathing made any noise.

Where the sewer emptied into the North Outfall's ten-foot concrete passage, there was a small drop-off. Ignacio stepped down into two inches of water and sludge, relieved he could finally stand upright. Even Arbol could stretch his heavy fists high overhead. Everywhere there were the sounds of trickling sewage and underground air movement.

"Where the fuck are we?" the big homeboy asked.

"In hell," Romy answered. "All that's missing is the furnace."

"And *el diablo,*" Arbol added.

"You got that right." Ignacio couldn't disagree. He aimed the light and revolver to his right and left. He saw nothing, not even a rat. He checked for the footprints.

"Fregado," he cursed softly. The tracks ran in both directions. He listened.

SLSHSH.

"What the fuck," Arbol hissed.

Ignacio almost lost his balance swinging the gun and light to his right side. The tunnel curved out of view not a hundred yards away.

SLSHSH.

Ignacio heard Romy's switchblade engage.

"Come to yo' momma," El Cuchillo beckoned.

Though Ignacio didn't look, he knew both Arbol and Romy would also have their small-caliber revolvers drawn. The final countdown to confrontation was imminent. One thing disturbed him, though. Ignacio had no way of knowing how distant the noise was. He swallowed and flicked off the light. But there was no mistaking the intensifying stench that creeped over him.

"Mierda," Arbol cursed.

All three crouched and waited. Ignacio's gun rested on his thigh. He was scared. And ready. He was confident the two other homeboys were prepared for battle too.

SLSHSH.

Ignacio squinted into total blackness. He controlled the overwhelming urge to flick on the light.

SLSHSH . . . SLSHSH.

Ignacio put his finger on the pistol's trigger. He could almost hear his own voice saying, "Turn on the fucking light." Still he resisted.

SLSHSH . . . SLSHSH.

"Hey, *buey,* the light." Arbol's voice had taken on a plaintive tone.

Ignacio pressed his back against the wet concrete, molding it to the wall's curve. He was trembling. Though he'd once bragged to Roberto and Romy that he *had,* Ignacio had never really shot a person before. But tonight would be his time. For Irene, for Roberto, and for himself.

SLSHSH . . . SLSHSH . . . SLSHSH.

He heard Romy suck in his breath.

Closer, ever closer. Ignacio raised the gun and aimed. With his free hand he pointed the flashlight. He began to count to himself. At ten he would turn on the light and pull the trigger.

"What are you waiting for, *bato?*" Arbol urged. Now there was no masking the big gangbanger's fear.

Ignacio ignored him. This was his show.

Uno. Dos. Tres. . . . He gagged. The stench was unbearable. It was the same smell from Irene's abandoned car. The footsteps slowed.

SLSHSH.

Quatro. Cinco. . . . It was so fucking dark.

"Ignacio," Arbol croaked.

SLSHSH.

"Give me the fucking light," Arbol whispered.

"Stay cool," Romy breathed.

Ignacio squatted as if in a trance. Come on, you motherfucker. *Seis. Siete. Ocho. . . .*

SLSHSH . . . The sound stopped.

Come on, you fuck. Ignacio held his breath. *Mierda,* that odor.

Nueve. Diez. Ignacio flicked on the light. His eyes widened.

"Dios mio!" His voice barely squeaked.

Two shots exploded from his Beretta's barrel. Then he felt himself heaved viciously upward through the dark. With a sharp crack the back of his head whiplashed off the concrete ceiling. Dropping with a heavy plop, he landed on his stomach with such force, all the air escaped his lungs. For a split second he heard absolutely nothing, then two more shots. An instant later, the screams began.

Twenty-six

Vicki rolled out of her two-day bender late Sunday morning. Forty-eight hours had just been neatly erased from her memory slate. When the phone did ring, she imagined it was Ben summoning her to a place where the dead could still wing a good joke and pass the time of day reliving past triumphs and glories while shackled to their private ball and chain in the cold and silent great beyond.

She did it with straight-up Ezra Brooks and Jim Beam, chased down with chipped ice and Thunderbird. When she'd pickled her cranium to the point that her brain felt like two bricks buried in a pile of sawdust, she lay down and slept.

She dreamt of frozen wastelands and ice deserts, all strewn with bloody body parts, sloshing from rusted dewars in a never-ending search for their natural owners.

When she awoke, she felt like her head had been pounded with a ball peen hammer. However, four aspirin, a stelazine capsule, a glass of orange juice diluted with Ezra Brooks, some dry toast, and a Montclair returned her to the land of bills and debts and where emotions such as fear and guilt were as real as yesterday's news.

Much of Vicki still felt numb when she pulled the discarded mortuary letterhead from her purse. Images of severed appendages and necrotic organs had melted away under the stelazine's antipsychotic lift and she was able to pull enough bits and pieces from the edges of her memory to recall her abortive visit to the foundation. Kovacs hadn't lied about an accident in the storage unit.

Ben *was* missing and unless she pushed the search, she would never see him again, dead or alive.

Vicki strapped herself in behind the wheel of her van and drove into the sunshine, wondering how the sky could remain so blue in a world of burnt-out dreams and unfinished fairy tales. The cool air on her skin, though, imbued in her fresh hope and cleared her mind to the point that she once again began to believe most fairy tales have happy endings, if only one read far enough. In her case, that meant traveling east.

Evergreen Manor sat atop a well-manicured rise overlooking the Foothill Freeway in Pasadena.

Vicki found only two other vehicles besides her van in the lot—a hearse and a pickup truck with an assortment of lawn equipment stacked in its bed.

Vicki entered the mortuary's chapel half expecting to see an open casket and an altar lined with flowers. Instead an older, bearded man in coveralls approached.

"Can I help you?" he asked in a raspy voice.

"I'm looking for the director," Vicki said, conscious of his staring.

"That'd be Mr. Forester. His office is in the building next door. I'll show you." The man passed Vicki with the slow, methodical gait of a man who has all day to complete a task.

Vicki followed the gardener back outside to a white marble one-story building behind the main structure.

"In there," he said, fixing her in an uncomfortable gaze.

Inside, an older woman sat behind a desk in the anteroom.

"Hello," Vicki said. "I was told I could find Mr. Forester here."

"Mr. Forester is busy with procedures on Sundays," the woman said. "Do you have an appointment?"

"No." Vicki paused. "But this is rather urgent."

"Perhaps I can be of assistance. Do you have a personal request?"

"I'm not here to make any funeral arrangements." Vicki smiled awkwardly. "However, I did have an inquiry I'd like to discuss."

"Concerning a client?"

"A friend. I've been away on business for several months, and as unfortunate as this may sound, my friend passed away while I was gone. I wasn't able to attend his funeral service."

"That is quite unfortunate. And he was buried here at Evergreen Manor?"

"Yes, I believe so."

The woman rose and disappeared behind a door located at the rear of the anteroom. Almost immediately she returned with a thick loose-leaf binder and set it on her desk.

"We're in the process of updating our computer system," she explained. "In the meantime, we use this." The woman opened the binder. "Now if I could have the deceased's name and the month he was buried." She looked up. "He was buried, wasn't he? The other option is cremation, of course."

"No, he was buried," said Vicki, realizing she had no idea.

The woman cleared her throat. "I will need the deceased's name," she repeated.

Vicki tried to think. If Kovacs did transfer Ben's body here, it made perfect sense. What better way to continue the experiments' charade than to bury Ben in a mortuary? But would he have used the same name as on the fabricated death certificate? She really had no other alternative.

"Ben Simmons," she finally said.

"And what month?"

"I'm not sure. Definitely not this month. Perhaps if you try March or April." Vicki paused. "Yes, try March. Please." Hadn't Kovacs hinted the accident was several months ago?

The woman flipped the pages back to the third month. "S's,

S's, S's," she mumbled as she ran her finger down one page then the other. "I see a Gerald, here's a Sally. And a Mark. I remember Mark. He was a forty-eight-year-old ex-pro-football player, even spent a year in L.A. playing for the former Rams, I believe his wife had said. She found him lying in bed one afternoon after jogging. Dead as a cucumber. Casket had to be specially made. He was big." She finished the last page. She looked up. "Nope, no B. Simmons in March."

"Can you check April?"

The woman did. And May.

"I'm sorry," she finally said. "Perhaps it was another mortuary."

Vicki slowly nodded. "I really thought it was Evergreen, but I could've been wrong, I guess."

"I'm sorry," the woman said again. "If in the future we can be of any further—"

"Thank you." Vicki was ready to leave.

The room suddenly seemed stifling. Vicki felt thirsty. If the woman had offered her a good shot of anything amber and greater than forty proof, she would've gladly accepted.

On her way out, Vicki grabbed a mortuary pamphlet and almost ran smack into the bearded man.

"Excuse me," Vicki mumbled, stepping around him. He made no attempt to move aside.

All the way to her van, she could feel his eyes boring between her shoulder blades. She left the vacant lot never looking back.

That afternoon, for the first time since arriving in L.A. Vicki seriously considered packing up her few belongings and driving north to Seattle. As she'd told Dr. Charmaine during their first encounter, she could live with the nightmares. She'd done so for years. The foundation could surely live without her and if she was forced to accept the fact she would never see Ben again, well Ezra

Brooks, Jim Beam, and stelazine had already proved themselves a worthy threesome of living crutches. The only tangible reason she could think of to justify her continued stay was her intense desire to see Kovacs ruined professionally. Was risking her own life worth satisfying her quest for revenge?

Sunday evening, though, any resignation evaporated as Vicki watched the first television news she'd heard since crawling out of her alcoholic cocoon.

As the name and picture of the only known male victim of the Sewer Stalker broadcast over the airwaves, Vicki felt a cool tingling creep over her breast where Case had groped her. The involuntary flood of images—Evergreen Manor, Kovacs's empty dewar, the Shilden Hotel, and her old photograph—made her feel even colder.

Twenty-seven

Vicki's phone call came early. Julie turned her Monday-morning clinic over to the chief psychiatry resident and they met upstairs.

Julie ushered Vicki into her office. "I tried returning your calls several times," she said, fetching two cups of steaming coffee.

"I was indisposed," Vicki said. She received the Styrofoam cup with both hands. "Thanks."

Julie noted Vicki's mottled skin, especially over the cheeks and nose that the makeup failed to hide, the fine tremor involving Vicki's hands, and the bloodshot eyes and sensed what Vicki had meant by "indisposed".

"How was your weekend?" Julie asked.

Vicki appeared to concentrate on the blackness of the coffee as if answers she was seeking lay just below its hot surface. "I heard about those two people they pulled from the sewer."

"I saw that on the news too. Quite disturbing." The reference to the Stalker case made Julie think of Matt. Saturday night seemed less real to her now, more like an imagined event or a scene from someone else's video.

"How are you handling the recent events?" Julie inquired.

"If you're asking whether my nightmares have been worse recently, the answer is yes. Friday evening I drank myself into a coma and it was like a piece of my life peeled away. Only what was left underneath turned out to be more vile and wretched than the layer discarded." Vicki started to bring the cup to her lips but stopped. "Doctor, are you familiar with dewars?"

Julie shook her head.

"They're metal canisters used to keep body parts frozen. Kovacs used them in his research."

"Is this Dr. Wesley Kovacs?"

Vicki nodded. "All weekend I dreamed of dewars, Dr. Charmaine. I saw body parts crawling from one open dewar to another like they were lost and unable to find the right one. I counted arms, and legs, and hands and my impression was they would continue to search until they encountered their missing owners."

Julie watched her patient's eyes become unfocused. When Vicki didn't continue, she said, "This dream was different than your others, then?"

"Yes. I felt I was responsible for each separate part to find its rightful home, but because of my isolation, I couldn't reach them and therefore I couldn't fulfill my responsibility." Vicki paused briefly before adding, "And would never be able to fulfill it."

"And this failure to effect your responsibility made you feel guilty."

She nodded again, more slowly. "And then last night when I listened to the news, that sewer pipe reminded me of a giant dewar and . . ." Her voice trailed off.

"Vicki, you can't allow yourself to feel responsible for those two people. I agree, the circumstances are unfortunate, but experiencing guilt over a situation you exert no control over is not the answer."

"Even if you knew one of them?"

Julie felt like she'd been slapped in the face. "You were acquainted with one of the victims?"

Vicki almost started to smile, then stopped. The brief gesture again threw Julie off balance. This wasn't the look of an individual burdened with guilt.

Vicki's expression looked cast in stone. "He kidnapped me, then tried to rape me."

"You're referring to Mitchell Beeden."

"He called himself Case. He was a brute and deserved whatever pain he might have experienced." Her gaze softened a moment. "I don't feel that way about the girl."

"Are you sure about what you're saying?"

"You never forget someone who holds a knife to your throat, believe me."

"Have you spoken to the police?"

"No."

Julie watched her patient sip at her coffee. Beneath Vicki's vulnerable exterior, she detected a slab of steel. This woman's reaction to an attempted rape was not falling within the normal bell curve. She appeared entirely too calm. It was as if the assault, if it indeed had taken place, was secondary to a far larger issue. Then again, Julie surmised, Vicki could be simply experiencing a late-phase shock to the experience.

"Do you feel comfortable discussing it?" Julie asked.

"There's really not much to discuss. He was waiting for me in my van, we drove to a secluded spot, and fortunately I was able to escape before any real damage was done." Vicki glanced at the wall clock above a bookshelf. "I think he would have killed me if given half the chance. The bastard."

"The rage you feel toward this man is entirely normal," Julie said, "and the fact that Mr. Beeden is dead doesn't make your emotions any less appropriate. And some of the most intense rage can be found in these random acts of—"

"This assault wasn't random," Vicki interrupted. "Kovacs sent him."

It took a moment for Vicki's statement to sink in. "The same Dr. Kovacs who treated Ben Simmons?" Julie said.

"Case was one of Kovacs's patients."

"He told you this?"

"With the point of a knife on my neck and his hand under my bra."

"I'm sorry."

She shrugged. "It's over now. What goes around, comes around."

There were a hundred questions she wanted to ask Vicki, though many of them she realized belonged more in the realm of a police investigation than a counseling session.

Julie wondered whether Wesley Kovacs had prescribed the Haldol. If so, that could indirectly link him to the Sewer Stalker case. Her reasons for having Matt talk to this woman had just increased a thousandfold.

"Vicki," Julie started. "I know the detective in charge of the Sewer Stalker case. I feel it's vitally important you talk with him as soon as possible."

"He's not that Kincaid guy."

"No, his name is Matthew Guardian. In fact, I asked him to meet with you this week to go over some details regarding the Shilden Hotel episode." Julie reached for the phone. "I'm going to try to reach him now."

Vicki sat immobile, her sight fixed on some indiscriminate point visible only to her. "Go ahead. If you think it's important."

"I do."

The Parker Center dispatcher passed Julie through to the Robbery/Homicide division, but the detective answering told her Detective Guardian wasn't available.

"What about his partner?" Julie asked.

"Both Detective Guardian and Ramani are involved in an investigation."

Julie requested he page Matt and have him call her as soon as possible. She noticed Vicki now stood before one of her bookshelves.

"I never realized there were so many titles on dreams," Vicki said. She turned. "He wasn't in, was he?"

"I left a message."

Vicki touched one of the bound journals before returning to her chair. "The night Case attacked me, I dreamed it was Ben who'd committed the assault. Is that significant?"

"Dream interpretation is a complex process," Julie said, noting the troubled look behind Vicki's eyes. "There is no single answer, but I will say that anything a patient dreams in which the recollection of a particular scene causes any undue discomfort or ill ease would be considered significant."

"You still don't think dreams can predict the future."

"There has been no conclusive proof, no." Julie rose and moved to Vicki's side of the desk. "Vicki, do you feel your life is in any danger?"

"Not at the moment. Case is dead."

Kovacs turned the switch to off and waited for the centrifuge to slow enough to stop the spinning with his hand. The ten vials of monkey blood would be separated into two fractions, serum and whole blood cells. Both would then be cryoperfused and stored separately for analysis at three-month intervals. The metabolic transformation of cryonic enzymes that had begun to concern Kovacs four weeks ago would need to be documented from its inception, if in fact such a cryo biochemical change was occuring. Kovacs hoped the initial results had been spurious.

He transferred the tubes to a metal rack and placed them in a refrigerator. Eisler would handle the cryoperfusion process later.

The rear door to the laboratory opened and his associate director entered from the loading dock. He approached Kovacs with the unsure slow gait of a preoccupied man.

Setting his clipboard on the wood bench, Eisler pulled a stool under him. "The thermosensors for the remaining dewars will have to be recalibrated once they're positioned in the new facility."

"Is that a problem?" Kovacs asked, figuring there was more on Eisler's mind than the thermosensors.

"No."

Kovacs gave a curt nod of approval and started for the front exit.

"Wes."

"Yes."

"They'll be by asking questions."

Kovacs faced his associate. He himself had wondered why the police hadn't come around yet.

"I suppose you're correct. I feel as bad about Case as you do, but there's nothing we can do at the moment."

"What about notifying the police ourselves?"

Kovacs had been afraid Eisler would propose that route when the news broke.

"No, I disagree on that option," Kovacs said. "I think it best we allow the investigation to proceed at its natural pace and when the detectives come calling, we simply tell them what they already know. Mr. Beeden was a patient of the foundation and we are very sorry for his unfortunate mishap."

"What about the Zampisi woman?"

"Ms. Zampisi can fabricate any story she wishes. As for ourselves, we have no idea what Case was doing on the night he vanished."

Kovacs watched Eisler consider his words, hoping they would be enough to ease any disquiet. Since the Simmons debacle, Christian had been acting strangely, more anxious, nervous. He was also losing weight. Though Kovacs had been especially careful to ensure his colleague never directly witnessed Ben's removal from the dewar, it was possible, he supposed, that Eisler had seen parts of Ben's corpse before the transfer to the mortuary. Yet he doubted this. Eisler would've said something if he'd actually seen Ben's body. Maybe even resigned and this was a move Kovacs could ill afford at this time. His assistant's technical expertise would be mandatory for the successful priming of the new facility in Tucson. Not to mention the added weight Eisler's advanced degrees carried. Having one less PhD on the corporate prospectus could hinder the foundation when it came time again to apply for private grants and wooing investors. Not to mention the detrimental effect any unfavorable news would have on future venture capital.

Kovacs motioned toward the counter refrigerator, hoping to get Eisler's mind back on more familiar territory. "The rhesus samples have been spun and fractionated."

"Looking for anything specific?" Eisler asked, reaching for his clipboard.

"Any variations between intra- and extracellular metabolic enzyme levels from the presuspended state."

Kovacs waited until Eisler had started the cryoperfusion computations before returning to his office. He collected a stack of data sheets from the recent experiments and placed them in his briefcase. Some of these he would evaluate tonight in an attempt to determine when the metabolic aberrations had begun to take place.

Seeing Case's unfilled prescription for lithium on his desk, he tore it to pieces and tossed them in the trash. At least Case had had a valid reason for not returning his pages.

Now what was Devlin's excuse?

The steamy spray of the shower relaxed Julie's tense muscles. Matt had returned her call late that afternoon with more bad news. Two more bodies had been removed from the sewer.

Now Julie couldn't get the two gangbangers out of her mind.

God, they were barely past their teens.

In an effort to expedite matters, Matt had requested her assistance. Her single meeting with Ignacio Chavez had left her as the most accessible person able to ID the bodies. Only the young homeboy had not been among the unfortunate pair spread across the two metallic autopsy tables in Dorfman's forensic lab. She prayed Arbol, positively ID'ed as Jorge Salazar, had died before the dismembering. Ultimately he had bled to death. Quite rapidly, according to the deputy coroner. The smaller man, Romeo de la Cruz, had succumbed to a crushed skull and massive chest trauma. She was relieved Ignacio Chavez had not been among the body parts. In their only encounter, Julie had detected more humanity in the young gangbanger than he probably would have wanted to reveal. As far as she knew, he was still on the streets. Unless his body just hadn't been discovered yet. She quickly dismissed this last thought.

Julie let the water run down her chest and abdomen. Even the warmth of the shower pelting her bare skin couldn't ease the growing pit of apprehension in her midsection. It now seemed critical that Vicki open up to Matt and her. The meeting was set for first thing in the morning.

And it wasn't just Julie whose life was being affected by the Sewer Stalker. Since Brenda Nixon's apparent abduction in the hospital, the entire medical center staff seemed more uptight and less willing to double-book patients and stay late. The requests for security escorts had mushroomed, especially from the female employees.

Julie cracked open the shower door. Her Smith and Wesson sat on the counter within easy reach. She felt foolish taking the gun with her into the bathroom, but she also felt somewhat vulnerable standing stark naked in her own home. The front door was locked and armed and she knew Jake waited by her bed. All things considered, though, the sight of the .38 gave her an unequaled sense of security.

Matt allowed himself a trace of optimism about his upcoming interview with Vicki Zampisi. Not only would he be seeing Julie again—which he couldn't deny he was looking forward to with more than professional interest—but if the woman's story panned out regarding a purported rape attempt by Mitchell Beeden on the night he vanished, as Julie had relayed, then that would place her in the approximate vicinity of the scene where two of the Sewer Stalker victims had been pulled from underground. For the moment, she was all he had.

Matt had contacted the Investigative Support Unit at the FBI. They had access to an enormous amount of computer files complete with psychiatric profiles, MO's, and unpublished or unreleased details. They promised to get back with a profile as soon as possible. What was the delay? This must be the first sewer serial killer. Fucking fantastic. And it belonged to him.

Matt pulled into the Parker Center parking lot. A meeting with Craig Lichstein, the chief engineer for the city of Los Angeles wastewater program, had lasted thirty minutes. As he climbed from his car, he recognized a woman storming out the glass doors of the building. Isabelle Ramani's imitation Gucci purse swung at her side.

"Matt," she said, not unfriendly.

He loved her accent. "Isabelle," Matt replied warily.

"You win," she said, still no venom in her tone.

"I . . . ?"

Isabelle forced a smile and strode right by him into the lighted lot.

"Isabelle," Matt called after her. She didn't stop. "Isabelle." He knew it was futile to follow her.

Upstairs, the look on Ramani's face confirmed his suspicion.

"I just saw Isabelle," Matt said.

"She smiling?" Ramani wasn't.

"Sort of," Matt sort of lied. "So what's up with you two?"

"She's going back to Guatemala."

"Damn, that's bad. She coming back?"

"Don't know." Ramani wore the look of a defeated man. "You know, I really loved her. Still do. I mean I love her as much now as I ever did. And the funny thing is I think she knows this. But this damn case, the hours, the press, the T.V. pictures, it's getting to her. Sometimes I'm sick and tired of this whole goddamn city."

Matt collapsed in his chair with a sympathetic plop.

Ramani shrugged. "She said to call her when I can spend more time with her."

"You mean when this bitch is shut down," Matt said. He swiveled around so that he faced the L.A. wastewater division blueprint of the city's sewer system tacked to the wall.

The rules of the game were about to change.

Twenty-eight

Parker Center was much larger than Julie had imagined. Though not as immense as University Hospital, its pre-sixties architectural style made for an imposing edifice nonetheless.

Julie waited while Vicki parked her van. The two women met near the entrance. Both were dressed conservatively, Julie in a cotton skirt and blouse, and Vicki in pants, blouse, a light jacket, and obvious makeup.

She smiled awkwardly as Julie shook her hand. "I'm glad you decided to come, Vicki. I know you feel uncomfortable about this."

"It's one thing to tell my doctor I was almost raped. But a total stranger . . ." Vicki shrugged.

Julie smiled reassuringly. "He's a detective. He'll listen."

But inside, Julie wasn't feeling entirely at ease either. Since their weekend dinner together, she'd only seen Matt one time and that was to try to identify the two murdered gangbangers. Standing beside the detective at the autopsy table, she couldn't help noticing his exaggerated effort to be polite and courteous. She didn't know how to interpret this minor change. Though on Saturday they'd shared a few intense moments on her couch, she *didn't* sleep with him. By mutual agreement. And now Detective Sarcasm had molted into Mr. Polite. She preferred the old Matt. For now, she decided to just be herself and let the chips fall where they may. Even if nothing else happened though, she didn't regret discussing *all* the circumstances concerning Janine's accident with the detective. For two nights now, she hadn't dreamed of her dead sister.

The officer at the entrance booth issued each woman a visitor's badge and pointed them to the elevators.

Matt picked them up on the third floor and led them to a room with a glass door. "I thought we'd use the interrogation room. It's quieter and it'll be more private."

Ramani was already seated at the table. Julie thought both detectives looked enervated, especially Matt.

She introduced her patient.

"Coffee?" Ramani pointed to each woman.

"Please," Julie said.

Vicki declined. Her hands looked steady.

Matt sat directly across from both women, a legal pad in front of him. "Ms. Zampisi, try to relax as much as possible. I want you to know my partner and I appreciate you taking the time and effort to come in. This isn't an interrogation and you're not a suspect. In fact, if it wasn't for Dr. Charmaine, you wouldn't even be here."

Oh, thanks, Julie wanted to say, but she remained quiet.

Matt continued, motioning to a small tape recorder on the table. "I usually record these interviews; however, if you have any reservations, the recorder can be dispensed with."

"I don't mind," Vicki said.

"Very well, then." Matt pressed the RECORD button and indicated the time, date, and all individuals present. "Dr. Charmaine has filled me in briefly, but why don't you start from the beginning and tell Detective Ramani and me what you know."

"Well, I'm not really sure where to start. I've been under Dr. Charmaine's treatment for these incessant nightmares and . . ." she stalled.

"But you're not here because of these dreams," Matt said.

"Yes and no," Vicki said, reaching for her purse. "Does anyone mind if I smoke?"

No one objected. As Vicki lit up, Julie noticed her tremor had returned. She noted Matt's curt sideways glance at Ramani.

Vicki pulled an ashtray close. "I returned to Los Angeles a little over three weeks ago. I'm from Seattle, I mean I'm originally from Los Angeles, but in 1985 I left and moved in with my mom up north." Vicki took a long drag. "Occasionally over the last four or five years, while in Seattle, I'd have trouble sleeping. I figured, no big deal, everybody has trouble sleeping every once in a while. Right? Then approximately two months ago, I read a brief article in the local paper about a company I used to work for. They were moving their headquarters to Arizona. That same night, I woke up with this terrible fear something terrible was going to happen if I didn't return to Los Angeles. I disregarded it at first, but the nightmares became unbearable. So yes, detective, in a way I am here because of these dreams. I moved back to confront a situation that happened years ago in an attempt to elicit a cure." She cleaned an ash from the Montclair with the glass edge of the ashtray. "I just didn't realize I'd land myself smack-dab in the middle of a high-profile murder investigation."

Ramani shifted position in his chair. Julie saw him check his watch.

Matt shuffled back several pages of his legal pad. "Ms. Zampisi, why don't we return to the evening of the sixteenth. That was the night Officer Kincaid found you outside the Shilden Hotel."

Vicki smiled wryly. "You mean arrested. He didn't believe me." She tapped her knee. "My stitches come out tomorrow."

"We're listening now, Ms. Zampisi," Ramani interjected.

Julie caught Matt's stare. She touched her patient's forearm. "You're doing fine, Vicki. Just tell your story like you told me."

Vicki's gaze roamed above the detectives' heads. "Before the earthquake, the Shilden Hotel had been a private, tranquil respite from city drudgery. I always thought it belonged in New England or in a travel guide magazine for B and B inns. It saddened me to see what it had become." Her eyes returned to Matt. "On the night of the sixteenth, I parked my van a half block away in front of an all-night laundromat. There was a breach in the security fence next to the alley from some type of construction work. I entered the building from a ground unit by climbing over a damaged balcony railing," Vicki said, reaching for her cigarette.

"According to Kincaid's report," Matt said, "you heard a call for assistance from inside."

"Thought I heard," Vicki corrected him. She exhaled the smoke toward the ceiling light, watching it disperse until all that remained was an invisible scent. She pulled the ashtray next to her Styrofoam coffee cup. "That part wasn't exactly the truth. I never heard anyone call out for help."

"I assume you had some reason to risk a trespassing charge," Matt said.

"I had my reasons. But they have nothing to do with why I came here."

Julie watched Matt's reaction. His expression remained neutral.

"What happened once you were inside the hotel's premises, Ms. Zampisi?"

"Like I told the cop," Vicki went on, "the assault occurred just as I was leaving. I'd just stepped into the hall when someone grabbed my wrist. The hand was large. It went completely around my forearm. I was only able to break free after I hit him with my flashlight."

"Him," Ramani said.

Vicki doused her cigarette. "Most definitely. He was big with very large hands. No woman could ever have a grip that strong."

Ramani tapped a pad in front of him. "Then you saw him."

"No. Only his arm. It was as thick as a tree limb and covered with some sort of shiny material, maybe plastic."

"But you had a flashlight," Ramani said.

Vicki shook her head. "I lost it when I hit him. It flew down the hall. That's when I ran and injured my knee."

"By tripping." Ramani was reading from a file.

"Yes," Vicki said. "I fell against a wooden beam."

"And then ran into the alley." Ramani closed the file. "Did he chase you outside?"

"No. But I'm sure he must've left fairly quickly because your officer was right there and didn't see anyone."

"You didn't see the alleged attacker leave?"

Vicki shook her head. "He was gone by the time I looked back."

"And that's when you confronted Officer Kincaid."

"Yes." Vicki placed another Montclair between her lips and lit up. "He summoned the ambulance."

Matt set his pen down. "Ms. Zampisi, I'd like to go back to your statement regarding some sort of shiny material. You mentioned plastic. This wasn't in the original police report."

"Some things become clearer later, detective."

"Any ideas?"

Vicki shrugged.

"A raincoat," Matt offered. "It'd been raining around that time."

"That's a possibility. It felt like a sheet of thin rubber," Vicki said, replacing the cigarette with more coffee.

"What does come to mind?" Ramani asked.

Julie saw her patient's jaw muscles tense briefly, then relax.

Vicki stared at the recorder. "You ever been to the meat section of the grocery store?"

"I'm not following you, ma'am," Ramani said.

"It was similar to that plastic wrap the butcher places around the steaks under the display windows."

"You mean cellophane," Matt said.

"Only thicker. And it wasn't transparent."

"Color?" Ramani asked.

Vicki frowned. "It all happened in a split second. No, detective, I can't give you a specific color."

"Was it black?" Matt asked.

"No, it wasn't black."

"White?"

"Somewhere in between, maybe closer to brown, I don't know." Vicki's tone carried a trace of irritation.

Julie tried to catch Matt's gaze but his eyes remained focused on his legal pad.

"Ms. Zampisi," Matt began. "Let's move ahead to a topic of more recent mutual interest. Are you familiar with the name Mitchell Beeden?"

Julie wanted to interrupt, citing one specific area the interview had failed to explore thus far. She hoped Matt would get back to it.

Vicki nodded. "It was only after I saw his picture on the news that I realized who he was. He told me his name was Case."

"You watch the news then?" This question came from Ramani.

"Some."

"A lot?"

"Detective, if you're insinuating that what I'm about to tell you I got solely from the news, the answer is no." Vicki fidgeted awkwardly. "I do watch enough to know the stalker didn't stop with Beeden or that pretty black girl."

Julie saw Matt's attention shift her way, perhaps checking her reaction to Vicki's allusion to the stalker's latest victim. Julie could still see Arbol's dismembered body on the metal autopsy table, gunpowder residue peppering his right hand. She kept any feelings hidden and when she met Matt's gaze, Julie detected something in his expression on a different level than a routine police interrogation. But he looked back to Vicki before she could get a read.

Matt flipped to a fresh page. "Can you describe the sequence of events involving your relationship with Mr. Beeden?"

Vicki flinched. "Sure, if you want to call an attempted rape a relationship."

Matt backpedaled. "I apologize, poor choice of words. Let's try encounter."

Again Julie felt tempted to intervene but held her tongue.

Vicki killed her second cigarette. "It happened two nights after the attack at the Shilden. It was a Friday evening. He was already in my van when I came out of the grocery store over on Clarence. He was waiting for me in the backseat."

"You routinely lock your doors," Ramani said.

Vicki ignored the comment. "I wasn't aware of his presence until he placed the knife against my throat. He said if I didn't do exactly as I was told he'd slit my throat."

"Those were his exact words," Matt said.

"No. His exact words were, 'Bimbo, do as your pretty ass is told or I'll fill up the fuckin' van with your blood.' " Vicki wet her lips with a sip of coffee. "He ordered me to drive to the Fourth Street bridge where I pulled off onto an access road. We parked in a secluded area out of view from the street. That's where he tried to rape me." Vicki opened her purse and took out the packet of Montclairs. The cigarette was slow in coming, forcing her to slap the pack several times against the table. She lit up and exhaled, staring at the recorder. "How long's your tape?" she asked.

"An hour," Matt said. "There's plenty of time."

"Wonderful."

Julie saw Matt and Ramani exchange glances. This time Matt met her gaze and seemed to understand her look of concern.

"You want to take a break, Ms. Zampisi?" he asked.

Vicki shook her head. "Is there any charge for more coffee?"

Ramani filled everyone's cups and once he was seated, Vicki continued.

"I was able to fend him off by opening the driver's-side door. We both fell outside, I slipped out of his grasp, and ran down under the bridge. That's where I lost him in the dark or, rather, he lost me. When I emerged on the other side, I was alone. I didn't see him again until I saw his photo on the news."

"What do you think happened to him? Did he fall?" Ramani asked.

"I don't know. And frankly, I don't give a damn."

Matt scribbled on the legal pad. "Ms. Zampisi, you used the words 'tried to rape.' I assume then Mr. Beeden was unsuccessful in his endeavor."

"The bastard barely made it to second base, detective," Vicki said, dislodging an ash into the ashtray. She reached for her coffee cup. "Your next question's probably going to be why I took so long in reporting it."

"That did cross our minds," Ramani said, scratching the top of his head.

"It's simple, detective," Vicki said. "I didn't think you'd believe me. I also didn't want the police involved. Dr. Charmaine convinced me otherwise."

Matt glanced Julie's way briefly before asking his next question. "Do you believe rape was Mr. Beeden's primary motive?"

Vicki looked at Julie, then Matt. "I don't, detective. He was sent to scare me, possibly kill me. Rape was a fringe benefit."

"Scare you?" Ramani asked. "Into what?"

"Leaving California."

"You're alleging Mr. Beeden was working for someone else then," Matt said. "Do you have a name?"

"Dr. Kovacs," she said. "Mr. Beeden was a patient of Dr. Wesley Kovacs."

Matt's posture stiffened. "A doctor sent one of his patients to rape you?"

"I said scare me."

"How do you know Mr. Beeden was one of Dr. Kovacs's patients?"

"Beeden told me."

"And you believed him?" Ramani asked.

"I had no reason not to," Vicki said. "I was a psychiatric aide, detective. I've seen enough mental patients strung out on antipsychotics. Mr. Beeden spoke like he had a mouthful of half-cooked oatmeal." She didn't add stelazine occasionally had similar effects on her.

Matt looked Julie's way. She shook her head slowly to indicate she hadn't revealed a thing of their past conversation regarding Beeden's medical history. He returned to Vicki. "What do you mean when you say antipsychotics?"

Vicki shrugged. "There are many, stelazine, thorazine, Haldol."

"What about lithium?" Matt asked.

"Technically it's not an antipsychotic. But it's often prescribed in combination with the others."

"Were you aware that a prescription of Haldol was found with Mr. Beeden's body?" Matt asked. "Also several capsules of lithium?"

"That doesn't surprise me," Vicki said. "The man talked like a fucking zombie with a hard-on."

Julie felt an intensity in the room that hadn't been there moments earlier.

Vicki sat implacably immobile, both hands resting on the table, the smoke of her cigarette tracing haphazardly toward the ceiling in a single undulating plume.

Matt asked the obvious question. "Who is Dr. Wesley Kovacs?"

Vicki started to answer but stopped when the recorder made a soft click. While Matt turned the cassette over, she pulled out a Montclair.

"Dr. Kovacs was a research psychiatrist at the medical center years ago when I was an assistant there. I worked for him."

"Medical center as in CUMC?" Ramani asked.

Vicki gave a curt nod. "He was interested in cryogenics."

Matt looked at Julie. "Cryo . . . ?"

Julie explained. "Cryogenics, also known as cryonics. It's the study of tissue and its reactions to extremely low temperatures. Essentially the science refers to freezing subjects for future revival."

Both detectives exchanged glances, clearly lost.

Vicki attempted to clarify herself. "Dr. Kovacs thought cryogenics might lead to improved methods of treating mental illness. He even incorporated it in his practice, a company he calls the Phoenix Life Extension Foundation. His office is on Pacific in Huntington Park."

Matt stopped his note-taking. "Are you indicating Dr. Kovacs's practice involved this . . . freezing procedure?"

Vicki continued as if the question hadn't been asked. "Dr. Kovacs would conduct his research with small animals, freezing them for certain lengths of time and then reviving them from their period of suspension, as he used to call it. Many would die; but a few survived. The more cryonic trials he attempted, the greater the number of survivors. The doctor actually became quite adept at this process."

Matt glanced at Julie in disbelief.

She ignored him, concentrating on Vicki. Her patient's demeanor had become less hostile and more evasive. Julie wondered if the interview's direction had suddenly entered a realm of discussion Vicki felt less inclined to delve into.

Matt narrowed the focus. "Ms. Zampisi, is it your contention then that Dr. Kovacs instructed his patient, Mr. Beeden, to . . ." he checked his notes, "scare you into leaving California?"

"Yes."

"Have you formulated an opinion why a doctor might resort to such drastic tactics?"

Julie noticed a trace of cynicism creep into Matt's tone. She hoped her patient didn't.

Vicki looked troubled.

Ramani pressed. "Ms. Zampisi, why did Dr. Kovacs wish you out of California?"

"I don't . . ." Vicki started and stopped.

Watching her patient fidget nervously, Julie felt inclined to confront her patient's reluctance to answer, but this wasn't her interview and she felt uncomfortable intervening. She sat silently as did both detectives.

When Vicki spoke, it was an inaudible mumble.

Matt leaned closer. "Do you understand the question, Ms. Zampisi?"

Closing both eyes, Vicki nodded. "Because of . . . an experiment."

"I'm not following you," Matt said.

Vicki's stare locked onto the detective. "Dr. Kovacs wanted me out of California because of what I know about an experiment he conducted years ago."

"What type of experiment?"

The detectives waited while she lit up another Montclair. After two puffs, Vicki continued. "There was an individual at the clinic who participated in Kovacs's research. His name was Ben Simmons."

Julie shared a look with Matt.

Vicki didn't miss it, but went on anyway. "During the periods that Kovacs wasn't studying Ben, he would occasionally use him to frighten the other patients. Many of Dr. Kovacs's patients had been mentally ill for so long and gone so many months and sometimes years without proper treatment, that they could be very difficult to control. Even violent. At least initially anyway, before their medicines took effect. So the threat of Ben's presence was used to help maintain order in the clinic. By instilling fear. This was ludicrous because Ben was more gentle than a puppy dog. But it worked. You see, Ben was incredibly strong, and scary if he became riled. He weighed over two hundred fifty pounds. The meanest, craziest schizophrenics wouldn't touch him. They were all afraid. Then one day, Ben was gone. Dead. And the next time I saw his body, it was . . ." Her voice broke briefly.

Vicki shifted awkwardly in her chair.

Julie realized her patient appeared nervous now, some of her former unease returning. Julie was hearing some of this for the first time. But it was Matt's next question that really captured her attention.

"Ms. Zampisi, how did Ben fit into Dr. Kovacs's research?"

Vicki's expression turned to ice. "Dr. Wesley Kovacs froze Ben almost twenty years ago."

"Jesus," Julie mumbled.

Ramani spent several seconds staring at his watch while Matt showed no visible reaction.

"Do you have any evidence corroborating your statement?" he asked.

"Not yet," Vicki said—almost too quickly, Julie thought.

"When you say freeze," Matt said, "you really mean Dr. Kovacs's cryo experimentation?"

"Yes," Vicki said. "But I couldn't tell you how it was done. Kovacs was very secretive about his work."

"But it was because of this Simmons experiment that Kovacs

wants you out of the picture, now that you've returned. Is that an accurate assessment?"

"My knowledge of the experiment, yes. Public disclosure would hurt him both financially and professionally," Vicki said.

"Even though this happened close to two decades ago?"

"Yes."

"Twenty years is a long time."

"Yes."

Matt pondered her words with a single "um" while rubbing the linear ridge of scar tissue over his eye. "Why would Kovacs feel threatened by your knowledge of Mr. Simmons, a deceased patient from the distant past?" he asked.

She stared fixedly at the ashtray.

"Ms. Zampisi."

Ramani scratched at his elbow. Julie thought both detectives appeared impatient.

"Because," Vicki began, "Dr. Kovacs is a paranoid individual and sometimes paranoid people do irrational things."

"That's your hypothesis, then, simple paranoia," Matt said.

"Like you said, we're talking twenty years. What else could it be?" She ground out her cigarette and produced another one.

Matt gave her a moment to embellish on her statement while she lit up. When she refused to meet his eyes, he asked, "How did Mr. Simmons die?"

"An accident. He choked during a therapy session."

"Then he was refrigerated," Ramani said.

"Frozen."

The short detective grunted.

Matt scribbled several words before moving on. "What about Mr. Beeden's attempted rape? Can you give us any proof?" he asked.

"Besides a busted passenger-door lock?" Vicki indicated "no" with a puff of gray smoke. "He wore gloves."

"What kind?" Ramani asked.

"Latex."

Matt flipped back a page of his legal pad. "Ms. Zampisi, I'd like to return to the assault scene a moment. You indicated Mr. Beeden chased you under the Fourth Street bridge. Did you see anything unusual?"

Vicki started to shake her head but stopped. "I think I saw someone in the shadows. I remember wondering how Beeden could catch up so quickly."

"But it wasn't him."

"I can't be sure. I don't think so."

Matt glanced Julie's way briefly before his next question. "What about smell? Did you notice anything unusual?"

Julie quietly cheered. So he hadn't forgotten.

Vicki didn't answer immediately. "There was a horrible smell in the air just before Beeden vanished."

"Similar to the odor in the Shilden Hotel?"

Vicki frowned. "Possibly."

"Possibly?" Ramani prodded.

"One dead dog smells like any other, detective."

Julie sensed Vicki was on the verge of saying more, but she simply tended to her cigarette.

Ramani tapped the glass face of his wristwatch and got a reciprocal nod from his partner.

"How are your dreams?" Matt asked, setting his pen down.

Vicki shrugged. "With Dr. Charmaine's assistance, I'll get them under control." She reached for her purse.

"One more question, Ms. Zampisi," Matt said, watching her rise from her chair. "Any ideas regarding the sewer killings?"

Vicki managed to hold his gaze. "No, detective."

Twenty-nine

Matt waited until Ramani had escorted Vicki from the room before addressing Julie. "Your patient just accused her former employer of freezing another human being. Strange lady. Is she crazy?"

"No, I don't believe so. She told me Ben had died in a freak accident in the early eighties. She didn't mention anything about his body being preserved through cryonics, though. Frankly, I'm shocked."

Matt grunted and shut his legal pad.

Julie saw the consternation etched in the lines of his face. "I hope you don't think the interview was a waste of taxpayers' money."

"Definitely not," Matt said. "If what Ms. Zampisi stated is true regarding the Beeden attempted rape, then the Fourth Street bridge becomes an additional scene to check out. The location's consistent, at least in proximity, to the sewer well where he and the Humphries girl were removed. Also, her description of the odor at the Shilden Hotel draws a possible link to the smell under the bridge just before Beeden vanished."

"But you still don't believe her."

"I'll review the tape later," Matt said. "What's your read?"

"Vicki's a troubled woman besieged by nightmares that I feel are most definitely related to past experiences. It's even possible the ghastliness of the Sewer Stalker crimes is exacerbating her condition. I'll talk with her some more."

"But do you believe her?"

"She's my patient. It's my impression that what Vicki said today, she believes to be the truth."

Matt's tone lightened. "You sound like a defense attorney copping an insanity plea."

Julie remained serious. "Vicki's not insane."

"Let's hope not," he said, escorting her to the door. "Apprehending an insane killer's taxing enough without a lunatic witness assisting our side."

The old Matt had returned. "You're being too hard on her," she said.

His fingers touched the curve of her back. "Every homicide investigation requires making the right calls."

"And what's your call on Vicki?"

Matt frowned. "On the same par as the entire case. I don't know a goddamn thing."

Julie reached for his arm, feeling the hardness of the flesh beneath his sleeve. "You know Mr. Beeden's treating doctor now."

"Yeah," Matt said. "I got a name." He was quiet for a moment. "So how are you doing?"

"Fine," she said, acutely aware the investigation had just shifted to a more personal level. She allowed his hand to drift down over hers. "No more dreams."

"Talking helped."

"I think so." Julie felt as if someone had turned up the thermostat. The room was warmer, or maybe it was just her.

"Listen, about the other night—" Matt started.

Julie tensed, dropping her fingers away from his. "What about the other night?"

"Relax, I was just thinking," Matt said. "Maybe after this case is behind us and we both have some more time . . . ?" He gave her an innocent shrug.

Julie contemplated what remained unsaid. "We'll see," she told him, before opening the door.

Julie caught up with Vicki just as she was pulling her van away from the parking lot guardhouse. Vicki stopped and rolled down her window.

"I want you to know, I think you conducted yourself well in there. It wasn't an easy situation to be placed in," Julie said.

Vicki shrugged. "Thanks. We tried."

Julie saw a defeated look in Vicki's eyes. "Listen, the hospital sleep lab has a software program that I use in my dream research. It's proved useful in some of my more difficult cases."

Vicki stared ahead.

Julie wasn't even sure she was hearing. "Vicki, I think I can help you. I'd like to admit you into one of my sleep trials. Would you be willing to undergo a more in-depth evaluation?"

"What would it involve? I mean it sounds complicated and I'm not even sure I'd be a good patient."

"You'd get a free night's sleep in CUMC's sleep laboratory."

The tiny wrinkles at the corners of Vicki's eyes slackened. "Sure, why not? What's there to lose?"

"Great. I'll call you and let you know the details." Julie could see something else was still bothering her. She waited.

"We still haven't discussed the fees for all this. You're aware I don't have any insurance."

"Don't worry about my fees. I'm on salary at the medical center."

"Can't beat that price," Vicki said. She waved good-bye and pulled away.

• •

The clerk removed the bottle of cheap Martini & Rossi pink Chablis from the store shelf. Vicki dusted the cap. It was a 1990 blend. Inexpensive, not much more than a Thunderbird or Night Train, but without the stigma.

With the bottle three-quarters empty before dinnertime, Vicki was still debating the merits of the interview. On one point she did agree with Dr. Charmaine. She had conducted herself well under the circumstances. Though she hadn't been entirely forthright, she hadn't lied either. Yet how would the detectives have responded to all the facts? The interview would've ended on the spot and she would've been whisked away in a strait-jacket. Especially if they ever found out about Kovacs's private tapes. Ah well, withholding the truth was never as bad as just twisting it a little.

One part of her doubted anything she'd revealed would assist in the investigation. Kovacs would simply acknowledge treating Case Beeden and that would be the end of it. A smaller, darker part, though, kept returning to the gloomy interior of the Shilden Hotel room with its stained mattress, the frigid confines of the foundation storage unit, and the dampness under the Fourth Street bridge. However, no matter how her inebriated mind juggled the possibilities, any conceivable connection remained blurred and unfocused.

Maybe she was still crazy, as the attitudes of the detectives had tacitly conveyed.

Why else am I seeing a goddamn psychiatrist? And now Dr. Charmaine wants to put me in her dream laboratory. I should feel proud. I must be really fuckin' crazy.

Vicki was long past any earlier jitters when the phone rang. Her physical response was sluggish.

"Hello." Vicki weakly attempted to mask the slur in her voice.

"Is this Ms. Zampisi?" a man asked.

Vicki waited a moment, before speaking. She'd heard that gravelly voice somewhere.

"Who's asking?" She was feeling more sober.

"Ms. Zampisi, this is Johnny Devlin. I'm the gardener out at Evergreen."

The overall man. She suddenly felt stone sober. "Yes?"

"Ms. Zampisi, I overheard you discussing a client with Mrs. Pischenko. I believe the name you used was Ben Simmons."

Vicki was silent.

"Ms. Zampisi, you still there?"

"How'd you get my number?"

"Information, Ms. Zampisi. Can we talk?"

Vicki's mind was racing in circles. Why'd she been drinking, dammit? She needed a stelazine. She couldn't think straight. What did this Devlin character want? And when was she at Evergreen, was it only yesterday? Or the day before?

"Ms. Zampisi?"

"What do you know about Ben?" Vicki asked, a little too quickly, a little too interested.

"I'd rather not do this over the phone. Let's just say the situation with Mr. Simmons is somewhat awkward at present."

"Okay. Where?" Vicki wondered if Johnny Devlin was even his real name.

"Where do you live?" the gardener asked.

What, you think I'm stupid? "I don't feel comfortable meeting at my place, Mr. Devlin."

"I understand." He paused.

Vicki had the strangest impression he was talking to someone else. She could almost picture him with his hand over the receiver.

After several seconds, he was back on the line. "Can I call you later? We got a funeral this evening and the flowers just arrived."

"I'll be here."

"Good-bye." He was gone.

Vicki pushed aside her Martini & Rossi. But only long enough to find her purse and the pamphlet she'd picked up at the mortuary.

She dialed the funeral home.

"Evergreen Manor." It sounded like the receptionist she'd met.

"Yes, I'd like to speak with Mr. Devlin, please," Vicki said.

There was a moment's hesitation on the other end. "Mr. Devlin's unavailable. How may I assist you?"

"But Mr. Devlin does work there." It was more a question.

"Yes, but like I said—"

"Thank you."

Vicki replaced the receiver. She would wait for Johnny Devlin's call.

The mortuary served Holmby Hills and Rodeo Drive clients. The rich were buried here, along with their sons and daughters. In some cases the personal, favorite pets of the rich were buried here. With few exceptions, the mortuary provided fast, efficient, costly, and quite private services.

The landscaping engineers, as the gardeners at Evergreen Manor preferred to be addressed, were responsible for maintaining the twenty-plus acres of vibrant green lawns in mint condition. This was a virtual dictum. As Mr. Forester prided himself on phrasing it, "Though what is under the ground turns brown and rots, the ground above must at all times be alive." Always. There were no exceptions. When it rained, water. During the dry Santa Anas, water more.

Evergreen employed five full-time landscape engineers. The head engineer was Johnny Devlin. He sat in his air-conditioned office adjacent to a building equivalent in size to a three-car garage. Inside the structure were the mowers, the hedge trimmers, weed eaters (even grave sites grow weeds, especially fresh grave sites), ant killers, and a hundred other plant and grass fertilizers, herbicides, insecticides, and horticultural vitamins.

The four other landscape engineers were, in the parlance of landscaping, out in the field. But Devlin wasn't sitting alone.

Christian Eisler looked out of place in his dress slacks, shirt, and clean white hands. He was adept at handling Erlenmeyer flasks, not pushing lawn mowers.

"When are you going to call her back?" There was a sense of urgency in Eisler's voice which wasn't missed by Devlin.

"I'll call her. I do it too soon, she gets suspicious."

"She's already suspicious. She showed up here didn't she?"

The gardener held up one callused hand. "Hey, don't give me that look. I never seen the broad before."

Eisler nervously rubbed his chin. "Let her pick the spot."

"Whatever you say." Devlin never liked the nerdy types and Eisler was no exception. But money erased many dislikes a man might have.

"You never made contact with the Mexican drivers?" Eisler was fidgeting with a small grass clipper.

"Careful, just sharpened them blades," Devlin feigned concern. He didn't really give a shit if Eisler cut his fucking fingers off. Just don't bleed on the grass. "Nah, told you, they be miles south of Tijuana somewhere. You wanted someone out of this area, hell, them *mojadas* didn't even speak *inglés*. But I'll keep trying."

"Has Kovacs called back?"

"Twice."

"You speak to him?"

"Your instructions stated otherwise."

"Don't tell him a goddamn thing."

"Relax before you blow a fuse," Devlin said while using the blade of his pocketknife to chip some dirt from under a nail.

Eisler set the clippers on a bench. "Why would he do this without my involvement? The first human cryonics experiment is worthy of the Nobel prize. I told him the body should be preserved. I even pleaded with him."

"Fuck Kovacs. Can't preserve a body if you can't find it." Devlin tossed Eisler a sick grin. "You sure he was dead?"

"Hell yes he was dead. Why would Kovacs lie? You can't bury someone alive. God, man, that'd be murder."

Devlin snapped shut the knife. "Yep, if he wasn't dead."

"I swear he was dead."

"Okay, he was dead."

Eisler reached for the door. "Just find the drivers. If they took the body to Mexico, I want it returned. It belongs to the foundation. And as soon as you find out where this Zampisi woman wants to meet, page me."

"Yes, sir."

Thirty

Matt waited at the podium while the ten officers settled in their seats, then laid out the mission in detail. Five specific segments of L.A.'s underground sewer would be meticulously searched. This would entail, in some instances, crawling through pipes three feet in diameter with six inches of water and sludge around the knees and hands. The search would include the CUMC basement, where the nurse had last been seen.

The police volunteers had all been chosen because of their size. Each man was five foot eight or less and none weighed more than one hundred and fifty-five pounds, though all had scored highly in the physical fitness phase of their evaluations.

Behind Matt, a transparent overlay of the City of Los Angeles Wastewater System hung from a metal stand, marked conspicuously with five numbered plastic dots, two bluc and three red. The red represented female and the blue, male. Dots one through four fell within an area of ten city blocks or about four square miles. Dot number five, a blue one, lay south of dots three and four by almost two miles. But they all had several things in common in addition to the fact that they were round and plastic. Each corresponded exactly to some segment of L.A.'s sewer system.

Dot number one was Irene Inez. It sat just off the intersection of Cincinnati and Soto in an alley without a name.

Dot number two, Brenda Nixon, marked Fourth and Chicago.

Dots three and four, a.k.a. Humphries and Beeden, were clumped in a bi-dot pattern near the L.A. River basin on Willow. And dot number five, the unfortunate homeboys who had literally been broken like wishbones, lay near Santa Fe and Sacramento, slightly west and six blocks south of the East L.A. Interceptor Sewer. Matt had already put out an APB for Ignacio Chavez. It wasn't coincidence that the gangbanger's cousin and two friends were dead.

Five dots. Six corpses. And over ten miles of city sewer lines.

Matt reviewed the numbering system for the city's sewers as described to him by Craig Lichstein, the wastewater division's chief engineer.

"The sewer vaults are all delineated by eight digits. The first three correspond to a particular map page of the wastewater division's procedural manual." He held up the thick blue binder. "We don't need anyone getting lost."

There were a few chuckles.

"The second set of digits," he went on, "denote the quadrant of that map, and the third set, the specific manhole cover for providing access to that vault. Comments? Questions?"

There were none.

Again he informed the men, "We're simply looking for physical evidence. You hear, find, see, or smell," a few more nervous chuckles, "anything, you radio."

Besides the usual yellow sanitation rain uniforms, rubber boots, and gloves, each man would be equipped with a head light (thereby freeing their hands), a wireless radio, and an air-purifying respirator. Of course, they'd carry their weapons.

"All clear?" Matt asked.

They nodded.

Matt glanced at Ramani. "Anything I left out?"

"You mention the rats and snakes?"

"Fuck you," someone grumbled.

Matt checked his notes. They'd begin in the order of the victims. "We'll start at Louis. Jenkins and Purcell, you're on."

He folded the sheet of paper and downed his coffee. It was cold.

Assuming Irene Inez was carried or dragged underground from Louis Street to the service alley off Cincinnati five blocks away, her torturous trip could've followed but one route. Only one sewer conduit in the immediate vicinity was accessible for human transportation, accessible being a relative term.

Matt leaned against the hood of his Monte Carlo. The map and printouts sat on the front seat, but he'd stared at the Public Works drawing so long, they were practically imprinted in his brain. He used the brief interlude to check past developments. The previous evening, as a result of the Zampisi interview, he'd obtained the address of the Phoenix Foundation and driven out to the Huntington Park location. The building appeared vacated and it was only a fortuitous coincidence that he'd met up with a white Lexus pulling into the lot.

The driver, identifying himself as an associate director, confirmed that Mitchell Beeden had been a patient of Dr. Wesley Kovacs and both he and the good doctor, who happened to be unavailable, were saddened by their personal loss. Nothing else of importance had been revealed.

Matt had left his card and departed, dubious that anything Beeden's physician said would have any significant impact on the Stalker case. Regardless, he'd make a point to have himself or Ramani follow up.

Regarding Julie's comments about the homeless man she'd seen behind the Shilden Hotel, so far his men had been unable to locate the transient. That was not unexpected. L.A.'s homeless became invisible as soon as the police began asking questions.

His radio mike crackled and he picked it up.

"They're off." It was Ramani.

"Who's down?" Matt asked.

"Jenkins. Purcell's point."

"Ten-four."

Matt was out on a limb on this operation because his assumption that all the victims had been transported underground was a big one. Many details did support the hypothesis, the most significant of which was that three of the victims were actually *found* in a sewer pipe and the other two ended up close to a sewer vault entrance. Of course, the biggest assumption of all was that all the crimes were committed by a single entity, although Matt found it difficult imagining more than one crazy fuck in this city insane enough to drag a body through shit and piss and whatever else Dorfman had isolated in the black sludge.

Unfortunately only two of the cases had a finite beginning and a finite end. These were the Inez and Nixon murders. The Inez crime, initiated at her car on Louis and concluded somewhere in the alley off Cincinnati. Brenda Nixon, assaulted in the CUMC Tunnel and left to die in a Hollenbech Park culvert. For the other three victims, only segments leading to the sights where the corpses were discovered would be searched. No beginning point had been identified. Or ever would be without witnesses.

Matt checked his watch. Fifteen minutes had passed. In another ten, the fire and sanitation crew would arrive and set up at the vault in the alley off Cincinnati where Matt now waited. Vault #012-09-111.

The portable crackled again. Matt picked it up. "Guardian."

"Purcell here. Nothing yet, chief. Jenkins is entering A now. Claims he saw a rat as big as a cat."

"I hope he doesn't plan on shooting the sonofabitch."

Purcell grunted. "Not while I'm in his line of fire. Out."

Matt figured another twenty minutes to complete this first sweep. The going would slow some since Jenkins would be leaving the sixty-three-inch La Cienega line for the forty-eight-inch A segment.

Ramani called next. "Matt." His voice had taken on a more serious tone.

"What's up?"

"Jenkins got something."

Matt found the "down" officer. "Jenkins, it's Guardian. You read?"

"Yessir. Not real clear." The patrolman sounded taut above the static.

"Where are you?"

"In A, about a hundred yards east of the La Cienega cutoff. Should meet up with Purcell in five minutes. Man, it's dark down here."

"You wanna climb out?"

"I'm fine."

"So whaddaya got?"

"Bodies, man, all kinds of fucking carcasses."

Matt almost smashed his head on the car's roof. "What?"

"No, I mean rats, a big pile of 'em. Man they're all fucked up. Legs missing, heads, tails. There's some other shit too. Looks like a couple of possums and maybe a raccoon or two. They've been eaten or something, I guess. Man, I'm glad I got this fucking breathing mask."

"Don't puke, it's hell on the respirator," Matt said. He reached for the sewer map highlighting Jenkins's route.

"Don't touch any shit," Matt heard Ramani warn as he studied the grid.

The Sewer A segment was constructed of vitrified clay and reinforced concrete. Along its route, a total of five other sewer lines with diameters of twenty-four-inches and less intersected it at various points. If any one thing had impressed Matt most during his meeting with the Public Works director, it was that somebody, if they were crazy enough, could literally travel anywhere they wanted under the city and never come up for fresh air.

Jenkins's voice crackled. He was talking to Purcell. "I see the light, bro."

"Hallelujah," Purcell said back.

Ten minutes later, fire and sanitation were setting up for Jenkins's exit in the alley. Purcell and Ramani were with them, as was Matt. The entire trip had taken thirty-five minutes, slightly longer than anticipated.

Once out and stripped of their water-resilient suits and respirators, the two officers came over to Purcell's squad car while sanitation closed up the vault.

"You guys look like shit," Matt said. He looked at Jenkins, the shorter, squatter of the two. "Rats, huh?"

Jenkins shrugged. He looked relieved to be up top again. "Piles of 'em. Mostly near intersecting pipes. Eerie, man."

"And they were all dead?" It was Ramani.

"Seemed to be."

"What about you, Purcell?" Matt asked.

"A few. Mostly the furry fucks kept outta my way. Lucky for 'em. I hate goddamn rats."

One man of the two-member fire crew approached Matt. Breland was a member of the HAZ-MAT team. His assignment was to determine there were no excessive levels of toxic fumes or gases prior to any of the patrolmen's descent.

Breland wiped some dark goo from one glove onto his uniform. "If you're set here, detective, we can get on over to CUMC. Or is it going to be the Hollenbech site?"

Matt wasn't sure. He gazed at the manhole cover ten yards down the alley from his Monte Carlo. Officially, it was 012-09-111. To Matt it was where the Inez girl was found.

Breland followed Matt's gaze. "Or we can pop the lid again and have your boys take another look down there. Your call, chief."

Purcell and Jenkins didn't appear real eager. Matt could easily understand why. Someone would have to be insane to keep wanting to go back down. Obviously *someone* was. And Matt meant to find him.

"Give me five minutes," the detective said.

Within three minutes, the manhole cover was reopened and the sanitation crew was surveying the vault from above with two Mag Carbide flashlights.

Matt waited by the ladder.

"You want Jenkins's shit?" Ramani asked, holding the yellow sanitation garb.

"I won't be long."

Matt positioned the respirator and started down with one of the lights. He stepped onto the concrete floor. It was slippery but there was no sludge. Shining the light, he was amazed at how much like a cave it was. Or a tomb. There were two exits, one was directed west back to the La Cienega line and the other serviced areas further east.

Matt's light reflected dully from the moist concrete walls. Nothing looked out of the ordinary. He moved over and shined the light first west and then east along the A segment sewer line. The east branch curved out of view fairly quickly. There was nothing. But the west . . . Matt grimaced. Not ten feet away, he saw what Jenkins had just described—a neat pile of decomposing animals. Matt assumed they were rats, though some of the bodies had been eviscerated and mangled.

Matt found a small pebble and tossed it along the clay conduit. It made a hollow clinking noise, but there was no movement from the pile of rodents. Raising the beam just a little, Matt thought he spied another pile farther down.

"See anything?" It was Ramani again.

Matt abruptly waved him off as if Ramani's voice was going to suddenly shock the dead rodents back to life. He shivered. And it wasn't even cold.

Taking several deep inhalations of purified sewer air, he spent another minute examining the rusty metal attachments where the ladder was secured to the concrete wall of the vault. They appeared safe enough. Careful to disturb the ladder's integrity as little as possible, Matt reemerged into the alley.

"How'd it go?" Ramani took the respirator.

"Like a walk in the park."

Jenkins brought over a clear jug of Evian water.

Matt chugged a good third of it. It was amazing how a tense, alien situation could dry a person out.

"You see the rats?" the cop asked.

"You weren't lying." Matt found one of the sanitation crew replacing the iron lid to the vault entrance. "That normal, all those dead rodents?"

The sanitation man gave one last kick and the cover slammed into place. "It happens sometimes, especially after some heavy rain. A bunch of the critters drown then get washed into piles. The ones that survive get hungry and start feeding. No different than south central L.A. after a quake or a bad jury verdict. Survival of the fittest. Also some bozo buys some rat poison, bags his neighbor's cat, then decides to toss the corpse and the poison. Where's it go? The sewer. Rain washes it down and presto, a bunch of dead rats."

Matt listened. For some reason, which he had trouble placing a finger on, these rats didn't look like they'd been poisoned. Some carcasses weren't even complete, just pieces.

The crew man spit a chaw of tobacco. "Then, again, could've been a virus. They get viruses just like humans. Or a bacteria. Who knows? Anything."

That sounded plausible too.

"Hey, we gonna investigate a shitload of dead rats or get to the Nixon scene?" Ramani fingered his watch.

"Jenkins and Purcell," Matt said, "you guys are officially off the Inez case. Thanks."

"Don't forget to wash your hands," Ramani said.

• •

The Hollenbech Park culvert yielded no dramatic new pieces of evidence. Fossa and Reeves were out of daylight less than twenty minutes and did not find any dead rats.

The same resulted at the Willow Street site, where Humphries and Beeden had been discovered.

The two patrolmen working with Ramani in the CUMC basement search considered themselves fortunate. After receiving permission from the hospital administrator, they removed the iron grille in the generator access room. It took less effort than anticipated because the bolts and nuts were rusted. They knocked two of the bolts loose with a screwdriver.

Adams and Kowser descended into the Tunnel's vault complete with miner's lights. The nine-foot-high concrete conduit which at one time served as the medical center's wastewater disposal system ended after only thirty feet at a set of vertical bars spaced at six-inch intervals. That appeared to leave no visible means of reaching the sewer from the basement, unless an individual was built like a rail. However, upon closer inspection, two of the bars nearest the wall were found to be severely corroded at their cement bases and actually bent out at an angle away from the floor, leaving a clearance of approximately eighteen inches. Conceivably, someone could've squeezed through the opening and gained access to the basement.

The two police officers crawled under the bars and followed the sewer channel back for a quarter mile before returning with nothing more of significance to report. A dog's carcass and the remains of a possum were not considered relevant to the case. The officers terminated their search by dusting the vertical bars as well as the ladder back up into the medical center basement, but detected nothing useful. The few smears they lifted demonstrated very poor ridge detail and could easily have belonged to the last individual to inspect the Tunnel's vault. The search was not considered a total failure, though. At least it offered a possible explanation of how the abducted nurse could've been transported to Hollenbech Park via the sewer.

The fifth and last search was vault 121-12-418, the massive North Outfall Sewer at Seventh and Santa Fe. Whereas only days previously, the 121-inch conduit had yielded the mangled remains of two L.A. gangbangers, today nothing so prodigious or monumental lay inside. Only the presence of more rat carnage seemed noteworthy, though neither detective could make a concrete link between the mangled rodents and a possible killer. Unless, as Matt said disgustingly, "The sick bastard's gotta be eating something."

Ramani caught up with his partner at his car. With Isabelle gone, he didn't feel like eating alone. "Who's on for dinner?"

Matt sat in the Monte Carlo's front seat, staring blankly at the sewer map. "Rats didn't carry off the Nixon girl."

"Nor the Inez girl, the Humphries, or the others. I know."

Matt gripped the wheel. "Where's this guy live?"

"Huh?"

"Where's this sewer suck live?"

"Shit, crazy people can live anywhere."

"No, not anywhere. Not this one," Matt said as he traced one index finger along the blue curved line of the map representing the L.A. River basin. Paralleling this same blue line were the major segments of the city's wastewater system. His finger stopped where the 60, the 10, the Santa Ana, and 101 freeways touched. Hand-penciled in red letters was the single word SHANTYTOWN followed by a question mark.

"Not this one."

Thirty-one

Though the small crucifix barely reached the edges of his palm, this particular evening the tiny religious token offered Ignacio more solace and comfort than any Beretta or thirty-eight caliber ever did. The young gangbanger hadn't looked at it—nor held it—since his mother had sent him to catechism classes with his *primo* Roberto well over a decade ago. Now he couldn't make himself put it down.

Ignacio turned the cross over in his hand, studying the crucifix more closely. It'd been a gift from his godmother and as a child, he'd never appreciated the carving's intricately ornate design. If observed from the front, it was what it appeared to be—the body of Christ, in exquisite detail including even the crown of thorns, nailed to the cross. However, when the wood carving was turned over and held upside down, a finely crafted sculpture of the Virgin de Guadalupe, Mexico's most revered national saint, appeared along the long axis of the cross.

Shivering under his long-sleeve shirt—more from anticipation, and perhaps fear, though he'd never admit this, than cold—Ignacio gently set the crucifix down so that its small weight anchored the piece of paper to his mother's nightstand. Once Soccoro returned from her job as a nighttime janitor and read what her son had written, he knew she'd go to the police. He didn't care. By then he'd be well south of the Mexican border. In his confused and agitated mind, he'd already rationalized he wasn't running, rather simply regrouping. There would be a time for retribution and revenge but tonight wasn't it. He wasn't thinking clearly. Damn, he couldn't even make sense of what he'd observed the other night in the sewer. Part of him wanted to admit the adversary had been . . . he groped for the right word. Inhuman? He shook his head, refusing to accept that choice. What the hell had Arbol and Romy run into, a *chupacabra,* that legendary Mexican half-man-half-beast vampire? No way. He'd never believed in that Mexican bullshit before and he wasn't going to begin now. No, what they'd come against was simply one tough motherfucker—in fact, the toughest he'd ever had to fight. There was no way around it. This dude was huge and incredibly strong.

Still somewhat awed, Ignacio sat back on his mother's quilt. He never dreamed he'd see the day that one individual would be able to take out both Arbol and Romy. Simultaneously. And not just take them out—murder them. Brutally.

He could sense his blood beginning to boil again. He was seething.

"Calmate, calmate," he muttered. Relax. He'd achieve his revenge for both his *prima* as well as his homeboys. But first he wanted to pay homage to Roberto way down south. He owed his cousin that much, especially after he'd failed so miserably in keeping his promise to watch his sister, Irene. And he'd already convinced himself this trip was his only option.

Originally, after regaining consciousness in the sewer, and unable to find either his flashlight or his gun, Ignacio had scrabbled in the dark and sludge to locate his two best friends. Failing that, he'd crawled out, still with a shred of hope his *batos* had survived the carnage. He'd searched all their favorite hangouts—the barrios, clubs, *chiche* bars—to no avail. Then after the news broke that Arbol and Romy had become the Sewer Stalker's most recent victims, Ignacio realized he'd be called in for questioning, in all likelihood as the prime suspect. Fuck the cops—the racist, prejudiced bastards. He'd debated, only briefly, calling that pretty psychiatrist, the one he'd turned over Irene's gun to, but nixed that idea too. She was nice, but nice wouldn't help him now.

After carefully replacing the canvas envelope behind the nightstand, Ignacio grabbed his pack and despondently walked across the threadbare rug toward the door. In less than thirty minutes, he'd meet his ride. He'd hated having to borrow out of his mother's emergency cash fund, but he desperately needed the money. She'd understand. Besides, he'd pay her back later.

He cast one last look at the crucifix and mouthed a silent prayer. Then, walking out, he locked the door behind him, telling himself again he wasn't running.

The occupants, mostly drunks, derelicts, and down-and-outers called it Shantytown. CalTrans and some city officials referred to it privately as the Shithole. But everybody who lived there called it home.

The four-level was where the 60, the 10, the Santa Ana, and 101 freeways converged to form a virtual spaghetti bowl of concrete and exhaust fumes.

It was here, under the concrete and along the weeds and tall grass of the dusty Los Angeles riverbed where Shantytown first bloomed ten years before. Since its birth, the population had steadily increased every year so that the current residents, give or take the few who got lost, got found, or just plain gave up, numbered more than a hundred. The primitive place had no running water, no electricity, no bathrooms. It had only the L.A. River to absorb the human excrement.

For several years the city had tried to get the place bulldozed and cleaned up, but with homeless advocates comprising ten percent of the makeshift town's population and a few even claiming to be lawyers, it was no easy task. So on this very early Friday morning, a couple of hours before the sky lightened in the east, little commotion disturbed the plywood shacks and nylon tents that cluttered the area under the 10 and 60 overpasses.

Frazier Stoops ambled along the river bottom, kicking at a feral cat, which hissed and darted into the shadows. With a half pint of Night Train in his hand and the rest in his bloodstream, the ex-con mumbled incoherently to himself. For the past two months Stoops had been serving time in the Parker Center jail for urinating on a woman at a bus stop. Last night he'd been released and he had headed home.

Upon his arrival several residents had warned him the cops had been out, asking about any strange newcomers to the homeless encampment. Stoops had to chuckle at the news. Where were the cops from, Mars? Hell, everybody that lived here was strange.

The ex-con pressed onward. He still had just enough brain cells functioning to know his particular place was not far ahead. Fuck the goddamn cat. This was his home too.

While the other occupants preferred cardboard boxes and shacks, Stoops preferred a six-foot concrete culvert under Interstate 10 that served as a flood control for the Los Angeles River basin. The pipe usually remained dry and its thick walls sheltered him from the racket of auto traffic overhead. He never ventured back in it too far, though, so he had no idea it led to a connector sewer that eventually emptied underground into the massive North Outfall Sewer a quarter-mile west.

"I'm gonna knock your dick in the fuckin' dirt," Stoops grunted to no one as he paused in the predawn dark to relieve himself. The emptying of his bladder made him groan. He peered ahead.

Somewhere in the cemented slope of the riverbed lay the culvert. He squinted and took another swig. "I'm gonna knock . . ."

He saw it—its black entrance beckoned him. He moved forward. An eighteen-wheeler rumbled by overhead, its vibration reaching all the way to his callused and stinking feet.

"Eat shit," he cursed.

"Shut the fuck up," a hoarse voice shot from a nearby tent.

At six-two and close to two-thirty, Stoops was tempted to walk over and rip the tent up by its stakes. But this was Shantytown. He'd let it pass. He was home. He ambled over in front of the culvert.

He cursed under his breath. A whiff of fetid stench suddenly filled his nostrils. He squatted down and peered inside. He lit a match. In the flickering flame, he saw something that irritated him more than the smell. Someone was sleeping in his place. Some stinking dick. A tattered blanket was wrapped around him.

The match blew out. Stoops cursed again and stepped inside. He'd share the culvert tonight but tomorrow the newcomer would have to find another place to lie. As Stoops walked along the concrete, he stumbled on something. He reached down and immediately pulled back his hand. It was furry, warm, moist, and soft.

Stoops found another match and struck it, only to gasp in revulsion. He stumbled back from the pile of decomposing rodents.

"What the hell," he cursed. Just as the match went out, he heard a noise.

SLSHLSH.

Fumbling for another match, he struck it and reeled back in shock. A dark form shuffled toward him.

"Git away," Stoops muttered as he stumbled back outside.

This big, bad, stinking dude could keep the goddamn culvert.

Still chagrined from the relative failure of the previous days' sewer searches to turn up anything of evidentiary value, Matt skipped breakfast and a morning workout and drove by the foundation headquarters again, hoping to catch Dr. Kovacs this time.

Pulling into the lot, he saw two men loading two large silver canisters onto a U-Haul. Neither looked his way as he parked out front, three spaces down from a black Mercedes.

The entrance doors were locked and the glass tinted, making it difficult to see any details inside. A small video camera was mounted several feet above the door frame.

Matt pressed the doorbell but heard no response. He was on the verge of knocking when a figure appeared on the other side of the glass.

The lock disengaged and one door swung open.

"Yes?" a man said.

He was large with a puffy face of smooth skin and white hair cut close on the side and longer on top. He wore a white smock over a sports shirt and slacks. His shoes looked freshly polished and on his hand Matt saw two large gold rings.

Matt identified himself and showed his badge.

"You're here regarding the Beeden affair, I presume," the man said. "I'm Dr. Wes Kovacs." He didn't offer to shake hands.

"Do you have a few moments, Doctor?" Matt asked.

"If it won't take long. I'm in the process of moving and we're on a strict deadline."

"I'll make it as brief as possible."

Kovacs glanced at his watch once, then motioned Matt inside.

"We can talk in my office," he said.

Kovacs led through the reception area and down a corridor stacked with small cardboard moving boxes. Before entering the first office, Matt saw two other doors at the end of the hall, one of which had NO ADMITTANCE stenciled on it.

"Please, make yourself comfortable." Kovacs pointed to a chair. "I'd offer you a drink but I'm afraid you'd refuse my hospitality."

"Some other time perhaps," Matt said. "On the clock."

"I suspected as much."

Matt watched Kovacs move to an oak credenza laden with texts and open a small compartment from which he removed a decanter and one glass. He filled it halfway.

"Nineteen-ninety chardonnay," he said, returning to his desk. "Researchers say a glass a day's supposed to prevent atherosclerotic buildup in the blood vessels. I'm not sure about the theory but the wine sure as hell tastes good."

He didn't smile when he said this and Matt waited until he was seated behind his desk before speaking.

"Dr. Kovacs, a prescription with your name was found with the deceased," Matt began, skirting the truth. For the moment, he preferred not to bring up Vicki Zampisi. "How long had you treated Mr. Beeden?"

Kovacs rubbed one finger across his temple. "Six years. And as my associate expressed to you last evening, the entire foundation is feeling his loss. Mitchell was an exemplary individual."

"What exactly was Mr. Beeden's condition?"

"If you're referring to his diagnosis, it was manic depression with an underlying paranoid psychosis. However, at the time of his disappearance his condition was stable."

"Was Mr. Beeden also employed here at the foundation?"

"Strange that you should ask that, but yes, I occasionally supply employment for some of my long-term patients. Especially those that would find it difficult to hold down a permanent position on the outside."

"And Mr. Beeden fit into this category?"

Kovacs took a long sip and then set the glass down. "When Mitchell was first referred to me, he was homeless, suffering from tuberculosis, and experiencing delusions that his family in Louisiana wanted him dead. He even claimed they'd hired a hit man from the New Orleans Saints. I promptly placed him on the appropriate medicines, in this case Haldol and lithium, and once his condition was controlled, kept him on here at the foundation because frankly he had no place else to go. It seems the current attitude toward mental health problems is commensurate to their feelings toward wayward alligators. The only good one is a dead one."

Matt opened a notepad but didn't write. "When did you last speak to the deceased?"

Kovacs glanced at the ceiling momentarily. "That would be around last Thursday. I'm only guessing, of course. I knew it was several days before he was found."

"And how would you describe his demeanor at the time?"

"Pleasant. Oriented. I had him assisting the movers with some of the heavier laboratory equipment."

"Dr. Kovacs, would you consider Mr. Beeden a potentially violent individual?"

At the word "violent," Matt noted a subtle change in Kovacs's expression. He appeared more on guard.

Kovacs set down his wine, uncrossed his legs, and leaned forward. "That would depend of course on the therapeutic levels of his medicine. A paranoid psychotic with subtherapeutic levels should always be considered potentially violent, 'potentially' being the key word. However, many of these individuals will not exhibit violent behavior unless confronted with stressful or awkward situations." He paused.

Matt pressed. "So for two days you had no idea of your patient's whereabouts?"

"Not specifically, no. Mr. Beeden's a free man. My patients are not kept on a leash."

Matt decided to switch gears. "Doctor, Mr. Beeden was extracted in separate pieces from a sixteen-inch pipe down by the L.A. River channel. Did he tell you he was meeting anybody on the night he vanished?"

"No."

"Did you ask Mr. Beeden to meet anybody?"

Kovacs's eyes narrowed, making his puffy lids look like putty. "I'm beginning to understand your line of questioning now. It seems we have a mutual acquaintance."

Matt's expression remained unchanged. His silence forced Kovacs to speak first.

"In deference to both our busy schedules, let's cut through the preliminary crap. To begin with, Vicki Zampisi is a depressed, demented woman who at one time was employed at the foundation. This was years ago. I hired her more out of pity than anything else. She had no resume, no experience, just to look at her you weren't sure whether to laugh or cry. I don't know what she related to you, but the day after Mitchell disappeared she came here to my office accusing my patient, a man she's never met, of trying to rape her. The charges are totally without merit and if she persists in these ludicrous statements, I'll be forced to hire an attorney, which of course I'm not inclined to do. Lawsuits take time, a commodity I have little of."

"So Ms. Zampisi came here, to your laboratory?"

"Not laboratory, detective, office."

"What was the nature of her visit?"

"Besides her groundless babble, she wanted to discuss her nightmares. I presume that's why she's back in Los Angeles. She heard about the foundation's move and felt I might be able to help her."

"With her nightmares?"

"Yes." Kovacs reached for his wine.

"Have you treated her for nightmares in the past?"

Kovacs fixed Matt with a hard stare. "No."

He started to drink but halted at Matt's next question.

"Doctor, are you familiar with the name Ben Simmons?"

Kovacs tensed. "What did she tell you?"

"Actually, she was quite vague. She expressed a concern that her knowledge of a past experiment might be related to her abduction."

The physician smirked. "Alleged abduction."

"That's being considered."

"She said nothing else?"

"Is there more?"

"No." Kovacs appeared to relax some. "Detective, our research delves into the cryonic preservation of living tissue for future use."

"As in organ transplants."

"That and whole-body suspensions as well. That, I'm afraid, is the root of Ms. Zampisi's skewed ideations."

"So Ben Simmons was never frozen?"

"Of course not, detective. The knowledge of cryogenics was only in its infancy at the time of Ben's death. However, I admit, we do presently have a number of whole-body clients suspended. A few rather well-known locally. If you'd like to examine the contracts, I'm sure you'll find the signatures and terms valid."

"That won't be necessary, Doctor," Matt said. He watched Kovacs check his watch. "Why did Ms. Zampisi think you could help her with these nightmares?"

"I am a psychiatrist. Unfortunately in Vicki's case, I feel the nightmares are a sign of much deeper problems and because of the time restraints of my research, I would have simply referred her to a colleague."

Matt wanted to return to the primary subject matter of the interview. "Then you have no idea what Mr. Beeden would be doing down by the L.A. River channel."

"No."

"Did he have any enemies?"

"None that I'm aware of."

"Did he ever mention the name Jezebel Humphries?"

"Never heard him."

"Ever see him angry?"

Kovacs offered his attempt at a smile. "We all get angry at times, detective, even the mentally ill."

"One last item. Did Mr. Beeden go by any other name?"

"We called him Case."

Matt nodded, closing his notepad. He handed Kovacs one of his cards. "That should about do it, Doctor. Think of anything else, let us know. I appreciate your time." He stood and walked to the door. Before exiting, though, he turned and asked the one question he thought Kovacs would have asked but didn't.

"Doctor, any theories on who killed your patient?"

"Only one," Kovacs said, rising from behind his desk. "The Sewer Stalker."

Long after the detective departed and the entrance doors to the foundation re-locked, Kovacs remained in his office, unwilling or unable to return to his laboratory. It wasn't like him to suffer cracks in his concentration, yet the detective's last question had done just that. And this was no time to experience a mental softening. The foundation's move was imminent and he could ill afford any loose ends.

He supposed he could've simply told the detective the truth, at least as far as Ben was concerned. But that would've adversely affected the foundation's status in the closely connected scientific community. Initially the experiment had been such a success. Now, an utter failure. From bonanza to bane, all because of a tiny goddamn leak. No, he couldn't risk his reputation. Or his pipeline of investor funding.

Let the police handle the serial killer. The Sewer Stalker had nothing to do with the foundation's research, Kovacs reminded himself. He chided his momentary cerebral lapse. The self-admonishment helped only minimally.

Though he considered the interview a nonevent, Kovacs remained at a loss to explain the sensation of cold fingers crawling up the back of his scalp.

Vicki watched from the steps of the Federal Building as a group of elementary-school children filed through the entrance doors led by two women. From her vantage point above Wilshire Boulevard, she'd seen the group exit an orange school bus. Now, listening to the children's laughter, she found herself envious of their innocent happiness. There had been far too little laughter during her own childhood.

Vicki didn't need to check her watch to know that Devlin was late. Their meeting had been set for 3 P.M. today. She'd arrived at her spot at 2:30 and she'd already been waiting at least an hour. Initially she'd been so anxious about this meeting that she'd forgotten about lunch but now as the wait stretched on into mid-afternoon, her hunger pangs had become more prominent.

There was a cafe just down the street and although Vicki had planned to talk inside the Federal Building lobby, she decided Elenas would be just as safe. It appeared to be doing a brisk business and if this gardener from the mortuary attempted anything foolish, at least there'd be plenty of witnesses.

For a moment she stared up at the sky and let the warm sun caress her face.

"Vicki Zampisi?"

The voice startled her. She jumped as a man paused on the same step but a few feet to her right.

"I'm sorry, I didn't mean to scare you," he said.

"You didn't," Vicki lied. Shading her eyes, she stared at the youngish-looking man who could easily have been a college professor. He was dressed neatly in slacks and sports coat but he seemed fidgety.

"Do I know you?" Vicki asked.

"No. My name's Christian Eisler." His eyes hung on Vicki's face. "I believe you spoke with a Johnny Devlin."

"Yes. And that's who I agreed to meet with here."

For a moment neither said a word. Several seconds passed before the recognition bloomed in Vicki's mind. This was the same man she'd seen on the loading dock of the foundation talking to Case Beeden. She felt a brief twist of rage deep in her chest.

Eisler cleared his throat. "Well, to be perfectly honest, I was the one who asked Mr. Devlin to arrange this, ah, rendezvous."

"Why?" Vicki asked, growing angry again.

"I want to help you."

"How do you know Mr. Devlin?"

"We did some business together. Do you mind if we talk somewhere else?" His voice was strained but he said it with a feigned smile.

"There's a little restaurant just down the block."

When they sat at an outside table, a waiter took Vicki's order for iced tea—she was suddenly no longer hungry—and Eisler's for some obscure brand of water she'd never heard of.

Eisler appeared relieved to wet his lips. "You must be familiar with this area."

"I used to live in Los Angeles. It was a long time ago."

"I see." Eisler paused to drink. "Mr. Devlin mentioned you were inquiring about a Ben Simmons."

"Do you know Ben?"

"You ask that as if you feel Simmons is still alive."

Vicki's gaze sharpened. "*Did* you know Ben?"

"No," Eisler said, quickly adding, "not personally. I never met him."

Vicki stared hard at the younger man. "I was at Ben's side when he choked on his own vomit twenty years ago." She saw the shock in Eisler's eyes. "And you're most certainly aware of my relationship to Dr. Wes Kovacs. But before we go on I'd like to see some identification."

"What?"

"ID. You know, visa, passport, a driver's license will do nicely."

"Why?"

"Because I don't know who the hell you are."

"I told you, my name's—"

"ID." Vicki started to rise.

"Wait." Eisler reached for his wallet.

Vicki noted a new tremor in his hand as he held out his California driver's license. She nodded. "Dr. Christian Eisler. A PhD."

Eisler replaced his wallet. "Yes, I'm a molecular biologist. Actually a molecular cryophysicist. I work directly with Dr. Kovacs as his associate director." Eisler leaned forward just a little. "I want to set the record straight right now, Ms. Zampisi, that I had nothing to do with the actions of Mitchell Beeden."

"Save your statements for the police," she said.

"I already told all I know to a detective." Eisler settled back in his chair. "So what you say is true about actually being present when Mr. Simmons died?"

Vicki nodded. "I also know what happened to Ben after. I stayed on for nearly two years and assisted with the experiment. Should I lay out the details for you?"

"I'm well aware of Dr. Kovacs's early research in cryonics. That initial attempt took monumental nerve. And his recent human preservations have been published in numerous journals. He's quite famous in the cryonics field, you know."

Vicki grinned acerbicly. "A real saint."

"There are those who would agree," Eisler said, missing Vicki's sarcasm. "What I'm having a problem with is trying to determine what it is you're looking for now."

"Why is what I want so important? Did Kovacs send you?"

"No. And frankly, I doubt he'd approve if he did."

Vicki met Eisler's gaze. "Are you afraid of Wes Kovacs?"

Eisler answered with a sip of water. "What do you want?"

"Why do you want to know?"

Eisler set his drink down and watched some passing vehicles. "Ms. Zampisi, in the years I've been associated with the Phoenix Foundation, I've seen it grow from an obscure laboratory with freezers packed with frozen rodents to a potentially multimillion-dollar human research facility. Once we complete our move to Tucson, this potential will be realized. Unfortunately, there was a mishap, a leak, and the first-ever human cryogenics experiment was terminated. It was a failure. And failures in the scientific community, especially one of this magnitude, can pose an insurmountable liability for an upstart research institution when attempting to apply for financial grants, whether they be governmental or private investors. Do you understand what I'm saying?"

Vicki felt her anger lessen. So Eisler didn't know the entire truth either. Kovacs really was a snake, the lying bastard. She held back a tiny grin. "Are you calling Ben an embarrassment?" she asked.

"No, not Ben. But the experiment was and is an embarrassment."

"And you'd like it to just . . . disappear."

"It has, Ms. Zampisi. It's over."

Vicki took a deep breath. "You asked what I wanted."

"I'm listening."

"I'd like to see Ben's body."

So would I, Eisler resisted blurting out. Instead he countered, "That's impossible."

"That's what Kovacs said."

After a pause, Eisler said, "If I allow you to view Ben's grave so you can weep or cry or whatever you feel is necessary for your own mental well-being, will you agree to leave California and let Mr. Simmons rest in peace?"

Vicki didn't hesitate with her answer. "I might live with that."

Vicki had barely unlocked the door to her apartment and was only thinking of her next drink when the phone rang. She expected it to be Eisler about viewing the body. It was Julie.

"Hello, Dr. Charmaine."

Julie came right to the point. "Vicki, I've arranged for you to spend tomorrow night down here at the hospital. You'll use our sleep lab. I hope you don't have any plans."

"None that I can't break. You really think this can help me?"

"Yes, Vicki, I do."

That was enough. Vicki could sense Julie's excitement and it was infectious. Things were finally beginning to happen.

Julie replaced the receiver. On her desk, Vicki Zampisi's chart lay open to the last dictated note. Julie reread the diagnositic impression and almost found herself second-guessing her decision to formally submit Vicki to a dream study this early in her evaluation.

It was not a question of whether Vicki's present condition was linked to events from her past. That much would be obvious to any first-year psychiatry resident. What wasn't so obvious was how significant a role the current media hype surrounding the Sewer Stalker case was playing.

Studies had already demonstrated individuals with underlying psychological disorders tended to suffer relapses when confronted with situations over which they exerted little control. Natural disasters, floods, war, and commercial plane crashes were all examples of these situational-induced exacerbations.

Serial killings were associated with a specific type of situational-induced exacerbation. *Projective identification* occurred when the patient projected her own emotions onto the dead victim, and in turn, allowed the perceived emotions of the victim to be projected back onto the patient, thus acutely intensifying any feelings the patient might be experiencing—fear, for instance.

Julie worried that projective identification could at least in part be to blame for Vicki's worsening nightmares. If that was the case, submitting Vicki to a dream study in the middle of a serial-killing spree could, in theory, make for an explosive situation if Vicki's coping mechanisms became overwhelmed.

Julie closed the chart and set it on top of the DO NOT FILE stack. Despite any lingering doubts, though, she still felt confident she was making the correct therapeutic decision. Vicki had already demonstrated a strong inner constitution and unlike the difficulty associated with attempting to reverse any untoward effects from a pill, if the dream study turned the least bit inauspicious, she would simply wake Vicki.

Julie felt her tensions lessen. What could go wrong with that?

Thirty-two

Across the desk from Matt and Ramani, Dorfman took another bite of the chocolate bar. "How many cases have I worked on for you?" he asked between swallows. The question wasn't directed at either detective in particular.

Ramani shrugged. "I've been on RHD for seven years. Maybe forty."

Dorfman took another bite. "And in all those cases, did I ever hedge on a physical or laboratory finding pertaining to a cause of death? Ever?"

"Luis Filipo," Matt said without batting an eye.

"Shit." Dorfman slapped his free hand down hard on the desk. "Shit, you would resurrect that SOB from the grave."

Luis Filipo had been a homicide Matt got hung with his first year on RHD. It involved a sixty-two-year-old ex-con, heavy into porn, who was found hanging from the ceiling of a urinal stall in a topless nightclub. Dorfman was the coroner and he couldn't decide whether it was a suicide or a homicide. That's because although the victim's hands were free at the time he was discovered by the night janitor, indicating self infliction, faint residues of hemp were discovered embedded in his wrists. This could lead one to surmise that if his wrists were in fact tied, it would be a homicide.

"The case's still open, Dorf. Your record's clean," Matt said.

"Yeah, I completely forgot poor Mr. Filipo. But you know,

technically speaking, I didn't hedge on his cause of death. In fact, it was a pretty straightforward case of death by asphyxiation. Check the death certificate. I just fudged on whether it was a homicide or suicide."

"So?" Ramani said.

"So, have either of you ever known me to hedge on any physical or laboratory finding pertaining to a particular case?" the coroner asked again.

Dorfman took their silence for a no. He reached for the top folder in a three-chart stack. He brushed some chocolate off the manila cover. "I'm hedging on the Inez case," he confessed. "More specifically the hedge refers to that goddamn material isolated from the victim's nails, and not just from Ms. Inez but the others." Dorfman quickly listed the other stalker victims. "For the time being, each of these samples is simply being labeled amorphous necrotic debris of unknown etiology. You'll find this term in each report, though there's a wrinkle or two I'll touch on later."

"Amorphous necrotic debris," Matt repeated.

"Of unknown etiology," Ramani said.

Matt scratched his chin. "Sounds like a hedge, Dorf."

Dorfman shifted his bulk. "Then I'm glad we're clear on this minutia of forensic glossology," the coroner said, setting the Inez chart aside. "Also those small polyurethane fragments I mentioned, the ones isolated from some of the nail samples. Similar material can be found in over a thousand household and industrial products. The trace-evidence lab can give us the precise chemical makeup which might help us nail down a specific trade name. Then we can begin compiling a list of potential manufacturers."

"That doesn't help a whole helluva lot," Ramani griped.

"You haven't heard the wrinkle yet." Dorfman shifted his gaze to Matt. "How'd the sewer search go?"

"We think we know how the Nixon girl got from point A to point B," Matt said.

"That's a start," Dorfman replied, producing another candy bar from a desk drawer. He tore off the wrapper. "Low blood sugar."

"Jesus, Dorf," Ramani said. "Thought you were on a diet."

"Just like you quit smoking." He reached for the other two charts in front of him. "Incredible," he said, eyeing number 1096, and the name, JEZEBEL HUMPHRIES. "In over twenty years of forensic pathology, these two are the absolute worst I've ever seen. Incredible. Goddamn incredible."

"What's so goddamn incredible?" asked Ramani.

"For starters," Dorfman was referring to chart 1097 now, "Mr. Beeden was not a small man. A guestimation of his street height would put him at around five-nine or -ten and his weight at two-thirty, and that's being conservative. Anyway as I was about to say, normally for a man, or woman for that matter, to be wedged into a sixteen-inch-diameter pipe, the body would have to be physically sawed up and dismembered first. You know, to get the parts to fit. But in this case," Dorfman tapped the appropriate file, "he wasn't even hacked up."

"Heaton says he and the girl were removed in pieces," Matt said.

"Correct. But that's only because he'd already been dead seven to ten days, therefore well on the road to the decomp heap. Naturally, when attempting to extricate a necrotizing piece of flesh wedged into a tight space, it's highly probable that a single piece of flesh will end up in several pieces once it's removed. A human body, any body really, tears differently after it's been lying around a while. The difference between tissue disruption in the living state and tissue that's been decaying is like night and day. I emphasize this anatomic variation in response is only evident through the lens of a microscope. I guess what I'm getting at is that both Ms.

Humphries and Mr. Beeden were in all probability very much alive when they were crushed into that connector sewer pipe."

"Ouch," Ramani echoed Matt's thoughts.

"I'm not saying they were conscious—Lord knows I pray they weren't, and I'm not known for my goddamn religious convictions—but I am saying that many of their wounds, lacerations, and havoc in general affecting their vital organ systems occurred as a result of the severe pressure exerted on them during the wedging process. And this damage occurred while their hearts were still beating. This is demonstrated not only by the pattern of the blood in the capillaries immediately adjacent to the wounds I sampled, but also by the relatively little amount of blood present in their vascular systems. Indicating most of the blood loss transpired only after the victims were placed in their final resting place."

This point was critical to any homicide detective. At every crime scene it was always important to determine whether a victim actually died at the location where the corpse was found or if the victim was killed elsewhere and then deposited at the scene later.

"That explains all the blood Heaton described in the pipe," Matt said.

"Exactly. The cause of death in both cases was extensive head and thoracic trauma resulting in exsanguination. Basically they bled to death. Although any number of single injuries would have been fatal. Including ruptured spleens, fractured necks, fractured skulls, severed spines, bilateral premothoraxes, cardiac tamponade, et cetera. There's a list in each report. I already told you that the severed ear you picked up in the hospital basement belonged to the Humphries girl. I guess the killer's trying to demonstrate his sense of humor."

Ramani's stare turned cold. "Yep, I'm laughing, real hard."

Dorfman paused long enough to finish off the second Snickers bar. "What's really amazing is the strength it'd take to stuff just a single body into a space that confined. And we're talking two bodies, adult bodies. Unfuckinbelievable."

"Toxicology screen show anything?" Matt asked, thinking about his conversation with Dr. Kovacs.

Dorfman reviewed a page from each folder. "The girl's came back negative. She was clean. Beeden's was positive on four. Alcohol, point oh-six—not considered legally intoxicated—and THC, the active metabolite in marijuana. Also Haldol and lithium, both consistent with the unfilled prescription and capsules found. For what it's worth, the Haldol was in the therapeutic range, but the lithium subtherapeutic."

"By how much?" Matt asked.

"Normal is one-point-ten to one-point-five milliequivalents per liter. His was point seven, not that it makes any difference after being crammed head-first into a cement pipe."

"Received any records from his treating physician yet?" After the Zampisi interview, Matt had released Kovacs's name to the coroner's department.

Dorfman shook his head. "Usually takes two or three days."

"I spoke with Dr. Kovacs today," Matt said.

"How'd he come across?"

"Preoccupied, busy. Can't say he was uncooperative. Didn't express much remorse for his patient's demise."

"That significant?" the coroner asked.

Ramani shrugged. "It means he's a cold sonofabitch."

Dorfman grinned briefly and leaned back in his chair. It groaned as he reached for a cardboard flat used to hold micro slides. On top was a sheet typed up with the microscopic findings. "Now for the really strange part. And here's why." He moved the charts aside and briefly reviewed the typed reports before continuing. "I took some samples from Humphries's and Beeden's nails and compared them to samples isolated from the first victim, Inez, as well as the Nixon girl and those two 'bangers. And guess what?"

"All amorphous necrotic debris," Matt said. "With a wrinkle."

Dorfman held up one finger. "Very astute. But this is where it starts getting somewhat sticky. Sure, all the samples are organic in nature, meaning flesh, skin, even some empty hair follicles. Oh, by the way, did you know hair was one of the last things to decompose on a corpse?"

The detectives shook their heads.

"It is. That's excluding bone, of course. Anyway, I'm not a hair expert myself, but I'm having a colleague of mine, a forensic professor at UCLA take a look at the slides we made of the hairs from the Nixon hospital scene. Get a second opinion. If they are animal hairs, we might be able to narrow down a species."

Ramani frowned unenthusiastically. "Hell, those hairs might just be wild hairs. For all we know some asshole had been relieving his pet sheepdog under the hospital."

"True," the coroner agreed.

Matt sat up. "Dorf, you know as well as I do the only kind of animals that rape and murder young women are *Homo sapiens*. What about DNA testing?"

"I've sent some samples from each victim to Cellmark Diagnostics, a DNA testing lab in Maryland. They'll be able to confirm what I already believe to be the case. The problem is explaining the results in a rational manner."

The coroner was really piquing their interest now.

"I've concluded that all the tissue samples were in various stages of decomposition," he said.

Matt interrupted. "That would make sense since the Humphries girl and Beeden were both dead for some time before being found. The same process would also affect any tissue under their nails. Right?"

"If only the answer were that simple. You're forgetting Inez,

Salazar, de la Cruz, and Nixon. The samples under their nails were also undergoing some form of decomposition. And presumably these samples, especially from the Inez girl, would be fresh if they came from the attacker. But they weren't. And also the samples from the two pipe victims should've been in a far more advanced state of decay but they weren't."

"How so?" Ramani asked.

"Let's take Beeden. I estimated his time of death at seven to ten days. So presumably the samples from under his nails should've been seven to ten days old as well. But they weren't. In fact, I can't give you an estimate. It's impossible to tell precisely when they began to decompose. It's almost as if they were fixed in formaldehyde. And that brings up another point.

"There was no evidence of blood in any of the collected nail samples. Not one blood cell. There was hair, skin, and even some remnants of skeletal muscle from the Humphries girl; she had the longest nails. But no blood."

"Is that unusual?" Ramani wasn't sure.

"Hell, yes. If I scrape a good chunk of skin off your arm, I guarantee I'll be able to isolate some blood. In the capillaries at least. But none of these samples had any blood at all. And in some slides, I was able to find vestiges of a capillary or two and even these were devoid of blood."

"How the hell you explain that?" Matt asked.

"Can't. I'm having our trace-elements lab take a look and see if they can come up with anything else. And one more thing. The DNA evaluation will give us a genetic profile of the killer. Humans have forty-six chromosomes normally, though in rarer cases this number may vary."

The coroner put a hand on each of their shoulders as he led the detectives to his door. He patted Matt. "Hey, Ramani, keep an eye on this dildo. He's gonna owe me some money after the Jones/Whittaker fight."

Ramani glanced at his partner. "I thought you were gonna quit betting with this bum."

Dorfman chuckled and showed them out. "Hell, Guardian'll quit betting when you quit smoking and I quit eating."

As the two detectives made for the elevators, the smile melted from the coroner's face. He checked his lab-coat pocket but he'd eaten the last Snickers bar. He turned and stepped back inside his office. He had failed to reveal one piece of information. And this had been on purpose as he'd seen no use in raising the issue until he was sure.

He'd sent six thin paraffin slices, four microns in thickness each, for SEM analysis. One slice per victim. All contained material retrieved from under the nails. He was fairly positive the skin and muscle samples were human. At least mammalian. That was not in question. But what was odd was the appearance of some of the individual cells from the foreign samples. Especially those elongated cells isolated from the muscle tissue. They were missing something. A tiny structure one would normally observe in all mammalian cells. But *absent* in these particular tissue samples. He wondered if the scanning electron microscope would validate his odd interpretation of the histopathologic sections. He realized, of course, as he leaned his rotund figure back in his chair, that if the paraffin tissue slices *were* validated by the SEM analysis, the resulting conclusions would cross the fine line between reality and impossibility.

Dorfman found himself almost wishing that the electron microscopy would prove his initial conclusions incorrect, because the coroner had no trouble dealing with reality. It was the *impossibility* that caused him to lose sleep.

Thirty-three

Kovacs cursed under his breath as he studied the glycolytic pathway of enzymes on the flow chart before him. Thank goodness Ben's body hadn't been cremated as he'd originally contemplated.

Twenty years ago, Dr. Wesley Kovacs had purportedly accomplished what no other doctor in the history of the world had ever attempted. He'd frozen a complete human being for the specific purpose of preserving the body for resuscitation at a later date. Originally the length of time was designed to be one year. One year became two. And two lengthened to three. And so on and so on. The longer the elapsed time, and the more prestige and notoriety he garnered, the greater the fear of failure dogged the doctor's psyche.

But now a crisis had emerged—one that Kovacs had not remotely anticipated. And if what the pages of data before him indicated was correct—and he had every reason to believe it was—then the surreptitious disposing of Ben's body might have cost him far more than the invaluable documentation of the long-term effects of freezing living tissue.

Originally, the disposition plan had been simple enough. The experiment, terminated because of the dewar's inability to maintain a constant minus 196°C, was written off as a total and utter failure. Kovacs discovered the nitrogen leak too late to salvage much of anything. In his haste to rid not only himself, but the foundation of any embarrassment, Kovacs had decided the best solution would be to dispose of Ben's remains. Eisler didn't know the entire story, just what he'd been told, that Kovacs had obtained legal permission to freeze the body and these same documents also granted the foundation full legal guardianship of the "cryo subject."

A large sum of money went to the gardener of a major but very private mortuary and two months ago the body was transported from the loading dock on Pacific Avenue to a cemetery in Pasadena via an old ice cream delivery van. The stench made the cold transfer necessary. Once the transfer of twenty-five thousand dollars in foundation cash was complete, Ben was buried under a false identity.

That should've been the end of it. Kovacs's reputation for integrity would remain intact. But the research side of Kovacs's brain now cried out for access to Ben's remains, tissue he was convinced held priceless groundbreaking information. Data that the foundation would find absolutely essential if it was to be more successful in future endeavors to cryotreat the human species.

Kovacs detested the idea of getting the gardener involved again, yet his services would be necessary in order to retrieve an arm or leg from Ben's grave. In fact, it would cost the foundation an arm and a leg just to get Devlin to exhume the corpse.

Multiple biopsies of the vital organs would be necessary as well. The job would have to be completed quickly and discreetly, within the next few days. The longer the corpse remained under the ground, the greater probability of further tissue deterioration affecting the usefulness of the data.

Kovacs checked the time: 8:20. Eisler was due in at ten that morning. The doctor went back to his notes. The foundation had more than fifty subjects presently on "ice," ranging from pets to whole-body suspensions. Only one subject, though, a rhesus monkey named Stephanie, had been suspended for more than ten years. However, two others, a couple of rats named Tom and Jerry, though both female, were frozen a short while before Ben. Prior to the Simmons experiment, a host of other dogs, cats, monkeys, and rodents had been frozen, thawed, and refrozen. All yielded pertinent cryonic data and had since been discarded. Except Tom and Jerry.

It was only after the nitrogen leak was discovered and the Ben Simmons experiment terminated that Kovacs decided to "thaw" the oldest known rat popsicles in experimental history. This decision was a natural one since the dewars holding the rodents and Ben had been linked to the same nitrogen source. During the reviving process, miraculously, one of the rodents, he guessed it was Jerry, developed a heartbeat. She lived two weeks. If one could call it living. She barely ate, drank less, never defecated, and most of her hair fell out where the skin had blistered from cryo burns. She simply wasn't all there. She'd sit and stare, occasionally gnashing her teeth or flicking her tail. She never even closed her eyes.

Meanwhile, Kovacs dissected and biopsied Tom (the one whose revival had been unsuccessful). And it was this initial data, Tom's cryodata, that gave Kovacs such grave concerns. He'd hoped it was an error. He repeated the tests with more of Tom's tissue but the results were always identical, except for variations explained by the different biopsy sites.

Concerned, Kovacs decided to keep these findings to himself. He wanted to be sure. And more than ever, he wanted to be wrong.

Five weeks ago to the day, he sacrificed Jerry, the rat he'd resuscitated, hoping to solve the enzymatic puzzle. But it only deepened the mystery. Just killing the rodent had proved to be a challenge. Normally he'd sacrifice the nonhuman subjects in a way that was least damaging to the tissue, both structurally and metabolically, as well as being least traumatic to the individual animal. He used a chamber that resembled a microwave oven, except instead of using microwaves, various ports allowed the introduction and removal of gases. Kovacs could still recall his surprise, shock really, when he'd returned only to find Jerry sluggishly clawing at the glass trying to escape after breathing 100 percent carbon monoxide for more than one hour. Kovacs's immediate response had been to ensure all the valves and ports were working properly. They were. Irritated, he replaced the sealed atmosphere with 100 percent nitrogen. This only antagonized the rodent.

Cursing, Kovacs put on a thick pair of gloves, yanked open the door, and grabbed the slow-moving rat. She seemed almost robotic. He carried her to the sink, filled the basin with water, and promptly submerged the creature. At first the rat struggled, though not in the way one would expect a drowning animal to struggle. Kovacs waited.

Jerry moved in slow motion, making little dog-paddle attempts, though her head and nose remained three inches underwater. Normally this action would cease after thirty seconds to a minute. But oddly enough, the damn rat kept moving. Kovacs checked the time. Ten minutes passed and the goddamn rat was still paddling. Kovacs was dumbfounded. *The damn rodent wouldn't die.*

Kovacs wasn't used to drowning his test subjects but the few he did, he always noted a steady stream of bubbles flowing from the animals' nostrils and mouth to the surface. However, not a single bubble escaped from Jerry's lips or nose. Thinking the rat was holding its breath, Kovacs used his free hand and compressed the rat's rib cage like a boa constrictor. Still no bubbles. Angry now, he applied more pressure. It only angered Jerry. She fought ferociously, sinking two front incisors through his glove.

Kovacs yelled, but kept the rat submerged, now holding her underwater by her tail. What happened next, Kovacs would never forget. Jerry turned back on herself and coolly *gnawed through her own tail.* The stunned doctor could only watch as the almost tailless rat climbed out of the sink and crawled across the counter after being submerged underwater for almost a quarter of an hour. That was the last straw. Kovacs found a scalpel and promptly decapitated the stubborn rodent. Even then, the body continued to move for almost twelve minutes and the jaws snapped for the same length of time.

It was only after the rat's final muscle biopsies had returned and he'd carefully analyzed all the data from an outside biochemical lab that Kovacs began to understand what had taken place. That had been two weeks ago. Reviewing the complex tables, flow charts, and histopathology data again only confirmed his theory. And what a theory it was.

Kovacs jumped at the sound of a car door outside. He'd lost track of time. He heard the outer office door unlock and recognized the deliberate gait of Christian Eisler. He leaned back in his chair and waited for his new associate to knock.

A minute later a haggard-looking Eisler sat before him.

"You look hungover, my man," Kovacs said.

"Didn't sleep well." Eisler left it at that.

Kovacs had come to ignore his assistant's nervous tic but this particular morning it seemed more prominent. "How'd the meeting go yesterday?"

"What . . . oh, the transportation. Everything's been arranged. We'll have access to a fully refrigerated and insulated van capable of maintaining the required temperature."

Eisler pointed at Kovacs's voluminous pile of notes spread across his desk. "Problem?"

Kovacs stood. "Christian, what happens to a living cell when its intracytoplasmic temperature is lowered to minus one-ninety-six degrees Celsius?"

Eisler obviously didn't like the question. It was elementary, too much so. The kind of question on board exams meant to trap you, coaxing you into giving an obvious answer even though you suspect that the obvious answer is the incorrect one. Eisler offered the obvious answer anyway.

"All the cell's metabolic and biochemical activity comes to a halt."

Kovacs chuckled again, this time smugly. "Wrong, Doctor. In *theory* that's what's supposed to happen. But you know what?"

Eisler shook his head.

"You're dead wrong. *I* was wrong. Come here." Kovacs motioned toward the door. "I want to show you something."

Eisler followed Kovacs down the main aisle of the warehouse to the cold-storage unit and waited while Kovacs deactivated the electronic lock combination. Once both had donned insulated gear, Kovacs swung open the heavy freezer door. Midway down the center aisle under the blue fluorescent lighting, a lid had been removed from one of the smaller dewars, one about three-feet tall, the approximate size necessary to cryofreeze a child.

"You've revived Stephanie," Eisler said, his breath frosting his goggles. "I was under the impression she was to be transferred to Tucson."

"This was a special case."

Kovacs examined the temperature gauges on several neighboring dewars. He wiped the frost off one and stepped back, pointing. "What does it read?"

Eisler bent closer. "Minus one-ninety-six. I don't see a problem."

"Follow me."

Kovacs led Eisler back outside. "Do you happen to recall any of your undergraduate biochemistry?"

"If you're asking whether I can recite verbatim the precise sequence of chemical reactions in glycolysis and the Krebs cycle, no. But if you'd like to hear an overview, I'm confident I could still maintain an A in Biochem One-oh-one."

"That won't be necessary." Back in the laboratory, Kovacs motioned to a stool. "Take a seat, Christian. I'd like you to meet Stephanie." And with that, Kovacs reached across the counter and yanked the brown blanket off what Eisler had assumed was a box or some other small packing crate.

It wasn't. It was a twenty-gallon aquarium with a glass top. And it was completely filled with water.

Eisler gasped. Inside, completely submerged, crouched Stephanie, the rhesus monkey. Denuded of fur, broken skin lay open in ulcerating lesions. Her front paws, hands really, were held against the glass wall, palms outward as if she were trying to push herself free. But she wasn't struggling. In fact, she wasn't moving at all.

"My God, you've killed her," Eisler said.

Then he saw Stephanie's tail move. "Jesus Christ, she's alive!"

Kovacs chuckled. "Of course she's alive. As much as any anaerobic organism is alive."

"What are you talking about?" Eisler couldn't take his eyes off the bizarre sight.

Kovacs moved his hand in front of the monkey. She bared her teeth and snapped at the glass. "Stephanie was frozen eleven years and four months ago. During this period of suspended cryopreservation, no one, including myself, could've predicted the unforeseen effects long-term supercooling would have on an organism's enzymatic and metabolic machinery."

Eisler leaned closer.

"Come closer, Stephanie won't bite." Kovacs wasn't smiling.

Eisler stepped up to the aquarium, looking for any pipes or other means by which the monkey could be breathing. There were none. "It must be a supersaturated medium." Eisler referred to the process of forcing oxygen into a liquid medium under tremendous pressure.

"It's simply water. Turn on any faucet and you'll find more of the same."

Eisler shook his head as he studied the monkey's face. It was expressionless, its eyes dull. "How does she breathe?" he asked.

"She doesn't."

"What?"

"I said she doesn't breathe."

"That's impossible." Eisler ran his hand across the sealed glass top. Other than a tiny air pocket at one end, the aquarium was devoid of any other source of inhalable oxygen.

"At least not the way you and I define breathing," Kovacs added. "Sit down, Christian."

Eisler ignored him. "She belongs in a fucking carnival."

"Stephanie's not a sideshow freak. She's a problem in a world-class research lab. A problem that must be solved if our species are ever to be successfully cryopreserved for any length of time."

"Simmons," Eisler gasped and spun around to face Kovacs. "Are you saying—"

"Sit down, Christian," Kovacs repeated. He motioned Eisler back to his stool. He didn't like the almost fearful look in his PhD's eyes. Poor dear Stephanie was certainly shocking, but nothing to fear.

Eisler seemed to mumble something as he took a seat. He still couldn't look anywhere but at the monkey, so Kovacs tossed the blanket back over the aquarium. "What does minus one hundred ninety-six degrees Celsius mean to you?"

Eisler looked at Kovacs like the foundation director was insulting his intelligence.

"No, just answer it. It's not a test of your genius," Kovacs said.

"Minus one hundred ninety-six degrees Celsius is the temperature at which liquid nitrogen evaporates. It's also the temperature that all cellular functions reversibly cease."

"So it's like . . . death."

"I said *reversibly*."

"Ah, yes. Reversible is the key word here. But let's suppose that the minus one hundred ninety-six degrees Celsius was not low enough. Let's assume that the temperature should've been minus two hundred degrees Celsius. Or even absolute zero. What would be the consequences?"

"It's quite simple," Eisler answered quickly, then paused and continued more slowly. "If the organism in question was not fully suspended, over a period of time it would continue to carry on some metabolic processes. And an energy source would be required to sustain these processes."

"And once this energy source was drained?"

"The cell's functions would irreversibly cease. It would die."

Kovacs raised one finger. "Now let's assume that although minus one hundred ninety-six degrees Celsius was not cold enough to reversibly shut down a cell completely, it was cold enough to slow it down to such a point that the cell had time to adapt to a new energy source." Kovacs briefly shook his head. "No, that's not quite accurate, let me rephrase it. Let's say the energy source, in this instance, glucose, remained the same, but it was the cell's metabolic machinery that actually changed. Became new. In other words, this metabolic adaptation enabled the cell to survive in this cold environment in an unpreserved state. Far longer than anyone would've ever anticipated. Or predicted."

Kovacs read Eisler's uncertainty. "I'm saying that in the process of cryopreserving a living organism, we've unfortunately succeeded in converting that aerobic organism into an anaerobic one." He yanked the blanket back off the aquarium. "Look at Stephanie. She's proof. She doesn't require goddamn oxygen to survive. She's like a fucking fish without gills."

Eisler shook his head in disbelief. "Is that possible?"

"It's not only possible, but it goddamn happened." Kovacs passed his notes of enzymatic sequences across the counter. "I first suspected something after I saw the histopath stains on Tom's tissue. There were enormous amounts of glycogen, lactic acid, and pyruvic acid present. Much more than in any freshly killed rat. If Tom had been truly cryopreserved there shouldn't have been any more than when the subject was put under twenty years ago. Next came Jerry. I couldn't kill the rat. Not by conventional means, anyway. She refused to suffocate, even refused to drown. I was forced to decapitate her. I then subjected both specimens to an intense histobiochemical analysis."

"Why wasn't I informed?" Eisler asked, examining the data.

Kovacs ignored the question. "And their results were remarkably similar. Within one standard deviation. Not only did each of their tissues exhibit abnormally high levels of glycogen, pyruvic, and lactic acids, but also markedly increased activities of their glycolytic enzymes, especially the hexokinases and phosphorylases. None of it made sense. That is until I saw the electron microsopy data."

Kovacs paused. He could see Eisler was too intrigued with the written data before him to really be listening. He decided to give his associate an hour to review the notes.

It took Eisler only thirty minutes to absorb the data. And the strange part was it actually made sense. It was totally unbelievable, but they were reflecting scientific fact.

Eisler took a break from the diagrams to observe Stephanie. *An anaerobic monkey.* In all likelihood, the first anaerobic monkey. *Anaerobic.* It meant without oxygen. Versus *aerobic,* meaning with oxygen. Anaerobic organisms were classified as anaerobic because they survived in environments with little or no oxygen. A prime example were some viruses and certain bacteria such as anaerobic streptococcus or peotpsteptococcus. On the contrary, aerobic organisms required oxygen to carry on their cellular functions. Homo sapiens were aerobic. So were dogs, cats, horses, and pigs. Also monkeys and rats. They all required oxygen to survive.

However what really separated the two classes, aerobic versus anaerobic, was how they chose to utilize their food substrates as a source of energy. They did share some common characteristics. To survive, they both ingested food. The food was usually converted to a simple sugar, in most cases glucose. The glucose supplied the physiologic requirements of the organism, but here the similarities ceased.

In anaerobic organisms, the energy was released from the glucose molecule through glycolysis. Glucose was broken down to two pyruvic acid molecules which were subsequently converted to lactic acid. This sequence of biochemical reactions, requiring hexokinase and phosphorylase enzymes, was all the anaerobic organism needed to sustain itself. It was primitive but highly adaptable and successful. Anaerobic life was well over five hundred million years old. Only much later did aerobic organisms evolve, with their far more complex enzymatic machinery. It revolved around a sequence of reactions known as the Krebs cycle. Here the pyruvic acid, which was formed from glucose, was further metabolized in the presence of oxygen to carbon dioxide and hydrogen. Its major enzymes were the dehydrogenases and decarboxyleses.

There was one other important distinction between the two classes. All aerobic metabolism took place in specialized microstructures inside the cell. These power-plant-like structures were called mitochondria. And all aerobic organisms contained mitochondria. All anaerobic organisms did not.

Eisler suddenly felt a shiver as he began to understand Kovacs's hypothesis. He looked up, only to catch Stephanie staring at him.

Kovacs's initial assumption that minus one hundred ninety-six degrees Celsius was not cold enough to completely shut the organism metabolically down was correct. It had to be. How else would the conversion have taken place? And the electronmicroscopy data confirmed it *had* taken place. Without a doubt, Tom and Jerry were anaerobic organisms. Their cells, at least each one examined, contained only the atrophied remnants of mitochondria. Eisler presumed Stephanie's would be the same. The monkey would have to be sacrificed later to know for sure. And this conversion hypothesis also explained the markedly elevated levels of glycolytic enzymes in their tissues and the total lack of Krebs cycle or aerobic enzymes. They'd disappeared along with the mitochondria. There was no need for them. For years the organisms had been sequestered in a medium devoid of oxygen. So they did what was necessary to survive. They had to use whatever energy source was available anaerobically. Why? Because their cells had not been completely shut down. *It hadn't been cold enough.*

Of course they found no shortage of energy substitutes. Eisler wanted to laugh at the simplicity of it all. It was all so goddamn simple.

The organisms, in this case Tom, Jerry, and Stephanie, and in all likelihood the other subjects presently preserved under the auspices of the foundation, required glucose, as all living creatures did, to carry on their life processes. And where did they get the glucose? They were literally bathed in glucose. *The cryoprotectant.* The cryopreservative or protectant was a glycerol:alcohol:sucrose mixture. And what was sucrose? It was a disaccharide, a simple chain of sugars. Glucose and fructose. Even the simplest of bacteria would have little trouble converting fructose to glucose.

There it was. Though it read like science fiction, the scenario was reality and in place long before Eisler ever graduated from high school. Three formerly aerobic organisms, two rats and a monkey, were cryopreserved in a vat of liquid "glucose." Only technically, they weren't 100 percent cryopreserved. Instead, entombed in their sugary mausoleums, they continued to carry on their metabolic processes, though in a much inhibited state.

Darwin would've been proud. *They survived and evolved.* Backwards. They went from being aerobic to anaerobic. They no longer required oxygen. Use it or lose it. They lost the mitochondria and adopted the much more efficient anaerobic process of energy formation—the glycolytic process. They formed massive intracellular chains of glucose, called glycogen. When energy was required, the glycogen was broken down to glucose, and subsequently to pyruvic acid and lactic acid. Whatever lactic acid or pyruvic acid wasn't burned was then converted back to glucose and glycogen. And the process rejuvenated itself.

Eisler shut the journal. These organisms no longer even needed blood to carry oxygen. They only needed nutrients. The cryoprotectant filling their arteries and veins sufficed as a nutrient transport medium. As long as they had a pump that would periodically move it around. And every medical student knew the heart could run just fine on lactic acid. And that was an aerobic heart. Think what an anaerobic heart could do. It'd literally pump forever, as long as its cardiac cells had access to glucose. In fact, every cell in the body possessed the ability to use glucose. All it needed was food.

Eisler looked up just in time to see Stephanie start clawing at the roof of the aquarium. She wanted out. She was already looking stronger and moving faster. She'd obviously adapted well to her new metabolic machinery. It was only when Stephanie bared her teeth did Eisler suddenly realize his own mouth was dry. He covered the aquarium with the blanket again.

Only after he left the laboratory to find Kovacs, however, did his subconscious mind allow the true impact of the data to hit him. He froze outside Kovacs's closed door and stared in horror at his hands. His own, aerobic hands.

Simmons. He'd almost forgotten about Simmons. *Not Simmons.*

Eisler barely breathed. *Goddammit, not Ben Simmons.*

Thirty-four

Matt took the Imperial Street exit from Interstate 10 and drove the short two blocks to Sacramento, where he parked.

Across the concrete basin of the Los Angeles River, he could see the decrepit collection of makeshift wood shacks and nylon tents. Within five square miles of this exact spot, three of the victims had been found. The Nixon girl at Hollenbech Park and only a mile north the two corpses, Humphries and Beeden, had been removed from the sewer under Willow and Santa Fe Avenues. And the Fourth Street bridge where Beeden supposedly accosted the Zampisi woman and subsequently vanished was in the same general proximity.

Matt called in his location on the radio and followed the concrete walkway across the river and into the outskirts of Shantytown from the south. As he walked along the cement embankment, he saw several men fishing from the rain-swollen river.

Along the way, he counted numerous piles of refuse and garbage, littering the various paths used by the residents to make their way to and from the river bottom. It was fitting, Matt thought, the city's namesake river was used as one giant latrine. Rusted shopping carts were strewn about and Matt spotted several rats and more than several mite-infested roaming dogs. The air smelled of raw sewage, rotting garbage, and animal feces.

In his suit and sports coat he stood out like a ruby in a pile of dog shit. But no one paid him any mind. He was mostly ignored as he made his way through the encampment. He was a cop and cops spelled trouble. Matt read it in all their eyes, the homeless, the deranged, the mentally ill, and the drug abusers.

He stopped and asked one old geezer if he'd heard of the names Mitchell Beeden or Benjamin Simmons. The old man simply coughed up a mound of green phlegm and left it on his tent floor. Matt moved on, wondering if this trip would turn up anything worthwhile. But his jaunt wasn't over.

A man sat huddled in a blanket until the detective was almost upon him, then he stood.

Matt barely flinched.

"Detective," the man said.

"What's going on?" Matt studied the vaguely familiar face but couldn't place it with a name.

"Frazier Stoops. Just got out on a two-eighty-eight (lewd conduct charge). But your partner run me in, two years ago on a five-oh-one." A 501 was the code for armed robbery. "My PD talked it down to a simple assault."

Matt still didn't recall the incident. He did know most PDs; public defender cases involved bottom-feeders. Stoops was a prime example.

"This your home?" Matt asked, his tone nonjudgmental.

"Maybe. For a while till I get established. You?"

"Just passing through."

"Anything I can assist you with, detective?" Stoops asked.

Matt accepted. "Ever hear of Mitchell Beeden or Ben Simmons?"

Stoops thought for a moment. "This guy big and ugly? Real ugly?"

Matt shrugged. "Ugly's sort of relative. I mean some of my own dates call me ugly, but we both know that ain't true."

Stoops grinned. Two teeth were missing. "I mean big, and

thick. And ugly like in some fuckin' accident. I could hardly see him but it looked like he was burned real bad. You know, his skin all fucked up. Smelled like shit too."

"Where you see this ugly cat?"

The ex-con shook his head like he hadn't heard the question. "I was scared. And I'd go in the ring against most any man, even you, chief, but not this big bad stinkin' dude. Didn't fuckin' piss for a day."

Matt was hearing every word. He repeated the question. "Where'd you see this man?"

Matt perhaps looked a little too interested or Stoops recalled too vividly the encounter because he backed down. "Don't rightly recall, sir. He might've been passing through. Sound like your man, detective?"

Matt sensed the change. "Could be, Stoops." He dug out a card and handed it to Stoops. "You see him, call me."

"Sure thing, detective."

Matt turned. "Be careful of that third strike, Stoops."

Returning to his car, Matt figured he'd only hear from Frazier Stoops if the felon ran into a jam. That didn't bother him nearly as much though, as Stoops's description of this big bad stinking dude.

Thirty-five

*The drizzle began Saturday eve*ning, soon after Julie arrived at the hospital. Though the precipitation was light and gave the air an acrid muggy smell, she couldn't explain the blanket of foreboding that hung in the dark like an invisible veil. Except it was on a night very similar to this that Janine had died.

On her way over to the sleep laboratory, Julie counted four guards. The increased security made her feel more comfortable, though not entirely safe.

In the lab, while Jim Nelsen ran a checklist on the VEROC software, Julie made sure all the polysomnographic equipment was in proper working order. By 6 P.M., they were ready to go.

Julie found Vicki waiting for her in the main lobby. She'd just come from the emergency room where her sutures had been removed.

"How's it feel?" Julie asked.

"The knee feels fine. It's me I'm having doubts about."

Julie took her hand. "Ready?"

Vicki smiled uneasily. "It's not everyday I get to have someone watch my dreams."

Upstairs, Jim watched from the observation window, while Julie, assisted by another technician, applied the monitoring devices to the appropriate points on Vicki's body.

Vicki tried to relax on the firm mattress but it was obvious she was anything but relaxed. "Maybe I should take a sleeping pill or something."

"I know all these wires and gadgets look intimidating, but there's really nothing to be concerned about." Julie finished with the last one on Vicki's right gastrocnemius muscle. "None of this will hurt and we'll be watching you the entire time."

"What's that for, Dr. Charmaine?" Vicki indicated the electrode strapped to her leg.

"The four sensors on each of your extremities measure your muscle activity. Though you don't feel it, your muscles contract many times during a normal dream cycle. And those small wires attached to your head, there's six in all, lead to an instrument called an electroencephalogram."

"An EEG."

"That's right. You were a psychiatric nurse. Anyway, the EEG will tell us when you enter REM sleep. It's during that time that we'll be able to quantify your dreams." Julie liked the word "quantify" better than watching. It sounded less voyeuristic.

The technician finished connecting the five ends of the EMG and EEG sensors to the monitoring devices and Julie made some last-minute checks on the various monitors in place. All seemed to be in working order.

Vicki slowly shook her head. "I'll be glad when tomorrow gets here."

"Relax, Vicki," Julie said. She rubbed her patient's shoulder. "You'll do just fine."

"I hope so."

Julie shut off the lights.

It was 11:45 P.M. "You hungry?" Jim asked.

Julie shook her head. She'd barely touched a sandwich she'd

brought from home. She was far too wired to even think of eating.

"Nervous?" Jim's eyes remained on the computer console.

"A little."

Julie had never monitored a dream study when she didn't feel that vague lightness in her chest or the butterfly wings fluttering in her midsection, both connoting a controlled adrenaline rush. On occasions like tonight, it became impossible for Julie not to envision herself in the bed below, attached to the electrodes. What would *she* see?

Julie shifted position, relieving some stress from her back. Two hours ago, Vicki had entered the first Stage IV non-REM sleep period. This initial stage had lasted twenty minutes and was followed by a brief period of REM sleep. During the five minutes of desynchronized-wave activity recorded by the EEG, the overhead video monitor remained visually silent. Since then Vicki had passed through two other short REM sleep periods, most recently only a half hour ago. Still nothing showed on the video screen. Yes, Julie was nervous and more than a little impatient. Was Vicki dreaming and the VEROC sensors missing it? Or was there a malfunction in the software somewhere? Or was Vicki just not dreaming?

Jim must've read her thoughts. "The software's algorithms are running fine." He shrugged.

Julie studied the EEG. The waves were large amplitude delta waves characteristic of Stage III and IV deep sleep. "We have another sixty to ninety minutes of this before another REM period," she said.

She saw Jim suppress a yawn. "If you want, you can go take a nap in the next sleep room. I'll wake you at the first sign of REM."

Jim shook his head. "Thanks, but I'll stick it out. Besides, I like to run the image reconstruction calculations every ten minutes or so."

Julie went back to checking a smaller monitor with three parameters digitally updated every fifteen minutes. So far, Vicki's pulse, blood pressure, and respirations had not changed significantly since falling asleep.

When she looked back at the main video terminal, the once blank screen had become a snowstorm of static.

"Dr. Charmaine." The tech motioned to the EEG tracing.

"It's too early for REM—" She never finished.

The monitor's static instantly transformed into ever-changing confluent patterns of grays and blacks.

"Jim?" Julie's attention remained on the EEG pattern. It showed only delta waves, deep Stage IV.

"It's working."

Jim didn't need to hit the keys. The program had been kicked into high gear by Vicki's dream. A dizzying array of graphics and equations flashed across the computer screen. The green glow reflected off both their faces.

Julie was obviously shocked. She gazed down at Vicki. "This is incredible, a non-REM dream."

"Are those rare?" Jim asked, never taking his eyes from the computer console.

"Unfortunately, there hasn't been much research into them. The only study I'm aware of is one conducted by a psychologist in Denver. He claimed non-REM dreamers experienced a higher incidence of insomnia." Julie studied the video screen. A splash of deep red shattered two converging gray waves and all three patterns disintegrated into one amorphous blob. "What do you see, Vicki?" Julie asked, more to herself than anyone else.

Jim read out the vitals. "Respiration's twelve, BP one hundred over seventy, pulse eighty and regular."

Julie nodded her satisfaction as the shapeless images formed on the screen. The only sound was Vicki's respirations over an overhead speaker. "This is being recorded, right?" she asked.

Jim checked just to make sure. It was.

The EEG still indicated Vicki was in a deep Stage IV sleep. As Julie's eyes were glued on the screen, the video abruptly darkened. "What's wrong?" she asked.

"It's not me," said Jim. "It's the program. There must not be any generic images in the dreambank that match what Vicki's dreaming."

"Vitals?"

"Respirations sixteen, pulse ninety-two."

"BP?"

"It's climbing. One hundred and thirty over eighty."

Julie frowned. This was Stage IV. Vicki's vitals should've been dropping, or at least staying constant. Definitely not rising.

Julie looked at the screen. Only darkness.

"BP one hundred and forty over ninety." Jim's voice sounded strained above the whir of the computer hardware.

"Damn it, why aren't we seeing anything?"

"I don't know. This has never happened before."

Suddenly the entire screen went back to static.

"What happened?" Julie asked.

Too engrossed to answer, Jim worked feverishly at the computer terminal.

Down in the sleep room, Vicki moaned.

"Respirations twenty, BP one hundred and fifty over ninety," Julie read the vitals.

"Should we wake her?" Jim asked.

"No, not yet."

Above Vicki's moans came the first *beep* of an EMG sensor.

"Julie," Jim warned.

Vicki was struggling. There were more beeps as the electromyographic sensors fired with the sleeping subject's muscle contractions.

"Julie." This time Jim pointed toward the observation window. Vicki was moving.

Suddenly, the static was wiped out by a wave of black. Then a wave of red. Julie asked the screen, "Why are you so angry, Vicki?"

"BP one hundred and seventy over one hundred and ten."

In the background Julie heard Vicki's labored breathing.

Then suddenly over the speaker, a voice. "Get away, no." It was Vicki, talking in her sleep. "Get away!"

A blot of yellow appeared in the center of the screen and rapidly spread outward, displacing the red.

Julie's head jerked toward the observation window. Vicki wasn't angry. She was terrified.

Vicki continued to cry out. "Stay away! Stay away! I'm sorry. It wasn't my fault. He made me do it! No! No!"

The pleading voice instantly motivated Julie to action. The dream was going too far. She lunged at the speakerphone. "Vicki, it's all right. I'm here. I'm here, Vicki!"

Vicki's voice cried out. "God, not you. Get away! No, please. It . . . It's me . . . me . . . *No!*"

Julie froze. "Oh my God, what's happening?" she breathed.

A second flash of yellow exploded across the screen.

Vicki screamed.

Jim's voice came almost as loudly. "BP two hundred over one hundred twenty!"

"Wake her!" Julie ordered. "We have to wake her. Now!"

Vicki screamed again.

Julie yelled into the speakerphone. "I'm here, Vicki! I'm here!" She rushed for the sleep room door. "We have to wake her!"

Jim was right behind her.

The entire room filled with a high-pitched shriek. It sounded like Vicki's vocal cords were being ripped out.

"Look at the screen!" Jim clutched at Julie's lab coat.

Julie turned, totally unprepared. All she could do was stare at the video screen. For there on the monitor, was the generic figure of a monkey. The image lay perfectly still, solitary, and impenetrable, until tiny islands of static began to eat away at its silhouette.

A cold sweat broke out on Julie's skin.

In the sleep room below, Vicki began to sob uncontrollably.

While Vicki slept, courtesy of a mild sedative, Julie reran the dream sequence tape five times and in each instance she found herself unable to complete the video without stopping. The sticking point was always the same.

Vicki's cries of terror filled the tiny sleep-lab conference room for the sixth time.

"*God, not you. Get away! No, please. It . . . It's me . . . me . . . No!*"

The monitor exploded once again in a burst of yellow.

Julie pressed STOP.

This point in the dream she was convinced held the key to Vicki's nightmares. Yet even after her patient's vital signs had returned to normal, Vicki had remained inconsolable. Julie had attempted a brief interview but witnessing her patient's persistent distress had forced her to abandon any type of counseling session. And in Vicki's current state of mind, having her patient watch the video would have been tantamount to asking for disaster. Julie had never witnessed such an intense reaction to a nightmare. Even as an observer, it was unnerving.

She pressed START again and tensed, preparing for Vicki's terminal cry of anguish. When the monkey image filled the monitor, goose bumps broke out on Julie's skin a second time.

More than a little unnerved, she ejected the tape and was on her way back to the sleep room when a security guard met her outside the observation bay.

His face wore the wide-eyed expression of someone abruptly awoken from a light doze. Rain stains soaked his uniform.

"Dr. Charmaine?" he said.

"Yes."

"I'm supposed to escort you to the surgery suites. Stat."

Thirty-six

The girl was discovered in the shadows of Old Red. By 1 A.M. she'd been stabilized and rushed to the operating room where the neurosurgeons and orthopedic surgeons on call had worked a minor miracle. In the coming twenty-four hours, they rated her chances of survival at fifty percent. Not for the first time in her life, Julie felt utterly helpless.

At the nurses' station, she found Matt Guardian and three other policemen. As soon as Matt saw her, he excused himself and came her way.

Together they went to Melanie Balsam's bedside. She lay comatose in a monitored bed, oblivious to the cardiac electrodes taped to her chest, the IVs in her arms, and the urinary catheter dangling from under the sheets. Worst of all was the halo brace, that metallic cage that was literally screwed into her skull in four places in order to prevent even the most minimal movement of her cervical spine.

A nurse worked mutely while she finished noting the patient's vital signs. She avoided Julie's gaze, though Julie couldn't avoid staring at the teenager's swollen and battered face. Images of Irene Inez flashed in Julie's mind. As with Irene, one of Melanie's eyes had completely swollen shut.

"Fill me in," she told Matt.

He waited for the nurse to finish adjusting the IV rate. "You familiar with the Mary Nunn House?" he asked.

"Yes, it's a halfway home for battered women affiliated with the medical center. I discharged Melanie there a week ago."

"From what we can ascertain, the administrator reported Melanie missing for her ten P.M. room check. A roommate was under the impression the girl had been trying to contact you."

"By walking to the hospital?"

"That's the assumption we're working on at the moment. The distance is approximately four blocks."

Julie couldn't stop shaking her head. "In the rain? At night?"

"Yeah, I know." Matt rested a hand on her shoulder. "How you holding up?" he asked.

Julie felt like her home had been broken into and she was powerless to intervene. Something had been taken from her. Melanie had been her patient, still *was* her patient, her responsibility. And as Julie waited in grim silence, feeling utterly frustrated almost to the point of being mentally numb, she wondered if she'd ever be able to get her back.

"Janine's anniversary is tomorrow night," she said. She saw no relevance in the statement. It was just something to say, as if bringing the past and present together under the somber glow of the ceiling lights might somehow alter the final outcome. She rechecked Melanie's radial pulse at the wrist.

Matt waited as the respirator completed a cycle, the gentle rising and falling of Melanie's chest told him when it was complete.

"Who did this?" she finally asked.

"We'll find him. I promise."

"It was the Sewer Stalker, wasn't it?" Twenty-nine years ago she might have said Worm Man.

"There are a helluva lot of similarities. The victim, young, female, the location—close proximity to a sewer outlet—the crime scene, raw sewage splattered over the walls and concrete."

Julie continued to watch Melanie. The teenager's dark hair contrasted sharply with her deathly pale face. "There's no excuse for this. She was—" Julie shook her head "—*is* a beautiful girl. It shouldn't have happened. Goddammit, it shouldn't have happened."

"We'll nail the bastard." Even as he spoke Matt found himself studying Julie's profile against the recovery-room lights. Though he could see she was tired and emotionally taut, she looked every bit as beautiful as that day on the hospital wards almost three weeks ago. Paint in a radiant white gown, a stormy night, the edge of a craggy cliff and she would make the perfect heroine. As the respirator completed another cycle, this thought was shoved aside by another more worrisome thought. For the first time, Matt realized Julie had some of the same characteristics as the other female victims. Young, at least younger than he was, attractive, long dark hair. He also realized now wasn't the time to bring these details up.

"I saw her X-rays," Julie said. "A fracture of C-four, and a third degree subluxation at C-six-seven. A broken neck. He must've shaken her like a rag doll."

Matt touched Julie's hand. Neither spoke.

It was Officer Blocker who finally interrupted them. "She could've used your right cross, Matt," he said, motioning to Melanie. "You see the delivery alley behind the hospital?"

Matt nodded. "Not now, Blocker."

Blocker understood. He momentarily eyed Julie and kept it brief. "A hospital security guard heard two screams. He found the girl prone on the concrete. This was approximately eleven fifty-five P.M. We still haven't been able to nail down a single goddamn witness."

"Keep trying," Matt said.

He lightly patted Julie's hand once more and was about to turn away when her fingers gripped his wrist.

"What did Officer Blocker just say?" she asked, the monotone gone from her voice.

"About no witnesses?"

"Yes, that." For the first time since standing by Melanie's bed, Julie met Matt's gaze directly. "I want you to listen to something."

• •

With Vicki resting in a room on the fourth floor until her sedative wore off, Julie led Matt to Conference Room A in the sleep lab.

He sat before the monitor and waited for Julie to insert the tape.

Before pressing PLAY she turned to face him. She could read and understand Matt's reluctance. He was probably wondering what he was doing inside a sleep laboratory with the police choppers still conducting their searches outside. Yet Julie would have been uncomfortable not bringing the tape to Matt's attention. She could not ignore what Vicki had seen in her dream.

"I recorded these images earlier this evening," Julie explained. She pressed PLAY. The screen briefly filled with static before solidifying into a homogeneous black background. Two sets of times represented digitally could be seen, one in each corner. One read 12:10 A.M., the other 5:22 A.M. and included a moving second column. "The time to the right of the screen is the time these images were actually recorded. It was just past midnight this morning. The numbers on your left represent the present time."

"Don't remind me."

Matt's eyes traveled from Julie's face to the screen which had now begun to undulate in shades of grays and blacks. As the detective watched the images unfold exactly as Vicki had dreamed them earlier, Julie attempted to succinctly explain the principle behind what Matt was observing. She kept it as elementary as possible, realizing Matt possessed neither the background nor inclination to fully comprehend the methodology behind the dream-reconstruction process.

At several points, Julie paused, allowing Matt the chance to ask any question or at least make a comment. The detective did neither. There was not much to see—shades of black and the fiery waves of red and yellow, accompanied by the audio of Vicki's respirations.

"Red generally signifies anger, and in some cases fear. Yellow if the fear is extremely intense," Julie explained.

"You're telling me this was recorded from Ms. Zampisi's dream? While she was asleep? Tonight." His reluctance had turned to skepticism.

"Exactly as you see it, Matt. The computer program that made this possible was years in development. But wait. This isn't the part I brought you here to see. It's coming up. Here."

Even though Julie knew what was about to happen, she couldn't suppress a shiver as she listened to Vicki's terrified pleading. She jumped when Vicki's scream shattered the conference room's stillness.

Matt reflexively reached for his revolver. "Jesus Christ," he muttered.

Julie froze the tape. "Whatever Vicki was dreaming, many of the images fell beyond the generic images provided by the VEROC software. However, one image did match. That of a monkey."

Matt waited. "What is *that* supposed to mean?"

"I don't have an explanation."

"Did you ask her?"

Julie frowned. "Vicki was unable to discuss tonight's experience in any depth. I had to sedate her. She did say she was intensely afraid of dying."

Matt's eyes remained glued to the monitor. "How the hell did Vicki dream up a monkey? Isn't that what the Inez girl said?"

Julie nodded. *"Chango."*

"Shit," Matt shook his head. "Shit."

"Believe me, Vicki wasn't faking this. She was emotionally involved."

"And she hasn't seen the tape?"

"It wouldn't serve any therapeutic purpose. I'll wait till she calms down before going over it with her." She caught Matt watching her. "Thoughts, comments?"

Matt didn't wait long to answer. "Relative to tonight's victim, I think it's totally irrelevant and entirely coincidental. You never mentioned to Vicki what Irene Incz had said, did you?"

"No, nothing."

Matt looked back at the monitor. "I admit the timing's bizarre. Sort of reminds me of a case six years ago. A lady's only child, a four-year-old girl, was snatched from her while she was using an ATM. The getaway car, a Ford Taurus, was later found abandoned. It'd been stolen. The driver and kid were gone. The lady was a young widow, no enemies and no money. For six months, nothing, not even a ransom note. A psychic was eventually brought in, by the distraught mother I might add, and using one of the kid's tennis shoes, claimed the kid was in a dark box. A cold dark box. She also described a broken set of skis. Four weeks later, the girl's decomposing body was found in an abandoned freezer near one of the local ski resorts. Nearby, sticking out of the ground with some other trash, was a broken set of skis."

"Did you find the killer?"

"Still open. The mom OD'ed on barbiturates the day after the girl's funeral."

"Sad." She couldn't imagine losing a child that way. Losing a sister was painful enough. "Are you insinuating you think Vicki's psychic?" she asked.

"Do you think she is?"

Julie wasn't willing to step out on that limb. Not yet. "No," she said.

"Neither do I."

Thirty-seven

Even with the intense police activity, after discharging Vicki, Julie spent much of her Sunday at the hospital. She received several calls of condolence regarding Melanie, including one each from Terry Kalone and Dr. Finny Todd. Todd's fractured nose was healing well and he was back in the ER rotation.

At 1:30 P.M., Julie entered the surgical intensive care where Melanie had been transferred. She arrived just as Dr. Statler, the neurosurgeon, was finishing his weekend rounds with a group of surgery interns.

"Any change?" Julie could see Melanie's bed against the far wall.

"Status quo, Julie. I'm sorry." He motioned for the interns to continue rounds while he hung back. He followed Julie to Melanie's ICU spot. "She's developing more swelling around the fracture site. We increased her dexamethasone and started a mannitol drip. I ordered another MRI too."

Julie gazed at the telemetry. At least Melanie was in a normal sinus rhythm and her other vitals were stable. "How long will it be before you know if she'll regain any use of her extremities?" she asked.

"It's hard to tell. Statistically speaking we're looking at close to a zero-percent use of her lower extremities and possibly some minor use of her upper extremities. According to the literature—"

"Thanks." Julie had heard enough. The last thing she needed was a rehash of last month's *Journal of Neurosurgery*.

Julie spent another several minutes by Melanie's side. It was painful seeing how fragile and small Melanie looked in the maze of high-tech equipment. As she looked at the comatose patient, the figure from Vicki's dream suddenly flashed in her mind. Was that generic image Vicki's interpretation of the Sewer Stalker or just a vision from her patient's past? Up to discharge, Vicki had still been reluctant to discuss the dream, which itself was not unusual—many patients exhibited similar reactions when confronted with recurring nightmares—though Julie sensed Vicki recalled more than she admitted. Though prior to her discharge, she'd denied remembering saying the words "God, not you" or any knowledge of what she'd dreamed, Julie believed otherwise. Vicki was holding back. Why? Maybe her behavior would change when faced with the actual video, but for now, without answers, Julie's sense of frustration only increased.

All through her training she'd been taught to believe only what could be palpated, seen, smelled, or auscultated. If a patient exhibited an abnormality on an electrocardiogram, it meant heart disease. If a patient complained of delusions and hallucinations, it meant a possible diagnosis of schizophrenia. But what if a patient's dream coincided so vividly with an event that actually happened? With Melanie lying near death and another patient terrified of falling asleep again, Julie felt compelled to believe this link was more than just a hypothesis.

She returned to her office and spent the next thirty minutes transcribing her interpretation of the last twenty-four hours. Her book project would have to be placed on hold, but in the interim she was determined to keep accurate notes.

On the way out, she dropped by the medical center library but was disappointed, though it wasn't unexpected, that their inventory didn't contain one text or journal on parapsychology. She did find one reference, though, some obscure article written by a psychologist who taught at the Institute of Parapsychology in Durham, North Carolina. She asked the reference librarian to order her a copy before leaving. A security patrol walked her to the parking lot.

Jake anxiously awaited Julie when she pulled into her drive at seven. She could hear him barking through the door.

Julie playfully cuffed him, stopping only after she noticed the call light on her answering machine blinking. She suspected it was the hospital or maybe Matt. She didn't expect Vicki.

"Hello, Dr. Charmaine," the tape replayed. "It's Vicki Zampisi. Please call me as soon as you receive this message."

Julie copied the number down and promptly dialed it. There was no answer. She tried again just to make sure she hadn't inadvertently dialed incorrectly. After seven rings, she hung up. Vicki wasn't home.

Julie replayed the tape. Vicki sounded less anxious than during her discharge. But maybe watching the news about the most recent assault had jarred her memory of the nightmare.

Julie dialed the number again.

Still no answer.

Benny Slade had been six foot four and an ex-USC defensive end. Though he never graduated, he would've been the class of '73. Unfortunately for Benny, the pinnacle of his existence had been the 1972 Rose Bowl, in which he sacked the opposing quarterback three times. From that point to his fiery death thirty-one years later, his life had been unemployment lines, Thunderbird, some coke when he could afford or steal it, and three children out of wedlock.

The '89 Le Mans had skidded out of control three weeks ago during a rain shower and crashed into a cement embankment, where it burst into flames.

Devlin stared at the body lying at the bottom of the aluminum coffin. Eisler had been very particular. The corpse needed to be large, male, and most significant, unrecognizable. Eisler had been adamant that the body be mutilated beyond visual identification. How he'd arrived at those specific parameters Devlin hadn't asked. So what if Benny had been black. The corpse was big, burned beyond recognition, and male. It'd have to suffice.

With one foot, the gardener kicked the coffin shut and walked over and waited by the backhoe. From the hilltop located at the east end of the mortuary, the lights twinkling twenty miles to the west in Los Angeles made a serene sight. And to think all these people here could enjoy this heavenly view for all eternity. Or until the next big earthquake.

Devlin swatted a bug on his arm. He wished Eisler would hurry up with that Zampisi lady. The nervous PhD had called him earlier to set up this show-and-tell. Now standing alone, the quiet glare of the grave excavation lights gave him the creeps. He wondered what old Benny would think of all this. Probably not much. If the sparcity of his funeral attendance was any indication, he'd obviously not done a whole lot of thinking while alive, either.

Tires on gravel caused the groundskeeper to turn. Downhill, at a turnout, two vehicles pulled in and stopped. One was Eisler's Lexus, the other he recognized as the van Zampisi had driven. As the two figures made their way up the well-manicured cemetery hill, one carrying a flashlight, Devlin checked the sky. A few clouds were building, but he could still make out many stars. Good. He wanted to get the casket back in the ground before any chance of rain.

Eisler led Vicki into the illumination. "Mr. Devlin, I'm sure you remember Ms. Zampisi."

Devlin would've shaken her hand but his were dirty. "Of course. Ms. Zampisi." He smiled, thinking about the extra ten grand this was going to cost Eisler and his associates.

Vicki's eyes rested on the closed casket. It was one of those inexpensive kinds and sat perpendicular to the long axis of the grave. A pile of dirt lay heaped to one side. She didn't speak. Devlin thought she appeared strained, even more so than a couple of days ago.

Eisler motioned her toward the grave, obviously in a hurry to get this charade over with too. "Ms. Zampisi, I'm sure you can understand why the foundation preferred to keep his burial confidential. That's why the mortuary had no record of him ever being here. Of course, Dr. Kovacs still requested all the proper procedures be carried out as far as the embalming and preparation of the body. He even went so far as to have a priest bless the grave site."

Vicki leaned down and touched the casket. "When was the funeral?"

"Six weeks ago," Eisler said, glancing at Devlin.

Vicki opened her purse and took out an envelope of the size used to mail Christmas or birthday cards. This one was stenciled with a pattern of little flying angels.

"I'd like to see the body," she said. She set her purse on the ground.

Eisler moved the purse out of the dirt. "I wouldn't recommend that, Ms. Zampisi. Because of the accident, Mr. Simmons was in a very advanced form of . . . decomposition. It's not a pretty site. Please rest assured, the body in that casket belongs to Ben Simmons."

Vicki never removed her eyes from the coffin. "I'd like to see Ben, Dr. Eisler."

Eisler shot Devlin a concerned look.

The gardener removed a crowbar from the backhoe. He kneeled down beside the coffin and inserted the flat end under the top. He paused and looked at Vicki. "Are you sure?"

Vicki didn't hesitate. "Please."

Devlin popped the seal and raised the top, revealing the body. He had anticipated this very request because he'd situated the lights so that as the top opened, it would cast a shadow over the contents of the casket.

Even in the dark, though, the corpse was evident. It was dressed in a black suit and its skin revealed charred and coagulated tissue. The face was barely recognizable as human, much less of the Negroid race. No hair was present except for a remnant of a mustache. Most had been burned off.

Vicki's eyes studied the entire length of the body, stopping only momentarily at the head.

"I warned you, Ms. Zampisi," Eisler said, watching her reactions carefully. "Here, let me help you." He attempted to pull her back.

Vicki shrugged him off, saying, "This isn't Ben Simmons."

Eisler's expression hardened. "This is Ben Simmons, Ms. Zampisi. Now forget him. The scientific community has."

Eisler and Devlin stepped back and waited for Vicki to drop the envelope inside the casket.

Instead, she turned and without a word, walked away.

Eisler stepped after her. "Remember our deal, Ms. Zampisi," he shouted.

In the dark Vicki didn't answer.

The dark blue, two-door sedan followed Vicki's van from Evergreen Manor all the way back to her apartment. Once Vicki had clearly gone inside, the car pulled halfway down the block and parked. Two hours later the sky clouded up. An hour after that, it began to drizzle.

Thirty-eight

Vicki stared stonily at the portable monitor set up in Julie's office.

Julie pressed PAUSE and the monkey image froze just before dissolving into static.

"I can back it up if you'd like," she said.

Vicki shook her head. "Listening to myself scream once like that is enough."

"I understand."

Julie allowed the video to complete its cycle, then ejected the cartridge. She'd adjusted her Monday clinic schedule to accommodate Vicki's morning request to be seen. And now seated across from her patient she couldn't help but be intrigued at the change she saw.

Dressed in jeans and a plain cotton shirt, Vicki no longer exhibited any fear or inhibition at watching her own dream sequence. She'd barely flinched at the plaintive sounds of terror in her voice. Something had transformed this woman's demeanor from one of fright to acceptance, or apathy maybe. Julie wasn't sure. She would almost have labeled Vicki as angry.

Julie returned to her desk. "Can you recall what the monkey was doing in your dreams?"

"He was trying to kill me."

"Why do you say *he*?"

"Because I never dreamed of a she monkey."

"Is that all?"

"No." Vicki sat quietly a moment before saying, "I believe the monkey represents Ben."

"When did you first feel it was Ben?"

"Can you read me what I said again?"

Julie found the place on the transcript. "Initially you said, 'Get away. Get away.' "

"Keep going."

Julie read further. "Then 'Stay away.' You said that twice, followed by 'I'm sorry.' "

"I think when I said I'm sorry. That's when I knew it was Ben."

"How did he appear?"

Vicki chose to look at her purse. "I can't really say. Dreams are funny, I guess. I just know Ben was there and wanted me dead."

Julie gave Vicki more time but when she didn't elaborate she asked, "What did you mean, 'I'm sorry'?"

Vicki shrugged. "The accident. The manner in which Ben died. This was almost twenty years ago. Maybe I just feel bad I'm alive and Ben is dead."

"Being alive is no crime." How many times had Julie told herself the exact same thing? She hoped Vicki took it to heart quicker than the years it'd taken her to accept the statement's validity.

"I know. But still it hurts. If I hadn't listened to Kovacs . . ." Vicki's voice trailed off.

"If you hadn't listened to Kovacs, what?"

A long silence followed, finally ending with Vicki shaking her head. "It doesn't matter anymore, Dr. Charmaine. The past is fixed, it can't be changed."

"But how you perceive past events can be altered. Believe me, I know."

Vicki sat impassively.

Julie couldn't tell whether anything she'd said was getting through or not. She felt reluctant to force the session further, though. There came a time to push but today wasn't that time. She waited for her patient to speak.

"There's another reason I needed to talk with you," Vicki said.

Julie set the transcript aside.

"An associate of Dr. Kovacs arranged for me to view Ben's grave," Vicki began. "I thought if I finally saw Ben in the ground and buried, I could put an end to all this baggage I've been hauling around for so long." She paused in thought.

"How'd it go?"

Vicki's icy gaze returned. "The bastards tried to pass off another corpse for Ben."

"You're serious."

"Yes. According to Kovacs, two months ago there was a nitrogen leak at the foundation resulting in the interruption of Ben's suspension. His body had to be destroyed. Yet, the body I witnessed definitely was not Ben's."

"You're sure."

"Believe me, there could be no mistake."

"But why would Dr. Kovacs even attempt such a stupid stunt?"

"It's obvious," Vicki said. "They can't find the real Ben."

The trees form an interlocking mesh of green and brown over his head. A comforting ceiling, far more satisfactory than cinder blocks, rusted pipes, and concrete. But as always, he feels exposed and vulnerable whenever he emerges from the sewer's confines and wends his way over the ground, searching. Always searching.

He smells the air, picking out rancid odors from a nearby mendicant camp—human and animal excrement, rotting food, and stagnating water. He shuffles from the isolated copse of trees, mostly short-lived shrubs, a few eucalyptus, and bounds across a blacktop round before diving back into another island suburban forest that has taken root and flourished along the Los Angeles River corridor.

He passes a pump house vault, a storm sewer entrance, a sequestered pond rife with algae bloom, and in short order arrives at the outskirts of the small homeless encampment, one of many tiny transient communities that sprout up each month only to vanish the next.

The ground is wet and littered with Dumpster trash—cigarette butts, liquor bottles, beer and soda cans, old soft-drink crates, and used condoms, wrinkled and wadded together like huge dead snails. Two tattered tarps lie stretched over a tripod of broom handles and he approaches the two figures lying beneath them with caution. Not out of fear, simply instinctual behavior. Neither glimpses him until he's almost upon the shelter. His shadow eclipses the early evening's moon's rays and the two stuporous derelicts look up languorously.

He recognizes neither face and shuffles past, vanishing back into the gloom before they have time to register anything amiss. A third person he catches from behind, relieving herself over a shallow hole scooped in the dirt, and just as the woman shifts and turns, a huge flat hand wallops her across the side of her head, effectively silencing the bag lady for the remainder of the night.

This foray will continue until almost dawn. Then thirty minutes prior to sunrise, he will descend back below ground.

Ronny Bledsloe found Ramani and Matt at their respective desks. He paused by the coffeemaker long enough to see it was out of cups. "Shit."

Ramani opened his drawer and pulled one out. He tossed it to the shift detective. "You owe me," he said, yawning.

Bledsloe retrieved the cup from the floor. "You hoarding Styrofoam now, Ramani?"

Matt waited while Bledsloe poured himself a cup. "So what did you find out?"

"Not a thing, except she drives a beat-up van in need of an oil change, shops at some liquor mart on Pennsylvania, and she spent thirty minutes visiting a mortuary up in Pasadena last night." Bledsloe found a vacant desk and sat down. "Then she drove to her apartment where she stayed the entire evening."

Matt agreed it wasn't much. After listening to Julie's tape, he'd followed a hunch and decided to put a tail on Vicki Zampisi. Ramani thought it was a waste of time till he heard Bledsloe was assigned to the stakeout.

Matt eyed Bledsloe. "You say a mortuary?"

"A place called Evergreen Manor. Tony place that overlooks the Two-ten freeway. Next time she goes I'll let you drive up there."

"Why would Ms. Zampisi spend thirty minutes at a mortuary?"

Bledsloe shrugged. "Maybe her mom died?"

"Her mom lives in Seattle. Anyone else with her?"

"She followed some guy driving a white Lexus. License number GE6425. I broke off at the entrance. The place looked closed for business and I would've been too obvious. She left alone."

Matt motioned to his partner, who'd already copied down the license number. Ramani would run a search first thing in the morning.

"That's it?" Matt asked, hoping it was. He still sensed Zampisi was in no way linked to the sewer killings and he didn't want to waste any more man-hours on her than necessary.

Bledsloe downed his coffee.

Matt took that as a yes. "Get some sleep, Ronny. You look like shit."

• •

Tuesday afternoon Matt and Ramani were scheduled to meet with Al Loren, chief of security at CUMC, this time about the Balsam assault.

Though the crime scene had been thoroughly investigated the night of the attack, Matt chose to initiate this follow-up meeting in the alley behind Old Red.

Ramani reset the scene. "The girl was found there," he said, pointing to the rear wall of one of the outpatient clinics. "She was facedown, positioned roughly north-south with her head abutting the south wall."

Matt looked from Old Red to the roof of the two-story clinic. "Lighting," he said.

"Two." Ramani motioned one building down. "Above the loading dock," he swung a hand behind him, "and a streetlamp on Medical Center Drive. That's fifty yards away."

Loren interjected. "Any time past six P.M., the service docks would be shut down. Leaving only the streetlamp which would have been partially blocked by the upper floors of Old Red."

"Plus the rainstorm," Ramani said.

Matt began to walk south toward Medical Center Drive. "Meaning that night the girl was pretty much in the dark." He stepped through a shallow puddle which Ramani and Loren hiked around. "So she leaves the halfway house, takes the shortest route to the medical center which would be east on Marenga and north on Bristol. She takes Medical Center Drive and decides to shortcut it behind Old Red. Why?"

Loren kicked some mud from his loafers. "At that late hour and under those inclimate conditions she probably just wanted to get out of the rain." The security chief swiveled and pointed back past the four-story Old Red. "Follow this service alley and turn right at Old Red and you can see the emergency room entrance, which would be the only building accessible at that time."

Matt stared at the asphalt. "So this scum nabs her in the alley, then vanishes." He gazed up at his partner. "The rain sure as hell didn't wash him away."

Ramani consulted his notepad. "The nearest sewer vault entry point is on Medical Center Drive. There's also one on Marenga, but both roads are fairly well traveled twenty-four hours a day with the shift changes and emergency traffic. Thus far no one's reported anything suspicious. The patrols are still checking."

"Maybe he didn't use the sewers," Loren said.

Matt turned and started retracing his steps. He'd already considered other options, especially since both vaults emptied into twenty-one-inch-diameter connecting pipes, severely limiting each as an efficient means of travel for any human, if not impossible. In fact, the only vault on hospital grounds large enough to easily accommodate a man was located in the medical center's basement. He could effectively rule that out because the Tunnel had been regularly patrolled since the Nixon murder.

Did the perp use the streets and then enter a vault elsewhere? Possibly. Or did someone other than the stalker attack Melanie Balsam? A copycat, for instance. He looked up and saw only the sheer concrete walls of the surrounding buildings. The stalker sure as hell didn't climb out of the alley. Unless he had suction cups for hands, which Matt wasn't ready to consider just yet.

The security chief's voice rose. "I said I believe I've rectified the problem in the Tunnel."

Matt caught his partner's eye. "We through here?"

"Our wad was shot the night the girl was brought in," Ramani said, shoving his notepad into his shirt pocket.

Matt felt the same frustration. "I'll meet you both down below," he said, swinging back down the alley past Old Red.

• •

Loren took the lead, Matt and Ramani followed.

"I must admit I was skeptical at first about your sewer theory," the security chief explained, "but after reading about the other victims, well, it's beginning to make sense, especially after considering those corroded bars, which by the way have been replaced."

They were approaching the generator room so everyone had to speak louder. Matt paused at the hall leading to housekeeping. Several vacated carts stood idle against the wall. Nothing out of the ordinary.

"And gentlemen," Loren pressed forward, "I've taken the liberty of adding one additional obstacle, just in case this asshole decides to play the long shot and come roaming our way again." He waited for the detectives to catch up.

Matt passed the generators. The next room was the one where the lone sewer well was located. Loren was waiting. There was a certain gleam in the security chief's eyes.

Ramani didn't miss the chance. "You're about to tell us you have Mr. Sewer Stalker tied up and waiting with a signed confession, right?"

The gleam vanished. Loren hustled the detectives into the ten-by-ten-foot generator access room. Overhead Matt could hear water running through the four-inch pipes that led to and from the adjacent generator room. Loren pointed to where the large sewer grille was located.

Lying securely on top was a square panel of metal. The edges just covered the greatest diameter of the circular grille's circumference.

Ramani walked over and kicked it. It sounded as solid as an armored tank.

Loren smiled confidently at his engineers' work. "We got two inches of solid cast iron bolted five inches into the cement floor." His foot kicked one of the four large bolts at each corner. "Here, take a look at these fucking screws. Hell, they're not even screws, they're three-quarter-inch metal pylons. This baby would stop Superman."

Matt kneeled closer and inspected the workmanship. It looked solid enough. He noted only a minimal amount of concrete chipping at the points where the bolts securing the iron lid entered the cement. "This is the only connection between the hospital's sewer system and the basement, correct?"

Loren kicked the iron cover once more. He was making this an irritating habit. "The only connection large enough for a human body to pass."

Ramani nodded approvingly. "It looks like you've just solved the problem, Mr. Loren." The compliment was cloaked in sarcasm. With a single motion of his head, he let Matt know he was out of there.

"What's eating Butthead?" Loren asked.

Before Matt could think of an appropriate response, the security chief's radio crackled. He listened briefly. "You got a call, detective. There's a phone in the main hall."

Julie reread the business card Vicki had given her. The Phoenix Foundation address was only twenty minutes from the medical center. Before leaving, Vicki had warned Julie to be careful, Kovacs was a dangerous man.

As Julie waited for Matt to arrive, she set the card aside and thumbed through the article she'd requested from the Medline search. It'd been faxed over from the medical center's library this morning. This particular scientific publication was more than fifteen pages and authored by Dr. Seward Brighton from the Institute for Parapsychology. The title of the journal was simply *Parapsychology.* The article, "The Parapsychological Evaluation of Violent Crime." The abstract summed up the article fairly well. The pages contained summaries and exposition concerning almost one-thousand cases over the last twenty years in which paranormal phenomenon were used to solve crimes against persons. The brief dissertation concluded with a quote by Franz Kafka. Julie recalled he was a writer who died in the early 1920's. What really struck her as odd was the quote's content.

> *". . . The dream reveals the reality which conception lags behind. That is the horror of life—the terror of art . . ."*

Julie had barely begun going back over the paper in more depth when Matt appeared in the doorway. She set the article aside while Matt found his customary chair. "I think you're spending more time at the hospital than I am," she said.

"Loren's sealed off the Tunnel from any access by way of the sewer," Matt said.

"He's closed off the basement vault?" Julie said.

"The room where we found the ear."

"Yes, where that nurse was abducted."

"He says the seal's designed to stop Superman."

Julie sensed the sarcasm. "I hope we aren't dealing with Superman."

For a moment they watched each other, fully aware of the truth to Julie's words. The detective leaned forward just a little. "How's the girl?"

"Melanie's still critical, though she does respond some to deep pain. And her EEG demonstrated enough activity to remain optimistic of her regaining consciousness soon. Now if you were to ask when, that's an entirely different set of predictions."

"I won't ask when."

"Her progress for any neuromuscular recovery is still very much guarded. But she's showing improvement. She's a fighter."

Matt's eyes wandered to the journal paper on Julie's desk. "I see you've widened your reading list. What does it say? That we should find a crystal ball and toss it under the first manhole cover we find?"

"I was only starting to read this when you came in."

"I still find it difficult to accept that tape as reality."

"It wasn't reality. It was a dream. The computer did what it was supposed to do. It matched an image from Vicki's dream."

"And you're convinced that image is linked to the Balsam assault. Parapsychologically?"

Julie was tempted to ask if Matt's tone was naturally sarcastic or just sarcastic on Tuesdays. She didn't. "No, but I can't ignore what Vicki saw. And even more so after talking with her again."

"You spoke with her today?"

"Just before I called you."

"How is she?"

"She's had a rough couple of days."

"I wonder if that has anything to do with her trip to the mortuary."

This caught Julie unprepared. "How—" There was only one way Matt could know. "You had Vicki followed."

"After I saw the tape."

"So you are taking her seriously."

Matt leaned back. Telling Julie how pretty she looked right now would've been entirely inappropriate. So he said what was appropriate. "I have one victim who was frightened to death, four more in the morgue who resemble hamburger meat, a dead nurse, and a teenage girl upstairs who isn't even aware she's still alive. Yes, Julie, I'm taking everything even remotely related to this case seriously. Just look at the city's overtime tab for the Stalker task force."

Julie picked up the business card and handed it to Matt. "Vicki left this with me."

Matt took the card, reading the corporate name and logo.

"The Phoenix Foundation." He looked up. "I already questioned Kovacs about Mitchell Beeden."

"And . . ."

"He didn't strike me as the remorseful type."

"Did he strike you as someone who would falsify a corpse?"

Matt used one corner of the card to clean a nail. "Is this your question or Ms. Zampisi's?"

Julie took this as a sign to proceed. "Sunday afternoon Vicki received a call from one of Dr. Kovacs's associates. His name was Christian Eisler. Supposedly he's some PhD Kovacs hired."

"I know, I met him."

"Anyway, Eisler basically propositioned Vicki into agreeing to forget the entire Simmons experiment ever took place on the condition he showed her Ben's grave. For some reason, Vicki believed that if she actually viewed Ben's burial place, she'd achieve closure and her nightmares would stop. So she agreed."

"Go on."

"Vicki drove out there last evening. You know that. Did you know Eisler met her there and led her to an unmarked grave?"

"No. Why unmarked?"

"Eisler explained the foundation preferred Simmons's burial be as discreet as possible. Anyway, when Vicki arrived, a grave had been excavated. Eisler claimed it was Simmons's. But when she viewed the body . . ." Julie shook her head.

"Didn't this Eisler character realize Vicki would recognize the real Simmons?"

"No. Eisler must've assumed that Ben's body would be unrecognizable after the experiment's failure so all he had to do was find any poorly preserved or, in this case, badly burned body and as long as it resembled Ben's gross dimensions, he would be able to pass it off as the real Ben Simmons. Needless to say, Vicki wasn't tricked. Or pleased."

"So where is Simmons's body?"

"Vicki doesn't know. And that's not all, Matt. She told me on the night she was nearly assaulted in the Shilden Hotel, she recalled seeing a shiny material covering the attacker's arm."

"Right, the cellophane."

Julie went on. "Vicki also remembers seeing a similar material on the floor in the foundation's cryostorage unit where Ben's body should've been, but wasn't. And then there was the same odd smell in both places. Not the sewage—an aseptic odor. Vicki swears Kovacs and Eisler are involved in Ben's disappearance." Julie paused briefly before dropping the bomb that Vicki had laid on her earlier. "She also believes Ben could've killed that nurse in the basement, and maybe the others too."

"She does? Why?" Matt's calm expression belied his incredulity.

"Because of her nightmares and because Ben's body is still unaccounted for."

"Is Vicki aware of the Balsam attack?"

"Yes."

"How's she taking it?"

"It shook her."

Matt needed time to think. This wasn't logical. "Maybe Kovacs and Eisler are covering something up, but how does what you just told me make them suspects or in this case accessories in six homicides?"

Julie shrugged. It did seem illogical. "Why would Eisler go through the trouble of showing Vicki the wrong corpse, unless they were attempting to hide something big? Let's suppose what Vicki said was true. Ben Simmons did suffer an accident that left him incapacitated. And Kovacs did try to cryopreserve him. Then there was a second accident and he began to thaw. Then—"

Matt rubbed his chin. He'd clearly forgotten to shave. "You know what I think? Vicki's batshit crazy."

"No, Matt, hear me out. Ben is missing. He's thawed out and

now he's *decomposing*. The tissue samples under the victim's nail. Even your coroner can't explain those."

"Please don't throw Vicki's dream monkey at me."

"Irene Inez did say *'chango'*."

Matt looked exasperated. "I don't know. I don't have witnesses. Hell, what's my motive? Frostbite of the brain."

Julie was losing him. She could see it in his face. She had to push harder. Her eyes settled on the business card. She suddenly grabbed it. "Let's call him."

"Who?"

"Kovacs."

"I told you I already talked with him."

She ignored him and dialed. "Don't worry, I'll ask the questions this time." She pressed a button that activated her speakerphone.

Matt ran his hands through his hair. "Jesus Christ. You're as crazy as your patient." He quieted when the number began to ring.

Julie waited. Five, six, seven rings. She was almost ready to hang up when someone answered.

"Hello." The voice was deep.

Julie read from the card. "Yes, I'm looking for a Dr. Wesley Kovacs of the Phoenix Foundation."

"I'm Dr. Kovacs. However, the foundation is in the midst of transferring all operations out of state."

"And what operations might those be?" Julie asked.

There was a pause, not drawn out, but long enough to make Matt give Julie a look.

"Are you a reporter?" Kovacs's voice wasn't friendly.

"No. I'm Dr. Julie Charmaine. I'm a friend of Ms. Vicki Zampisi."

This time the silence on the other end was almost audible. Matt leaned closer to the phone.

"I'm not acquainted with any Vicki Zampisi."

"How about Dr. Eisler then?" Julie asked.

There was another pause before Kovacs spoke. "Please don't ever call here again." This was followed abruptly by a dial tone.

Julie hung up. "He's lying," she said.

Matt barely heard her. That's because in his mind, he was already replaying the entire bizarre conversation. Of course the guy was lying. He already knew that. However, only someone with experience in interviewing hundreds of suspects would've been able to fathom that not only was this man lying, but more significantly, he didn't give a shit that whoever he was lying to, knew that he was lying. He was bold. And this type of brazen lie was always characteristic of a certain type of suspect. One who was convinced he'd just gotten away with something and no one would ever be able to prove otherwise.

Matt reached across Julie's desk and picked up the business card.

Thirty-nine

Julie gave Matt a lift back to his car in the coroner's lot. Neither looked at each other during the two-minute drive.

Matt remained silent, as if waiting for the question he knew would come. When it did, it came in the form of a statement.

"You're going to interview Kovacs again, aren't you," Julie said as she pulled in beside his Monte Carlo. She didn't wait for his comment. "I'd like to be present when you question him."

"Thanks for the lift." Matt opened the door.

"Matt, I said I'd like to go with you."

"It's against departmental policy," he said, avoiding her gaze.

Julie reached across for his arm. "Don't just get out."

"My car."

"I said I want to go with you."

Matt paused. "And I heard you. And I repeat, it's against departmental policy for a civilian to accompany a detective while questioning a suspect."

"So he is a suspect."

"Jesus Christ, this is crazy. No, he's not a suspect. Not yet. But he is a potential witness who just may know more than he's saying."

"Don't forget I have a sixteen-year-old patient with a fractured neck who may never walk again. If this guy had something to do with it . . ." Julie didn't mask the threat.

"This *is* about Melanie?"

"What the hell is that supposed to mean?"

"It means you've been on your own one-woman guilt trip since your sister's—"

Julie's palm flew toward Matt's face like it'd been launched from a missile.

The detective deflected it, catching her wrist with his own hand.

Julie's eyes bore into his. "You don't know me well enough to say that, detective."

Matt released his grip and rubbed the scar along his brow. "Ramani says cases like this bring out the best and worst in law enforcement." He worked his jaws a couple of times, before speaking again. "I'm sorry. What I said was uncalled for." He stepped out onto the pavement.

Julie thought his movements seemed mechanical. She decided to press the issue. "So what about it?" she asked.

Matt watched a pigeon fly to its roost above the coroner's building. Once the bird had landed, he turned and rested one elbow on the roof of Julie's car.

He said, "I'll have some men run over and check out Vicki's mortuary story, though it's unlikely Kovacs had anything to do with Melanie's assault."

"Then why was he lying? And don't tell me—"

"Wait just a minute. If, and this is a mighty big if, if I do let you come along, I, and I repeat, I do all the talking." Matt waited for her tacit agreement. "Get in," he finally said with obvious resignation.

Once inside his car, Julie said, "There is one advantage to having me come along, you know."

"What's that, early retirement?"

"Kovacs is a research scientist. What do you know about cryogenics, freezing coefficients, and cryoprotectants?"

"Nothing." Matt patted his side. "But I have a bigger gun."

Julie frowned. "Let's hope it doesn't come to that."

After fifteen minutes on the 10 freeway, Matt exited Alameda and drove south. Julie wasn't familiar with this primarily light-industrial section of the city, but Matt was. "Twelve blocks north of here is where those two gangbangers were discovered," he said.

Julie held back a groan. She could still see their mutilated corpses on the coroner's steel slab.

Matt turned left onto Pacific. "There's still time to change your mind."

"No way," Julie said.

The mostly one- and two-story houses and low-tech industrial buildings were not what Julie would have expected for a scientific foundation. She was used to CUMC and before that, UCLA. However, she was also cognizant of the fact that some of the most useful and innovative discoveries of this century had come out of structures that on the outside looked more like rental properties than sites of genetic and medical research.

The light turned red on Forty-sixth. Matt stopped. "There she be," he said, pointing to his right.

Julie checked the business address at the one-story rectangular warehouse. "Two twenty-five," she said.

The light turned green and Matt pulled into the lot and parked next to the only car visible out front. A black Mercedes.

The front entrance was locked as before.

Julie tried peering through the glass. Through the tint, she could see a light from under a door at the back. "There's someone inside." She stepped back, looking briefly at the surveillance video. "This really isn't what I had in mind for a foundation that supposedly freezes bodies for a business."

Matt shrugged. "What did you expect, Dr. Frankenstein and Igor waving a can of freon from the curb?"

He pressed the buzzer by the door. No sooner than he'd

released the button, they heard footsteps inside and the door to the reception room opened.

Reflexively, Matt pushed Julie away from the doors when Kovacs stepped up and released the lock.

He wasn't smiling. "This is private property. You're trespassing," he began but stopped when he recognized Matt. "Detective . . ."

"Guardian."

"Yes, Detective Guardian."

Kovacs turned to Julie. The corners of his mouth moved but it wasn't a smile. "And you're Dr. Charmaine, I presume."

"Dr. Julie Charmaine."

"We'd like to ask you a few more questions if it wouldn't be too inconvenient," Matt asked.

Kovacs's facial expression told them it was. "As a matter of fact, you've caught me at an awkward time. As I mentioned before," he waved, motioning to the empty lot and lack of reception furniture, "the foundation is in the midst of vacating the premises. I'm quite busy. If this pertains to Mr. Beeden, I thought that business was taken care of. Like I told you—"

Matt held up a hand. "Dr. Kovacs, I'm here on the matter of Ben Simmons."

The doctor met both his visitors' eyes with a piercing stare. After a moment of silence, he made his decision. "I apologize if I misled you earlier, Dr. Charmaine," Kovacs said. "We can talk in my office. But please keep it brief."

Kovacs led them through the reception and back down the front hall. Julie noticed the sparcity of furnishings and packing crates.

"I recall you introducing yourself as a doctor," he said to Julie.

"That's correct." She wasn't sure how much Matt wanted her to say so she kept her comments brief. "I'm a psychiatrist at CUMC."

"Ah, the university. At one time I was a visiting staff physician there. I, too, am a psychiatrist by training. The field has certainly changed over the years."

"Yes and it continues to change. For the better I hope."

"We shall see." Kovacs's gaze shifted to Matt. "So, detective, how can I satisfy your curiosity with Ben?"

"You previously stated Mr. Simmons was deceased," Matt said, removing a notepad from one pocket. He turned to his past notes.

Kovacs nodded. "That's correct. Ben died while undergoing a procedure. A terrible, terrible accident. And totally unpredictable. That was years ago." The doctor pointed to one of the photos on the far wall. "That's him there."

Julie and Matt walked over for a closer look. The man in the photo was young, blond, and certainly good looking. He also appeared rock-hard like he was some sort of weight lifter. Another individual was also present in the photo. She recognized a younger version of Dr. Kovacs. The two men had struck similar poses, arms crossed over their chests.

"For a period Ben assisted my research," Kovacs continued. "That is until he became too difficult to control."

"How do you mean?" Matt asked.

Kovacs seemed to enjoy elaborating. "Ben was mentally compromised. His views of reality became increasingly distorted. One time you'd find him courteous and cordial, a minute later he was transformed into a different individual. Angry, distrustful, even psychotic. It was scary even for me and I'm not a small person." He paused. "After one particularly violent outburst, I committed Ben. You see he was given up for adoption early and had lived in a succession of foster homes. Once I brought him to my clinic, I became his legal conservator. Unfortunately, one morning Ben suffered a massive seizure and aspirated while in my care. This led to the development of a fulminent aspiration pneumonia which was unresponsive to antibiotics. He succumbed a short time later."

Julie moved forward in her chair. "Vicki said this accident occurred during an electroshock session."

"Ms. Zampisi's correct."

"Was an autopsy performed?" Matt asked.

"No. As the treating doctor, I already knew what killed him. A postmortem exam wasn't necessary."

"Dr. Kovacs," Matt began. "Your business here at the foundation is freezing individuals."

"Or individual parts," Kovacs said with a smile. "We prefer to use the more accurate term, suspension."

"Did Ben Simmons undergo any form of suspension?"

"You asked me that before and the answer remains the same. An emphatic no."

Matt flipped to a page of his notepad. "I assume you're familiar with the Sewer Stalker investigation."

"An individual would have to be in suspension not to be," Kovacs said, putting his full weight back in his chair.

"Doctor, if I was to tell you that each of the victims had collected necrotic tissue samples under their nails, how would you respond?"

"You want an explanation?"

"This is only rhetorical, Doctor."

Kovacs's gaze moved between Matt and Julie, settling on Matt. "I'd have to say I have no explanation. If I may offer a suggestion, though, your city's coroners would in all likelihood be more adept at supplying a satisfactory answer. I would ask them."

Matt ran a finger along the length of the scar above his eye. "One more scenario, Doctor. Again, simply rhetorical. If an individual were frozen—"

"Suspended."

"I stand corrected. If a person were suspended, then underwent an unscheduled thawing, what would be the consequence?"

"How do you mean, consequence?"

"Could this person survive?"

Kovacs inhaled and exhaled deeply, glancing at his watch. "Depends on a variety of factors. Length of time of the suspended state, circumstances of the thawing, and, most important, support systems in place once this individual returned to a normal body temperature; by support systems I mean oxygen, respirator support, cardiac monitoring, et cetera. In short, detective, your question cannot be answered with a simple yes or no."

Julie watched Matt ponder Kovacs's response and waited for him to ask the question which was on both their minds.

Matt allowed Kovacs one more look at his watch. "Doctor, if Mr. Simmons had been suspended—"

"He wasn't."

"Your former employee states otherwise."

"I told you she is unstable and depressed. Prevarication is a symptom of dementia."

"Then humor me, Doctor. If Mr. Simmons had been suspended for ten, fifteen, twenty years," Matt continued, "what would be the physical state of his body once he was revived?"

Kovacs drew his chair nearer his desk. "I make it a practice, detective, never to postulate on the absurd, impossible, or irrational. Ben never was, is not currently, and never will be a client of the Phoenix Foundation. Now I really must ask you both to leave. Any prolongation of this meeting can be directed to the foundation's law firm."

Matt seemed to be on the verge of ending the interview when Julie abruptly leaned forward and asked, "How's it done?"

"How's what done?" There was more than a modicum of disdain in Kovacs's tone.

"Cryogenics. How's the tissue frozen?"

Matt cleared his throat, waiting.

"Being a psychiatrist, entrenched in academia," Kovacs said, "you'll probably be unable to fully understand. It's a very complicated process."

Julie smiled ingenuously. "I appreciate your concern, Doctor, but I'm really just curious. I've read a little about the process in the paper and—"

"First," Kovacs cut in, "the tissue is drained of all blood. Then, once the specimen is permeated with a cryoprotectant, the entire sample is placed in a suspension of silicone oil. The suspension tanks are called dewars. In the dewar, the temperature is cooled to minus seventy-eight degrees Celsius. For your reference, dry ice is between minus seventy-eight to eighty degrees centigrade. Liquid nitrogen cools the sample to minus one hundred and ninety-six degrees. At this extreme cold, all metabolic activity ceases and the sample is considered to be in a state of permanent hibernation, if you will.

"That's as simple as I can make it," he said. "I hope the explanation will suffice." Without waiting for a response, he rose and walked around his desk. "Now, I really must—"

Julie wasn't finished. "But what about ice crystals forming in the blood? Aren't they damaging to the tissues?"

Kovacs faced her, his words were slow and deliberate. "As I just said, all the blood is drained and replaced with a cryoprotectant. An organic antifreeze. There are no ice crystals."

"What kind of cryoprotectant?"

Kovacs forced a smile. "Is the university planning on entering the cryonics business?"

"What kind, Dr. Kovacs?"

"Without divulging any trade secrets, the cryoprotectant the foundation utilizes is actually a combination of three solutions. Glucose, alcohol, and glycerol."

"Alcohol is very flammable," Julie said, but her mind was already moving back to the Irene Inez case.

"Ether is also very flammable, Dr. Charmaine, as are a host of other chemicals used in the field of medicine. I trust you'll believe me when I say I'm well aware of the combustion coefficient of alcohol. Thank you for your concern." With that he walked across the carpet and swung open the door. "If you'll excuse me."

Matt stood. "Once more for both our consciences, it's safe to say then that Ben Simmons never underwent any sort of cryoprocedure."

"Detective, Ben's remains were donated to a research facility, the name of which has escaped me."

Julie waited until Matt was in the hall before pressing the doctor one last time. But as she opened her mouth, a scream silenced her. Almost as soon as the first cry ended, a second, more prolonged and louder, split the air.

"What—" Kovacs started but was cut off by a third cry.

The doctor's skin paled.

Matt unholstered his revolver. "What's behind those doors?" he asked, stepping in the direction of the caterwauls.

"The laboratory," Kovacs said.

Julie made it to the double doors just behind Matt and the foundation director.

Matt held up a hand. "Wait here," he told her and shoved inside, right behind the doctor.

Julie followed before the doors closed. She saw Kovacs lumber up a central aisle with Matt on his heels.

The disturbance came from a corner of the laboratory behind a counter topped with several microscopes, a centrifuge, and a glass aquarium. Two men in work clothes stood staring at something blocked from view by boxes.

Seeing Kovacs, one of the men yelled. "It's got James by the hand! Hurry! I think his fucking finger's gone!"

Matt kicked a box aside and stopped in midstride. A third man kneeled on the floor, curled in a fetal position, bent over both arms. Only agonized whimpers escaped between his clenched jaws.

"What happened?" Kovacs pushed through the two men.

The man who'd yelled said, "James thought it was dead."

"And he removed the weight," Kovacs finished.

No one said anything.

"Damn it." Kovacs knelt beside the injured man.

Matt motioned the other two movers back and he squatted down near the man's head.

Julie could see a small pool of blood forming under the man's abdomen where one hand was still held out of sight. The man rocked back and forth. "Get it off me, Doc, get the fucking thing off me."

"I'll call the paramedics," Julie said.

"No." Kovacs looked at Matt's gun. "You won't be needing that. Now if you'll help me roll James over, I'll take care of Stephanie."

Holstering his pistol, Matt and Julie gently coaxed the injured man on his side. His face was purple with swollen veins and tensed muscles and both eyes were squinted shut, squeezing out clear droplets of tears.

Only when he was successfully rolled over did the source of the injury become obvious.

"What the hell is that, Kovacs?" Matt reflexively pushed Julie back.

"That, detective, is Stephanie."

The monkey lay balled up around the man's right hand, its incisors buried in the thickest part of the man's index finger. Blood continued to dribble down along the wrist and forearm, coalescing in the expanding pool on the floor.

Instantly, Julie noted the smell of infected and diseased tissue.

She guessed the putrid stench originated from the small mammal because its skin contained multiple festering sores and much of its body and tail were devoid of fur. Only isolated stringy brown patches remained, mostly on its head and upper back.

When Kovacs attempted to disengage the animal, the man screamed. "No, it's biting harder."

"Calm down, its just a monkey," Kovacs said, looking up at the counter. He pulled the blanket from the aquarium and covered the animal. "Don't move, James."

Matt lifted one corner of the blanket. "That animal looks dead."

"As James will attest, Stephanie is far from dead." Kovacs stood and began shuffling through a drawer.

Julie kneeled beside Matt. "What happened? Is she rabid?"

"Not rabies." Kovacs pulled pliers from a small toolbox. "Okay, James, I'm going to remove her."

The man groaned, but didn't speak.

The other men moved away a step.

Kovacs pointed to one. "Throw me some gloves."

Matt passed the canvas gloves to Kovacs. "You may have to kill her," he said.

"True, detective, but she's too valuable to sacrifice now." Once Kovacs had the gloves on he pulled off the blanket. "For the moment I simply want her off James's finger and back in her cage."

Julie glanced around but saw no cage, only the aquarium filled with water.

"Now, detective," Kovacs said, positioning himself behind James's back. "If you will slowly raise the man's arm, I'm going to vise grip one of Stephanie's paws. She should release James's finger and when she does I'll grab her."

"Careful, Matt," Julie warned.

"Use these," the other worker said, passing Matt his gloves.

On the count of three, Matt raised the man's arm, giving Kovacs access to one of the monkey's front paws. The pliers bit into the dark flesh with such force, a tiny digit popped free and landed on Kovacs's sleeve.

The reaction of the monkey was nothing that Julie would've predicted. The animal didn't panic, jerk, or jump or try to free herself. No sound came from her mouth. She simply opened her jaws and swung her head toward the metal gripping her paw. Her controlled movement reminded Julie of a mechanical stuffed animal whose batteries had run low.

James cried out and pulled his hand free.

Kovacs grabbed Stephanie by the tail, lifted her over the aquarium, and dropped her in. Once the lid was in place, he set a twenty-pound weight on the top.

Julie felt nausea twist in her midsection as she watched the diseased animal sink below the water's surface. She noticed Matt step nearer for a closer look, a similar expression of sickening disbelief on his face.

Julie shivered, yet couldn't remove her eyes from the brown mass crawling rhythmically along the bottom of the aquarium, its mangy head swinging from side to side, as if foraging for food. "Is *this* part of your research?"

"I revived Stephanie from a cryosuspension less than a week ago," Kovacs said, flicking the severed monkey digit off his sleeve.

"I find that difficult to believe," Matt said.

"Believe it, detective. Stephanie's no dream."

Forty

Julie and Matt returned to the hospital in relative silence. Julie still couldn't completely accept seeing a mammal submerged underwater for that length of time without coming to the surface to breathe. Especially a dying mammal. And there was little doubt in Julie's mind Stephanie was dying. Keeping an animal alive in such poor physical condition was grotesquely inhumane.

Kovacs's terse explanation left too many questions to be even remotely credible. It was obvious to her and she guessed to Matt too, that the research scientist had purposely skirted the truth. She did recall Kovacs calling Stephanie a metabolically transformed mammal. What had he meant, *metabolically transformed?*

She looked over at Matt. His same somber expression hadn't changed since they'd left the foundation. She had no clue to his thoughts. He drove, staring straight ahead.

"I'm not sure whether to call Channel Two News or the Humane Society," Julie said.

Matt's gaze didn't waver. "That monkey was no longer a monkey. It was a . . ."

"Freak," Julie said.

"Yeah, something like that." Matt briefly watched while a highway patrol car pulled a pickup truck over. "You know, not breathing could have its advantages."

"Sure, if you wanted to swim the English Channel underwater."

"Or," Matt said, glancing her way, "if someone wanted to spend all his time crawling through the sewers."

"Are you suggesting Stephanie's the stalker?"

"Not Stephanie, though I have to admit the idea is consistent with Ms. Zampisi's dream."

Julie clearly deduced Matt's inference. "Two times Kovacs denied Simmons ever underwent cryonic suspension," she said.

"He also denied being acquainted with a certain former female employee."

Julie stared at the traffic from her passenger-side window. "I just can't conceive that scenario. If long-term freezing did that to some poor animal, think how it might affect a human."

Matt grinned. "He'd be a real gem, wouldn't he?"

"God, he'd be a monster."

Matt slowed and pulled into University Hospital's main entrance.

Julie stepped out onto the walk. "Kovacs never did elaborate specifically on the final disposition of Simmons's body. If it was donated to a research facility, there must be records of the transaction somewhere."

"Twenty-year-old paper trails have ways of disappearing."

"That is a long time," Julie said, reminded again of Simmons's missing hospital file. "I'll run the question by our medical school director."

"Don't get too involved or I'll have to put you on the city's payroll."

Julie waved. "Thanks for the lift."

After seeing that she made it safely inside, Matt shifted gears and exited the medical center grounds. He needed Dorfman's assistance and a search warrant for the foundation's records and property. If he could seize samples, the coroner's forensics lab might be able to determine whether the monkey tissue had undergone changes similar to the tissue collected from the victims' nails. Stephanie sure as hell wasn't the Sewer Stalker but if any findings matched—the possibilities seemed too remote to even consider, yet at the moment, the stalker task force had failed to unearth any other potential suspects worthy of serious consideration. Suddenly Dorfman's decomposing animal hairs were looking less and less like wild hairs.

Matt headed back to Parker Center. Filling out the police report and affidavit declaring what evidence he was seeking would be the easy part. Finding an understanding judge to affirm and sign it might take a little more explaining.

The UCLA medical director was attending an out-of-town conference when Julie called so she left a message with her work phone number. She hoped her inquiry would settle an issue that had gnawed at her since returning to the medical center.

Julie could understand a prominent physician like Dr. Kovacs flatly denying ever undertaking a cryonics experiment involving a human subject, but to claim Simmons's body had been donated to a local research facility for cadaveric purposes while a foundation associate tried to show Vicki Simmons's grave created a dangerous contradiction. Cadavers donated to science were normally cremated. There should never have been a grave site.

Kovacs and his associate obviously hadn't coordinated their stories. Julie found it impossible to go back to her work. She decided to confront this inconsistency as she would any other question or problem in her practice. She'd research it.

Leaving the clinic in the hands of her house staff, Julie dialed information to the county registrar's office. She called the number. The address was 12400 East Imperial Highway and the office would be open till 5 P.M. Julie identified herself and stated she would be researching a former patient's death. All she needed would be the patient's death certificate. She gave the clerk the patient's age, and treating physician.

Julie found the county clerk's office on the third floor. Amazingly, the clerk had retrieved the microfilm containing Ben Simmons's death certificate and left it waiting for her when she arrived.

Julie showed the clerk her driver's license.

"You're young to be a doctor," the clerk smiled.

Julie returned the smile. "I appreciate your efficiency," she said, receiving the box of microfilm.

"We have death certificates back over forty years and I've worked in this particular office for almost one third of those years," the clerk explained, pausing as Julie checked the box labeling. "We have detectives and coroner's investigators periodically, but not psychiatrists. This an unusual case?"

"Somewhat," Julie said, not wanting to be curt but not wishing to discuss any details either.

The clerk didn't press further and showed Julie to the microfilm imagers.

None was occupied and Julie picked the newest-looking one. She opened the box and inserted the roll. She recalled Kovacs saying he'd been Simmons's legal custodian, and as Simmons's treating physician as well, Kovacs would've been the one to certify the death certificate.

Julie had signed several death certificates herself during her training and she was familiar with the space for the body's final disposition. By stating medical research on the body disposition line, the mortician would be bypassed and the body would be transferred directly to the facility where the research was to be scheduled. Ninety-five percent of the time medical research meant the bodies were being donated to cadaver programs. Sometimes other research such as tissue harvesting was involved. She wondered what she'd find on Ben Simmons's certificate. Regardless, if a coroner was not involved, Kovacs could've listed any final diagnosis within medical reason and he would not have been second-guessed.

Julie perused the S's. More than fifty individuals with the last name of Simmons expired that year according to county records. From here it was relatively easy to pick out the one she was interested in. There was only one Benjamin.

She adjusted the fine focus dial. She knew she was close. The patient had died August 6, 1983 and he'd been twenty-eight. Julie searched for the signature of the certifying physician. DR. WESLEY KOVACS M.D. This was it. He'd treated Simmons and certified his death. He was at least telling the truth on that account. The diagnosis was more complex. There were three lines.

IMMEDIATE CAUSE OF DEATH: CARDIORESPIRATORY ARREST
Contributing Causes:
1) Aspiration Pneumonia
2) Status Epilepticus

She found no coroner's addendum. As Kovacs had said, the disposition line was marked MEDICAL RESEARCH.

Julie jotted down the pertinent details.

As she wrote, several things concerned her. The receiving facility for the body on the medical research line was abbreviated with three letters: CPC.

Kovacs had mentioned Simmons had been donated to some medical school, but Julie couldn't think of any school with the initials CPC. The other thing that bothered her was why Simmons hadn't automatically become a coroner's case making a coroner's investigation mandatory. There were two red flags in the diagnosis list the registrar should have questioned: the seizures and the aspiration pneumonia. Each by itself would be enough at CUMC to automatically flag a coroner's postmortem exam. Oddly, a space for race was left blank.

Julie finished writing and reexamined the certificate. In a way it vindicated Kovacs's statements but in another way it raised even more questions. Did Ben Simmons have a long history of epilepsy? Vicki never mentioned it. And without any coroner's second opinion, Kovacs was free to certify any cause of death he felt was accurate. He could even go so far as to falsify certain key elements, including the entire certificate if he so desired. Without a body, since it was donated for medical research and therefore unavailable for exhumation, who could disprove him? No one.

"CPC." Julie read the letters out loud. What did CPC stand for? All the way back to CUMC, Julie played the acronym game. There was UCLA, USC, LL for Loma Linda, and a host of others, but she could think of no research facility with the initials CPC.

Bledsloe had just finished off a double-double from an In-and-Out Burger when Vicki emerged from her apartment. She gazed once up and down the street, checked the darkening sky, then proceeded to her van.

Vicki drove west on Pennsylvania and stopped at the red light on Soto. Overhead, she heard the deep rumble of thunder and outside her window, the air smelled laden with smog and moisture.

The failed mortuary deception had been the final straw. Ben obviously wasn't buried, and a body didn't just evaporate. Kovacs knew where he was, and Vicki meant to find out. And if the tapes were available she'd confiscate those too.

The light turned green and the traffic moved slowly across the intersection. Looking ahead, Vicki could see the next traffic lights in a continuous blinking-red pattern. That was the hold up. Only one car could pass at a time.

Vicki pulled out of the line of cars and took a quick right on Soto and sped up to Michigan where she turned left. From behind, she heard a squeal of brakes and in her rearview she saw a dark sedan swing wide, barely averting a collision with a pickup truck.

The lights on Michigan were functioning normally and Vicki steered toward the freeway. Keeping an eye on the car ahead, Vicki pulled her purse close and reached inside. The pistol rested next to her compact. She couldn't really see herself using it but the gun's presence would give Kovacs something to seriously consider. And if push came to shove, Vicki would not be on the receiving end. This time, the answers she sought would be hers before she left Kovacs's home.

A train whistle came suddenly, blaring from her left. One car up, Vicki watched a furniture truck jump the tracks. Though the warning lights were blinking, the swing poles remained in their up positions.

"Hurry the fuck up," Vicki muttered, waiting while the car in front of her eked across. She let her foot off the brake.

The Metrolink barreled toward the intersection. Ignoring the mounting vibrations under her floorboard, Vicki stomped the accelerator and bounced over the railroad tracks just as the warning poles began their descent.

Feeling lucky, she entered the northbound lanes of Interstate 5. She wanted to make it to Elysian Heights before the rain.

"Goddammit, god fucking dammit," Bledsloe cursed, watching the Metrolink roll to a stop before clearing the intersection. The red warning lights continued their incessant blinking.

The shift detective opened his glovebox and grabbed a stick of chewing gum. The van was good as gone.

"Happy surveillance, Guardian." Bledsloe tossed the wrapper on the street.

Forty-one

The Sewer Stalker task force was in high gear, and because no legitimate suspects had been apprehended, the mayor was on Chief Williams's ass who was on Captain Osshoff's ass, and the ass-kicking progressed unhindered, downhill, like a runaway fusion reaction.

Earlier, Ramani had taken the search warrant declaration to the courthouse for a signature. Though the judge they were seeking was tied up in court, Matt still hoped for an affirmation before today's session ended. If not, he'd be forced to resort to a telephonic search warrant. Or wait until the morning, giving Kovacs even more time to "dispose of any evidence." Justice was a double-edged sword.

Dorfman was behind his desk when Matt arrived. Dorf had called him over to "discuss something." Matt hadn't like the tone of the coroner's voice.

Dorfman continued to study the contents of a manila folder. "You like puzzles?"

"No. Hated them as a kid."

"Well, I got one for you."

The blinds over the single office window were pulled up for a change, so Matt gazed outside. The overcast had turned to drizzle. The rain explained why the blinds were raised in the first place. If it'd been bright and sunny out, Dorfman would've had them shut as he did most of the time in sunny Southern California. He didn't like the sun, often referring to the tan of today as the skin cancer of tomorrow.

Watching Matt, Dorfman leaned back and shut the blinds. Before he could say anything else the phone rang. Dorf answered and handed over the receiver. "For you."

"Ramani?"

"Doesn't sound Ramaniish."

Matt took the phone. "Guardian here."

"Hello, Matt." It was Julie.

Matt glanced at Dorfman who simply shrugged.

"Matt, I found the name of the facility where Simmons's body was supposedly donated. It was typed on his death certificate."

"I'm over at the coroner's—"

"Great. I'm in my office. I can be there in ten minutes."

Matt cupped the phone. "Dorf, you mind if Dr. Charmaine sits in? She helped assist with the Salazar identification."

Dorfman, never averse to a pretty lady, said, "She might even be of assistance."

"We're on the second floor," Matt told her.

"I'll meet you inside."

Julie parked in the first open staff slot. She saw Matt standing at the entrance. As she greeted him, she could see he hadn't shaved and he appeared haggard. The Sewer Stalker was fraying everybody's nerves.

On their way back to Dorfman's office, she summarized what she'd discovered at the county registrar's.

"And CPC doesn't ring a bell?" Matt asked.

"No, but I made a note to ask Vicki. Maybe she knows. Also there's the question of why no autopsy. Today, a diagnosis similar to Simmons's would make a postmortem exam automatic."

"The laws haven't changed. Why no coroner's investigation then?"

Julie shrugged. "It's strange."

Dorfman was waiting at the door when they arrived. "Please, both of you, come in and sit down," the coroner said. "Hello, Julie."

Julie shook his hand.

When all were seated, the coroner placed several folders before him. "Frankly, Matt, I'm puzzled. It's the DNA analysis."

Julie listened quietly.

"What about the DNA analysis?" Matt asked.

Dorfman-opened one of the folders. It was thicker and was a different color, gray. "Ever since the first victim, this case has been particularly unsettling. For starters, there was Ms. Irene Inez. Official cause of death, cardiopulmonary arrest. Unofficially . . . I'm not sure. She exhibited nothing that should've been fatal."

Julie agreed.

"And the other victims," the coroner continued. "There at least we have causes of death. Massive injuries exhibited most blatantly by Mr. Jorge Salazar, a.k.a. Arbol, injuries that would've required tremendous strength to commit. And Señor Salazar's extremities weren't cut. They were ripped.

"But the most intriguing—I'm getting tired of saying puzzling—the most intriguing findings have to do with the tissue samples collected from the fingernails of each victim, especially the Humphries and Beeden victims, the two found stuffed inside the pipe," Dorfman reminded them.

Julie cringed. She glanced at Matt, who shrugged as if finding a corpse shoved inside a sewer pipe was an everyday occurrence.

Dorfman briefly waited till he had both their attentions before continuing. "Six days ago I sent fingernail samples from the initial four victims, Inez, Nixon, Humphries, and Beeden to a DNA specialty lab in Maryland. Along with those samples, I sent slides of the hairs found in the medical center basement after the Nixon girl's assault. Then two days ago I sent a rush order, samples taken from the most recent victim—" he pointed to Julie "—I believe Matt said she was your patient."

Julie nodded. "Melanie Balsam."

"How is she?" Dorfman digressed briefly.

"There's been some improvement. Hopefully she'll be conscious and talking soon."

Matt shifted impatiently in his chair.

The coroner got back on track. "I won't mention the hefty tab, but the results of their prelim DNA analysis arrived yesterday." Dorfman paused, only increasing the suspense. "And all the samples match. Perfectly."

Julie held up one hand. "You're saying the same person who attacked Irene Inez also murdered the other girls, then?"

Dorfman reached for another folder, this one the manila color of the coroner's department. "Hold on. I haven't gotten to the most intriguing aspect."

The coroner motioned to Matt. "You recall that conversation I had with you and Ramani after the discovery of Humphries and Beeden?"

Matt nodded. "Concerning the state of the tissue."

"Yes." Dorfman's gaze shifted to Julie. "It seemed so odd that all the samples we isolated exhibited minor variations in their states of decay."

Decay. Julie tensed.

Dorfman folded his hands across his belly. "It was bizarre because they reminded me of a case I had years ago, during my residency. A woman had fallen through the ice up north, and she'd remained semi-frozen until spring when the lake thawed. Her body was discovered two weeks after the first warm spell. And I distinctly remember the histopathology findings from the poor woman, though for the life of me I can't recall her name. Anyway, they were very similar to what we have here. If I were a betting man, I'd almost say the samples isolated from our victims were taken from a corpse that had at one time been frozen and subsequently begun to thaw out. And with thawing, came decomposition."

Julie looked at Matt but he wouldn't meet her shocked gaze.

"What's so odd is I've yet to see a frozen corpse commit a crime," Dorf said, "much less a homicide. Yet this tissue is decomposing. Or rather was."

"You're sure the tissue's human?" Matt asked.

"The human genome is characterized by forty-six chromosomes." The coroner motioned to Julie. "Feel free to jump in on this part because what I'm about to discuss actually falls more in your realm of expertise. The cells we identified from each of the victims contained *forty-eight* chromosomes."

Julie let out a soft groan.

"I'm awaiting the final karyotype," Dorfman followed up.

Matt tensed impatiently. "Forty-eight. Dammit Dorf, is this thing human or not?"

Dorfman pointed to Julie. "Your show."

Julie took a second to gather her thoughts. "That's correct, the normal human genome is made up of forty-six chromosomes, including two X's if female, or an X and Y if male. However, entire texts have been written about a myriad of conditions characterized by chromosomal abnormalities. I'm familiar with two that involve forty-eight, there's probably more. One of those two we can eliminate immediately. This condition is lethal early in life, death usually occurs in three to six months secondary to severe cardiomyopathy and total organ failure.

"The other condition, forty-eight-XXYY, concerns me. A variant of forty-seven-XYY syndrome, these individuals are all males of subnormal IQ's. Some are frankly retarded. The condition is also characterized by certain defects of the elbow joints and larger than normal dentition."

"And," Matt said.

Julie frowned. "Forty-eight-XXYY males are also known to be acutely antisocial and some studies have demonstrated increased incidents of aggressive or violent behavior."

Matt rubbed irritatingly at his brow. "What the hell was Kovacs doing back then in his lab?"

"Kovacs can't alter an individual's genetic makeup," Julie said. "No one can. You're born with what you have, the good, or the less than good."

"There's more perplexing news," Dorfman said. "All human cells also contain various other cellular structures, just as other animals' cells do, a cow, a pig, a bird. And this brings me to my next point. Though these samples appear to have originated from a human, albeit an abnormal human, they were all missing a significant kind of organelle—or subcellular structure. One that without, the cell should die. But these didn't. Then again, maybe that's why they were decaying. They were already dead."

"I don't follow you," Julie said.

"That's quite understandable. I don't follow the findings either. I first noted this abnormality after the Humphries autopsy. I saw it again with Beeden, so I went back and reviewed the samples from the Inez and Nixon posts. And they were all quite similar. None of the foreign tissue cells contained mitochondria. At least that's what I thought using conventional light microscopy. So I submitted all the samples to our electromicroscopy department. They confirmed my earlier observations. Only the increased magnification went a step further. The cells actually contained mitochondrial remnants, but the organelles were in a severe state of atrophy. They might as well have not been there at all because in their markedly atrophic state, they sure wouldn't function the way they were meant to function."

"Which is?" Matt asked.

Julie answered for Dorfman. "Cellular respiration. Breathing. Oxygen." She looked at the coroner.

"Some of the better-preserved cells also contained excessive levels of lactic acid," Dorfman went on. "Especially the decaying muscle cells. Also, all the foreign tissue samples contained an alcohol-glycerol mixture. No blood. Explain that."

Julie felt her facial muscles tense as she met the coroner's gaze. A human without mitochondria. Impossible. But she couldn't deny what she'd witnessed in Kovacs's laboratory.

"Stephanie," she said.

Seven times he's felt flesh and bone render under the shearing force of his fingers. Seven times he's heard their shrieking cries of agony and mercy. And seven times his instinctive thirst for recompense remains unquenched.

He passes numerous side tunnels, many far too narrow to accommodate his bulk. Small furry denizens of the wet and dark scurry and scatter to avoid his outstretched hands, the efforts of the unfortunate falling inches short. He stops and consumes, letting the discarded rodents' offal drop at his feet. Sniffing the miasmic air, he detects nothing belonging to his past, yet some unspoken code, innate and primordial, tells him he's nearer than he's ever been. He presses on, his nostrils quivering in anticipation.

The putrid stench of decay and underground methane no longer troubles him. But his recollections do. Where he once heard laughter and gaiety, he hears only the ineluctable drumbeat of bitter loneliness; where he once felt his teacher's gentle and tender caress, he feels only the cold and squalor; where he once tasted her warm moist folds flush with passion and blood, he tastes only filth and garbage.

He squeezes past thick rust-encrusted water pipes wet with rivulets of moisture and comes upon a partial wall of bricks, some approaching a century in age. A large part of the immense vault has crumbled into a mountain of stone rubble, exposing stretches of rough-hewn rock. He climbs over the debris and begins a slow, gradual ascent. Crouched on the circular rim of a huge valve, a ravenous rat leaps at his face for a quick meal and instead becomes a meal. Only the rodent's tail, as thick and long as a writhing night crawler, is tossed aside.

He shuffles past more tunnels and more vaults, many cracked and oozing with seeping water.

He knows the big house of pain and pleasure is not far.

Forty-two

Kovacs stuffed the research notes from the Tom and Jerry and Stephanie projects into his overburdened satchel, then locked his office door from the inside.

At the far end of the corridor, the laboratory sat dark and quiet. Earlier, the injured worker had been taken to a local medical clinic where he'd received several sutures in his finger, in addition to tetanus prophylaxes and antibiotics. His prognosis was good, in stark contrast to Stephanie's.

Unwilling to risk further accidents, Kovacs had resuspended the monkey, this time to minus two hundred degrees centigrade, four degrees cooler than the original suspension temperature. The formal dissection would take place in Tucson away from the prying eyes of detectives and inquisitive psychiatrists.

Alone at last, he inserted the last tape into the VCR. He began to watch.

The initial protocol had been innocent enough. After a two-month introductory get-acquainted period, Ben had taken a real liking to Vicki, captivated by her femininity. Lord knows the poor girl had needed a boost to her self-esteem, which was entirely understandable. When Kovacs had first met her, he'd thought she'd been in some terrible accident, so misshapen was her head. She'd reminded him of an ugly gnome out of a twisted children's fairy tale. But obviously Ben wasn't put off by her bizarre appearance. His friendship and the antipsychotics were a wonderful therapeutic combination for Vicki.

She taught him to eat with utensils, clean the room, make the bed, rudimentary reading skills, even showed him how to use the phone. Ben loved dialing different numbers.

When the touching and frolicking became more than just friendly, though, Kovacs's scientific curiosity really piqued. How far would their amorous relationship go? And more significant, would Ben demonstrate the identical social behavior after suspension that he'd demonstrated before? That was the million-dollar question. Kovacs had hoped the data would assist in extrapolating the effects prolonged freezing would have on the normal human brain.

The experiment's design, years in preparation, had been perfect, down to the fine details of medical consent forms, proper signatures, and even a genuine death certificate. The initial published data and prestige had been indispensable for drawing in new clients and investment money. Unfortunately the experiment itself had failed. The foundation's other cryo subjects would now have to provide Kovacs the fame and respect he sought. He no longer needed Ben, only a few of the deceased's organs. In fact, if the entire truth was ever made public, Kovacs's position in the scientific community would be severely damaged. The foundation had already received millions of dollars in venture capital. Carrying on without further funding would be impossible.

Pressing FAST-FORWARD, he slowed the tape when he reached the steamy scenes. Even years later, he couldn't believe what he was witnessing. Vicki being humped on like a bitch in heat. Quite entertaining, really. It was a shame all the tapes would have to be destroyed. Each would probably fetch a small fortune on the Internet. Computer porn was big money.

The tape ended and Kovacs wiped the perspiration from his face while the video rewound.

By the time he armed the building alarm and locked the foundation's front entrance, a light drizzle had become a steady downpour. He cursed at his lack of an umbrella and walked to his Mercedes, unwilling to use the satchel as cover.

Interstate 5 was a virtual parking lot and Kovacs resigned himself to the long rush-hour haul home, adjusting the wipers and windshield defogger to match the rain's barrage.

For the past two days, he'd collected the last of what he considered potentially damaging records from the foundation's soon-to-be abandoned headquarters. Though some of the less incriminating data had been delegated to his associate to handle, all of his personal notes, observations, and tapes—the ones meticulously recorded from before August, 1983 to present, including the pertinent details of the initial accident—he now held in his possession. Tonight he would destroy all he deemed expendable. He would expunge the doomed experiment from the foundation's past. Any inquiries would discover only a death certificate. No body. No leak. No decomposing corpse. What could anyone prove, except Ben Simmons had expired. Kovacs had never formally used the subject's name in his published reports, confidentiality has its benefits, so any digging into past funding documents would simply confirm Dr. Wesley Kovacs had been the first to cryopreserve a human, the identity of who would remain anonymous. Besides, he had other cryo subjects to take the limelight now.

His speed inched up to fifteen miles per hour. He decided to use the delay to make a call, only this time with a twist. Devlin never had returned his page and this was a source of sincere concern. He wanted to collect Ben's tissue samples by tomorrow evening at the latest. If nothing was amiss, why hadn't the gardener called him back?

Kovacs dialed the mortuary, hoping someone was still there to manage the phone. It wasn't yet 5:30 in the evening.

When a woman answered, he asked to be connected to the landscape engineer.

"I believe Mr. Devlin's left for the day," she said.

Kovacs expected this response. "I just spoke with him," he said. "Can you tell him Christian Eisler is back on the line? It's really quite important."

Kovacs waited while he was placed on hold. He heard a brief series of clicks until a man's voice came on the extension. "Hey, I said I'm working on finding them Mexicans, don't—"

"Evening, Devlin," Kovacs interrupted. "The rain keeping you from returning your calls?"

"Doc." The gardener instantly took on a more obsequious tone. "The sec's ears must need a cleaning. She said—"

"Quiet and listen. There's been a minor change in the foundation's itinerary. I'm going to require access to Ben's body. Probably not more than half an hour. It's mandatory I collect tissue samples."

Kovacs could hear the gardener breathing.

"When?" Devlin asked.

"Tomorrow, preferably in the evening."

"An exhumation will cost ten grand."

"Understood."

Kovacs heard the gardener cough and spit. The rain filled the void that followed.

"Is there a problem?" Kovacs asked.

"Your timing is not optimal."

"The ten thousand should cover any inconvenience to you. Now what's the fucking problem?" Kovacs snapped. The traffic had returned to a standstill.

"Ask Eisler."

"Listen up, you grass-stained piece of shit. Eisler doesn't sign the goddamn checks. I do. If there's a hitch, you tell me."

"Doc, I don't want to lose my job." Devlin sounded genuinely fearful.

Kovacs minced his anger. An uncooperative gardener would only exacerbate an already difficult situation. "Mr. Devlin," Kovacs said, "the foundation's willing to double your fee."

"Twenty thousand?"

"Consider it a bonus."

"I appreciate your generosity," the gardener said, "but there's still the little matter of Simmons's corpse."

"What about it?"

"Eisler didn't tell you?"

"Tell me what, Devlin?"

"The body's missing, Doc. And I can't locate the two fucking Mexicans."

Vicki drove slowly past the impressive gates and winding driveways of the Elysian Heights neighborhood until she came to the estate occupying one half of an entire cul-de-sac. Once she'd determined the address was the correct one, she turned and followed the street back to a four-way stop. She crossed the intersection to a tiny park with children's swings and sandboxes and swung into the lot.

For once, she was grateful for the rain. The park was deserted and the inclimate weather kept the neighbors off the streets and sidewalks.

Vicki sat and watched the entrance drive of Kovacs's very private residence. Though large trees blocked much of her view, what she saw of the house was every bit as impressive as she'd imagined. The English tudor-style mansion rose regally behind a vacant circular motor court and Vicki counted three separate massive chimneys and multiple overlapping gables. The patterned stonework and half-timbering blended magnificently with the oriel upstairs windows and large downstairs bay window. The entire estate appeared to be buried under blooming rosebushes and luxuriant ferns. She guessed Kovacs had paid a fortune to his landscape architect.

All she saw didn't impress her, though. The wrought-iron gate for one. Reaching to at least eight feet and supported by brick columns on either side, it stood too tall for her to scale. She'd have to devise another method into the estate.

Thirty minutes later, it was dark. Vicki grabbed her purse and shielded from the rain with her umbrella, she approached the residence from the sidewalk. The iron felt cold and wet under her hand and when she applied pressure, the gate moved only slightly. The top of each vertical bar ended in ornate spearlike points, further reducing any chance of using the closed gate as a place of entry.

A single electric light, one of which was burned out, crowned each brick column and the wrought iron continued from the drive as a fence, surrounding the entire estate until it disappeared somewhere behind the main residence.

After first glancing at the neighboring houses to make sure she wasn't being watched, Vicki walked as far as she could along the fence until the thickness of the vegetation prevented her from going further. When she returned to the sidewalk her clothes were wet and her shoes muddied.

She stared at the darkened house a good hundred yards down the drive.

The sudden illumination from a pair of headlights made her start. Shielding her face with the umbrella, Vicki began to walk away from the estate.

The car passed and began to slow.

Vicki turned and halted in her tracks. It was the white Lexus from the foundation.

Holding her breath, she watched the car stop at the entrance drive.

Nothing happened for several moments, then the gate began to roll open.

"Yes," Vicki whispered.

She watched the Lexus enter the estate. When the car was

halfway down the drive, she ran back to the gate and slipped through, just before the wrought-iron latch clicked shut.

Using the trunks of eucalyptus trees for cover, Vicki followed the car, keeping parallel to the drive and hiding herself in the trees' shadows.

The Lexus circled partway around the motor court and parked next to the mansion's main entrance.

Fifty feet away, concealed from view, Vicki watched Eisler knock at the front doors, his briefcase noticeably absent. She saw he'd kept the car lights on and engine idling.

When there was no response, he rang the bell twice and tried the door handle. When this action proved unsuccessful, he pounded on the doors a third time.

Vicki heard him swear. Then he crouched low and ran back to his car, using one hand to block the raindrops.

The Lexus continued around the court and swung back down the drive. Vicki didn't move until the car's taillights had vanished and the gate had rolled closed.

As Eisler's failed attempts had proved, the front doors were locked. Vicki stood in the dark a moment before walking in the direction of the attached four-car garage. The rain had lessened to a light mist and she closed her umbrella. Finding each garage door secured, she crossed the driveway to the side of the lot, stepping around two wide trellises laden with rose vines. The lack of any illumination forced her to walk slowly. The grass was thick and spongy and each step created a soft sucking noise. She hoped no one heard her. She wasn't worried about a dog. She knew Kovacs despised pets.

The backyard was expansive and included a swimming pool, elevated jacuzzi, and guesthouse. From the pool, the ground sloped gently to a wooden fence. Beyond the fence, Vicki saw only the deep shadows of trees and vegetation and she thought she heard the gurgling of runoff water from the recent rain. As in the main residence, the interior of the guesthouse stood dark and still and the only illumination was created by the pool lights which oddly enough were on, casting all they touched with a pale blue glow.

The reflection off two sliding-glass doors caught her eye and she proceeded across the pebbled agate and tile that bordered the pool. Resting one hand against the glass, she glanced through her own mirror image into an informal dining area connected to the kitchen. Stacked against one counter she saw a pile of cardboard moving boxes.

She tried the handle but the doors were locked. Stepping back, Vicki looked for another point of entry. Further from the pool, she saw another door. She crossed a shallow strip of grass and climbed up two steps to an elevated covered patio. As she approached the door, she began to notice an odor reminiscent of stagnant water. Glancing around, she could see nothing to explain the smell. She assumed it was the result of the rain. The pool appeared clean and well-maintained although at the shallow end nearest the guesthouse she did pick out some darker spots on the light-colored tiles.

Vicki turned her attention back to the door. Reaching for the doorknob, she abruptly stopped midway. The knob was missing. Around the hole where it'd once been, the wood was splintered and darkly stained. Glancing at the ground Vicki saw more dark spots as if someone with big muddy feet had stood exactly where she stood now. Next to the bottom of the door she saw the doorknob. She tapped it with her foot and it rolled, leaving two loose screws and a dark trail on the outdoor carpet.

Turning, she opened her purse and removed the pistol. With her eyes, she followed the splotches a short way down a covered concrete walk until they vanished under the open sky. For several seconds she stood perfectly still, listening. Yet all she heard was the water runoff. And the stagnant smell seemed less than only moments earlier.

Impatient to get inside, Vicki turned back to the door and hooked one finger in the recess left by the knob and pulled. The door swung open freely. She waited, wondering if she'd triggered any type of alarm, but heard nothing.

She stepped inside and found a switch on the wall. She flipped on the lights. She was standing in a utility room. Against one wall stood a washer and dryer. She looked at the floor. The tile, though a dull vanilla, was devoid of any of the ugly stains she'd noticed outside. From the utility room, Vicki entered a hall of plush carpet and oak-paneled wood. She found the switch and hit the lights. Several unframed canvases of abstract art hung on the wall. She then dashed back to the utility room and turned off the lights there.

For the next ten minutes, this was her modus operandi. After entering a new area of the house and finding the light source, she would reverse her path and kill the lights from where she just exited. Though she wasn't exactly sure what her plan would be, she was sure she didn't wish to broadcast her presence to Kovacs when he arrived.

In every room she explored, she saw indications of the planned move. Furniture covered, packing crates, bookshelves lacking books, pictures partially wrapped and leaning against the walls.

Entering the living room, Vicki paused at a wide balustraded staircase leading upstairs. If she'd had the time, she would have liked to have explored the second floor. She imagined the vastness of the master bedroom encompassing her entire apartment in Seattle. The thought of Kovacs's sleeping form, though, quickly dispelled any romantic ideations, and she moved on, passing under an archway into the sunken den.

The twenty-foot ceiling supported by one-foot-thick oak beams was certainly impressive, but what caught Vicki's eye first was the huge cobblestone fireplace hearth. Stretching eight feet from end to end and extending out three feet, it rose at least another two feet above the thick shag carpet covering the floor.

Vicki crossed over a Persian rug to gain a better view of the three storage boxes sitting on top of the recycled cobblestones. Each was labeled in bold marker, PHOENIX FOUNDATION I, II, III, respectively. Next to these lay a separate pile of folders, and a spiral-bound journal. She didn't see any of the tapes. Vicki set her purse and the pistol aside and sat down. The stones felt cold and hard under her, just the opposite of the warmth she envisioned them emanating when the fireplace was filled with glowing embers. Now only ashes buried portions of the iron grate.

The single lamp filled the room with huge oblong shadows, creating enormous two-dimensional shapes stretching across the floor, walls, and ceiling. Her own reflection gazed back at her in the large bay window. From her vantage point, she could see the drive and entrance gate. If Kovacs arrived now, he'd immediately sense something amiss. She rose and after a quick search, found the cord for the drapes. She pulled, eliminating all visibility to the outside.

Returning to the hearth, she began her inspection with the three storage containers. In the one marked I, most of the records were financial—she recognized receipts for equipment, legal contracts, and tax returns. She perused the most recent, never realizing Kovacs had received so much funding for his research. When she was through with him, he'd be worth less than a pauper. She moved to the second container. This one held records for past patients. They were in alphabetical order and she quickly found the S's, but, as she'd anticipated, there was no chart for Simmons.

The third container contained the videotapes. She set the box aside. Noting once again the ashes, Vicki sensed what Kovacs had been in the process of doing. As she suspected, he'd segregated all records pertaining to Ben, both published and private, and placed them in separate stacks. Their position on the hearth indicated he'd probably planned to burn them. She surmised he'd already destroyed some of the files. She hoped she wasn't too late.

Vicki grabbed the first folder and read. It was an old travelogue. Kovacs had documented his trips to Borneo. There'd been two. On the second one he'd returned with Ben. There were photos and notes.

Vicki hadn't understood how tortured Ben's infancy had been. Left an orphan when his parents were shot to death in cold blood, he'd lived in a string of temporary homes, until Kovacs obtained all the necessary papers. She felt Ben's loneliness as she set the travelogue aside.

Vicki reached for the bound journal. Though some of the pages were handwritten in Kovacs's script, most were typed in manuscript form. From the precise format, it indicated to her Kovacs's aim had been to continue to publish studies of his star subject. However, unlike the published reports, where Ben was only a code number, in the private journal, Kovacs had referred to Ben by name. How touching.

She'd just begun to read when the phone rang. She jumped. After four rings she heard Kovacs's recorded voice from another room. A dial tone followed briefly, then the line disconnected. No message was left.

Another noise made Vicki stiffen before she recognized the sound of drizzle. The rain had returned. Reflexively, she looked back past the stairs toward the hall from which she'd come, but saw only blackness. If Kovacs had been standing in the middle of the staircase she would have been hard-pressed to see him because of the lamp's dimness. She resisted the temptation for more illumination.

Pulling her purse and pistol closer, she returned to the first typewritten section with controlled elation. With what she knew, the journal would prove beyond a shadow of a doubt Kovacs's ulterior motives. The initial section contained a summary of Ben's early years. Vicki guessed it'd taken Kovacs months to gain his pupil's trust.

She started to read, feeling like only days had passed since she'd last experienced Ben's tender touch, not decades.

She flipped to the end section. Here, the manuscript referred to Ben only as subject, not by name.

The experiment's goals were outlined. Vicki experienced a sense of guilt. She recalled how Ben had started acting strangely around the time Kovacs had begun cryopreserving small animals. First frogs, then rats, then dogs and cats.

Reading further she understood why. The bastard had been spiking Ben's food, the very meals Vicki prepared for him, with lithium. Kovacs had diagnosed Ben with manic-depression, but in reality it was the lithium that had caused Ben's outrageous mood swings. *Ben had been slowly poisoned.*

A dead sensation filled Vicki's midsection. She skipped more pages. Her name appeared more often, creating a greater sense of impending doom. Tears began to form. She knew she was nearing *the time.*

Vicki forced her eyes down the page. It was 1983. Elsewhere in the house, a hinge creaked. Vicki looked up, listening. Only the rain. It repeated a second time, more prolonged. Had she closed the utility room door? She couldn't recall.

She turned another page, skimming the print until her eyes froze on a particular passage. *Once I was aware Ben had consumed a meal, I elected to proceed with his electroconvulsive therapy session. Timing could not be more perfect. All behavioral studies are complete.*

In the margin, underlined, were four handwritten words—*Ben has been humanized!*

Vicki groaned in anguish. The bastard knew Ben had eaten, yet he'd gone along with the ECT session anyway, knowing with near certainty Ben would aspirate. The accident wasn't an accident. Ben's demise had been carefully orchestrated from the beginning. Kovacs had done it on purpose. *For his precious research.* Investing in frozen tadpoles and frogs was small change compared to the financial backing he could receive from the first human cryonics experiment.

Vicki stopped reading. She could recite the rest. She'd lived with the guilt and pain for years. Now that same pain was buried behind a wall of unmitigated anger. Anger at the man responsible for betraying two lives.

She flipped to the last pages, but these contained mostly diagrams and equations which she had no desire to decipher or comprehend. Kovacs's scrawled personal thoughts and explanations she could do without. She'd heard them before.

Vicki wasn't sure how much time had elapsed since closing the journal when she felt the cool draft graze her ankles. She reacted as if a match had touched her skin.

Jerking suddenly, she looked past the staircase into the darkness of the house. She discerned no motion, yet when the wet muted sound continued, she knew. *Someone was walking in the hall.*

Clutching the journal, along with her purse and gun, Vicki dashed from the hearth and raced across the rug toward the only other passageway she saw. She stumbled, knocking over a small table. Glass shattered on the floor.

The first door she found, she opened and jumped inside, shutting it. Clothes hit her back. She was in a closet. She started to leap out when she heard a garbled sound. She was unable to make out any words. Positioning the pistol in front of her, she held her breath. How could Kovacs have arrived without her noticing his car or the gate opening?

From the den, she heard the crackling sound of paper being thrown about, followed by a lamp or vase crashing against a wall. Then silence.

Vicki listened but heard no other noises. For the briefest of moments she was tempted to leap from her cover and take Kovacs by surprise.

The sharp explosion of the shattering bay window stopped all thoughts of further action. For several seconds, all Vicki heard was the crunch of glass fragments on the carpet.

Why would Kovacs . . . then the realization hit her at the same time the sewage stench filled her hiding place. *It wasn't Kovacs in the house.*

Outside the closet, the wet, heavy steps grew louder.

Forty-three

Kovacs waited impatiently for the electronic gate to roll open. The jackknifed big rig had cost him nearly two hours. And Devlin's bad news could cost him much more.

"Goddammit," he swore, blasting the horn in frustration.

He hit the accelerator and the big Mercedes's rear tires spun on the wet pavement, causing a minor fishtail. The rear bumper tapped the gate, knocking a roller from its metal groove. The gate stalled three-quarters open.

Ignoring the bump, Kovacs steered up the drive and parked in the circular court as close as possible to the front entrance. He grabbed his briefcase and dashed for the door.

Standing in the dark, Vicki whispered a silent prayer of thanks. Whoever stood on the other side of the closet door had departed as soon as the car horn sounded. She now knew Kovacs was into something far deeper and far more evil than she or anyone else could have imagined. Kovacs had said Ben thawed. He'd begun to decompose. But there was no body. *That's because he wasn't dead.*

Vicki felt her knees trembling with the realization. At the Shilden Hotel, it'd been Ben who'd stained the bedroom mattress, waiting for her return, oblivious to the passage of time.

How he'd survived the lengthy cryonic suspension, she had no idea.

With her finger on the trigger, she swung open the door. The odor of sewage had dissipated, leaving only an odd residual smell of alcohol and necrosis. A draft of air caressed her face. She guessed this was originating from the broken bay window.

Traversing the short hall, she found more lights on than she remembered. The increased illumination made it easier to step around the sludge and mud curdled on the hardwood floor.

From the den, Vicki heard paper being shuffled. The entrance door remained open and she glimpsed the front fender of the Mercedes.

She found Kovacs bent over the massive hearth. He'd already turned on the gas and yellow flames licked around the iron grate.

For several seconds Vicki just watched him inspecting his precious records. In a small way, she felt sorry for the man, a brilliant scientist so obsessed with his research he'd destroy innocent lives to achieve his goals.

A shard of glass fell, breaking on the wood sill. She looked over at the bay window and when she turned back, Kovacs was watching her. His skin looked pale, his face prematurely aged.

"Is this your doing?" he asked, motioning at the room's disarray. If he saw the gun, he chose to ignore it.

Vicki held up the journal. "He was here."

"You're insane."

"I smelled him," Vicki said. She moved to a chair and sat. "He was so close I could've touched his skin."

"That's impossible," Kovacs hissed, but Vicki saw doubt etched in every line of his face.

"*He knows.* I smelled him in the Shilden, I smelled him in your lab, and I smelled him here." Vicki held the journal against her chest, protecting it like it was a tiny infant. "He's rotting, falling apart. He won't be around long, Kovacs. Will that make you feel better? Killing Ben twice?"

Kovacs reached for the journal and she pulled away. Vicki thought she detected sadness in his eyes.

"How did you get in?" he asked.

"The utility room door."

Kovacs nodded. "Logic dictates that I must ask, why are you here?"

"I came for Ben's medical consent form."

"Half is missing."

"I have it."

Kovacs smirked. "I suspected as much. No matter. It's useless without a signature. Ben's signature."

"Ben never signed it. You did. There're laws against perpetrating fraud. And with the photograph I have and proof that you forged Ben's name on a Consent to Treat form, plus the journal . . ." Vicki chuckled. "You'll be the laughing stock of the scientific community. When the truth comes out about your grand *human* experiment, your investors will treat you like you're the plague. You'll wind up in prison."

"You're forgetting one minor detail, my dear. The truth will remain buried."

"That's what you think. Now where the hell is Ben?"

"You think you can force me to tell you with that?" he said, gesturing to the pistol.

Vicki smiled ruefully. "It won't be necessary. Ben found us." She watched him studying her with a cold stare. She wasn't afraid. Not of Kovacs.

He stood perfectly still, unsmiling, seemingly mesmerized by the gun in her hand.

Vicki flipped the pistol's safety to the ON position. "We'll have to tell the police."

"About Ben?"

"About everything." Vicki rose. The trembling had left her legs feeling weak. "I lied," she said. "I think I really came here to kill you."

"What's stopping you?"

"Because I am not a monster. And you have become a monster."

"Your poetry touches me, Ms. Zampisi."

"Damn your foundation." Vicki started past him.

"Where are you going?"

"To see Ben."

"You are crazy." Kovacs waited until Vicki came within reach, then he lunged, catching her by the left arm.

"You bastard," she screamed, aiming the muzzle at his forehead. She pulled the trigger, which didn't move.

"You stupid bitch." Kovacs wrenched the pistol and journal from her hands. With a swift toss, the bound manuscript landed in the fireplace. Vicki's heart sank as she watched the pages crinkle in the flames, before turning brown, then black.

She raised a fist to strike him and he slapped her hard across the face with the gun's barrel. Blood welled from under her eye and she dropped to one knee. Kovacs released the safety and yanked her up, twisting her arm up behind her shoulder blade.

"You smell like a winery," he said, inches from her nose.

"Let go." Vicki started to struggle and he forced her arm higher. The pain made her gasp.

"You will not destroy all I've worked for," Kovacs said. "You will not. You will not!" He twisted a fraction more until Vicki groaned. "Now listen very good, my dear, sweet woman. If you ever so much as breathe Ben's name again, I will kill you. And I'll kill that pretty doctor of yours too. And I'll kill you both so bad, there'll be nothing left worth preserving." He paused, letting his words produce their desired effect before relaxing his grip. "Are we clear?"

Vicki's eyes blazed. "Fuck you."

She saw his arm raise and ducked, but the blow never materialized because of a loud splash from the backyard.

Kovacs shoved her to the carpet. "Not a word," he said.

Vicki watched him disappear down the hall and when he returned, he carried an elongated metal rod in one hand.

Vicki recognized the electric cattle prod, Kovacs's means of dispensing punishment.

"No!" she screamed, leaping to her feet. "He's not an animal!"

Kovacs lumbered for the kitchen.

Vicki ran after him. "Kovacs, I swear I'll kill you."

She ducked around the door frame and caught the rod's electronic prongs full on the side of her neck. The shock felt like she'd been hit over the head with a sack of coins. She hit the floor flat on her back. She saw Kovacs staring down at her.

"You really are a pathetic creature," he said. He turned and walked away.

Vicki heard the sliding-glass door open. Shaking the cobwebs from behind her eyes, she struggled to her knees and, half-crawling, half-stumbling, made it to the open door.

Kovacs was walking to the pool's edge.

She braced herself in the doorway. The rain had returned in force and wind gusts blew the fine mist in her face.

"Kovacs," she called out. She could see an empty metal animal trap lying on the bottom of the pool. "Leave him be!"

Kovacs ignored her, too busy inspecting the footprints around the pool.

Behind a small gazebo built near one corner of the guesthouse, she heard a wet slushing noise.

Kovacs heard it too, and stepped purposely over the tracks and into the rainy darkness.

Then she saw *him*.

"No!" Vicki cried.

• •

The bitch, Kovacs cursed as he stalked around the tile lip of the pool toward the gazebo. Once he finished with Ben, he'd teach Vicki a hard lesson she'd not soon forget. No one threatened the foundation—his life's work—without suffering severe repercussions.

The rain did nothing to dilute the stench of rancid flesh and momentarily the odious spoors caused Kovacs to gag. A blurred indistinct image of a huge mildewed dewar flashed in his mind and he stifled the ugly vision by coughing up a wad of phlegm. The plug landed with a concentrated plop in the pool. Behind him, he heard Vicki whimpering like a lost child but after only a few steps the sharp gusts of moist wind quickly drowned out her sobbing.

He tread imperiously past the house lights' perimeter where the dark was so complete the outline of the gazebo and guesthouse were just obscure black silhouettes. Abruptly, he stopped in his tracks realizing he'd been foolish to leave Vicki alone. What if she tried to escape? He briefly considered going back but the stench was suddenly so overwhelming, he spun, attempting to isolate its fulsome source.

"Ben," Kovacs commanded, brandishing the cattle prod threateningly out in front of him. "Come here, Ben."

The wet *sloshing* came from his right and sounded like someone walking across fresh concrete.

He whirled to face his attacker, realizing too late his egregious error in judgment.

The huge hand floated from the darkness and clamped around his neck. Instantly, Kovacs felt his two-fifty-plus pounds pulled forward. Gasping for air, he swung the weapon just as a vicious pain racked his face. He reached up and felt his fingertips dip inside a fist-size hole of ragged, tattered flesh. Too shocked to emit much more than an anguished groan, he watched defenselessly as the mouthful of teeth spat out a large portion of his cheek, then came at him again. Above the rancidity, he now detected a new, sweet, pungent odor— his own fresh blood.

Kovacs's scream was nothing more than a wet gurgling sound as blood filled his throat. Any anger and insolence had long-since evaporated as he felt himself begin to choke.

His only thought was escape. Flailing his arms, he tried to wrench free but a second set of fingers curled around the arm clutching the prod and instantly he felt and heard the two bones in his forearms snap like dried sticks.

Horrified with panic, he clawed at the dark form, clutching sinew and muscle so cold he flinched in revulsion.

"No, Ben," he begged as he was pulled further from the house.

Another audible *pop* and his left shoulder dangled loosely from its socket. He tried to kick and was tossed violently on his back, knocking the air from his lungs in a single *whoosh*. In quick succession, Kovacs felt both knees forcibly hyperextended until the cartilage stretched and snapped. He screamed mutely at the searing pain. He was sure his legs were on fire as he felt himself dragged over the ground like a sack of corn. His light-headedness mercifully progressed to a dying stupor but not before Kovacs lay helplessly and watched as two thick digits brutally gouged out both his eyes.

Falling against a packing crate, Vicki stumbled back through the kitchen, the den, and finally out into the damp night.

Forty-four

In the dream, the knocking never stopped, even when Julie called out from the top of the stairs. It was late, the night was deep and far from over. The rain had dampened Julie's skin and clothing, leaving her shivering in the dark. When she descended the stairs, the carpet under her feet made a wet sucking sound that threatened to swallow her up.

The incessant *tap-tap-tap* continued.

Julie reached for the doorknob.

Tap-tap-tap-tap.

Pulling the front door open, Julie had to shield her eyes as the fury of the storm drove against her face. The raindrops felt like pellets bombarding her skin. Far worse was the odor of insecticide. The sweetly pungent fumes assaulted her nostrils, making her brain burn.

"Hi, Jule, wanna play Worm Man?"

Janine stood in the drizzle, both arms hanging limp at her sides. The wet Tweety Bird T-shirt clung to her chest so tightly, Julie could count her ribs. Dirt and grime caked the cuffs of the child's bell-bottom jeans. Both bloodshot eyes bulged unnaturally and Julie watched her sister's lips curl up in a hideous sneer.

"Hey, Jule, you're all grown up now."

"Happy anniversary, Janine," Julie wished.

"He's coming for you too."

"Who?" But Julie knew.

Her sister began to sing. "The worms crawl in, the worms crawl out . . ."

As she sang, Janine began to grow older. Her hair lengthened and a feminine shape appeared, taller and fuller, just as Julie would have envisioned a seven-year-old girl maturing into an adult woman.

"Why didn't you open the door, Jule?" her sister asked.

"I tried, Janine."

"You let me die."

"I'm sorry," Julie said.

Janine's face twisted in indignation. "Not good enough, little sister. Not tonight. No way." She coughed, spitting up a glob of partially digested earthworms.

Sobbing, Julie watched the mangled writhing mass crawl into the grass and disappear. "I said I'm sorry," she bemoaned.

Janine pirouetted in the air like a ballerina, singing, "Not fucking good enough, not fucking good enough."

"What do you want from me?" Julie cried out.

Janine stopped spinning and grinned. "I want to play Worm Man. This time it's your turn to hide, little sister."

"No!"

Janine reached out with two bloody hands.

Julie felt their pull and recoiled. "No!" she screamed again, stumbling backward. She slammed the door and awoke in her bed.

Outside, the rain pattered the red tile roof. The drizzle's monotonous sibilance echoed so softly Julie at first mistook the sound as part of her dream. Somewhere downstairs, a tree limb rattled a windowpane with rhythmic regularity. *Tap-tap-tap-tap.*

Julie disentangled her legs from the bed linen and sat up. Her cheeks were moist and she could taste the salt on her lips. She'd actually cried in her sleep. Inside, she felt empty. She prayed there was a heaven that allowed a young life cut short to continue in some cosmic fashion, though sitting alone in the dark, she doubted a heaven of that sort really existed. The prayer only deepened her despair. Even Jake's sleeping form near her bedroom door failed to lighten her spirits.

Julie switched on the lamp. Jake stirred but remained locked in his somnolent state. It wasn't yet midnight. It felt much later. The dream had deprived her of more than sleep. It had nibbled away at her sense of self-worth.

Julie decided to dial the hospital and inquire on Melanie's status. The news did not help. No change.

The next number she also knew by heart.

"Hello." A woman's voice answered after the second ring.

"Hi, Mom—"

"You've reached the Charmaine residence . . ."

Julie hung up before the recording's completion. Her parents were probably spending the week at the cottage on Lake Texoma. Or asleep. Like she should've been. It would be almost 2 A.M. in Dallas.

The doorbell rang.

Jake was on his feet before the double tone ended. The hair on his neck bristled and a deep growl rumbled from far down in the center of his chest.

Julie opened the nightstand drawer and removed the .38. Crossing the floor, the carpet felt soft and dry under her bare feet, unlike in her dream. The doorbell rang once more when she was midway down the stairs. This time Jake barked. She made no effort to muzzle him.

She approached the door with all the trepidation of a five-year-old child entering a dark room. She wanted to call out but was afraid of what she might hear in return. The Sewer Stalker or Worm Man she could fight. But if she opened the door and confronted a seven-year-old dead girl in a Tweety Bird T-shirt . . .

She checked the peephole. Immediately her grip on the pistol relaxed, though her insides roiled, but from an entirely different mixture of emotions. After securing her robe, she unlatched the deadbolt.

The rain was coming down in heavy sheets. Matt's hair lay plastered across his forehead. He eyed the gun in Julie's hand. Attempting a smile, he said, "I can come back another time if you'd prefer."

Without a word, she lowered the pistol and motioned him inside.

"No, Jake," she said. The dog eyed Matt suspiciously a few moments before padding over to his spot by the fireplace.

"Can I get you anything?" Julie asked.

"No," Matt said, not taking his eyes from her. "I wanted to see you. You okay?"

She waited while his gaze filled the emptiness inside her. "I'm getting there," she said.

"Wanna talk about it?"

She slowly shook her head. "Later, maybe."

Two things went through Julie's mind as she led Matt upstairs. First, she hoped Jake wouldn't be jealous. And second—and a concern of a more morbid nature—she said a short prayer for Janine who would never experience lying next to a man she was slowly falling in love with.

The rain only heightened their feelings. In the dark, as their two bodies touched, the hurt and frustrations of the past surrendered to the passionate bond that had grown between them. They pulled each other close, their lips eagerly caressing the other's face, neck, breasts.

Julie felt herself jettisoned over the edge more times than she could remember, though later she'd want to remember them all. There was no shame or hesitation, only the freedom of pleasing and being pleased by that one person who could boil one's blood and cool it with a single stroke.

Later, while Matt slept, Julie lay awake refusing to think about tomorrow. Though the dream was less than two hours old, she felt relaxed, even refreshed. The gates to her prison had been unlocked. Janine would not visit again tonight. And next spring was a full year away.

Before closing her eyes, Julie kissed her finger, then gently touched Matt's scar.

Forty-five

Julie awoke to the ringing, thinking the caller might be either her mom or dad. She looked again at the clock to make sure she'd read it correctly. Another minute had passed: 2:31.

Recognizing Vicki's slurred speech, she was frightened by the desperation in her patient's voice.

"Don't leave," Julie said.

She kissed Matt and quietly dressed.

Pennsylvania Avenue was lined with cars when Julie slowed to check the street address. She parked next to the curb a half-block down from Vicki's van.

Overhead the sky was pitch black when she hit the sidewalk. The thick cloud-cover blocked any hint of the moon or stars. Carrying only an umbrella and her purse, Julie approached the small complex. She guessed Vicki's was the upstairs apartment. It was the only one with a light on.

Julie knocked and waited. Though physically standing outside Vicki's door, a part of her remained curled under her sheets next to Matt. She'd never seen him more at peace than when he'd been sleeping. It made her sad to think he might not be there when she returned.

Vicki opened the door. Her hair hung in damp tangles, covering a portion of her face, and she wore a robe over her clothes. A Band-Aid partially covered a bruise high on her right cheek. She motioned Julie in with an awkward gesture of her hand. Her fingers clutched a glass one-quarter full of an amber liquid. The smell on Vicki's breath left no doubt what it contained, the only question being the brand and proof.

They moved to the kitchen table where Julie saw the Ezra Brooks bottle was two-thirds empty. While Julie made coffee, Vicki sat silently.

Julie set a cup in front of Vicki and took the other one herself.

Vicki took a long sip. She used both hands when setting the cup back on the table. When she spoke, she still hadn't let go. "Kovacs is dead." She said this as calmly as if she were giving the time of day to a stranger on the street.

"Why do you think he's dead?"

"Because Ben killed him. Just like he's going to kill me."

"No one is going to kill you." Julie had treated enough paranoia to see the signs in Vicki. The most important thing now was reassurance. "Detective Guardian and I spoke with Dr. Kovacs only yesterday. He was fine."

"Not anymore."

Julie touched one of Vicki's hands. "Tell me what happened. From the beginning."

Vicki lit a cigarette, inhaling deeply. The smoke escaped through her nostrils. "Ben was always happier when I was around. I could see it in his eyes. Those stupid tricks of his." Vicki attempted a smile, if only to herself. "I accepted him for what he was. And for what he'd never be."

"Over the phone, you said you'd driven over to Kovacs's house."

Vicki barely nodded. "I got in through a back door and found all his records of the experiment, the accident, everything. All stacked on the fireplace hearth. Kovacs planned to destroy them."

Vicki's lips formed an inappropriate smile. "Only he was the one destroyed."

"Kovacs?"

"Back behind the pool. Ben took a bite out of Kovacs's face." She began to sob.

Julie reached for her hand. "How do you know it was Ben?"

Her voice hardened. "Because I saw him. Dr. Charmaine, you have to believe me. Ben's alive."

"Have you reported this to the police?"

"No," she said.

Though Julie's mind raced, she kept her tone calm. "Vicki, I'm your friend. And I believe you. What time were you at Kovacs's house?"

"I don't remember exactly."

"Okay, what time did you arrive back at your apartment?"

Vicki wiped at the tears and the Band-Aid came loose. Julie saw an ugly gash.

"I'm not sure. I drove around for a while. I was so scared." Her eyes opened wide. "What if he comes here?"

"He's not coming here," Julie said. She reached over and replaced the Band-Aid. "What happened to your cheek?"

"Kovacs hit me."

"It's swollen, I'll get you some ice."

"No," Vicki said, pressing the edges of the Band-Aid down. "It's nothing after what this face has been through."

"You may need sutures."

"Doesn't matter." Vicki shook her head once. "I hate myself, Dr. Charmaine. I should never have gone along with Kovacs. Never."

Vicki stared at the Ezra Brooks bottle. "Two months prior to Ben's death, he began acting strangely. I understand why now. Kovacs was poisoning him with lithium."

"Lithium's used to treat manic-depression."

"The drug only made Ben worse. While I helped divert Ben's attention, Kovacs administered a potent sedative. Ben fell asleep in my arms." Vicki's voice cracked. "I betrayed him. When Ben awoke he was restrained, confused, and angry. That's when he snapped. Everything he learned, he forgot. He hated me. He hated everyone. When he wasn't so sedated he could barely walk, he'd scream out in fits of rage."

She shuddered.

"I can still hear him. That's why I wanted to believe Kovacs could make him well again with the shock therapy. But something went wrong. It was like . . ."

"He wanted Ben to seize."

Vicki nodded. "Afterward, Ben was like a vegetable. He didn't move. He barely breathed. He didn't even recognize me. Every time I looked into those empty eyes, I wanted to die. I'm convinced the whole purpose of Ben's accident was to provide Kovacs with a cryonics subject. Once the death certificate was made up and signed, Ben was frozen."

"At CPC."

"Yes. Later it became the Phoenix Foundation."

"That explains the initials on the death certificate." The hard evidence made it no less difficult to believe. "He was frozen alive then."

"Suspended is the word Kovacs used. He said I'd be part of scientific history." Vicki stopped talking a moment and glanced at the window. "Ben was suspended for twenty years, Dr. Charmaine." Her face twisted in disbelief. "Now he's back."

Julie recalled Dorfman's aberrant chromosomal analysis. The thought only magnified her disquiet. "Even if Ben did kill Kovacs, why would he want to harm you?" she asked.

"That's easy." Any doubt vanished from Vicki's face. "He trusted me. And I betrayed that trust."

Forty-six

Julie watched Vicki disappear into her bedroom before dialing her own number. When the outgoing message had completed its cycle, she said, "Matt, it's me, pick up the phone." There was no response. Either he hadn't heard the answering machine downstairs or he was no longer there.

She decided to try him at home. She called the number he'd scribbled on the back of his business card.

Matt answered on the first ring.

"You're home," Julie said. He'd obviously found her note.

"Where are you?" he asked. She detected genuine concern in his voice.

"I'm still at Vicki's apartment," she said. "I'm going to admit her for observation. She claims she saw Ben kill Kovacs."

Julie heard a low-pitched groan.

"I hope this is good," he said.

"I'll meet you at the hospital."

Vicki's facial laceration took seven stitches to close. While the ER physician sutured, Matt listened to Vicki's version of events. He only asked a few questions during the time it took Julie to finish the admission orders.

She watched as her patient was wheeled toward the elevators.

"Besides being severely depressed, she's in a state of shock," Julie said. "How'd you find her?"

"Out of touch."

"But if her story's true . . ."

A clerk waved them down. "Detective Guardian, you have a call."

Julie waited while Matt grabbed the nearest phone. She could hear portions of the one-sided conversation.

"You're positive it's the correct address? Fine, don't make a move. Only if the guy tries to leave, then apprehend him." He listened a moment. "Yep, possible homicide. I'm on my way."

Matt's step had picked up a pace. Julie had to walk fast to keep up.

"That was about Kovacs, wasn't it?" she said.

Both slowed, yielding to a stretcher-bound patient destined for one of the cardiac rooms.

Matt nodded. "After your call, I had a patrol dispatched to Kovacs's home. They just got back to me."

"And?"

"Kovacs's black Mercedes is parked in front."

"Did they see Kovacs?"

"They reported seeing a man enter the house but he was driving a white Lexus. It's registered to a Christian Eisler."

"Vicki mentioned that name. What's he doing there this late?" She glanced at the wall clock above the triage desk. Almost 4 A.M. "Or should I say early."

"He's not going anywhere, at least until I give the say-so."

They arrived at Matt's car first. "A search warrant's in the works for the lab."

"That's good news, Matt."

Matt returned the mike to the radio. "Three-fifty-seven Roseview."

Julie sat on the passenger side. "Los Angeles?"

"Elysian Heights."

"That's money."

As if in affirmation they entered an enclave of large homes. Matt slowed in front of the one with the patrol car parked at the gate. He turned off his headlights. "Wait here," he said and got out.

Julie watched him approach a uniformed officer. Any calm she'd seen in his expression had long-since vanished. The two men talked briefly and Matt returned to his car.

"Eisler's still inside," he said. Matt circumvented the malfunctioning gate and parked behind the Lexus. The officer followed and positioned his vehicle at the circular court's periphery.

Julie pointed. "Look."

A loose fold of drape hung outside the shattered bay window and large shards of glass clung precariously to the wood frame. Light from inside escaped outside, reflecting off the row of hedges.

Matt shut off the engine. "This time I mean it. Wait here." He opened the door and unholstered his revolver. He approached the front entrance behind the cover of the Lexus. It was quiet until he stepped up beside the door, which was not completely shut. That's when he heard it. An odd noise. It sounded like scraping with an intermittent, coarser sound. He didn't recognize it.

"What's that?"

Matt jumped. Julie stood behind him. "I thought I told you—"

Inside, the noise stopped. With one arm shielding Julie, Matt pushed the open door with one foot. It swung in.

"I'm calling the police," a voice called out.

Matt, poised in a crouch, leaped inside. In one smooth motion, the 9mm sights settled on a thin man by the fireplace who held a poker in one hand, and some loose papers in the other. His use of the poker to sift through the thick black soot explained the odd sound.

"I am the police," Matt said with enough emphasis to demonstrate he meant business. He showed his badge.

Eisler seemed driven to destruction, obviously not recognizing the detective.

"Now please put down the poker," Matt said.

"It's not a weapon," Eisler stuttered.

"It's about to be construed as one. Put it down."

He complied, setting both the metal poker and papers on the brick hearth. Then he glanced at Julie who had entered and was standing quietly just inside the lighted entrance. Other than the front enclave, kitchen, and den, the remainder of the main residence was dark.

"Are you alone?" Matt asked, taking in the entire scene. He saw no sign of anyone else.

"Yes."

"That your car outside?"

"The Lexus."

"You don't remember me, Dr. Eisler? I spoke with you outside the foundation offices regarding Mr. Beeden."

"Vaguely. I was an associate of Dr. Wes Kovacs. This is his house."

Matt reholstered. "What are you doing here?"

"I came here to resign." Some of the fear had left Eisler, replaced with suspicion. "And I might ask the same question of you."

"We're looking for Dr. Kovacs. Is he around?"

The scientist met Julie's gaze and looked away. "No. I came by yesterday and called several times last night but there was no answer. When I returned an hour ago, I found this awful mess."

"Is that why you were digging through his fireplace?" Matt was tempted to join him, but he'd be way off-base if he conducted a residence's search without Kovacs's permission, especially since he wasn't in possession of a proper warrant. Regardless, all he could see beneath the metal grate were several piles of black and gray ashes.

Eisler didn't answer right away.

Julie said, "I remember Vicki called one of the men who showed her Ben's grave at Evergreen Manor Christian Eisler. Only according to Vicki, it wasn't really Ben."

Eisler's eyes widened in a look of muted surprise. Then suddenly appearing very weak, he slumped on the couch.

Julie glanced at Matt. He simply nodded. Julie stepped over and took a chair facing Eisler. "Dr. Eisler, my name is Julie Charmaine. I'm a neuropsychiatrist at CUMC and Vicki Zampisi is one of my patients."

Eisler avoided her eyes. "I haven't seen Kovacs in twenty-four hours," he mumbled.

"I believe you," Julie said.

"Have you seen the guest house?" he asked. He followed the simple question with a series of odd chuckles.

"No," Julie said. "Is Dr. Kovacs in the guest house?" The thought made her uneasy as much as Eisler's strange behavior.

Eisler stood. "I'll show you."

As he led them through the spacious den toward the two French doors leading into the backyard, Julie motioned to Matt who'd also seen the mud-stained floor.

The entire scene made her nervous. There was something in Kovacs's guest house that was causing Eisler to behave inappropriately. What would upset him to the point of *laughing*?

The French doors opened into the expansive, marvelously landscaped backyard. Jake would've loved it, but Julie was too anxious to think about it.

Eisler mumbled something else about being careful. "It's slippery."

Julie noted the sludge streaks around the pool. They led toward the rear of the guest house where they disappeared from view.

She noticed Matt had unholstered his gun again. He was feeling *it* too. She glanced behind her and saw the other officer waiting back, his revolver in his hand, covering their backs.

Everywhere, the stench clung to the air. Not strong, but a reminder that sometime in the recent past these immediate surroundings had reeked of death and decay. A small tree lay uprooted in a clay pot, its thin trunk broken in several places, the obvious victim of some sort of physical trauma. Lying on the ground, she saw an elongated metal rod. Its handle appeared to be coated in blood, making Julie wonder seriously about other victims. If there were other victims.

Matt paused, checking the dark stains on the concrete. He didn't say anything. Eisler waited till the detective had finished, then continued leading.

Julie half-expected to see a body or blood in the pool, but except for a few leaves the water was clean. She noted the animal trap eight feet below the smooth surface.

Eisler stopped at the door.

"Is this the only entrance?" Matt asked from just behind him.

"Yes, I believe so."

"Why the bars?" he asked.

The separate structure's windows and door were reinforced with vertical-running steel bars and a thick mesh screen.

"You'll have to ask Kovacs," Eisler said, chuckling.

Matt caught Julie's warning look. *He's cracking.*

Eisler swung open the guest house door. Smelling more of the offensive odor inside, Julie's pulse quickened.

"He wasn't in the main house so I checked out here," Eisler said. "Want to see?" He stepped in.

Matt went next, followed by Julie. There were no lamps on and with all the drapes pulled, it was quite dark. For Julie, the odor immediately triggered images of Irene Inez and Melanie's brutalized body.

Matt found the wall switch and turned on the single light mounted in the center of the ceiling.

The main room was sparsely furnished—a table, a couple of chairs, and a couch. The cement floor was covered with a faded green carpet and the wallpaper, worn and torn in places, projected a pattern of painted trees and lush forests. There was also a cramped kitchen, equipped with a sink and small refrigerator. A few cheap toys littered the floor. Julie saw a football and a plastic barbell set. A rusted pull-up bar was mounted on one wall. A bookshelf held only two books—Dr. Seuss's *The Cat in the Hat* and one other, but she couldn't make out the title.

Eisler sat on the couch, chuckling to himself, while Matt checked out a small second room located at the rear of the guest house.

From outside, the officer called, "You okay in there, detective?"

"Get a crime unit out here," Matt yelled, emerging from the smaller room.

"Yessir."

Julie saw Matt's eyes scanning everything in the main room. "Is anything missing?" he asked.

Eisler grinned. "Only Kovacs." He sat perfectly still, holding his hands between his knees.

The smell was getting to Julie. "Can we open a window or something?" The door was still open but it provided very little ventilation. She wondered why the smell was so strong. She saw Matt watching her.

The detective motioned to her. She followed him to the back room, a sleep storage room. Stacks of small animal cages filled one corner.

Julie gasped when she looked inside. A section of the back wall was ripped out. Splintered two-by-fours and wallpaper dangled in a space the size of one conventional door. She could tell a window used to be near the damaged area because a small portion of the frame, including the iron bars and steel mesh still hung from the ceiling. Shattered glass covered the floor, along with mud and sludge. Debris littered the sheets of the only bed, which was shoved to one side. A dresser lay haphazardly across the twin-sized mattress. The bedspread had been removed and was piled around the edges of the bed.

Matt stepped toward the new exit. "This room faces the back of Kovacs's property. Take a look. Careful of the glass."

Julie stepped across pieces of Sheetrock and wood. She ducked through and found herself alongside a fence that marked the back property line. A small portion of the wooden fence was also splintered, revealing a gap. Beyond this was a shallow wooded ravine, the bottom of which contained a cement storm channel.

"See the sludge streaks?" Matt pointed at the east corner. "They continue from the pool, around the back here, and then stop at the fence."

Julie followed his hand. The marks appeared to stop at the splintered gap in the fence. Beyond the perimeter she could see the earth was also disturbed, the ground mounded and cracked in places.

Matt bent down, looking at something hanging from a sharp piece of wood.

Julie started to look too, but Matt moved to restrain her. "It's ugly."

She grimaced. There was a large chunk of human flesh, at least two inches thick. Dark cloth was still attached to the tissue by coagulated blood. "Jesus, Matt, what is it?"

"I think it's a piece of leg. I'm not sure. Come on. Let's go back inside."

Eisler hadn't moved from the couch when Matt and Julie returned to the guest house's main room.

Matt reholstered. "A burglar might pick a lock or crack a window, but he sure as hell doesn't rip out a wall."

Eisler's face twitched nervously. He giggled. Julie thought his skin looked sickly pale. In the light's weak glow it was hard to tell.

"Maybe we should go back out," she suggested.

Matt agreed. "If I smell any more of this, my olfactory senses will never be the same."

He helped Eisler up and the three returned to the main residence. Julie was worried about Kovacs's associate. Ever since leading them to the guest house his demeanor had changed. He was almost childlike. The despair on his face was obvious, yet he would suddenly laugh with no provocation. She didn't feel comfortable with his bizarre behavior.

She brought him a glass of water from the kitchen. "I should check back in with the hospital," she said, observing Eisler drink with both hands.

"I'll have a patrol car give you a lift back." Matt had moved closer to an antique desk holding several framed photos. He pointed to one. "Here's another one of Ben and Kovacs."

Eisler giggled.

Julie walked over and recognized the same well-built man she'd seen in the photograph in Kovacs's office. "He's younger there. So is Kovacs. Here's one that looks more recent." She picked up a second picture. "This one includes Kovacs, Ben, and Eisler." The three were posing in front of a restaurant at San Francisco's renown Fisherman's Wharf.

Eisler looked up from his glass, and laughed again.

Matt turned. "What's so goddamn amusing?"

"Matt." Julie touched the detective's arm. He shrugged innocently.

Eisler giggled. "What's so amusing, Mr. Detective, is you said that was Ben in the photo."

A sudden chill touched Julie's spine. "Isn't it?"

Eisler grinned, staring up at the ceiling. "Kovacs, you're fucking unbelievable. You really pulled it off, you charlatan." His eyes drifted back to the glass in his hands. "It was all there. In a few pages of his notes he hadn't destroyed yet. There was even portions of a Consent to Treat form. And it was signed! Imagine that." Eisler appeared to want to laugh but couldn't. "The big secret that no one was supposed to know," he said. "Not his investors. Not even me, Dr. Christian Eisler, his trusted associate."

"What was in his notes?" Matt asked.

Eisler's grin melted into a blank gaze. "Kovacs was desperate to try out his theories on something greater, more important than rats and rhesus monkeys. So he created the almost perfect opportunity. With an almost perfect specimen. Or so he presumed." He restrained a giggle.

Suspicion crossed Matt's face. "Are you saying Dr. Kovacs did freeze Ben Simmons *alive*? Twenty years ago?"

Eisler smiled. "Oh yes indeedy, he did. And it was working. I fell for it. Even the cryonics community fell for it. He found investors. Reaped millions. All his success based on a calculated lie. Until the leak. Then Ben began to decompose."

"We have a witness who says she saw Ben here last night," Matt said.

Eisler laughed out loud. "We live in a strange world." When the laughing stopped, he continued. "It was Kovacs's decision to bury him. But to maintain the experiment's cover, he wanted to bypass the coroners and an autopsy. So a deal was set up and financed with foundation funds whereby the body would be secretly transferred to a local mortuary and be entombed in an unknown grave."

"Evergreen Manor," Matt inserted.

"A scintillating bit of deductive reasoning, detective," Eisler quipped. "Unfortunately at this juncture, Kovacs's judgment erred. He delegated the job to Evergreen's groundskeeper. Devlin hired two Mexicans who drove an old ice cream truck with a camper shell." He chuckled. "Then an amusing thing happened. Which even the great Dr. Kovacs wasn't aware of, though I suspect he might be very aware of it at the present time. Somewhere between Los Angeles and Pasadena the body vanished. According to Devlin, the Mexicans heard something in the camper. They stopped under a secluded overpass. There were more noises, followed by a loud crash. When they walked to the rear of the truck, the door to the camper was torn away and Ben's body was gone. The two Mexicans promptly found Interstate Five and are probably miles south of Tijuana now, telling tales of zombies in America," he added.

"Did you see the body?" Matt asked.

"No, I missed out on the memorable opportunity, but I saw the notes." Eisler wasn't too far gone to notice Matt's insinuation regarding Devlin's story. "Why would Devlin lie? He had an extra five grand coming to him once Ben was safely in the ground."

Julie listened in shocked silence. Again she thought of Stephanie, Kovacs's prized monkey. "Who's this man in the picture with Kovacs then?" she asked.

Eisler pointed with a shaking finger. "That good-looking fellow is Kovacs's younger brother, William. He's an internist in San Francisco."

"He's not Ben then?" Matt said.

Spittle flew from Eisler's mouth as he choked back more laughter. "Oh, most assuredly no, sir. Trust me. You'll know Ben when you meet him. I promise. Just ask Kovacs." His last two words barely made it past his lips before convulsive paroxysms of laughing and weeping ransacked his entire body.

Matt motioned Julie to the front entrance. Eisler didn't seem to notice as the two stepped just outside, where Matt could still keep an eye on him. "What do you think?" he asked.

"He's decompensating completely. We better summon an ambulance."

"He's going to need a long rest in a good institution when this is all over."

Julie's beeper interrupted them. She looked down, noting the number. "It's the hospital. Can I use the phone?"

"Not inside. I'll patch you through my radio."

Matt connected Julie and handed her the receiver.

"This is Dr. Charmaine." Julie frowned as she listened. "She said what?" She listened again, her frown deepening.

Obviously the news wasn't good. Matt hoped it wasn't Melanie.

"I'll be there as soon as I can," Julie finished.

"What is it?" Matt asked.

"That was Four West," Julie said. "Vicki's just checked herself out of the hospital."

Forty-seven

Officer Blocker dropped Julie off at the front entrance to the main hospital and she rushed inside. On Four West, she found Terry perusing Vicki's medical chart.

"No sign of her yet," the nurse told her. "She's been gone less than thirty minutes. The ward clerk said she was dressed in street clothes—it looked like she was going for a walk."

"Damn," Julie said softly. "Couldn't we stop her?"

"Dr. Charmaine, she wasn't a fifty-one–fifty. Plus she signed out AMA. What could I do, except page you stat?"

Julie examined Vicki's signature on the Against Medical Advice form. Terry was right. Everything had been done by the book, there was nothing else Terry could've done. Julie stepped over to the clerk who was filing the evening-shift's laboratory results in patients' charts.

"Did Ms. Zampisi indicate where she was going?" she asked the young woman.

"No, Doctor. She just asked me to call her a taxi. Here's the phone number." She handed Julie a slip of paper.

Julie took the scrawled note and walked the short distance down the hall to room 444. The door was open and Vicki's worn suitcase lay open on the bed. She hadn't even packed her things. Either she planned on returning or she never planned on . . . Julie refused to entertain the alternative.

Sitting on the bed, Julie tried to think logically. Vicki had been prescribed a short-acting sedative just before being transported upstairs. The chart notes had indicated her patient had been stable at that time. Now she was unofficially discharged. Where the hell had she gone?

Other than the bed's warming blanket, nothing else appeared to be missing from the room.

Julie reached for the phone and dialed the taxi company.

"Need a taxi? Where you at?" a dispatcher asked curtly.

"No. But one of your drivers recently picked up a fare at University Hospital. Within the last hour. I need to find out the destination."

"You a doctor?"

"As a matter of fact, I am. Dr. Julie Charmaine. Please hurry. This is critical. The woman's very ill."

"Woman's name?"

"Vicki Zampisi."

"Hold on." He returned in less than a minute. "That was easy. Been a slow traffic night." He released the information.

"Shit," Julie cursed, livid she hadn't seen Vicki's action coming. She replaced the receiver and dashed back to the nurses' station.

"Dr. Charmaine, is everything okay?" Terry asked, her tone registering alarm.

Julie had already started running for the elevators. She paused only long enough to say, "Terry, call the police. And page Detective Guardian stat. I'll be at the old Shilden Hotel. Hurry!"

Dorfman unlocked his office door the same time each workday, 6 A.M. This particular morning he was over half an hour early, anticipating an important fax from Germantown, Maryland.

The coroner flipped on the lights and strode to the facsimile machine. The laboratory report was the third item down.

He tossed it on his ledger and started heating some water for his morning coffee. Then, returning to his desk, he rifled through a drawer until he found a half-eaten candy bar.

He consumed two bites while returning his focus to the Sewer Stalker's DNA results. He scanned the normal karyotype, twenty-four pairs of tiny, dark, linear figures representing the forty-eight chromosomes.

Normal karyotype.

"Since when are forty-eight chromosomes considered normal?" he muttered, his wide face registering bewilderment. This rapidly progressed to exasperation, and finally shock as he moved on to the final impression.

"Those bastards," he yelled, lunging for the phone. He'd lay into those irresponsible East Coast technicians later.

Right now all he could do was wait until Guardian returned his page. He prayed the detective was prompt.

Julie braked across the street from the hotel's barricaded front entrance. The traffic was virtually nil, only two cars were parked in front of an all-night laundromat.

She scanned both directions for any police cars but saw no one, not even a passerby. Though it was only thirty minutes before dawn, the sky hung low, as black as jet fuel and the breeze smelled strongly of more rain.

She retrieved a flashlight from the glovebox and jogged across the pavement, jumping the curb to the opposite sidewalk. Her hands touched the NO TRESPASSING fence surrounding the condemned property. The metal felt cool and moist under her fingers. Gazing up at the monolithic silhouette, she scanned the windows for any sign of activity. None. Only blackness.

A dog barked and raced out of the alley that led behind the three-story structure. The animal's claws scraping on the asphalt were magnified by the overall stillness of the pre-dawn night.

Julie shivered and pulled her sweater across her chest. She walked to the place where she'd seen the dog and stopped.

"Vicki," she called out. Her own voice echoed weakly.

The streetlamp behind her glowed dimly, only partially illuminating the alley. With her flashlight beam, she could barely make out the orange construction cones. In the dark, they appeared almost crimson.

She took a step into the alley and stopped, suddenly afraid. Her respirations came in short bursts and she could feel her fingertips beginning to tingle.

Why didn't you open the door, Jule?

Forcing herself to stop hyperventilating, she faced the decrepit hotel. "You aren't old Mr. Ackerby's toolshed," she said.

Julie waited another thirty seconds for her breathing to return to normal, then swallowing her fear, she ducked down the alley.

She found Vicki's clothing—a pair of pants, blouse, undergarments—neatly folded and stacked in a pile just outside the construction cones and in front of an opening in the fence facing the back lot.

Julie knelt down and lifted Vicki's blouse. She saw no indication of any struggle. The clothing appeared to have been removed voluntarily. There was no blood and no buttons were missing.

She set the blouse back on the ground and stood, aware of a growing sense of impending doom. Why would Vicki remove all her clothes? The only answer that made any sense, Julie wasn't ready to consider.

She swung the beam across the edifice's back facade, illuminating cracked windows, piles of old lumber, stacks of Sheetrock, and clumps of vegetation.

"Vicki," she called out again. "It's me, Dr. Charmaine. If you see my flashlight, please answer."

There was none.

She stepped up on a wood plank bordering the construction pit and stopped, debating going further. Where the hell were the police? She admonished herself for leaving her cellular phone in her car.

She'd just shifted her weight to turn back when the breeze swung into her face, bringing her a new noise.

Julie turned her head so one ear faced the Shilden.

The new sound was *sobbing.* Someone was inside the hotel.

"Vicki," she called out louder.

The crying persisted. Julie forced the ghostly image of a sobbing Janine from her mind. This was real. Tonight was no dream.

"Vicki, please answer me. The police are on their way," she tried again.

The sobbing faded only to resume once more in strength. Though she couldn't tell whether the voice was male or female, she thought she could isolate its origin on one particular first-floor balcony.

She adjusted the beam. The light froze on a huddled form partially obscured by the wood railings. Julie recognized the hospital's white warming blanket.

She'd found Vicki.

Matt skidded to a stop in the NO PARKING zone. In the lobby, he found Blocker waiting behind the information desk with a security guard. Ramani arrived only seconds later.

"Dr. Charmaine still here?" Matt asked.

"You didn't get the page?" the officer said. "She's at the Shilden."

"Goddammit, I told someone to hold her here."

Blocker shrugged sheepishly. "Sorry, chief. She'd already left."

Matt spun on his partner. "I want two canine units and backup firepower at the old Shilden Hotel, just in case this is for real."

Ramani looked doubtful. "Dorfman's conclusion can't be right."

"I don't know what I fucking think anymore." Matt unholstered his 9mm Baretta 92F and raced for the exit.

Forty-eight

Using the light's beam to illuminate her way, Julie picked a path across the debris-strewn lot, dodging puddles of standing water and scraps of wood and Sheetrock. *Thank God I'm not in heels,* she thought, stepping over a pile of lumber. She'd sprain an ankle for sure.

She pressed on, and the nearer she came to the balcony, the more clear the sobbing became and at some point, she wasn't sure when, she recognized Vicki's voice.

She could also hear dripping water echoing from inside the hotel's hollow walls and the gentle plinking prodded her back in time to another rainy night, long ago. More than anything, even with Vicki in sight, she found herself tempted to turn around and lose herself in Matt's arms. But if she did, she'd award a childhood nemesis an easy victory. Again. And that was unacceptable. She was no longer a child.

"Screw yourself, Worm Man," she said and climbed up on the balcony.

Vicki sat on her knees, her feet tucked underneath her. The blanket was pulled tightly around her so only her head, neck, and a portion of her chest were visible. She rocked gently back and forth, her eyes staring back at the construction pit. Grime dusted her face, forming dark rivulets on her cheeks where she'd perspired.

Julie leaned down beside her. "Vicki, it's me, Dr. Charmaine."

Vicki's response remained unchanged. She simply rocked back and forth, seemingly unaware of Julie's presence.

As Julie knelt beside her, she shined the light back in the direction Vicki was staring. The beam fell on the open maw of the sewer construction pit, surrounded by the orange cones. A backhoe stood silently to one side like some huge, lifeless fossil.

Julie gently touched her patient's shoulder. "Vicki, I've come to take you back."

At the sound of Julie so close, Vicki stopped rocking. "Go back." The voice wasn't that of a woman cracking up, but of someone issuing a dire warning. It sent a cold tremor through Julie's body.

She gently tugged at Vicki's arm. "Vicki, we have to go."

Vicki was clutching two objects in one hand. She had them pressed firmly against her chest. One looked like a piece of paper. Julie wasn't sure.

"Vicki, get up," Julie ordered.

The beam from the flashlight caused Vicki's pupils to contract but she didn't blink. "No. It's too late for me. Please, Dr. Charmaine, go back."

Julie looked toward the alley. The police would be arriving at any moment and they would help coax Vicki back. If she didn't cooperate, then she'd have to be removed from the hotel by force.

Julie started to speak, but noticed the sudden strange stench of rotting sewage. She suppressed the urge to gag.

Vicki suddenly turned her way. The emptiness in her eyes made Julie shudder. *My God, Vicki is gone.*

"He's coming," she said, her voice still devoid of all emotion. "Do you hear him?"

This was total nonsense. Julie squatted down in front of Vicki and illuminated her own face to make her appeal seem more personal. "Vicki, we're leaving. Now get up."

Vicki ignored her. "Listen."

"Damn it, Vicki, no one's coming. I want you to return to the hospital." Julie began to pull Vicki up. Surprisingly enough she didn't resist. As Vicki's hands dropped limply to her sides, she dropped one of the items in her possession to the balcony floor. It was a photograph. She continued clutching the other, a cigarette lighter.

Julie retrieved the photograph, blindly shoving it in her pocket, but before she could take the lighter, Vicki grabbed her.

"It's him."

"No, Vicki—" The words lodged in her throat.

SLSHSH. SLSHSH.

A cold sweat broke out on Julie's face. She turned so fast that Vicki and she both nearly lost their balance. Her flashlight lit the faint mist rising from the rain puddles. She saw nothing. Yet she was sure she'd heard something . . .

SLSHSH.

Julie tensed. There it was again. The sound was echoing up from the construction pit. *Jesus Christ, someone was coming.* Julie thought of Kovacs, but deep inside her she knew whoever was approaching would not be the missing research psychiatrist.

"Go, Dr. Charmaine. You have to leave." Vicki's utter calm only magnified the deadly implication of the warning.

Julie listened.

SLSHSH. SLSHSH.

The sounds were getting louder. She grabbed Vicki by the wrist. "Goddamn it, we're leaving." She stepped toward the balcony railing, pulling Vicki with her.

The blanket fell open, revealing Vicki's naked torso.

Yet Vicki refused to budge. "I killed Ben. He wants me."

"No, Vicki. Dr. Kovacs killed him."

Vicki pulled her arm free of Julie's grasp. "You have to leave. Please." She stepped past a sheet of plywood into the dark unit.

Julie lunged after her. "No, Vicki! We've gotta get out of here!

Now!" She almost dropped the flashlight in her attempt to turn Vicki around. Her efforts were futile. In the distance, she heard sirens.

Then . . . *SLSHSH. SLSHSH. SLSHSH.*

The shaking beam magnified Julie's trembling hand as she spun and aimed the flashlight again, her breaths coming in short gasps.

She froze. Someone was climbing out of the sewer pit.

SLSHSH.

Julie stumbled backward. "Vicki, please come with me!" she pleaded, unable to remove her eyes from the figure emerging from the darkness.

SLSHSH . . . SLSHSH.

It was as if the cluttered lot was devoid of life one moment and the next, filled by a massive bipedal form.

Julie tried to speak but no words formed.

The figure appeared to pause and smell the air, before leaning forward and ambling across the ground. Briefly, Julie picked out a pair of close-set eyes, reflecting red in the light's beam.

She squinted in disbelieving shock at what she was actually seeing. Nothing Dorfman had said—the decomposing tissue, the abnomal chromosomes, the perpetrator's brute strength as evidenced by the victims' heinous injuries—had prepared her for what she was witnessing now, zeroing in on the canted balcony.

He was moving on all fours.

She flipped off the light. Maybe he wouldn't see them.

Shuffling agilely over piles of debris and scattered wood, the dark silhouette was nothing more than a shadow. He approached, splashing across rain puddles and sundering clumps of weedy vegetation.

She heard Vicki whisper, "Ben."

Julie turned, her face aghast. The night had lessened and in the early dawn's glow, she could see her patient's heavily made-up lips forming a vermilion smile. The inappropriate grin sent cold tendrils across Julie's neck.

The balcony shuddered suddenly from a heavy force.

Simultaneously, Vicki uttered, "He's come home to sleep."

Julie whirled around and was confronted by a huge figure suspended five feet in front of her. Waves of putrefying stench swirled past her nose. A second later the four-by-four railing cracked in the center and the figure crashed to the balcony floor on thick padded feet, leaving one muscled arm still holding fast to the second-floor ledge above.

Julie flipped on the light, landing the beam squarely on the ghastly form. The air turned as thick as water in her lungs. She could only manage a gurgled moan of anguish as she looked into the pair of red beady eyes mounted in the center of a head as large as a beach ball.

An ape. If she hadn't been so frightened for her life, she might have laughed at the absurdity of the realization.

Ben was an ape! His gargantuan stature rocked gently side to side, flexing the massive muscles of his trunk and thighs through skeins of decomposing skin. The face, frozen by mounds of scar tissue from years of sub-zero burns, framed the eyes that lay half-hidden behind long, matted red hair. Pronounced cheek pads and a distended throat pouch protruding from under his mandible gave the creature a hideous gargoylean countenance. Where the dermis was still intact, a translucent gray body glove covered portions of his thick terra-cotta body. The polyurethane's reflective surface gave his silhouette a preternatural sheen. His black lips smacked together with loud popping sounds.

With the swiftness of a cat, he twisted his neck to the side at the wail of approaching sirens.

Only then did Julie find her lungs. She screamed.

"Ben." It was Vicki talking. She tried to move toward the creature.

"No!" Julie gasped, forcing both of them away from the animal along the only possible route. Back into the hotel.

Vicki resisted. "I loved you, Ben," she said in the same tone a sad child would use when talking to a dead pet.

For an instant, the ape's eyes darted from Julie to Vicki, then back.

Jesus, it is him. It's Ben.

"Stay, Ben," Julie said with as much control in her voice as she could dredge up while gesturing with one palm.

The ape released the ledge above and reached out an enormous hand, slowly at first, then with more sense of purpose.

"Shit." Julie spun and, grabbing Vicki by the wrist, she splashed inside across the room's soggy carpet, finding the splintered door into the hall.

She heard the creature bellow in a rage. Under her shoes the floor began to shake as the ape smashed through a plywood sheet in close pursuit, emitting incensed combinations of growls and hoots.

Julie swung the light left. A ceiling cave-in blocked any hope of escape. She sprinted right, yanking Vicki with her.

"He wants me," Vicki cried, but at least her protests were not as vigorous.

Sprinting as fast as her legs would take her down the dark hall, Julie moved her light just in time to avoid colliding with a thick beam. She continued past, taking Vicki with her. The cracked walls and shifting shadows from the dangling ceiling panels made her feel like she was lost in a maze designed by a madman. There had to be some way out of here.

Behind her more splintering wood split the gloom, and she knew that Ben was gaining on them.

Outside the walls, the sirens seemed to be converging from all directions. They probably had the building surrounded.

"Matt!" she screamed, hearing only the terror in her own

voice. "Matt!" She and Vicki had to get out or be rended apart by Kovacs's creation.

SLSHSH. SLSHSH. SLSHSH.

The heavy sloshing across the wet carpet sounded like a stampeding hippo.

Julie tried to break into the nearest unit but the door was locked. She tried another. The knob froze under her finger. She banged the wood but the door wouldn't budge. She pivoted and, swinging the beam, she spied an open doorway at the end of the hall.

"Yes," she heard Vicki murmur and then her patient whisked past her toward room 5, the whiteness of her naked flesh glowing lewdly angelic in the flashlight's illumination.

Julie raced after her, trampling over the door lying in the hall. She leaped into the dark room and in the split second it took her to sweep the flashlight, she realized the magnitude of her mistake. The room had no exit. Two eight-foot plywood sheets blocked the egress to the balcony. Even the bathroom window was boarded over.

And she'd lost Vicki.

"Vicki," she cried out. She aimed the light at the sound of creaking springs and gazed in horrific disbelief.

Vicki kneeled completely exposed, her back arched against the bed's headboard. Her arms hung limply at her sides. Her expression looked as serene as if she were watching a sunset. If there was any doubt before that Vicki had drifted over the edge, there was none now. Debris lay piled around her body, giving Julie the impression of a helpless bird in a large nest.

An angry bellow exploding from the darkened corridor sent Julie's heart into her mouth. She scrambled for a loose sheet of plywood resting against one wall.

"Help me, Vicki," she screamed.

On her own she lifted the sheet and shoved it completely

across the open doorway. Then searching feverishly, she found a five-foot two-by-four and wedged the wood between the plywood sheet and the anchored bed frame, effectively barricading themselves inside the room.

Gasping for breath, she stepped back. She stared at the makeshift barricade, knowing fully ten sheets wouldn't stop the creature.

"Don't be afraid, Dr. Charmaine," Vicki said. "He wants me."

Men's voices sifted in through the building's cracked façade.

"Matt, we're in here!" Julie screamed. She took a step back further from the door.

Behind the plywood she heard nothing. Then a tentative step. And another. *SLSHSH.*

She moved back until her calf touched the bed frame. The flashlight illuminated the contact point between the two-by-four and plywood.

Silence. Then a soft sniffing sound, followed by a muffled thud against the plywood. The warped wood creaked. Julie felt the two-by-four start to vibrate against her leg. The ape was trying to push his way.

"Ben," Vicki whispered.

"Quiet," Julie said. From the lot, she heard barking dogs.

Suddenly, the plywood began to shake violently. A crunching noise followed, as heavy blows rained down on the barricade. Then the two-by-four bent in the middle and snapped, the separate pieces whizzing across the floor.

Julie ducked and jumped aside as the sheet flew through the air, bouncing off the ceiling and landing on the opposite side of the bed. She swung the light and held her breath as Ben shuffled into the room, filling the air with an odious stench. Snarling, he turned his massive head sideways as he looked about.

"Ben," Vicki said, holding her arms out, palms opened. "I've come back for you. Just like I promised."

With a throaty growl, his huge hunched form moved toward the bed on all fours, heavy knuckles sending bits of the two-by-four rolling over the carpet.

"No," Julie whispered, frantic for Vicki's safety as well as her own. She aimed the light directly into the primate's eyes. With wide swings of his fists he tried to shove the beam aside. His agitated response gave her an idea.

"Vicki," Julie whispered. "He can't see in the light. Climb off the bed and crawl toward me. Hurry." They might be able to sneak around the giant ape if she could blind him with the light.

The springs creaked as Vicki began to move. Julie cringed.

Vicki was moving *toward* Ben.

"No," Julie groaned, helpless to do anything but watch.

Vicki reached up and clasped one of the ape's wrists.

"Hello, Ben," she said, guiding the gargantuan hand toward her own chest. "It's me, Vicki. How you been, fella?"

For a brief second or two, Julie thought the ape calmed. His other fist ceased flailing at the air and he cocked his head inquisitively to one side. His thick fingers actually touched Vicki's face, leaving wide dark smudges. But that hope ended when a deep guttural noise erupted from Ben's throat. He grabbed Vicki's blond hair, his eyes absent of any recognition.

Julie saw her patient's face twist in terror as Ben yanked hard, driving Vicki's head down into the mattress. Then pulling again, he jerked her up and with his other hand sent her flying against the headboard with a single powerful blow to the side of her head, crushing the bone the years of plastic surgery had attempted to mend.

"Vicki," Julie cried, following Vicki with her light.

The naked body lay crumpled in a heap, one leg dangling awkwardly off the edge of the mattress.

The ape smacked its lips and, hopping up and down on two legs, began searching for another target.

Julie leaped to her feet and slipped, almost going to the floor. Catching herself with both hands, she dropped the light. With less than inches to spare, she rolled away from the colossal grasping fingers and scrambled for the doorway.

In the corridor she heard running footsteps. Beams of light danced in the dark.

"Matt!" she screamed, sprinting for the exit.

The ape's reaction was lightning-quick, blocking her retreat. A strong grip tugged her sweater and then she felt her scalp burn as Ben yanked her against his putrid body with a sharp pull.

"No," she screamed, gagging from the fetid odor. She flailed her limbs, struggling to break the inhuman grip, oblivious to the ape's bellows and snarls. She glimpsed two long, yellow, canine teeth descending toward her, and she raised an arm to shield her face. The stench was suffocating. Somewhere in Julie's mind, a tiny portion suddenly understood what the other victims must have experienced. Adrenaline surged through her veins and she clawed at the arms pinning her, only to feel the rotting flesh and hair pull away under her nails. She felt the ape's fingers clamp completely around her neck.

Darkness began to descend around the edges of her consciousness.

You let me die, Jule.

"Help me, Janine," Julie gasped silently.

Matt's voice broke through the thickening cloud.

"Let 'em loose, Ramani," she heard him yell.

A sleek black form shot by her like a heat-seeking missile. The German shepherd's teeth sunk into the ape's shoulder.

Barking drowned out the ape's enraged bellows as three more police dogs tackled the huge primate.

Dropping Julie, the ape stood on two legs to fend off the challenge.

"Get away!" Matt yelled at Julie, trying to aim his revolver but refrained from firing for fear of hitting Julie or one of the dogs.

"Where's Vicki?" he yelled.

"The bed!" Julie screamed.

"There's a woman at the head of the bed!" he warned.

Ramani had also unholstered and raised his revolver. For a short moment, it appeared the over four-hundred-pounds of canine fury would be a match for the enraged primate, but after two violent swings from a broken piece of two-by-four, suddenly two dogs lay still with crushed skulls.

Howling at his attackers, Ben adroitly shifted his bulk, dodging another shepherd's rush. He swung again, catching the dog in the ribs and sending the shepherd whimpering back into the hall. The fourth hesitated, growling unenthusiastically, before retreating on its own.

Matt saw an opening and fired three rapid rounds into the primate's thick torso.

Ben fell back onto the bed, snarling in rage, clutching at his chest. He then rolled onto the floor, his teeth bared, and hurtled himself toward the detectives on all fours, his red eyes bright with fury.

Matt and Ramani stood in the doorway, firing point-blank a fusillade of bullets.

Julie saw clear liquid spouting from Ben's wounds but the ape wouldn't go down. He charged into the detectives like a wounded water buffalo. Julie heard the snap of bone and Ramani scream in anguish. The short detective fell to the floor clutching his thigh.

Panicked voices filled the narrow corridor as more police crowded into the hall.

"It's a fucking gorilla!"

"That's not a gorilla!"

"What the hell is it?"

With lightning speed, Ben turned on Matt, knocking the gun

from the detective's grip with a short arcing swing and grappling furiously for a hold.

Matt responded with two lightning punches to the ape's face, instantly shattering the bones in his right hand.

He ducked away. "Don't shoot!" he yelled, realizing Julie and Vicki were once more in the officers' line of fire.

The ape whirled back on Julie.

"Matt!" Julie screamed, pushing back against the wall. She saw Ben's eyes fix on her face. During that half second when the ape didn't move, she thought his expression actually did look almost human.

Then he bellowed, beat his chest with both fists, and came for her.

"No, Ben!" she cried in terror.

Matt grabbed Ramani's gun and aimed.

"Ben," Vicki's voice rose above the commotion. Matt held his fire.

The big ape froze and swiveled around on his thick legs.

Julie stared in horror at the bed.

Vicki was kneeling unsteadily, half her face crushed, holding a six-inch piece of glass in one hand. On top of the headboard she'd set her cigarette lighter. How she'd been able to hang onto it through the mad dash down the hall and Ben's attack Julie would never know.

With one smooth flick of her fingers, Vicki slit her wrist just above her hand. Bright red blood spurted from the laceration in tiny pulsating geysers.

"Ben," she coaxed, holding up the bleeding extremity. She let the blood run down her arm, her bare chest, until it stained her breasts and lower abdomen.

The huge red ape sniffed the warm pungent scent and took a purposeful step toward the bed.

When Julie saw Vicki's hand discard the glass and reach for the lighter, she suddenly understood what her patient planned on doing. There should've been massive amounts of blood from Ben's wounds but Julie had seen only a clear fluid. Kovacs's cryoprotectant. A glycerol and alcohol mixture. *Alcohol.*

"No, Vicki!" Julie screamed just as the great ape let loose an ear-piercing shriek and launched its gargantuan form into the air.

Matt fired with one hand, blowing off a portion of the metabolically altered creature's skull.

Ben landed on top of Vicki, pinning her body to the mattress. She made no attempt to struggle. Instead, she calmly flicked on the lighter and tried to find Julie's horrified gaze.

"Please don't think too badly of me, Dr. Charmaine," she said. Then she held the tiny flame against the alcohol-permeated giant.

For a fleeting moment, Julie detected something in the huge ape's eyes—something that wasn't revenge or hatred. For a single instant, he was young again, a young, frightened creature devoted to a disfigured girl named Vicki Zampisi.

Ben and Vicki exploded in flame.

Forty-nine

It was a miracle no other lives were lost in the Shilden Hotel conflagration. In less than thirty minutes, the four-alarm blaze was contained, but only after the entire structure had been consumed by the intense fire and heat.

Julie stood by one ambulance while an attendant splinted Matt's broken hand. Another ambulance had just left the scene with Ramani, diagnosed with a fractured femur, for the medical center emergency ward.

Matt thanked the attendant and walked over to offer Julie an umbrella. The rain had begun again in earnest soon after the morning light had transformed the black sky to a slate of gray.

They stood together, gazing at the charred remains of the old hotel.

Matt flexed the fingers on his good hand. "That orangutan had a jaw like a block of granite."

"I think you dazed him."

Matt grunted. "Shit, I just made the SOB angry."

Julie shook her head sadly, beginning to feel an ache in her neck where the ape had choked her. "I still can't believe it. Ben was an orangutan. I had no idea they had forty-eight chromosomes. So close to us, yet so different."

"Neither did Dorfman. Befuddled the experts out East too," Matt commented. "Until the final karyotype was completed. Then they had to call in an outside consultant."

"Unbelievable. The poor pathetic creature. Kovacs was a madman. To think he'd submit an animal to such a barbaric experiment." Julie turned and faced the detective. "And falsify a death certificate to make it appear Ben was human. All for funding his research. He was so afraid the world would see his failure, he risked everything to cover it up. In some ways, I believe Wes Kovacs thought of Ben as more human than anthropoid."

Matt ushered Julie to a waiting squad car. "What about poor Vicki?"

"God, I can't even conceive the tremendous burden of guilt and shame she carried with her. So terribly sad," Julie said. "But I honestly believe in her disturbed heart she really loved Ben."

Matt climbed in beside her. The rain had escalated to a downpour, making it sound like marbles clattering the car's roof.

Outside, the entire lot was cordoned off with yellow tape. Wearing raincoats and ponchos, the crime-scene personnel worked to remove the two corpses. Julie watched as one body was transferred to a stretcher. The corpse was small and frail; she assumed it belonged to Vicki. Four men were required to heave the other corpse onto a metal gurney. The two dead dogs were tossed beside the charred orangutan.

Luckily once the fire broke out, everyone else had managed to escape. She and Matt had literally dragged Ramani to safety.

"Simian," Matt said, observing the scene with a dispassionate stare.

Julie gave him a quizzical look.

"After you left for the hospital," Matt explained, "I found a reference to it in Kovacs's notes. Kovacs derived Ben's last name from Simian. What Ben was had been in his name all along."

"Another example of Kovacs's twisted logic." Julie felt sick inside. She removed the old photograph from her pocket. She still couldn't believe what it signified. "Look at this." She handed the picture to Matt.

In places the rain had stained the film, but the images remained clear. Vicki looked dwarfed by the huge, hairy red ape squatting beside her.

"I found her clutching this and her cigarette lighter," Julie said, looking up. "It's odd how small things stick out in your mind." She studied the photo.

"This is Vicki," she said, unable to remove her eyes from the odd couple.

Matt handed the picture back. "She looked like a different person."

Julie pointed to the photo. "She was much younger then and she hadn't had all her plastic surgeries. She also had dark hair."

"Vicki was a blonde."

"She dyed it. But twenty years ago, her hair was dark."

Matt's eyes went from the picture to Julie. "Like yours."

Julie paused briefly. "Like mine."

"And Irene Inez, Brenda Nixon, Humphries." Matt named them off.

"And Melanie," Julie added. "Ben was simply searching for Vicki. It was always Vicki. But he was searching for the Vicki he remembered, the young Vicki, the Vicki with dark hair. And he remembered the Shilden Hotel as the place where the two had spent so much time together. Before the experiment."

"A case of misdirected love," Matt said.

"An unnatural love." Julie returned the photo to her pocket. Initially, she'd debated destroying it but now realized it belonged with Vicki's medical file. She hoped Vicki wouldn't object. The photograph was an intricate part of the most bizarre case she'd ever been involved with. She wondered if she'd ever learn the entire story.

"Any word on Kovacs?" she asked.

Matt shrugged. "His body will turn up. They always do."

"You think he's dead then?"

"After what I witnessed tonight . . . yeah, he's dead."

Both sat pensively, staring at the raindrops until Blocker and another cop approached the car and rapped on the window.

Matt cracked the door.

"You busy?" Blocker asked.

"Who's asking?"

"Signelli wants you to give a statement to the press."

"Fuck the press."

"That your answer?"

"No, that's my statement."

Matt slammed the door. Turning, he touched Julie's hair. "See you later?"

She kissed his cheek. "Promise."

Julie watched him slog through the mud, tucking his chin down against the rain, until she lost him in the milieu of mini-cams and reporters. She gazed past the squad cars and past the yellow crime tape. Past the rivulets of moisture and past the blurred melange of flashing red-and-blue police lights. Past childhood games, past old toolsheds, past years of guilt and pain.

Until all that remained was the rain.

Epilogue

*The dreams come with less fre-*quency now. The nights are usually dark and rainy when Janine makes her visits. Julie senses her older sibling is friendlier, less vindictive.

"Hey, Jule," Janine says. "Play with me."

Julie never resists because she knows how the dream will end. It's always the same.

Janine pauses in front of Mr. Ackerby's old toolshed and smiles mischievously.

"There's someone who wants to meet you," she says, gloating like big sisters do. Then she swings open the toolshed door.

Julie hears the rusted metal hinges squeak. "Not Worm Man," she begs.

"Don't be a crybaby, Jule," Janine teases. "Worm Man is only a game."

"Please don't make me go in," Julie pleads.

"You have to, li'l sis. You're not chicken, are you?"

"I don't want to."

Julie feels the hard tug of Janine's icy fingers and suddenly they're both inside the wood-plank walls. Over the fumes of insecticide, Julie smells the rotting flesh of dead corpses—they're all around her—and when she attempts to escape, the doorway is blocked by a massive dark form.

"Meet my new pal, Jule," Janine taunts her.

Before Julie can scream, she awakens. But not before she sees her dead sister's newest friend—a huge red ape.